LENN EVAN GOODMAN earned his doctorate in Arabic Philosophy at Oxford University three years after his graduation from Harvard College, where he specialized in Philosophy and Near Eastern Languages and Literature. Since 1969 he has taught at the University of Hawaii, where he holds the position of Associate Professor of Philosophy.

Dr. Goodman's articles, reviews, and translations have been widely published in magazines and journals. His translation and extensive annotation of the twelfth-century Arabian classic *Hayy Ibn Yaqzan,* by Iban Tufayl, was published in 1972. He has traveled and lectured throughout the United States and in Europe, Australia, and the Middle East.

Dr. Goodman lives in Honolulu with his wife, Madeleine, and their two daughters, Allegra and Paula.

The Jewish Heritage Classics

SERIES EDITORS: David Patterson · Lily Edelman

Already Published

THE MISHNAH
Oral Teachings of Judaism
Selected and Translated by Eugene J. Lipman

RASHI
Commentaries on the Pentateuch
Selected and Translated by Chaim Pearl

A PORTION IN PARADISE
AND OTHER JEWISH FOLKTALES
Compiled by H. M. Nahmad

THE HOLY CITY
Jews on Jerusalem
Compiled and Edited by Avraham Holtz

REASON AND HOPE
Selections from the Jewish Writings of Hermann Cohen
Translated, Edited, and with an Introduction by Eva Jospe

THE SEPHARDIC TRADITION
Ladino and Spanish-Jewish Literature
Selected and Edited by Moshe Lazar

JUDAISM AND HUMAN RIGHTS
Edited by Milton R. Konvitz

HUNTER AND HUNTED
Human History of the Holocaust
Selected and Edited by Gerd Korman

FLAVIUS JOSEPHUS
Selected and Edited by Abraham Wasserstein

THE GOOD SOCIETY
Jewish Ethics in Action
Selected and Edited by Norman Lamm

MOSES MENDELSSOHN
Selections from His Writings
*Edited and Translated by Eva Jospe, with
an Introduction by Alfred Jospe*

*Published in cooperation with the Commission
on Adult Jewish Education of B'nai B'rith*

RAMBAM

*Readings in the Philosophy
of Moses Maimonides*

*Selected and Translated
with Introduction
and Commentary by*
LENN EVAN GOODMAN

The Viking Press · New York

First published in 1976 by The Viking Press, Inc.
625 Madison Avenue, New York, N.Y. 10022
Published simultaneously in Canada by
The Macmillan Company of Canada Limited

LIBRARY OF CONGRESS CATALOGING IN PUBLICATION DATA

Moses ben Maimon, 1135–1204.
Rambam: readings in the philosophy of Moses Maimonides.

(The Jewish heritage classics)
Bibliography: p.
Includes index.
1. Philosophy, Jewish. 2. Philosophy, Medieval. 3. Ethics, Jewish. 4. Moses
ben Maimon, 1135–1204. I. Goodman, Lenn Evan, 1944– II. Title. III. Series.
B759.M32E5 1976   181'.3   75-14476
ISBN 0-670-58964-0

Printed in U.S.A.

Thanks to the Morris Adler Publications Fund of B'nai B'rith's Commission on Adult
Jewish Education for making the Jewish Heritage Classics Series possible as a memorial
to the late Rabbi Morris Adler, former Chairman of that Commission.

TO MY WIFE
MADELEINE JOYCE GOODMAN

PREFACE

The perplexity which Maimonides wrote the *Moreh Nevukhim*—the *Guide to the Perplexed*—to answer is far more widespread in our days than it was in his. For, if genuine and not merely expressive of a clash between secular and religious values, this perplexity is the natural response to an apparent incongruity of scientific and philosophic modes of thinking, on the one hand, with traditional religious categories of thought, on the other. Far more people today than in Maimonides' time are aware of the possibility of such a conflict. And it is not uncommon for a modern reader to open the *Guide to the Perplexed* with some hope of discovering whether that celebrated title actually indicates the possibility of some guidance in what we sometimes regard as largely modern intellectual problems. Usually these hopes are disappointed, and the modern reader comes away wondering whether the object of the work is to diminish or to increase perplexity.

There are three reasons why this is so. One involves translations; a second involves backgrounds; and the third and most important concerns Maimonides' method of operation.

Regarding translations: There is a natural tendency on the part of a translator to confuse literalism with accuracy. When consistently followed, this tendency can render any translation of a medieval Arabic work unintelligible. Arabic syntax is not English syntax; and, as every translator must admit, the unit of meaning is the sentence, not the word. Arabic words, like words in all natural languages, have numerous senses; and, since the set of senses attached to a given term in Arabic does not always correspond exactly with the set attached to another term in English, it is impossible to translate from Arabic to English simply by substituting one English term consistently for a given Arabic term. By ignoring these fundamental facts Arabic scholars have produced fairly extensive shelves of books which are of great value to other Arabists (since they show how one's colleagues have construed a given text) but are of no particular use to anyone who does not have a good Arabic text before him and the ability to use it. Yet, in the case of Maimonides in particular, we have an author who writes a clear, flexible, and direct Arabic, not overburdened by cumbrous terminology and jargon. There is no reason why the same clarity cannot be rendered in English.

Regarding background: It is no longer possible to presume that those who have reached the point of articulating a perplexity as to the possibility of an intelligent theism will have the grounding in Biblical and Rabbinic literature, or in the natural, moral, and metaphysical sciences which Maimonides regarded as absolute prerequisites to any comprehensive theological inquiry. Maimonides clearly never contemplated the possibility that large numbers of individuals would be exposed haphazardly and superficially to a welter of theological difficulties without being afforded any means of resolving those problems. He certainly would not have called such a process education, and he did his best in his *Guide to the Perplexed* not to be guilty himself of such an unprincipled offense. This problem of background is the source of the third and most serious cause of difficulty to the modern reader in penetrating the *Guide to the Perplexed*.

Maimonides' *modus operandi*: Maimonides followed a long tradition which made a point of writing in such a manner that only those who had a fairly clear understanding of their own philosophical perplexities regarding theism would make any headway whatever in comprehending generally a serious theological work. He does not state the perplexities he is addressing but suggests them through a complex system of allusive references which are opaque to the modern lay reader but which to the intended audience of the *Guide* would have called to mind immediately vivid associations regarding difficulties which they themselves had long pondered. Given a familiarity with the principal issues of monotheistic thought, the alternative views which Maimonides sets forth and the doctrines which he elaborates and defends would fall clearly into place in a lucid and well-ordered exposition. But for those who were not part of Maimonides' intended audience, namely those who had not pondered the problems he addresses, the book would remain obscure. This indeed was part of Maimonides' intention.

These two latter difficulties leave the modern reader somewhat in a quandary. For the general stock of knowledge of the educated layman today may be vastly different from that which Maimonides expected in his reader, and the associations that we make when thinking of the major problems of theology—the problem of the idea of God, the divine nature and existence, the possibility of knowing God, and the meaning of doing His will—are quite largely altered from what they were for Maimonides' original audience. Yet we do think about those problems and, to that extent, rightly belong in the intended audience of his philosophical work.

These are the considerations that have governed the preparation of the present book. My object has been to select the central passages from the *Moreh Nevukhim* and from Maimonides' ethical work the *Shemonah Perakim* (the *Eight Chapters*—originally written as an introduction to the section on the *Pirkei Avot* in his Commentary on the Mishnah, but often studied as a separate work); to present them in as lucid and intelligible a translation as I am capable of producing; [1] and to provide backgrounds, comments, explanations, and above all situations of the problems and analyses of Maimonides' conclusions sufficient to the needs of the thoughtful nonspecialist reader. I do not claim to have done this infallibly; where I have erred I shall be most

---

1. The present translation is based on Rabbi Salomon Munk's critical edition of the Arabic text of the *Moreh Nevukhim* and Joseph Gorfinkle's critical edition of Ibn Tibbon's Hebrew translation of the *Shemonah Perakim* (see Bibliography). All omissions from these texts have been marked. References to Biblical and Talmudic passages and cross-references within the Maimonidean corpus are generally supplied. Italics for emphasis have occasionally been added where Maimonides' intention seems to require them.

happy to be corrected. Nor do I pretend that I have exposed every atom of meaning to be derived from the hints and allusions which Maimonides provides. A fuller interpretation naturally would require a more comprehensive treatment than is possible in the present volume. I do claim that Maimonides' thought is not a document "sealed with seven seals." The serious reader who is willing to pick up the skein of Maimonides' thought will readily make sense of his principal themes, and may well find him most apposite. Given the necessary groundwork, he may find Maimonides as clear, fresh, and relevant as he was when his works first appeared some eight centuries ago. For, like all true philosophers, Maimonides makes a contribution which is timeless and perennial.

Thanks are due to B'nai B'rith for its sponsorship of this series and to the editors: to Dr. David Patterson, who initially invited me to undertake this project, for his kind help and careful editing, to Mrs. Lily Edelman for her patience, tact, and care in seeing the volume through the press, to Naomi Thompson of B'nai B'rith, and to the editors and staff at Viking. I am deeply indebted to Dr. Bertram Schwarzbach for applying his vast learning and keen analytic sense to the criticism of my manuscript. Where I have not followed his good advice, I shall have only myself to blame. I must thank my father and mother, Mr. and Mrs. C. J. Goodman of Los Angeles, for their constant encouragement and support. I express warm Aloha to my students, to the Jewish community of Honolulu, and to the gracious people of the State of Hawaii. Finally I should like to thank my wife, Dr. Madeleine Goodman, for her love and patience, for her unique combination of goodness and competence in all things. It is fitting that this book be dedicated to her.

LENN EVAN GOODMAN

Honolulu
April 1974

CONTENTS

GENERAL INTRODUCTION

The Life of Maimonides

Mosheh ben Maimon, called Maimonides by Latin authors and known to the Arabic-speaking world as Musa ibn Maimun, Moses son of Maimon, was born at one in the afternoon, March 30, 1135 C.E., a Sabbath day on the eve of Passover,[1] in the city of Cordova, where eight generations of his ancestors had served as rabbis and rabbinical judges. Capital of the Umayyad emirs and caliphs of Spain since the eighth century, Cordova had remained even in their political decline the center of a brilliant and prosperous civilization in which Jews and Christians as well as Muslims were active participants.

There had been Jews in Iberia since the times of the Visigoths, and the Jews of Spain were a prosperous and self-confident community. Wealth, learning, prestige, and even power in the theoretically Muslim state hierarchy reinforced one another as the Jews competed freely for

---

1. 14 Nissan 4895, by the Hebrew calendar. Maimonides is traditionally known as the Rambam, an acronym of his Hebrew name, Rabeynu Mosheh ben Maimon. The affectionate styling *Rabeynu,* "our master," coupled with the name of Moses must have suggested to Maimonides' admirers a parallel between the work of Rabeynu Mosheh and that of Mosheh Rabeynu, the prophet Moses.

1

the favor of the ruling princes. The Jewish physician Hasdai ibn Shaprut (d. *ca.* 990), for example, became finance minister to his royal patient Abdurrahman III, the Umayyad caliph at Cordova in whose long and prosperous reign (912–961) the Jews enjoyed far better fortunes than in many another period of their history. Ibn Shaprut gave honor and support to Jewish scholars and poets whose works became an ornament of the age. In Granada another Jewish leader, Samuel ibn Nagrela, served as minister to the monarch Habbus (r. 1024–1038) while distinguishing himself not only by his own work in philology but also by his patronage of (among others) the great Jewish poet and philosopher Solomon ibn Gabirol.

Even after the downfall of the Umayyad state, when all professing Jews were persecuted and forced ultimately to abandon southern Spain, there were many who carried on in new surroundings the traditions of wealth, influence, and cultural excellence familiar in the Umayyad era. Such was Maimonides' contemporary and admirer Sheshet Benveniste, physician and bailiff to Kings Alfonso II and Pedro II of Aragon. Benveniste was one of the wealthiest men in Europe, a man of formidable intellect, and a leader of the Jewish community of his time.

To Maimonides, as to many of the most cultured persons of his age, it was evident that wealth, leisure, security, even health, were not ends in themselves but means to study and contemplation. When Maimonides argues that the function of the state is to create the conditions of peace and security enabling man to perfect his human nature and, through thought and science, to come closer to God,[2] one can almost sense him looking back to the relative tranquillity of the vanquished Cordova of his childhood and his parents' memories. Clearly, these memories would not have been pure pleasantness. Even in their best days the Jews of Spain were a persecuted minority. But in the relative calm prior to the shattering of their world the Jews of Spain had built an intellectual capital from which Maimonides was to profit immeasurably even after the world which had produced it had ceased to exist. Poetry, astronomy, medicine, philosophy, scriptural exegesis, grammar, history, and mysticism in the century before the Rambam's birth

---

2. *Cf.* Parts Three and Five of this book.

were not separate worlds rigidly cut off from one another by barriers of incompetence. They were instead organically related arts and sciences which had a place in a comprehensive education. Abraham ibn Daud (*ca.* 1110–1180), historian of the generation prior to the Rambam and author of the *Book of Tradition*,[3] was a chronographer whose learning spanned Jewish and universal history. Ibn Daud's history was imbued with a structure and symmetry derived from the theme of continuity of cultural transmission from epoch to epoch in history. An active polemicist in behalf of rabbinic Judaism, Ibn Daud was also a philosopher. His *Emunah Ramah* (or *Lofty Creed*), as we shall see in the next section, comes closer than any other book to providing a precedent for Maimonides' *Moreh Nevukhim*. Even in exile ibn Daud seems to have remained productive. Thought to be identical with the Avendauth who translated Avicenna for the Christian scholars of Toledo, he thus seems to have had his share in sparking the Renaissance.

Ibn Daud credits one Judah ibn Hayyuj with reviving and reorganizing the study of Hebrew grammar on scientific principles. Along with Jonah ibn Janah and Moses ibn Gikatilla, according to Ibn Daud, Ibn Hayyuj restored Hebrew grammar to a level of comprehensibility which might otherwise have been lost forever. We know in fact that there were others who contributed to the same goal. Maimonides' ability to move effortlessly and indeed creatively through the entire scriptural canon with all its philological difficulties and, indeed, to choose to write his largest work, the fourteen-volume *Mishneh Torah,* not in his native Arabic but in Mishnaic Hebrew was the direct result of several generations of intensive work on Hebrew grammar which preceded his undertaking.

The Biblical commentators in Spain, again, were more than mere Bible scholars. Abraham ibn Ezra (1092–1167), a founder of scientific exegesis and a touchstone for all later Biblical interpreters, was a poet, philologist, and philosopher as well. Moses ibn Ezra (1070–1138), whose poetry fills the Sephardic mahzor, was a philosopher and secular poet whose intellectual and poetic gifts met in his liturgic works.

Finally, in Halakhic studies, the crucial legal core of rabbinic schol-

---

3. *Sefer ha-Qabbalah,* edited and translated by Gerson Cohen (Philadelphia, 1967).

arship, the West had gained self-sufficiency generations before Maimonides was born. Ibn Daud's notion of the continuity of Jewish tradition was accepted by Maimonides as a fundamental Jewish tenet, so it is difficult to see how Maimonides could have undertaken legal writings on the scale that he did had he not been able to see himself as standing in the mainstream of Halakhic tradition. But in fact Jewish Spain as it existed prior to the birth of Maimonides could make good such a claim.

Near the end of the tenth century an admiral of Abdurrahman's had abducted four Babylonian rabbis, whom he sold as slaves in North Africa and Spain. One, Rabbi Moses, was ransomed by the Jews of Cordova along with his son. Discovering his learning, the Cordovans made him their rabbinic judge. His son, Rabbi Hanok, by fulfilling the Talmudic injunction to raise up many students, made Cordova an independent center of Talmudic scholarship. The arrival of the illustrious Talmudist al-Fasi at Lucena had a comparable effect. For al-Fasi had studied at the feet of some of the last Babylonian Talmudists. His efforts at a new codification of Jewish law were to have a decisive formative impact on Maimonides' own attempts to render systematic and rationally comprehensible the immensity of Halakhah. Thus, in a way, Maimonides could see that Ibn Daud was right: as the academies of Babylonia waned, the authority of Cordova and Lucena grew. When Cordova was eclipsed, it seemed to fall to the most able refugees to carry on and develop the Halakhic tradition.

The efflorescence of Jewish culture and letters in Spain, in part the product of prosperity and a more pluralistic social structure than may be found almost anywhere else in the Middle Ages, was deeply shaken by the Almoravid movement, which had conquered western North Africa and the southern half of Spain by about 1100. Among the Almoravids' acts in Cordova was the public burning of *The Revival of Religious Studies,* the masterwork of Abu Hamid al-Ghazali (1058–1111), who had been recognized in the East as one of the most profound theologians of orthodox Islam. If the reading of this book was to be made a capital offense, there is little wonder that the Almoravids, flushed with the zeal of conquest, rigorously persecuted Christians and Jews. Jewish officeholders were purged systematically from government posts. The Jews of Lucena, who had long dominated the town, were forced to pay a heavy indemnity for their insistence on retaining their religion.

Thus the Jewish position in Spain, even before the birth of Maimonides, had been growing increasingly untenable as the militant wing of the Almoravid movement tightened its control in the face of threats from Christian Spain to the north and the loss of its foothold in North Africa to the Almohads in the south. Theologically more sophisticated than their predecessors, the early Almohads were nonetheless even more intolerant in the propagation of their faith. Within a few decades they overran southern Spain, totally defeating and displacing the Almoravids. In 1148, the year Maimonides became bar mitzvah, the Almohads took Cordova, destroying the great synagogue and much else besides. Jews, like Christians, were forbidden on pain of death to profess their religion openly. Many were martyred; many succumbed, publicly professing Islam, but often remaining secretly faithful to their own religion. Still others, among them the family of Maimonides, fled into exile.

Leaving Cordova with his family, Maimon, a rabbi and judge of the rabbinical court, wandered from city to city in Spain and North Africa, settling at last, strangely, in Fez, center of the Almohad movement. "This seems to us like going from the frying pan into the fire," Isaac Husik says in his account, "for Fez was the lion's den itself." But in Fez the Maimon family seems to have found the eye of the hurricane, as it were. During the years 1160–1165 they found a temporary respite from persecution.[3a] Later there were stories that Maimonides was among those who converted, at least nominally, to Islam. These reports remain unverified and seem to be based in part on conjecture, in part on the desire of subsequent historians to claim the celebrated Jewish savant for Islam. But it seems most improbable that the family would have uprooted themselves and undertaken the wanderings which were to be their lot for nearly twenty years had they accepted a verbal apostasy which would have freed them from such hardship. Maimonides himself clearly viewed his family's wanderings as a successful

---

3a. The truth is that the Almohad monarch, who would not allow even exile to his Jewish subjects as an alternative to death or Islam, died within a month of promulgating this decree; and his son, who succeeded him, did not see fit to enforce compulsory conversion with the rigor his father had demanded.

flight from forced apostasy.[4] It is possible, however, that in Fez the Maimon family revealed their Jewish faith only to a small circle of trusted friends.

Throughout his family's travels, the young Maimonides was attempting to educate himself as well as the circumstances would permit. His brilliance and love of learning were noted early (Maimonides himself, like many scholars of his day, believed that there are individuals who have an innate facility for learning), but since his father's library had been left behind in Cordova, he was forced to rely on what books he could find and, as was the custom, commit to memory.

Maimonides' first essays into scholarship show a vital interest in science, mathematics, and logic,[5] but the impact of his early scientific and logical studies was far greater than his two first slender volumes indicate. His interest in these areas permeates his life and all his subsequent writings—no doubt because those early studies sounded a note of affinity with his own profound rationality and penetrating analytical sense.

During his family's period of more or less underground existence the Rambam undertook to write commentaries on several portions of the Talmud,[6] but he seems to have abandoned his plans of a commentary on the entire Talmud and turned instead to the more unconventional task of writing a commentary on the Jewish legal canon, the Mishnah (*Kitab al-Siraj*), which laid the foundation for his reputation as a jurisprudent. Because of the rigors of his family's nomadic existence, the writing of this work took ten years, spanning the crucial decade of maturation between Maimonides' twenty-third and thirty-third years. Always keenly sensitive about the disruption of his education, Maimonides begged forgiveness from the reader for any errors his

---

4. See Maimonides' statements at the close of his Commentary on the Mishnah and those reported by R. Eleazar Askari of Safed, *Sefer Haredim,* quoted in Friedländer, "The Life of Moses Maimonides," *Guide for the Perplexed* (London, 1904), p. xviii. Cf. D. S. Margoliouth, *Jewish Quarterly Review,* o.s. XIII (1901), 539–41.

5. Maimonides' first book was probably his *Millot ha-Higgayon,* a brief conspectus of logical terminology said to have been written when he was sixteen. His second, published when he was twenty-three, was a handbook on the Jewish calendar (*Maamar ha-Ibbur*) combining rabbinic learning with mathematical and astronomic scholarship. (See Bibliography.)

6. Including tractate *Hullin* and orders *Moed, Nashim,* and *Nezikin.*

book might contain, parts having been written on shipboard, parts on the road. But, while he might fear openly—as he does in his famous Letter to Yemen—that he had not reached the level of his ancestors in learning, his legal work was to raise the study of Jewish law to a level of accessibility and rigor it had not reached since Talmudic times.

In 1165 the Maimon family's sojourn in Fez, which could never have been very secure, came to an end. Maimonides' father had written an epistle of consolation and encouragement for the Jews,[7] urging them to believe that God would not change His religion, abrogating the Torah in favor of the Koran, as was the Muslim claim. (The denial of this Koranic claim later became one of the thirteen articles in his son Maimonides' famous Creed.) Maimon implored his fellow Jews to hold fast to the Torah, comforting those who had paid lip service to Islam by assuring them that their true faith was the sincere belief preserved within their hearts. Al-Ghazali himself had made a similar claim in his *Revival;* for a coerced or insincere confession of faith had no spiritual significance. Maimon assured the distraught victims of cruel attempts to extract conversions at the point of the sword that such professions of Islam had no standing in Jewish law. The thrust of his argument parallels the force of the Kol Nidre prayer, which frees the mind from the tyranny of language by declaring both vain vows and vain oaths null and void.

There was, however, an opposing point of view, for the issue was an extremely sensitive one. Moved, perhaps, by the memory of those who had died as martyrs rather than utter the hateful words, an anonymous author rebutted the Maimon consolation, claiming that the words of the mouth *did* count as apostasy. Maimonides had come to his father's defense with a brilliantly argued legal and theological tract on apostasy and martyrdom [8] intended to tip the scales in favor of consolation for the living rather than adding to their sense of remorse for the sake of the dead.

The publication of this response inevitably brought Maimonides' Jewish views so much into the public eye as to make the family's pres-

7. Maimon's Letter of Consolation is edited and translated by L. M. Simmons in *The Jewish Quarterly Review,* o.s. II (1890), pp. 62 ff.; also F. Kobler, *A Treasury of Jewish Letters* (Philadelphia, 1954).
8. See Bibliography.

ence in Fez gradually untenable. They therefore set sail for Palestine on Apirl 18, 1165. By Maimonides' own account, the ship was nearly lost in the long and stormy sea voyage. Arriving in Acre, Maimonides journeyed to the site of the Temple in Jerusalem, where he prayed in solemn gratitude for having been preserved to accomplish this pilgrimage. He traveled to Hebron as well, the traditional resting place of Abraham, who held a special place in Maimonides' vision of history, not only as the first spokesman of a universal monotheism but also as the first to base theological claims on arguments derived from reason. Palestine, then under the rule of the Latin Kingdom of Jerusalem, proved a disappointment as a potential home. Persecution was severe, the land undeveloped. There were few Jews, and existing Jewish communal life was weak. After a few months, the family journeyed to Egypt, and, finding at last a measure of toleration and a major center of Jewish life, they finally settled in exhaustion.[9] Soon afterwards, Maimonides' father died.

Despite the shattering of the delicate globe of security, prosperity, recognition, and achievement which he had enjoyed in Jewish Cordova, and despite his own profound sense of having been cheated out of a formal higher education in his homeland, Maimonides did not assume the posture of a refugee in defeat. Through his private efforts he had more than made good what he had lost in communal education, and soon after arriving, he took the place of leadership to which his learning entitled him. After some two years' stay in Alexandria, he transferred to Old Cairo (or Fustat, as it was called). His name is prominently recorded on a manifesto of 1167 addressed by the rabbinic leaders of Cairo to the Jews of Egypt declaring that the Jewish world had not been destroyed; it was to be raised up, reorganized, and reformed, "reconciling the hearts of the fathers to their children," by the rallying of the fragmented and demoralized community to the banner of rabbinic authority. The Commentary on the Mishnah was finished about 1168. That same year he was appointed judge of the rab-

9. Possibly in violation of what Maimonides may have understood as a prohibition against Jews returning to Egypt. There were mitigating circumstances—and there is always the possibility that he regarded this prohibition as having lapsed with the abandonment of idolatry in Egypt.

binical court, and legal work remained a major occupation thenceforward.

In Cairo Maimonides found the Jews polarized between the Karaite and Rabbanite movements. As an upholder of the continuity of the Jewish tradition and thus a defender of the legitimacy of rabbinic authority, Maimonides was naturally a member of the Rabbanite party. He rejected categorically the Karaite contention that every man might develop his own authoritative interpretation of the Law. It should be acknowledged that both Karaites and Rabbanites in his time were progressive in outlook, in that both recognized the necessity of a process by which the entire Jewish law might grow and develop. But Karaites understood this process to take place by radical steps in which precedent had no binding force, while Rabbanites sought a more organic mode of development. What they most feared was that Karaite individualism represented a desire to found one's interpretation of the Law on personal preference. And this, as Maimonides insisted, implied a rejection of the very concept of divine legislation upon which Judaism is founded.

The conflict between the Karaites and Rabbanites was not confined to problems of theology and law. It had a political dimension which often threatened to grow beyond proportions which either set of antagonists could control. One Karaite leader, Zuta, who adopted the Biblical messianic title *Sar ha-Shalom*, "Prince of Peace," was lampooned by the Rabbanites as *Shor ha-Shalem*, "Perfect Ox." Maimonides helped to block Zuta's vengeance against one Rabbanite leader, and as a result lived afterwards under the by-no-means-unfounded fear that Karaite reprisals might place his life in jeopardy.

Communal leadership in the Rambam's time was a responsibility fraught with peril and burdened with the ever-present external threat of persecution or new exile. The danger was very real that Jewish internal divisions might boil over into the hostile outside environment. Assumption of leadership in such times could only express a profound sense of responsibility, underlined in the Rambam's case by his refusal to exact material gain from his rabbinic role. Throughout his life Maimonides refused to earn his living "from Torah," as the saying went. Instead, like the Talmudic rabbis, he followed a trade; and he condemned rabbis who earned their bread from their calling, feeling that it was a debasement of learning and the surest means of destroying rabbinic authority to make judicial interpreters the hired employees of their communities. In Egypt the family was supported at first by Maimonides' younger brother David, who engaged in the jewel trade. According to one source, Maimonides also participated in the family business. But Maimonides himself remembers his brother as the mainstay of the family, who engaged in trade in order that he, the elder brother, might devote himself to scholarship. The tragic death of David during a business trip in a shipwreck on the Indian Ocean left Maimonides in a state of deep depression bordering on prostration, which, he writes, lasted nearly a year. The family's savings lost in the same disaster, Maimonides himself took up the responsibility of supporting the family as a physician, and he practiced medicine assiduously until his death.

It is not known to what extent Maimonides was clinically trained by any of the numerous Jewish or Muslim physicians who lived in Cairo in his time. His medical writings refer over a hundred times to physicians of the West, that is, North Africa, including two whom he knew in Fez. Most likely he first learned medicine by reading the Arabic texts of such authorities as Hippocrates, Galen, Razi, Avenzoar, and Avicenna, for his writings evidence mastery of these and other of the great exponents of the Greek-Roman-Arabic-Persian medical tradition. But he seems at least to have observed a great deal in Fez and then perhaps to have acquired clinical experience in Cairo, perhaps in a group practice.

Considering medicine not merely a trade but an art of vital importance to the maintenance of human life, Maimonides invested it with the same diligence and lucidity he brought to everything he valued. As a result, his reputation as a physician grew, and with it his practice— to the point that he was taken up as a physician by the Fatimid court. After the Fatimid dynasty was overthrown in 1171, Maimonides was retained and given a regular stipend by the Qadi al-Fadil, wazir and chief justice to the new ruler, Saladin. With the latter's death in 1193 and the ensuing struggle for succession among his sons, Maimonides became chief physician to Saladin's eldest son, al-Malik al-Afdal, a dissolute prince who ruled for the last two years of the twelfth century with neither the vigor nor the success his father had shown and who paid scant heed to the outspoken moral/medical admonitions of his physician.

Maimonides' medical duties at the court in this last period of his life were extremely demanding. He attended the sultan in the citadel daily and was responsible also for the health of his children, his harem, and numerous court officials. Afternoons, when he could break away from the palace, were devoted to a demanding private practice. Evenings, when not totally exhausted, Maimonides turned to his medical books, for he felt urgently the need to exercise full command of the science behind his art and was not satisfied unless he could explain his diagnoses and prescriptions scientifically according to the best knowledge of the day. Yet Maimonides was no slave to the old texts, but practiced flexibily, adjusting the treatment to the case. One wonders when he found time to write,[10] but it is clear that Maimonides' medical works (ten treatises are known) date from this late period of his life, the last twenty years of the twelfth century, and that he taught medicine as well.

It was not medicine alone which first attracted the Fatimid court to the Jewish physician but also his knowledge of philosophy and other "Greek" sciences, which were highly prized by the enlightened rulers of the day and which the best physicians often combined with a knowledge of medicine. According to the Muslim biographer Ibn al-Qifti, Maimonides was much sought after to lead groups in the study of these sciences. His conversation, no doubt, was valued as well, especially by those who, like himself, placed no value upon gossip or insipid small talk.

The completion of his great code of Jewish law, the *Mishneh Torah*, around 1178 brought even greater fame to Maimonides as a legal authority than had his earlier commentary on the Mishnah and increased the volume of requests for his legal opinions on all manner of questions. His hundreds of responses, covering his remaining years, range from brief answers to knotty legal puzzles to complete, balanced monographs on problems involving major issues of jurisprudence. Correspondents from all over the world seemed to sense, or else to

10. Cf. his famous letter to his translator Ibn Tibbon, translated in *A Treasury of Jewish Letters*, ed. Franz Kobler (Philadelphia, 1954).

learn from Maimonides' legal work, that their letters would bring them into contact with one of the greatest Jewish jurists of any time.

Fame also brought Maimonides a desperate plea for spiritual guidance and support from the ancient Jewish community of Yemen. Beleaguered by persecution at the hands of a Muslim sectarian movement which offered a choice of apostasy or death and bewildered by one of their own defected scholars who urged them to accept the Muslim pretender as Mahdi (divinely prophesied forerunner of Redemption), the Jews of Yemen appealed for reassurance through their leader, Jacob al-Fayumi, to the intellectual authority of the Rambam. In his response, written in 1172, which he urged be circulated throughout the Jewish settlements of Yemen, Maimonides refuted the Messianic pretensions of the self-styled Mahdi and rallied the Jews of Yemen by reaffirming the universality of the Jewish faith and reminding the disheartened of God's promises that the faith of Israel would never be displaced. In gratitude for the successful intervention of Maimonides, the Jews of Yemen inserted his name into the sacred Kaddish prayer, affirming their hope that the true Messiah would come in the time of Moses ben Maimon.

Although an active and decisive controversialist, and well prepared to operate on a popular level, Maimonides never sank to the level of parochialism or dogmatism. Even in the context of polemic, his positions were keenly argued and never partitioned off from the highest reaches of his thought. His voluminous correspondence is eloquent witness to the high regard in which his contemporaries held him as an intellectual and legal authority and a standard-bearer to the scattered Jewish people. Maimonides consistently combatted the tendency of some of his contemporaries to enlist vulgar superstition in the service of religion. This he did on legal as well as conceptual grounds, not hesitating to allegorize or simply to dismiss as minority opinions Talmudic views which reason showed to be unfounded. Belief in talismans, astrology, and amulets is, according to Maimonides' historical appraisal, no part of monotheism at all but a survival of pagan notions of religion involving localized, capricious forces operating not through but in spite of natural laws. It is thus directly inimical to the concept of a universal uncapricious (nonvenal) God as well as to the projection of a universal science of nature, through which alone God's wisdom can be comprehended.

The most difficult problem Maimonides' writings were to confront did not concern matters of law or communal faith and unity or even medicine, but the problems of theology, specifically the problems posed by a critical scrutiny of Scripture in the light of the truths of science and reason. To the ill-educated and the ignorant, of course, there were no problems in Scripture. For, as Maimonides remarks, to such a person nothing is imposssible. But to those whose contact with philosophy and science had brought them beyond this uncritical level, the Torah might readily begin to appear to be a deep morass of problems. Guidance was to be found only in reaching through the problematic apparent meaning of the Torah to its deeper message. It was *through* the problems indeed that the message was to be derived; the difficulties of the text were pointers, according to Maimonides, defining the parameters within which Torah's meaning must lie. Philosophy and science, far from being impediments to a proper understanding of Biblical truth, were means by which such understanding might be informed, and depth in such studies could only deepen one's understanding of Scripture.

Rabbi Joseph ibn Judah Aqnin, who had journeyed to Cairo to study under Maimonides, typified, in Maimonides' judgment, the need of those Jews nurtured in childhood on the stories of the Bible, brought up with a traditional respect for Biblical law, but educated (or semieducated) in the logic, cosmology, theology, and philosophy of the Greco-Arabic tradition. Rabbi Joseph and many others like him had not yet found the means of integrating the one experience with the other. They lacked, therefore, a fully developed understanding of the properly philosophical contribution of the Bible.

In teaching Rabbi Joseph, Maimonides became aware how urgently he and others like him needed a philosophic/scientific exegesis of the conceptual content of the Torah, which would place not merely the laws and stories but the underlying concepts of the Bible in relation to the ideas of Greek philosophy and monotheistic (largely Islamic) theology. Following a course of study as old as Plato, Maimonides initiated his student into astronomy and mathematics, then logic. Finally, perceiving an ability to comprehend rather than confuse the truths of "first philosophy," Maimonides introduced his student cautiously to metaphysics, not by presenting this central area of philosophy systematically as a science for study but by allusions to one or another of the problems of Scripture and thus indirectly to the truths which these problems both concealed and (to the prepared sensibility) revealed. To the student whose mind had already been primed by his own inquiries and doubts, this was sufficient. Maimonides found in Joseph an eager and able student whose need was equalled by his capacity to understand; for, in such a case, the need was the direct result of the capacity to understand. After Joseph's departure, Maimonides composed his greatest work, as if to meet the needs of all those perplexed by the apparent incongruity of Scripture with the teachings of philosophy and science.

The *Moreh Nevukhim*, or *Guide to the Perplexed*, was published in 1190. Its composition probably occupied as much as five years; like most of Maimonides' works, with the notable exception of the *Mishneh Torah*, it was composed in Arabic (*Moreh Nevukhim* is the Hebrew title; in Arabic it is *Dalalat al-Hairin*), although twice translated into Hebrew within a short time of its completion, independently by Samuel ibn Tibbon and Judah al-Harizi.[11] It was not, as it is often represented, a mere polemical or apologetic work. The doubts and difficulties of Ibn Aqnin, like those of Augustine long before Maimonides and of Descartes long after, rather serve as the occasion for developing a coherent set of philosophical ideas. The true subject of the *Moreh Nevukhim* is not merely the defense of scriptural faith but the definition of that faith, the development of an intellectually acceptable

11. Harizi was the better stylist, but Maimonides' son, Abraham, regarded his work as faulty. Ibn Tibbon, who undertook his translation at the suggestion of Maimonides himself and with some guidance from the author, was unfortunately a rather pedestrian writer, but he worked with a painstakingly literal faithfulness to the original text. Although quite out of keeping with the Rambam's own interpretive methods and his explicit admonition to the reader always to understand his words in the most intelligible and acceptable possible sense, Ibn Tibbon's version was thought of as the authorized translation and was heavily relied upon by Maimonists, possibly because they feared polemical misconstruing of the *Moreh*. Harizi's translation survives in a unique Paris manuscript, Ibn Tibbon's in many manuscripts. Latin translations of the *Doctor Perplexorum* date from the thirteenth century.

foundation for belief. The premise of a doubting inquirer gives Maimonides, as it had given Plato, a framework within which one might raise radical questions without appearing to question radically, and in that context to delineate the absolute conditions of rational belief. Most of the major problems dealt with in the *Guide* are represented by the selections in the present book. Its sources, assumptions, and the extent of its influence and relevance will be discussed in the remaining sections of this Introduction.

Maimonides apparently married twice, remarrying after his first wife died in Egypt. His only son, Abraham, born in 1187, followed in his father's footsteps in law, medicine, and rabbinics, and was also the *nagid* or official head of the Egyptian Jewish community, an office which was retained in the family for five generations, no doubt thanks to the Rambam's prestige. Maimonides died December 13, 1204,[12] and was buried, in accordance with his own wishes, at Tiberias. He was deeply mourned by the entire Jewish world and was honored as well by an official period of public mourning in Egypt affecting Jews and Gentiles alike. At the time of the Rambam's death his son was only seventeen; but, through his father's teaching and the subsequent study of his father's books, Abraham demonstrated enough of his father's influence to become a significant exponent of the Maimonidean point of view.

The epitaph inscribed on Maimonides' tomb by an unknown hand represents him as the pure effulgence of Divine Intelligence. But a universally known Hebrew saying is sufficient testimony to the man's place in Judaism and in the history of world civilization: *Mi Mosheh le-Mosheh lo kam ke-Mosheh*—''From Moses to Moses there arose none like Moses.''

The Intellectual Backgrounds of Maimonides' Philosophy

It is impossible to speak of philosophy in the western world without reference to the specific complex of philosophical schools or traditions

---

12. 20 Tevet is the yahrzeit.

which arose among the ancient Greeks, passed to the Romans and Greek-speaking Christians of the Eastern Empire, then to their Muslim successors, from them to the Sephardic Jews, to the Latin Christians, and ultimately to the entire civilized world. Thus when Maimonides speaks of Philosophy, he refers to the cluster of philosophical traditions or schools which first disentangled themselves from myth and began their independent development some six hundred years before the common era. When he speaks of the Philosophers, it is specifically to the adherents of these schools and, above all, to the representatives of the foremost and most long-lived philosophic school of his day, the fused tradition of Plato, Aristotle, and Plotinus.

THE GREEK TRADITION

From its inception, Greek philosophy saw itself as an attempt to give an objective rather than mythical or anthropomorphic account of nature and divinity. Thus the very birth of Greek philosophy is marked by the replacement of cosmogony by cosmology, of theogony by theology: The question for the first philosophers (very much at variance with that of the Greek mythologists) was not how the world came to be but how the world is constituted, *i.e.,* "What is it *made of?*" The question was not (as in mythology) "What are the family histories and quarrels of the gods?" but rather "How can man conceive of the divine in its relationship to nature?" Thus Thales of Miletus (who flourished around 585 B.C.E.) was called the first philosopher by Aristotle not because of any supposed cleverness in his notions that everything was made of water and that all things were filled with gods but because he was the first Greek to replace the question "Where did everything come from?" with the question "What is the underlying nature of all things?"; he was concerned not with the personalities and supposed passions of the gods but with the concept of divinity itself.

The course of Greek philosophy is long and various, and not only were numerous alternative answers proposed to Thales' questions regarding nature and divinity but the questions themselves were rethought many times. Yet there is a certain element in Thales' way of conceiving the two questions which persists with remarkable constancy throughout more than a thousand years of Greek philosophical development and projects a decisive influence into the time of Maimonides and far beyond that period: (1) The cosmological question was conceived of as precluding any sort of temporal or genetic answer. The notion of describing the world's origins was regarded, almost unanimously, by Greek philosophical thinkers as a mythopoeic (or story-telling) means of dealing with a basically analytic question as to the world's nature. Accounts of the world's origins, then, were inevitably to be treated by these thinkers (and by all who fell under their powerful spell) as crude or subtle efforts to symbolize realities which were not in actuality historical at all. (2) The theological question was so conceived as ultimately to involve a radical rejection of the applicability to the divine of any predication conditioned by the narrowness of human experience.

These two limitations go far toward defining what philosophy meant to the Greeks, in the sense that they differentiated philosophy from other approaches to the same broad areas. And they were, of course, responsible for the removing of the philosophical phases of Greek thought to a higher level of universality than had been achieved in Greek myth or epic. They are nonetheless limitations, as was to become evident when Greek thought came into confrontation with the theological and cosmological conceptions of the Hebrews, most notably with the Judaic concept of a creator God who brought all the universe into being—from nothing, by a free act of will, a finite time ago—and who governs that universe in wisdom, justice, and compassion.

The successors of Thales proposed numerous alternatives to the notion that the world was made of water, but most of them retained the presumption that there was a single changeless substance underlying all things. The nature of this "substrate" could not be accounted for without initiating the same sort of infinite chicken-and-egg regress which had made cosmogony seem futile, but it was something in terms of which all phenomena were to be accounted for.

It was Parmenides (fifth century B.C.E.) who transformed cosmology into metaphysics by transferring the inquiry from the composition of the world to the prior and more profound question "What is reality?" The underlying presumption that reality is changeless remained, elevated from an assumption to an explicit principle and conclusion. For if one were able to express in a single word Parmenides' answer to the question of the nature of reality, that word would be "invariance"—reality is invariance in time, in identity, in place. And it was Parmenides who first articulated the prejudice of the Greek philosophers against the concept of creation when he demanded to know, if being had come to be, *how* it had done so and *why* it had not done so earlier. Even Heraclitus (fifth century B.C.E.), who regarded change as the fundamental feature of reality and thus seems to disagree with Parmenides, saw in change a measured, ordered process, uniting opposites—a constancy, in other words, in change itself.

In his cosmological dialogue, the *Timaeus,* written near his eightieth year, Plato (427–348 B.C.E.) sounded the theme which was to become by the time of Maimonides the dominant motif in virtually all discussions of the relationship between being and change. The changeable as such, Plato argued, was, because of its inconstancy, incapable of truly being known or thought and thus incapable of truly (and eternally) being real. Only the ideal, the absolute and universal, was capable of the perfect changelessness and intelligibility required of true being. Plato characterized the relation between being and becoming as one in which the changeable particulars "participated" or shared in the true being of their eternal "forms" or ideas. He symbolized this relation as one in which the ideas were patterns, as it were, of changeable particulars, and he invoked the notion of a Demiurge or "craftsman" god who realized these patterns in matter. To Plato matter seemed to be the mere occasion for the realization of form, but to his followers it appeared that Plato had left ambiguous the question of whether matter had always existed or whether the operation of the Demiurge was to be understood temporally or as an act of absolute creation.

This was an ambiguity which the subsequent tradition of philosophy could not let stand. Aristotle alone, of all Plato's followers, took Plato "literally," *i.e.,* as having asserted the creation of the world. (For had not Plato argued that the nature of becoming was not such that it can always have existed?) All the rest of Plato's principal interpreters took the Demiurge as one of Plato's many excursions into the philosophical use of myth to symbolize an abstruse concept, in this case that of participation. Matter, they argued, had in Plato's view predated the application to it of form, which Plato called the giving of being. Even Aristotle did not agree with what he took to be Plato's intended meaning.

Aristotle (384–322 B.C.E.) did more than any other Greek to identify philosophical cosmology with eternalism, for his entire account of causality, change, and being itself was founded on the notion that nature's order is eternal, that alteration is a mere interplay of "forms" in matter (although he did not conceive of forms in just the same way as Plato), and that the nature of being is to be, *i.e.,* to be *in* becoming. It was Aristotle who followed the hints of Parmenides to formulate systematic arguments in favor of the eternity of the cosmos, with which Maimonides and indeed all monotheistic thinkers were compelled to grapple. (See Part Two of this book.)

Greek philosophical theology began with a discomfort with the anthropomorphic gods of the mythic tradition, and much of its history may be seen as a progressive unbuilding of the myths, an effort to transpose the personified abstractions of mythology back into abstract or concrete "principles," related to but not always identical with those from which the mythic persons themselves had sprung. Xenophanes (sixth century B.C.E.) is typical of the early response by critical Greek thinkers to traditional mythology. "Mortals suppose the gods are born and have clothes and speech, and bodies like their own," he said. "The Ethiopians say their gods are snub-nosed and black; the Thracians, that theirs have blue eyes and red hair." Animals too, if they could draw, would picture the gods in their own images. But in truth there is one God above all gods and men, unlike any mortal thing, unmoved, but moving all besides Himself by the power of His mind, seeing, thinking, hearing in all His parts.[1] Xenophanes still believed that God had a body, although different from the body of any mortal thing, yet in the few sentences of his theology which survive he had already taken radical steps toward transcendentalism, recognized what was to become a classic problem of philosophical theology, the problem of the relation of a transcendent God to the world, and suggested one classic philosophical solution to that problem in the notion that God governs the world as the mind governs the body.

The various substrates proposed by the earliest Greek physicalists (or *physikoi,* as they were called) were all attempts to replace anthro-

---

1. Xenophanes fragments 16, 15, quoted in Clement of Alexandria *Stromateis* VII:22., V:109.3, tr. after Geoffrey Kirk and J. E. Raven, *The Presocratic Philosophers* (New York, 1961), nos. 171, 172.

pomorphic representations of the basis of stability (*e.g.*, Atlas bearing the heavens on his shoulders) with naturalistic ones. In this sense their materialism itself was an outgrowth of the move away from anthropomorphic theological concepts. But more fruitful than materialism, from a theological point of view, was the approach of Anaxagoras (fifth century B.C.E.), who introduced a ruling and self-ruled, "unmingled" principle into his universe of mixtures within mixtures, a principle he called Mind. The Mind of Anaxagoras and the *Logos* or "Word" of Heraclitus (that is, the underlying principle of unity and measure in change) became the food for thought which led Plato and his student Aristotle to their own conceptions of the nature of a transcendent deity beyond matter and yet ruling matter as mind rules body or as idea "governs" its instance.

To Plato it was plain that the Idea of the Good was not only the highest Idea; but, since Ideas were the true reality, the highest reality as well. Ideas were bodied forth in matter by a gradual declension of the absolute into the particular. Identifying the Idea or "Form" of the Good with God, Plato found it possible to envision absolute divine transcendence of all finite categories while maintaining that the world itself, in every affirmative aspect of its being, was the expression of the nature of God.

Aristotle was unable to maintain Plato's faith in the independent existence of pure ideas, but he did not depart completely from the elegant synthesis created by the man who had been his teacher for nineteen years. While ideas might not be self-subsistent, minds were, and ideas might exist in minds. Thus God became a disembodied mind, and the ideas or essences of things might have become its thoughts had Aristotle's transcendentalism not made him hesitant to say that the Highest Mind thinks anything but Itself. Totally self-absorbed, the Mind or God of Aristotle is an Idea, a thought thinking itself. It moves the world without itself being moved because it is the highest Good, and as such draws all things toward its own perfection. It is in fact the source of being in all things, since all reality or realization must, according to Aristotle, stem from the highest and most perfectly self-sufficient reality.

The kindred schools of Plato and Aristotle thus offered a brilliant resolution of the problems of transcendence and immanence as posed within the Greek philosophical world. The Stoics, by contrast, in identifying the divine with physical nature, carried immanence so far that they risked turning all religious discourse into one great equivocation, which left a profound ambiguity as to whether the divine was natural or nature was divine. The Epicureans, on the other hand, with their express intention to find divinity irrelevant to nature in general and to man's ethical choice in particular, carried transcendentalism so far as to cause medieval theists to wonder what significance the notion of divine existence can have had for them at all. The balance of Plato and Aristotle between these two extremes did much to enhance the impression shared by most medieval philosophers that these two and their followers alone were worthy of being taken seriously.

Cosmology and theology, Plato and Aristotle, therefore, met in the post-Aristotelian traditions of Academic (*i.e.*, Platonic) and Peripatetic (Aristotelian) philosophy. One of the finest Peripatetics, Alexander of Aphrodisias (flourished at Athens 198–211 c.e.), who was a prime source for Maimonides, did much to expose the confusions implicit in the Stoic pantheism while developing a far more careful and critical view of both cosmology and theology. Plato's Academy, after fully recovering from a long *mésalliance* with Skepticism, enthusiastically adopted and developed the philosophy of Plotinus (*ca.* 204–270 c.e.), an Egyptian-born Roman who transformed the static "participation" of Plato into a dynamic but timeless interaction between the many and the One, which he termed "flowing forth" or emanation. Plotinus was aware of Judaeo-Christian concepts of creation and carefully distinguished the eternal flow of emanation (the logical outcome of the very nature of divinity) from the abrupt and arbitrary act of creation, which appeared to him as it would have to Aristotle or any of his Greek followers to be a particularly crude regression into mythology.

Galen of Pergamon (*ca.* 129–199 c.e.), one of the most celebrated physicians of antiquity and an eclectic philosopher as well, affords an excellent illustration of the felt incongruity between the assumptions of Greek philosophy and those of Hebrew Scriptures. To Galen the Hebrew Scriptures seemed to depend too much on the notion of Will: Was God an arbitrary authority who laid down a law for man and nature which was not determined by what was the best? This seemed to be the implication not only of the Mosaic concept of divine self-revelation but of the very concept of creation as put forward in the Bible.

But while the theological notions of the Jews and Christians might well appear somewhat absurd from the parochial perspective of pagan Greek philosophy, it became clear very early to the Jews and Christians that there was something to be learned from the philosophers. Indeed, this willingness to learn may have contributed to the survival of the monotheistic religions long after the pagan tradition had died out.

The growth of Christianity and the resultant polemics, first of pagan versus Christian and then of Christian versus pagan, had accentuated the polarization between monotheist and Greek cosmology and theology. As a reaction to Christology, the Platonic Highest Principle grew more and more transcendent, "higher" principles being posited, even beyond the One. And, as if to compensate, more and more intermediary figures (demigods, demons, principalities, etc.) were introduced to mediate between nature and absolute Divinity, as the latter drew more and more remote, until the pagan philosophers' universe had grown so baroque as to appear ridiculous to the critical outsider. The very concept of divine transcendence began to seem a mockery of itself if this were the only means of securing it.

The more evident Greek philosophy made the problematic character of the nexus between a monadic and invariant Divinity and the diversity and changeability of nature, the more evident did it become to adherents of the monotheist traditions that the twin theological and cosmological concepts of divine will and divine creation were not as patently naïve as Greek philosophers made out. And this was to give monotheistic thinkers a philosophic foundation for a new spirit of self-confidence and intellectual independence. As Maimonides succinctly puts it: How without creation by something which we can conceive in human terms only as a will can the multifold and complex world we know emerge from the simplicity of God?

THE JUDAIC TRADITION

With respect to the particular issues of cosmology and theology which we have been discussing, the Jewish tradition in Maimonides' time was in certain ways the oldest, in others the youngest of the approaches to a monotheistic philosophy. Philosophy considered as an explicit, organized discipline which could trace its origins to Greek philosophical theory and practice was quite new in Judaism in the Rambam's time, for it derived from Muslim efforts in philosophy which themselves dated only from the ninth century. But the roots of Jewish cosmology and theology are planted deeply in the Torah.

The Torah, to be sure, is not philosophy in the technical sense, for it does not operate according to the Greek method of thesis-problem-argument-resolution. As Maimonides most emphatically states, it is law, religion, a guide to life. Yet embedded in the Torah are profound conceptions, not explicitly stated but implicit in the language, symbols, myths, and allegories of the text, as gold, to use the Rambam's image, underlies a filigree of silver. It would be absurd to imagine the Torah as a true guide to life if this were not so. This assumption underlies the work of all the great Jewish interpreters of the Law. The rabbis of the Talmud consistently ask not the fundamentalists' question, "What does the Bible say?" but their own exegetical question, "What does the Torah teach?" By this interpretive method, even apparent redundancies, ambiguities, incongruities, and grammatical irregularities become not shoals on which faith must founder but food for creative thinking which develops in a continuous tradition the authentic themes implicit in the text. In this sense one may say that philosophy is latent in the Torah.

To cite an example: The God of the Torah is described (Exodus 20:5) as *el kana*—"a jealous god," as the phrase is usually translated. And we are almost invariably told (and have been since the earliest days of Christianity) by scholars and critics of Hebrew Scriptures that the God of the Hebrews was a splenetic tribal deity (who shared, presumably, the narrowness and passions of his tribe). Yet if we look at this phrase in context (in the second of the Ten Commandments) and bear in mind that the Torah does not use abstract vocabulary, can we imagine a more graphic and direct way of symbolizing divine exclusivity? And was not exclusivity a corollary of the central theme of monotheism? [2] Attempts to derive any but the crudest representations

2. *Cf. Moreh* I:36. The later prophets of the Hebrew Bible, generally not implicated in the "splenetic tribal deity" accusations, evince no discomfort with the *el kana* theme

from the Hebrew Bible are often regarded as "reading something into the text." But such a conclusion can be sustained only by presuming categorically and *a priori* that nothing subtle, nothing deep underlies the Torah. And no one making such an assumption, as Maimonides argues, can possibly claim to do so in the name of defending the true sense of the Torah as representing a divinely given way of life.

The Torah, then, does contain cosmology and theology, albeit not of the explicit variety. Its concepts need not be read in the crudest and most primitive possible ways, and they were not so read by the philosophers (or Sages, as Maimonides calls them) of Judaism.

The most prominent features of Biblical cosmology and theology are in marked contrast to the established trends of Greek philosophical theology. The world and all things in it, according to the Torah, were created and thus are not eternal. The rule of causality in nature, therefore, is not regarded as conflicting with the world's having existed for a finite time. The existence of all created things is not regarded as being theirs simply by virtue of their exemplifying their essences but rather by virtue of their having been created by an act of God. God, then, is not seen as a "principle," not as a mere force or substrate of being, but as a voluntary, conscious, intelligent, and indeed in some ways arbitrary agent. Genesis eschews the effort to represent the creator God, as had been done so often in Semitic "creation myths." It thus achieves a sort of sublime transcendentalism of its own, by what it leaves unsaid. Nonetheless, the interjection of the category of will into the Godhead is from the Greek point of view a far more serious anthropomorphism than the carving of graven images, or even than the worshipping of many gods (of the Divine under many forms, as the subtlest of the "true" philosophers would have said).

And will was not the only remnant of "personality" in the God of the Hebrew Bible. Mercy, compassion, even providence and justice, as the Torah seemed to understand them, all appeared to show that the peculiar moral consciousness of the Jews did not allow their God to be reducible to a set of principles but required that He remain in some sense "personal." The reduction of the Godhead to first princi-

---

but develop it in terms of their symbolism of the relationship of God and Israel as that of lovers, often lovers who have fallen out as the result of jealousy over a rival, but who will ultimately surely be reconciled.

ples, however, is not at all an object of the Torah. And the fact that will as well as wisdom was inseparable from the Deity as conceived by the Torah does not at all imply that the Biblical categories are inferior to—or in any way more anthropomorphic than—those of the Greeks.

The earliest reaction of the Jews to the Greek traditions of philosophy, like that of the early Christians, was both strong and ambivalent. But while the Christians oscillated between blanket acceptance and outright rejection—Greek philosophical doctrines taking pride of place in the Gospel of John and extensive extracts of Neoplatonic philosophy being passed off as the work of a disciple of Paul, while Paul himself declared (somewhat disingenuously) that he knew no philosophy but Christ crucified and professed to prefer the "foolishness" of Christianity to the wisdom of the wise, and Tertullian announced impressively a faith in the absurd as such—the Jews took a different tack. To the Talmudic Sages it was clear that philosophy in general and cosmology/theology in particular (to which they allude, as was their custom, by a number of colorful names such as *Pardes,* or "the pleasure park") were both exceedingly dangerous and exceedingly precious:

> Four men went into the Pardes, our Rabbis taught, namely Ben Azzai, Ben Zoma, Aher, and Rabbi Akiba. Rabbi Akiba said to them: "When you reach the stones of pure marble, do not say, 'Water, water!' For it is said, 'He that speaks falsehood shall not be established before my eyes' " [Psalm 101:7].[3] Ben Azzai cast a glance and died. Of him Scripture says, "Precious in the sight of the Lord is the death of His saints" [Psalm 116:15]. Ben Zoma looked and became deranged. Of him Scripture says, "Have you found honey? Eat as much as is enough for you, lest you be filled with it and vomit it" [Proverbs 25:16]. Aher mutilated the shoots. Rabbi Akiba returned in peace [*Haggigah* 14b].

This startling and memorable account from the Talmud is a telling reminder of the forceful impact Greek thinking had upon the great

3. This gnomic remark, obviously intended here to symbolize Rabbi Akiba's critical and cautious approach, seems to suggest a warning against reductionism.

rabbis of the second century. Four of the greatest sages: Ben Azzai, a pure, ascetic scholar, whose tragic death occurred before his ordination as a rabbi and was ascribed directly to his philosophical/mystical researches so that he was reckoned as a martyr; Ben Zoma, who equated wisdom with an ability to learn from all men, defined might [4] as self-control and wealth as contentment (*Avot* 4:1), whose insanity was ascribed directly to his incapacity to digest the crucial problems which philosophy posed to Judaism; Elisha ben Abuya, called *Aher* ("another") after his apostasy, whose defection was ascribed to the troubling influence of speculative philosophy; and Akiba, the older contemporary of these three, who warned them of the dangers they confronted in these studies, yet engaged in them himself and emerged unscathed, even perhaps improved and all the more capable of taking his place as one of the greatest of the Talmudic rabbis. The philosophical problems with which these men struggled are explicitly situated by the Talmud in two crucial areas: (1) *maaseh bereshit*, the account in Genesis of the act of Creation and all that this implies regarding cosmology and the existence and nature of God, and (2) *maaseh merkavah*, the account of the Chariot (in Ezekiel), *i.e.,* the philosophical problem of theophany and all that it involves regarding God's manifestation to creation, divine providence and knowledge, the problem of evil, the immanence of a transcendent God, mysticism, prophecy, and divine revelation.

The earliest exposure to these matters as philosophical problems must have been a disquieting experience for the Sages. A telling experience for Judaism, it did not lead, however, to a reaction of complete recoil from philosophy, although the subject was recognized to be fraught with difficulty and danger. For the Torah itself (in Genesis, Ezekiel, and many other places such as Job, Psalms, Proverbs) demands that these problems be confronted and given most careful consideration. The Sages as a body had neither desire nor capacity to forbid study of these questions. That would have meant forbidding speculation on issues of philosophy which are not at all likely to leave men alone, issues to the resolution of which, in the rabbis' view, the

---

4. Equated by Maimonides with the prophetic quality of "boldness." See Parts One and Three.

Torah makes the decisive contribution. Their approach, therefore, was to attempt to regulate these studies by confining them (as Plato does) to those with the maturity and intellectual/moral capacity to benefit from them, and by demanding that instruction in these areas be most carefully and responsibly directed:

> The Act of Creation . . . may not be expounded upon in the presence of two, nor the Chariot in the presence of one unless he is wise and comprehends by his own understanding. . . ." [Mishnah cited in *Haggigah* 11b.]

This is the law laid down in the Mishnah. And it plainly does not preclude discussion of cosmology (Genesis) and theology (the Chariot), for the Gemarah or Talmudic discussion of the law proceeds immediately to discuss them in detail. Yet the mode in which this discussion is carried out is a remarkable tribute to the capacity of the rabbis, without the use of censorship, inquisition, or persecution, to regulate such inquiries. For, as Maimonides explains, the rabbinic method is not to explain but to expand upon the symbolism found in Scripture. The result is that forest of metaphors, parables, allegories and allusions known as the Aggadah (narrative material) in the Talmud, a forest in which the unprepared will grow weary long before reaching the heart of the matter, but in which the diligent and wise, "capable of understanding by themselves," will find much to help them in their quest. The shallow, superficial, and literal-minded are kept away from these rich, dangerous treasures by the admonition that all such material is legend and not legally binding. For it was entirely alien to the very constitution of the Jewish religion to attempt to bind belief (except in those few credal areas held to be vital to the continuance of society), and none of the rabbis stated as dogmas the results of his creative speculation into the most abstruse reaches of *maaseh bereshit* and *maaseh merkavah*. One result was that the forest grew, explored only rarely by the most penetrating Talmudic minds, and even then, for obvious reasons, not charted by them.[5] This might be called the tradition

---

5. Naturally this was not the only result. There were many who took the Aggadah literally, but our concern is not with them.

of "closet philosophy" in Judaism, which had a profound impact on Jewish thought but left the treasure, as it were, still in the mine.

There was, however, explicit philosophy in Judaism as well, one of the most brilliant exponents of which was Philo of Alexandria (ca. 25 B.C.E.–45 C.E.), a leader of the Jews of that cosmopolitan center. Philo was the first philosopher to approach monotheism in terms of the Greek philosophical tradition and to interpret it in terms of Biblical theology and cosmology. While Philo wrote in Greek for a Hellenized audience of Jews as well as non-Jews, he did not simply adopt the Greek mode of writing in thematic treatises or even dialogues but often couched his ideas in allegorical commentaries (a form common to Greeks and Jews) on the Bible.

To Philo it was plain that, despite differences of presentation, emphasis, and detail, there was a deep affinity between the prophetic message of Moses and the philosophic insights of Plato. Thus he viewed the account of Creation in Genesis as the philosophic prologue which Plato had declared all rational (as opposed to mere positive) laws must have, establishing the authority of the Law-giver (God) as the Author of nature and proclaiming the identity of the creative word or *logos* (*fiat, yehi,* "let there be"), by which an ordered world was called into being, with the divine imperative—the identity of the natural with the moral law. The same principle inspiring the prophet and affording the plan, idea, or design of creation was none other than an attribute of God, His Wisdom expressed as intelligence in man, as intelligibility in nature.

Philo exerted a profound impact on the fathers of the Christian church; they were captivated by his making philosophy the handmaiden of theology (as he put it) and saw in his discussions of the Torah as the Word/Wisdom of God the key to the solution of many of their difficulties regarding Jesus, whose person, after all, was regarded by Christian theology as having replaced the Law as "the way to salvation." Philo's immediate influence on the mainstream of Judaism beyond his community and time, however, was slight. Philosophy in Judaism continued to run in its deep but silent course, while Christian theologians and later Christian philosophers (that expression would have seemed a contradiction in terms to the earliest Christians as well as to their pagan philosophical detractors!) took up the task of integrating the truths of reason with those of revelation—often following the lead they had been given by Philo. Notable among these was John Philoponus (sixth century), who argued vigorously on philosophic and scientific grounds against the eternalism of the pagan philosophers.

When the new monotheistic faith of Islam swept across the Middle East and the southern countries of the Mediterranean in the seventh century, the Arab conquerors who settled down in the ensuing years to reap the fruits of their conquests found among their subjects, especially in the Greek-speaking provinces of Syria and Egypt, traditions of monotheistic philosophy going back hundreds of years. The Christians not only had engaged in spirited discussions on many issues of philosophy but had also preserved Greek texts and Syriac translations of what were to them the most crucial ancient works of philosophy, particularly those of Plato and Aristotle, which they studied and discussed with particular care.

It was probably the interchange of ideas between the Muslims and their Jewish, Christian, Zoroastrian, Buddhist, and Hindu subjects, converted and unconverted to the faith of the dominant group, which gave rise to the Islamic *Kalam* or dialectical theology. It was in the Kalam that the first truly radical and systematic defense of the concept of creation was undertaken (see Part Two). And the first major school of the Kalam, the Mutazilite, did much as well to set the stage for philosophical theology and cosmology in the context of monotheism by focusing on the principal problems arising out of the crucial monotheistic notions of God's unity (simplicity, uniqueness) and justice (fairness, rationality). It was in the Kalam that the issue of divine transcendence versus immanence, the latent tension between absolute infinitude and God's efficacy or immediacy, came to be expressed as a problem about the "attributes" of God, that is, about the characteristics of the Deity (which Scripture represents as personality traits) and the propriety or possibility of differentiating various attributes of a supremely transcendent and simplex God from one another, or from that God's Identity.

The growing interest of the Muslim peoples in Greek sciences such as medicine, astronomy, mathematics, and logic, not to mention their deepening awareness of the problems of theology and cosmology, led to an interest in Greek philosophy as well, and there followed a vast movement of translation from Greek (often via Syriac) into Arabic. The ensuing study of Greek philosophy and especially of Greek philosophical conceptions in theology and cosmology left an indelible impression on Islam and on all who came into close contact with the fruits of Islamic civilization.

The first Muslim philosopher of note, Kindi (ninth century)—an Arab prince, a physician, astrologer, and musical theorist—was a supporter of the translation movement and wrote a number of essays, often in letter form, on philosophical topics. Kindi, like Philo, believed that one should take truth wherever one found it. He assumed that it was possible to benefit from the insights of the Greeks without necessarily putting on the whole cloth of their views. Thus he adopted, for example, many Greek ethical prescriptions and even elements of the Platonic idealism on which they were based, but followed Philoponus in maintaining creation against the arguments of Aristotle. Kindi expressed his allegiance to his faith by proclaiming the subordination of the celestial spheres to the command of their Creator, and he exerted a decisive influence on the first medieval Jewish philosopher, the famous physician Isaac Israeli (d. early tenth century). Maimonides regarded Israeli as significant only as a physician, not as a philosopher.

Razi (d. 935), one of the greatest physicians of the Middle Ages, was also an eclectic, joining elements of Epicurean and Gnostic philosophy with his Platonism and rejecting Aristotle and all others who believed the world had always been as it is today. Razi denied special providence and special revelation (see Parts Four and Five), maintaining that God's share in the governance of the world consisted solely in the imparting of intelligence to an otherwise absurd existence and that even so the evil in the present human life outweighs the good.

To the Muslim philosophers who came after Kindi and Razi, such freewheeling eclecticism did not come so easily. To these men it became clear, as they studied and carefully commented on the ancient texts, that the Greek tradition, particularly that represented by Plato and Aristotle, was not such that one could simply pick and choose among its elements. The care and rigor of the greatest of the Greek philosophers had been bolstered by centuries of system-building enterprise on the part of their disciples. Thus to the serious student of philosophy Greek philosophical tradition represented an imposing and intricately organized system which one might criticize or even consider abandoning for a fresh philosophical start but which one could not adopt selectively without serious risk of running aground on some hidden inconsistency.

The two Muslims who undertook most seriously and comprehensively the task of integrating the philosophical tradition of Plato, Aristotle, and Plotinus with the insights of monotheism were the Turkish logician, political theorist, and metaphysician al-Farabi (870–950) and the Persian physician and philosopher Avicenna (Ibn Sina, 976–1037). Al-Farabi developed, *inter alia,* the philosophic notions of prophecy and prophetic revelation which Maimonides adapts, as well as contributing a great deal to Maimonides' conception of the good life for man (see Part Three) and the nature and function of the state (see Part Five). It was Avicenna who gave Maimonides his deepest insight into the problems of transcendentalist theology (see Part One). Many other Muslim philosophers contributed as well: Ibn Bajja (Avempace, d. 1138), for example, had conceived philosophical solutions to some of the most difficult problems regarding immortality and the relation of man's mind to the Divine. But in the process of confronting these grave problems, in the very act of creating a synthesis in which theological and cosmological values of the Greek and Judaeo-Christian-Islamic traditions fused, the monotheist philosophers often came under the spell of the logic of the Greek values, subordinating the scriptural God to what seemed a more rigorously philosophical conception, or even forgetting in some cases just how far the tradition of theistic philosophy might have taken them toward an appreciation of scriptural theology. For this they were severely taken to task by al-Ghazali, particularly with regard to their surrender in the area of cosmology by interpreting creation simply as eternal emanation and in the area of theology by reducing the divine attribute of will to that of wisdom before collapsing all attributes into the Identity of God.

None of the Jewish philosophers between Isaac Israeli and Maimonides accomplished in Judaism what al-Farabi and Avicenna had accomplished in Islam. Saadya (892–942), head of the Talmudic academy of Sura in Babylonia, was a systematic theologian as well as an eloquent defender of the Rabbanite position, a founder of scientific

Hebrew grammar and lexicography, and the first to translate the Bible into Arabic and write commentaries on it in that language. As a theologian, Saadya, like Kindi, was deeply influenced by the Mutazilite school. His assumptions were of immense importance to Judaism, but often they were naïve or inadequately developed.

The philosophy of Ibn Gabirol (*ca.* 1021–1058), the first philosopher of Jewish faith—indeed of any monotheistic faith—in Spain, was not well known among Jews. His *Fons Vitae* (or *Fountain of Life*) might have been helpful to Maimonides. But the latter regarded the work of Aristotle and his followers as providing a more sophisticated foundation in philosophy than did the tradition followed by Ibn Gabirol, and Maimonides would not have found in the *Fons Vitae* a single Biblical verse or Talmudic citation. Ibn Gabirol's ethical work, *On the Improvement of the Moral Qualities,* while making frequent reference to Scripture, did not systematically and thoroughly integrate the Biblical and philosophical perspectives.

The work of Bahya ibn Pakuda (late eleventh or early twelfth century) was of immense importance to the tradition of philosophical Judaism which reached Maimonides; *The Duties of the Heart,* Bahya's major work, was concerned not simply with restating the claims of spirituality over and against those of mere mechanical ritual but also with elevating the claims of belief (which, as Maimonides points out, must be cognized as well as affirmed) over and against those of mere lip service or cant. Thus *The Duties of the Heart* involved a careful analysis of the chief religious concepts, including an advanced concept of divine transcendence.

Judah ha-Levi (*ca.* 1075–1141) was a poet first and then a philosopher and physician. He knew the philosophical traditions of his day and, in a way, saw through the limitations of their rationalism. This made him, like al-Ghazali, by whom he was greatly influenced, at least as much a critic of philosophy as a contributor to it. While sharing ha-Levi's mistrust of the overextension of reason, Maimonides is less a victim of this traditional caution; he is buoyed by a spirit of confidence unparalleled within the prior Jewish tradition short of the ebullient spirit of constructive speculation which reaches an epitome in the optimistic rationalism of Akiba himself, who asserted that every word and letter of the Torah bears significance, and is thus, by implication, amenable to reason.

The work of Jewish commentators and glossators of the Bible (in large part because it was pervaded by the spirit of Akiba's method) was itself a vehicle of philosophical ideas, particularly regarding such concepts as creation, theophany, and anthropomorphism. For these are sensitive areas where glossators will be most prone to paraphrase and commentators to pause for a discussion. Maimonides was probably familiar with the philosophic work of Moses ibn Ezra and may have known the Biblical commentary of Abraham ibn Ezra as well.[6] He knew the ancient Aramaic translations of the Torah ascribed to Onkelos and Jonathan ben Uzziel. While such works no doubt heightened Maimonides' sensitivity to the problematic areas of Scripture, they can hardly have done more than offer points of departure. Maimonides finds commendable the efforts, say, of Onkelos to insulate with paraphrase the anthropomorphisms of Biblical texts; but a translation, as Maimonides himself observes, is hardly the place to open, let alone resolve, such problems as the complex issues of divine transcendence. Even a commentary hardly affords the scope for full thematic development.

The closest we come in the Jewish tradition to a philosophical model for Maimonides is the *Emunah Ramah* of Ibn Daud. For while commentaries and glosses could not adequately grapple with the problems of philosophy posed in (and resolved by) the Bible, neither was the purely thematic method of the Greek philosophers and their followers wholly adequate to the needs of the Jewish seeker after truth. For such methods only isolated the inquiry from the sacred and near sacred texts which were the lifeblood of Jewish thinking and the underlying ground of its continuity. Not only did the purely thematic mode of developing ideas lead the thinker off on tangents which had

6. While it is customary to regard Abraham ibn Ezra as a "philological" and "scientific" interpreter of the Bible, whose denunciations of allegorical interpretation are well known, it was also pointed out long ago that he himself indulges in philosophic allegorization (see Isaac Husik, *A History of Medieval Jewish Philosophy* [New York, 1916], p. 187 ff.). Maimonides for his part is no stranger to philological approach as a means to an end rather than an end in itself.

no bearing on the problems of Jewish concern—this was Ibn Daud's complaint regarding Ibn Gabirol's *Fons Vitae*—but they left untouched the textual problems as sources of perplexity to all those capable of juxtaposing science and philosophy with the Torah and the Talmud.

The task for the Jewish philosopher, then, which Ibn Daud posed clearly for his successor, was the task of integrating philosophy with Scripture. The groundwork had been laid, many of the basic concepts developed. But those which had been developed most fully in philosophical treatises had not been systematically and constructively applied to the understanding of the Biblical texts; and those which were most familiar in Biblical exegesis had not been worked up to the level of philosophic rigor and sophistication of which they were susceptible: hence, Maimonides' hybrid method in the *Moreh Nevukhim*, neither commentary nor thematic treatise but dialogue, as it were, between philosophy and Scripture, in which reason and text, argument and revelation alternate to enlighten and inform one another.

The Influence and Relevance of Maimonides' Philosophy

"In the post-Maimonidean age," writes Isaac Husik, historian of medieval Jewish philosophy, "all philosophical thinking is in the nature of a commentary on Maimonides, whether avowedly or not." Husik makes no effort to confine this remark to Jewish philosophy, and none should be made. Most of the central problems of modern philosophy in the West—those of time and space, free will and determinism, the existence and nature of God—trace their origins to the interchange of Greek and Hebraic views in which the Rambam's philosophic work played so large a part. Like Philo, Maimonides exerted an incalculable and unduplicated impact on all western philosophical thinking. Muslims, Christians, and Jews studied carefully the Arabic, Latin, and Hebrew texts of the *Moreh,* making the mental adjustments necessary to bring its arguments to bear on their particular creeds. Jews taught Maimonides in mosque colleges, and a Muslim commented on the text of the *Moreh.* The Bishop of Paris and the head of the Franciscan order read the Latin Maimonides. Albertus Magnus, a father of Christian scholasticism, found him indispensable; and to Thomas Aquinas, the greatest of the Christian scholastic philosophers, Maimonides was a trusted guide through the thorny problems lying between the data of Christian faith and a systematic Christian philosophy. The arguments of Maimonides were carefully culled by Aquinas to be quoted side by side with Aristotle and pseudo-Dionysius (the Christian purveyor of the metaphysics of Plotinus), and heeded as seriously. Duns Scotus among the late medievals and Leibniz among the early modern philosophers drew heavily on Maimonides for their understanding of the problems of philosophy. And through Leibniz, Maimonides reaches to Kant and beyond into contemporary thought, although, as Husik says, the influence is not always acknowledged or even recognized.

The *Moreh Nevukhim* became widely known and widely read among Jews almost as soon as it was published. The translation by Samuel ibn Tibbon was one of the most widely owned books of medieval Hebrew literature; nearly every major collection of Hebrew manuscripts contains at least one copy. Marginal notes of readers and names of copyists and owners—many of them eminent scholars in their own right—testify to the frequent recourse of Jewish scholars to the *Moreh* over the period of nearly three hundred years of manuscript circulation between the book's composition and the first printing of the Hebrew translation.

In his bibliography of the *Moreh Nevukhim* literature,[1] Michael Friedländer lists more than forty commentaries on the *Moreh* in whole or in part. With the notable exception of Leibniz's comments and those of the Muslim sage Tabrizi, all are by Jews. Some eighteen commentaries on the *Moreh* were known in 1591. Chief among them were those of Moses Narboni (1362), still a valuable source for the explication of Maimonides' intentions; Shemtov ibn Falaquera, who read the *Moreh* in the context of Averroës; Asher ben Abraham Crescas, identified by a later scholar with the "simple son" of the Passover Haggadah; and Israel ben Moses, the colorful false apostate from Judaism who satirized Christianity under the pseudonym Profiat

---

1. In his translation, *The Guide for the Perplexed* (London, 1904), pp. xxvii–xxxviii.

Duran. Other famous Jewish commentators included Isaac Abarbanel, Biblical exegete, philosopher, minister to Ferdinand and Isabella, and leader of Spain's Jewish community, who fought unsuccessfully to prevent the tragic expulsion of 1492; and Joseph ibn Caspi; and, among the moderns, Solomon Maimon, who took his European name as a tribute to Maimonides, and whom Kant recognized as one of his own most discerning contemporary interpreters. Commentaries are only the tip of the iceberg, a mere index of the *Moreh*'s vast influence on other independent works and the thinking of far wider numbers of individuals.

The *Moreh* was not universally welcomed nor understood, and approval or disapproval of the book cannot be strictly correlated with understanding of it. Comments on the *Moreh* (and its author) range from the full-scale and often thoughtfully critical commentaries and thematic studies of other philosophers and rabbinic writers to the intemperate praise of partisans and equally intemperate condemnation by opponents who read the book superficially—or, in certain cases, not at all. There were those who praised the *Moreh* because they did not fully understand it, and those who condemned it because they understood it all too well. The *Moreh Nevukhim* was anything but a collection of pious platitudes. It was a radical book addressed to persons confronting radical problems. To those who lacked sensitivity to those problems or to the hazards they involved, such a book, with its built-in challenge to both the believer and the doubter, could not fail to be profoundly unsettling.

Even before writing the *Moreh*, Maimonides was a controversial figure. The *Mishneh Torah,* by his own account his *magnum opus,* had raised the hackles of a number of his rivals in rabbinic law. Certain of its rulings were unprecedented. Some were based on rare or variant readings of texts or on unorthodox interpretations of traditional legal doctrines. But this was just a small part of the problem. The whole concept of a new, comprehensive, systematic code of the Jewish law was novel and, in many ways, disturbing. The *Mishneh Torah* makes no attempt to reflect the pluralism and fluidity of Talmudic law. It avoids the traditional focus on the study and discussion of the law and simply gives its sentence. It does not even systematically cite its reference texts in the Talmud. Some of these have as yet to be traced! The great power of the "Strong Hand" [2] lay in its making at least one comprehensive and authoritative statement of the law accessible to anyone who could read Mishnaic Hebrew, *i.e.*, to all Jews of any country who had a secondary education. This, to many of the rabbis of Europe, was the code's chief fault: one did not need to spend a lifetime in the Talmud in order to have an answer to any practical or academic question of law.

The reaction of some European Talmud scholars against Maimonides, however, was not a mere defense of their profession, or a natural resistance to the meteoric rise of a rival. For the *Mishneh Torah* was not just another book on law. It was a carefully thought out and challenging code whose comprehensiveness and logical clarity [3] were themselves implicit claims to conclusive authority. And conclusiveness was something many true Talmudists hated and feared. In the Yemen, where Maimonides was admired for his encouragement of the Jewish community in its blackest hour and revered for his Mosaic treatment of the age-old endemic problems of philosophy (long familiar to all who read Arabic), the *Mishneh Torah* became *the* authoritative code of Jewish law. But in France, where Jewish life was identified with Talmud and Talmud was identified with Halakhah (what Maimonides calls with humor the legal aspect of the Law), Maimonides' rising authority was resisted out of genuine fear lest the living law be ossified within the framework—no matter how imposing—of one man's views. Maimonides' staunchest defender in this bastion of legal pluralism and independent rabbinical jurisdictions, Aaron ben Meshullam, would only claim that there was nothing implausible in the Rambam's decisions. "The Torah," he wrote, "has seventy faces."

The reaction against the claims of the *Mishneh Torah* to legal authority was bound to spill over into the philosophical sphere. Even within the *Mishneh Torah* and the commentary on the Mishnah it was

2. The *Mishneh Torah,* which has fourteen volumes, is known familiarly as the *Yad Hazakah* or "Strong Hand" (*cf.* Exodus 13:14), the numerical value of the letters constituting the word *yad* (hand) being equal to fourteen.

3. Some of the most beautiful graphic work of the Middle Ages is found in the architecturally balanced columns of medieval manuscripts of the *Mishneh Torah.* It is as though the scribes and artists who illuminated these fourteen great volumes wished to represent graphically the keenness and analytic clarity they found there.

plain that the Rambam's rationalism and uncompromising rationality made demands within the realm of faith which required radical adjustments of those whose thought was organized on (and even defended by) the principles of tradition. The motto opening the *Mishneh Torah* was "Then shall I be not ashamed to scrutinize all Thy commandments" (Psalm 119:6). Its underlying purpose was clearly rationalistic. The opening theme, expressed in its first sentence, was the implicit rationality of the Mosaic laws. "Every commandment was given with its explanation" (see Part Five). The opening section of the *Mishneh Torah* dealt not with ritual but with doctrinal theology, clarifying the foundations of the Jewish creed, delineating and defining the elements of a religion which was, in essence and origin, not a set of actions but a set of beliefs, productive of action but stemming from a cognitive content, in short, from knowledge. Certain substantive issues of philosophy had necessarily to be dealt with in a comprehensive treatment of Jewish law: What is the God which Israel is commanded to obey and to love? What is a prophet? What is "the world-to-come," in which some men "have a share"; what is the eternal bliss promised for that world; and how does this relate to the notion of the resurrection of the dead?

Maimonides' answers to these questions were alarming to the tradition-oriented legists of Europe, whose theological sophistication often barely exceeded anthropomorphism (and that, in some cases, only debatably). To thinkers who had studied Saadya or who knew anything of al-Farabi and Avicenna, there was nothing shocking in the theology of the *Mishneh Torah*. It was merely a development of the logic of certain key theological concepts in their legal contexts. But for those experts in the "legal study of the Law" whose sensitivity to its vitality and dynamism did not extend to the perception of any invitation to develop the theoretical speculation of the Talmud as they had its Halakhah, the theological promise of the *Mishneh Torah* expressed itself as a threat, a threat fulfilled by the *Moreh*. Such minds were well warned by the ancient rabbis (and by Maimonides) to steer clear of metaphysics. Indeed, one of the harshest of the Rambam's critics, Meir ben Todros Abulafia, a younger contemporary of Maimonides and an instigator of the first wave of attack against his work, directed his critique against the legal work. Having scathingly denounced the

Rambam's philosophical treatment of immortality, he swore he would not look into the *Moreh,* a vow he claimed to have kept to his dying day.

Legal critiques of the *Mishneh Torah* were undertaken on specific points by Mosheh ha-Cohen, who showed himself to be a defender of legal obscurantism and the use of mezuzot as amulets and charms, and by the Rabad, Rabbi Abraham ben David of Posquières, another French contemporary of the Rambam, whose assault was more complete and more bitter. Like Abulafia, he attacked Maimonides' resurrection doctrine with special vigor. The fray was joined by Aaron ben Meshullam, defending the plausibility of the Rambam's legal and doctrinal position and his right to state it. Another defender of Maimonides was Sheshet Benvenisti, who added a touch of antirabbinical animus to his defense of Maimonides' frontal attack on legal obscurantism. As the issue broadened to include the *Moreh,* the great Hebrew grammarian and Biblical scholar David Kimhi spoke in Maimonides' defense, as did Abraham ben Hasdai, Samuel ben Abraham Saportas, and the Rambam's son, Abraham. Other supporters included Jewish leaders in Lunel, Saragossa, Huesca, Monzon, Kalatajud, Lérida, and Narbonne.

The controversy over Maimonides' work went on long after his death. Among those opposed to Maimonides was one Daniel of Damascus, whose strident attacks were silenced by the writ of excommunication issued against him by the Exilarch Rabbi David. More powerfully opposed were Rabbi Solomon ben Abraham of Montpellier and two of his disciples, who feared that Maimonides' methods, particularly his tendency to interpret problematic texts allegorically, might lend credence and the authority of his name to doubt and to unorthodox thinking. The eminent and respected Judah Alfakhar added the prestige of his name to the opposition of Maimonism. Moses ben Hisdai, who opposed the philosophy of Saadya, stood unequivocally in opposition to what Maimonides stood for, rejecting all open discussion of cosmology with the assertion "It is to the glory of God that such matters be kept hidden." And Nahmanides (the Ramban), leader of Spanish Jewry and defender of Judaism in the infamous Barcelona Disputation of 1263, who knew more philosophy than many of the Rambam's lesser opponents, joined them in the fear that Maimonides had given too free a rein to reason. To many disputants, such as Abba Mari Don Astruc and Rabbi Solomon ben Aderet of Barcelona, the issue was not simply one of Maimonides' thought but of the propriety and legality of Jews' studying philosophy at all.

Jonathan ha-Cohen of Lunel, a prime supporter, recognized in Maimonides an appreciation of Jewish law founded in reason. That is why he enlisted the aid of his great contemporary in combatting superstitious reverence for astrology in France. For the same reason he did not confine himself to legal queries on the *Mishneh Torah* but arranged for Harizi to translate the Mishnah Commentary into Hebrew, and ultimately he undertook to sponsor the Hebrew translation of the *Moreh.* This expains why Jonathan became an immediate target of Abulafia's ire. To many, among both the rationalists and their opponents, the Rambam's legal and philosophical work were of one piece. The controversy was fierce, and even the efforts of the wisest of those who stepped into the breach to moderate the passions it excited failed, in the end, to assuage the bitterness of the struggle. Harsh words about the effects of the Rambam's writings gave way to charges of hypocrisy and heresy against him. Bans on the public study of philosophy in general and of Maimonides in particular were met by injunctions from the philosopher's supporters against the enforcement of such bans and by writs of excommunication from Lunel and Narbonne against the anti-Maimonists.

Around the year 1232, the *Moreh Nevukhim* and Book One of the *Mishneh Torah,* the "Book of Knowledge," were denounced first to the Franciscans and then to the Dominicans—according to some partisan sources, at the instigation of Rabbi Solomon ben Abraham himself—and, after a cursory investigation by Church authorities, they were burnt at Montpellier. In the welter of subsequent recriminations, those found responsible for the denunciation (not Rabbi Solomon or his two disciples) reportedly had their tongues cut out for defamatory slander. Many of the scholars who had been drawn into the controversy now recoiled in horror, as did many more after the burning of the Talmud itself some eight years later. This act of fury seemed to have been brought down on the heads of Jewry by the initial denunciation of the *Moreh.*

Though the controversy cooled, it did not end. Maimonists continued to study and pseudo-Maimonists to adulate the work of the great philosopher of Judaism, while genuine and spurious objections continued to be raised not only against all Maimonides had accomplished but against all he represented. Long after the indispensability of the *Mishneh Torah* had been admitted by all, it was still possible for pious scholars to doubt that the *Moreh* was written in its entirety (or at all!) by the author of the great code: "Such heretic doctrines," wrote one rabbi, could not have come from the pen of the author of the *Mishneh Torah*.[4]

Throughout the storm of controversy, or in spite of it, many valid and significant questions were raised, perhaps the most pertinent being whether it was legitimate to interpret the same Biblical passage by two mutually inconsistent allegorical exegeses. But while there were numerous commentators and critics of all levels of seriousness and points of view, philosophical and nonphilosophical, there was not another Jewish philosopher of the stature of Maimonides until the time of Spinoza, when Holland gave a refuge to philosophy and to Judaism as the Islamic world had done some five centuries before.

Despite the Rambam's tremendous importance, philosophical literature on him is sparse. The claim has even been made that the teaching of Maimonides is incomprehensible from a modern point of view.[5] This would seem an untenable view, confining Maimonides' would-be students within the prisons of their own historicity. The problems dealt with in the *Moreh Nevukhim* are universal and alive for anyone who seriously regards theism as a possible or impossible option.

Of the philosophers whom Maimonides influenced, the two most profoundly affected and with the most significant impact on the subsequent history of western thought were probably Thomas Aquinas and Baruch Spinoza. The contrast is striking. For Aquinas, Maimon-

4. Rabbi Jacob Emden, *Mitpachat Sefarim* (Lemberg, 1870), p. 56, quoted by Friedländer, "The *Moreh Nebuchim* Literature," *The Guide for the Perplexed*, p. xxxvii. The story of the immediate controversy surrounding Maimonides' work is told at length in D. J. Silver, *Maimonidean Criticism and the Maimonidean Controversy, 1180–1240* (Leiden, 1965), and Joseph Sarachek, *Faith and Reason, The Conflict over the Rationalism of Maimonides* (New York, 1935, 1970).
5. *Cf.* Leo Strauss, "The Literary Character of the *Guide for the Perplexed*," in *Persecution and the Art of Writing* (Glencoe, 1952), p. 38.

ides was an insightful predecessor pointing the way to a philosophical mode of religious thinking which did not dismiss ancient Scripture as primitive or irrelevant but discovered in it hints by which reason itself might be enlightened. In the hands of Aquinas, the syntheses of Maimonides (along with other philosophers' ideas and the original contribution of Aquinas himself) became a system, the foundation of Catholic scholastic philosophy and thus of that Thomistic philosophy still alive today within the Catholic Church. This system was made possible in large part by Thomas's sensitivity to Maimonides, his questioning of what Maimonides questioned, his avoidance of questions Maimonides declined to ask.

To Spinoza, as to Aquinas, Maimonides typified the synthesis of Hebraic and Greek concepts upon which the edifice of medieval philosophy was founded. By following through to its ultimate conclusions the logic of Maimonides' approach, Spinoza actually succeeded in severely impairing if not totally destroying that edifice. Spinoza's "geometrical method" was no more than the placement in geometrical style of the medieval demands for rigor—conceptual clarity and coherence—which reach their epitome in Maimonides' terms, propositions, and arguments.[6] Spinoza's treatment of substance, of the attributes of God, of determinism and free will, are no more than the pressing to their logical limits of aspects of the conceptual content of ideas already present in the thought of Maimonides, Averroës, and certain of their Arabic-writing predecessors—the pressing of questions neither Maimonides himself nor any of his medieval predecessors or successors had ever been prepared explicitly to pursue so far: questions as to the relationship between God and matter, the locus of divine causality, the relationship between the rational pattern of causal law and the disordered play of chance, the nature of the Godhead and the mode of its being.

Where Aquinas had followed the synthetic bent of Maimonides, melding and smoothing to produce harmony between reason and revelation, Spinoza's keenly analytic mind untied all the knots between philosophy and Scripture, fulfilling the worst fears of Maimonides' direst detractors as to what would happen if the Maimonidean method

6. Compare particularly Maimonides' axiomatic treatment of the "propositions" of the Philosophers and the Mutakallimun (see Part Two).

were given its head. By rejecting Akiba's presumption of significance in the Torah and turning his back on the Maimonidean notion of Scripture as a quarry of theology, Spinoza paves the way for Voltaire's notion that Scripture is, at best, irrelevant to theological speculation; he destroys forever any possibility of a Jewish equivalent to Thomism. Yet, paradoxically, the concepts out of which Spinoza's philosophy is hewn are themselves Maimonidean, and thus ultimately (in the Maimonidean sense) Mosaic as well. The consequence for the future of any philosophy claiming to be Jewish rather than merely derivative of whatever intellectual fashions happen to be current is quite clear: Future Jewish philosophers may, in the end, find themselves engrossed by Philo's way of dealing with both Plato and the Torah. This remains to be seen. But where they must begin is plain: at the juncture between Spinoza and Maimonides, their rival approaches to the Torah, and their common conceptual vocabulary and method. This alone seems reason enough to study the philosophy of Maimonides with care, quite apart from its historical and intrinsic interest.

A PRELIMINARY WORD
BY MAIMONIDES

MOREH NEVUKHIM I:31

You ought to realize that there are some things which the human mind
has it in its power and nature to grasp, others which it cannot grasp by
any means whatever,[1] subjects which are closed books to it; and there
are other things still which the mind knows in one state but not others.
The fact that the mind is conscious does not imply that it is conscious
of everything. The senses perceive, but not at any distance whatever.
Similarly with the other bodily powers. A man can lift, say, two
hundred pounds; he cannot lift a thousand. That individuals vary in
these powers of perception and other bodily powers is plain to all
mankind. But there is a limit. These capacities do not extend indefinitely. The same holds true of human mental powers. They vary
widely from one individual to the next, as scholars plainly recognize.
Thus a given idea will be discovered independently by one person
while another could never understand it. Even if it were spelled out to
him at the greatest length with every possible illustration and in every
possible turn of phrase, his mind would not make the slightest headway with it but would only rebound from comprehension. Here too the

1. Not even through revelation.

variation is not infinite. There is surely a limit at which human reason stops.

There are some things man knows he cannot comprehend, and therefore does not find himself longing to know—the number of stars in the sky, for example, and whether that number is odd or even. . . . There are other things which man finds in himself a deep longing to investigate, things which every age and every thoughtful human group seek to master and to comprehend. Regarding such things there are many views. Disagreements arise among the investigators, and delusions as well, on account of the emotional attachment of the mind to the comprehension of such things, and everyone's supposing that he has discovered a way to the truth, when in fact the human mind is incapable of proving such things. For regarding demonstrable truths there is no disagreement, no give and take, and no rejection of the outcome of argument except by the untrained, who offer what is called resistance to argument. Thus you will find some people who deny that the earth is spherical. . . . But they have nothing to do with our object.

The things about which such confusions arise are very numerous in theology, few in science, and nonexistent in mathematics. Alexander of Aphrodisias says that there are three causes of disagreement: (1) competitiveness and love of supremacy, which blind men to the truth; (2) the subtlety, obscurity, or difficulty of the subject matter itself; (3) the ignorance or incapacity of the investigator in ascertaining what can be known. Thus Alexander. But in our times there is a fourth cause which he did not mention because it did not exist in his day: custom and tradition. For man by nature loves what he is used to and clings to it. Thus you may observe how desert people, despite the hardship of their way of life, where pleasures are few and food scarce, scorn the cities. They are not drawn by the pleasures of city life but prefer bad conditions which are familiar above more salutary conditions to which they are unaccustomed. Their spirits would not be at peace if they lived in palaces and dressed in silk; they would not enjoy baths, unguents, and perfumes. In just this way a man grows attached to the beliefs he is brought up with and to which he is accustomed. These he will defend, and others he will reject as alien. This is the cause too of man's incapacity to perceive the truth and his clinging to the familiar instead. It was this that bound the masses to anthropomorphism and many other theological delusions. All this was due to traditional upbringing, in which it was ordained that certain texts were to be held in awe and accepted as true which, taken literally, suggest anthropomorphism and other delusions. In fact these texts were symbolic and allegorical, as I shall explain.

Do not suppose that what I have said regarding the limitation of the human mind is said simply in behalf of revelation. The philosophers say the same things. They were well aware of this, without being concerned with any sect or dogma. . . . I preface this chapter simply by way of introduction to what follows.

MOREH NEVUKHIM I:32

You must know, dear reader, that to the extent that the intellectual apprehension is bound up with matter, it undergoes the same sort of effects as sensory apprehension does. When you look at something, you see what your visual sense is capable of seeing. But if you strain your eyes by staring or trying to see farther than they are able, or poring over minute script or a very fine drawing that you are not able to make out but force yourself to descry, not only will your eyesight remain too weak to do so, but this abuse will render it too weak even to make out what it *has* the capability of apprehending—your vision will become blurred, and you will not see what you would have seen before straining your eyes. The thinker investigating any field will find the same to be true of his mental processes. When he concentrates exclusively on one subject, he eventually becomes muddled and does not understand for the moment even things which are quite within his ken. For all bodily powers [1] are alike in this regard.

A similar problem can occur with intellectual apprehensions. If you rein yourself in before a problematic case, if you do not deceive yourself that there is proof where there is none or jump to conclusions, but do not ever categorically deny a proposition which has not been disproved,[2] and do not aspire to grasp what you are not capable of grasping, then you will be, in human terms, perfect—you will have reached

1. Being temporal, mental processes are matter-dependent.
2. Contrast the famous methodical doubt of Descartes, by which the mind is restricted from affirming what it is capable of doubting.

the level of Rabbi Akiba (on whom be peace), who "entered in peace and went out in peace" when he studied these theological matters [*Haggigah* 14b]. But if you aspire to grasp what is beyond your reach or hasten to deny things which have not been disproved or are possible (no matter how far-fetched), then you will go the way of Elisha Aher. Not only will you fall short of perfection but you will become as wanting as can be: Imagination will get the best of you and an inclination toward what is flawed, vicious, and bad, because of the darkening and distraction of the mind—in just the way that optical illusions appear when vision is weakened by illness or prolonged direction of the eyes toward minute or incandescent objects.

It is to this effect that it is said, "Have you found honey? Eat what is enough for yourself, lest you be bloated and vomit it" [Proverbs 25:16]. The Sages (of blessed memory) applied this symbolically to Elisha Aher. And how apt the symbolism was, likening learning to eating as I have explained [*Moreh* I:30], and citing the most delicious of foods, honey, which by its nature causes an upset stomach and vomiting when eaten to excess. Thus it says, in effect: This apprehension, sublime, awesome, and magnificent as it is, carried too far and not conducted with due caution may be perverted into a vice. . . . It is not the intention of the prophets and the Sages to interdict thinking or ban reason from apprehending what it can apprehend, as the backward and the overcautious may suppose, taking their own thick-headedness and inadequacy for strengths and mistaking the intelligence, learning, and achievements of others for faults, for irreligiosity—"taking darkness for light and light for darkness" [Isaiah 5:20]. On the contrary, the sole objective here is to communicate the fact that human minds have a limit beyond which they cannot go. . . .

PART ONE

LASHON BENAI ADAM /

THE LANGUAGE OF MAN

The Problem

of Religious Language

*T*he Lord spoke to Moses face to face, as one man speaks to another. . . . And Moses said to the Lord: ". . . Now if I have found favor in Thine eyes cause me, pray, to know Thy ways that I may know Thee and please Thee, and see that this nation is Thy people." . . . And he said, "Show me, pray, Thy Glory." And He said, "I shall cause all My good to pass before you. . . ." And He said, "You cannot see My Face. For man shall not see Me and live." And the Lord said, "Lo . . . it shall be that in passing My Glory I shall . . . cover you with My hand until I am past. Then I shall remove My hand and you shall see My back. But My Face shall not be seen." . . . And the Lord passed by His Face and proclaimed: "Lord, Lord, God, compassionate and gracious, longsuffering, and abundant of love and truth, keeping compassion for thousands, bearing sin, iniquity, and transgression, but not clearing the guilty. . . ."

from Exodus 33:11–23; 34:6–7

*M*oses said to God, "When I am come to the Israelites and say to them, 'The God of your fathers has sent me to you,' and they say, 'What is His name?' what shall I say to them?" Then God said unto Moses, "I am that I am. This shall you say to the Israelites: "I AM has sent me."

Exodus 3:13–14

(translated in accordance with
Maimonides' interpretations)

Introduction

If someone were to describe an elephant, Maimonides writes, as a talking animal with one leg and three wings, living at the sea bottom but capable of flying as well as swimming, with a human face and a body like that of a man but transparent, we would recognize at once that that person was either lying or mistaken. These characteristics are not only imcompatible with what we know of nature; they are incompatible with each other. The kind of being he described could not possibly exist. Yet, as Maimonides observes, many people who consider themselves to believe in God have no better idea of God.

It may seem surprising that Maimonides begins the *Moreh Nevukhim,* his *Guide to the Perplexed,* by speaking of the language applied to God in Scripture and the ways in which such language may and may not be understood. Should he not first prove the existence of the God of whose preferred epithets he seems to speak so knowingly? Such was the common practice in medieval treatises on theology. One first established the existence of God, then His unity and incorporeality. A fine medieval library might contain hundreds of books which proceeded in just this way. Yet Maimonides defers his discus-

52

sion of the existence of God until he has led the student deep into his book, recognizing a prior tangle of problems which must be confronted and resolved. His task is not the composition of another tome to tell scholars what they already know or think they know. Nor does he write for the casual reader (*cf. Moreh* I:2). Maimonides writes, with an urgency belied by his superficially ambling exposition, for a reader whose study of philosophy has brought him into a state of disturbance regarding the kind of theology the Bible, on the surface at least, seems to take for granted. To "demonstrate" the existence of God in such a context would be of little use. The perplexity in which the student finds himself extends beyond the question of God's existence to a questioning of the very concept of God itself. The student may have come to doubt not only whether God exists, but even whether it is possible for such a being as a Deity to exist at all.

Trivially one can "demonstrate" the existence of God (or of anything else, for that matter) using a schema such as the following:

> Premise 1: If grass is green, then God exists.
> Premise 2: Grass is green.
> Conclusion: God exists.

Technically this argument is valid, that is to say the conclusion follows from the premises, provided that they are true. The major premise (1) stipulates the condition for God's existence, the minor (2) asserts that this condition is met. The conclusion follows necessarily. So would the existence of square circles, if we substituted "square circles" for "God" in the same schema. Thus only two premises are necessary to "prove" the existence of God. The Aristotelian philosophers, as we shall see, required twenty-six.

The difficulty is that the "demonstration" proves nothing since it does not establish a connection between God's existence and the color of grass, it *assumes* one. But in order to know that there is such a connection, *i.e.,* in order to establish the truth of premise 1, we must know something about the nature of God and the world and the kinds of connections which can subsist between them. Since a relationship of implication might be postulated arbitrarily between any two alleged facts, it really makes no difference to this argument what "God" means. It might mean anything; or, like "square circle," it might mean nothing at all. Those who merely use words, as Maimonides puts it, without the faintest idea what those words mean or whether they mean anything at all, might, for all they know, be speaking of things which do not exist, indeed, which cannot exist.

Thus before the existence of God can be proved or even discussed it is necessary to establish what manner of being a Deity might be—and this in the context of doubts far more radical than those underlying the denial of God's existence. It is necessary (as we might say) to define "God," or if a definition of "God" proves impossible (see *Moreh* I:52.1), we must at least establish clear, acceptable criteria for the application of the concept of divinity if we are to employ that concept at all. Having such criteria is thus a precondition of any serious demonstration of the existence of God. In order to produce such a demonstration we must know which facts drawn from our experience are relevant to the question of divine existence, since it is a real being whose existence is to be proved, not the mere abstract outcome of arbitrarily stipulated relationships. And in order even to grasp a purported *demonstratio Dei,* we must have some way of knowing that the "being" whose existence it purports to prove is capable of existence and worthy of identification as divine.

The Bible tells us many things about God, yet rigorous investigation reveals that many things it says of God could not possibly be true of Him. Many, moreover, are incompatible with each other. And, worst of all, rigorous investigation of the concept of God seems to reveal serious rifts within the concept itself which appear to render impossible its use in any coherent fashion. To many, these difficulties might seem to demand that a choice be made between reason and revelation. The object of Maimonides' analysis of language about God as used in the Scriptures and as understood by reason is to show that such a choice is not only unnecessary but impossible.

To those who have not grappled with the problems Maimonides is addressing, his exposition may appear to begin *in medias res,* as though some part of the story had already taken place. But of course the *Moreh Nevukhim* does not tell a story. We cannot read it as we would a fable or a history—any more than we can read the Bible as a mere narrative (*Moreh* I:2). Still less, as we have seen, can we expect a strictly thematic or exegetical presentation of ideas. Rather the principle of development and exposition in the book is pedagogical—as the name implies, for *moreh* in Hebrew means "teacher" not in the sense of one who expounds but of one who "shows" or "projects" (*dalala* in Arabic means "guide"). Maimonides throws out ideas like a teacher, one or two at a time, constantly adding, repeating, making connections with ground already familiar, pointing again and again to certain markers and anchor points until they have become familiar landmarks and trusted pivots of thought, allowing the problems, alternatives, proposed solutions to percolate; gradually the whole terrain is imaged in the student's mind, and the logical relations among the problems and hypotheses have reconstituted themselves with all the clarity and articulation they had in the mind of the teacher. At that point the student sees for himself the way out of his perplexity.

In good pedagogic fashion, Maimonides begins with the elementary, the Bible's application to God of terms which, if taken literally, would imply God's corporeality. Even the least philosophically inclined reader becomes aware that such terms are not to be taken literally. Even small children should be taught, according to Maimonides, that God is incorporeal. What they do not know are the grounds on which incorporeality is established; hence they cannot know their full implications. It eludes them that the denial of divine corporeality is not an independent dogma but just one of the more obvious implications of a far more universal theme. For the student who wishes to "rise" from perplexity to a mature or "perfect" understanding of the concept of divinity, it is necessary rigorously to analyze the logic of the concept of God, although this is an investigation fraught with danger for those lacking the fortitude or firm bearing on moral principle needed to see it through.

Starting with the observation of the inappropriateness of corporeal language regarding God, Maimonides guides his student to the concept of absolute transcendence. This theme of radical transcendentalism is elicited from the Torah itself: only language popularly thought to denote perfection is applied to God. Investigation of the full implications of this theme reveals the core and source of all the problems latent in the concept of God; and this comprehension leads to their dissolution.

From *Moreh Nevukhim* I

Open the gates and the upright nation which keeps faith will enter [Isaiah 26:2].

MOREH NEVUKHIM I:1

Tselem u-demut: "form and likeness." It was once supposed that "form" in Hebrew denoted shape or configuration. This led to complete anthropomorphism on account of the divine utterance "Let us make man in our form and likeness" [Genesis 1:26]. People thought God had the form—*i.e.,* the physical shape and structure of a man. It followed that God was a purely material being, and this is what they believed. They thought that to depart from this belief would be to reject Scripture. For them a deity could not exist except as a body with face and hands like theirs in shape and lineaments—only larger and more splendid, as they thought, and with matter not of flesh and blood. This was as far as they thought transcendentalism regarding God should go. . . .

Now I say that "form" as understood by the masses, *i.e.,* the shape and configuration of a thing, is designated in Hebrew exclusively by *toar, e.g.,* "fair of form [*toar*] and visage" [Genesis 39:6], . . . "He marks its form with line and compass" [Isaiah 44:13]. This terminology is never applied to the Deity—far be it! But *tselem* designates natural form, *i.e.,* the principle which substantiates a thing and makes it what it is, its reality as that thing. In man's case this is the source of human awareness and it is on account of such intellectual awareness that it is said of man that "He created him in the form of God" [Genesis 1:27]. Thus it is said, "Thou despisest their form" [Psalm 73:20], for contempt applies to the soul, which is the specific form, not to the shape and lineaments of the anatomy. . . .

"Likeness" [*demut*] is a noun from *damoh,* "to be like." This again refers to conceptual similarity. For when he says, "I am like a pelican in the desert" [Psalm 102:7], he does not mean that he has feathers and wings like a pelican, but that he is as desolate. Man's distinguishing characteristic—rare indeed since it is not found in any other sublunary being—is intellectual awareness which does not require sense perception, limb, or organ. This resembles the consciousness of the Deity, which also has no instrument, although the resemblance is not real but superficial.[1] But on account of this resemblance, *i.e.,* on account of the divine mind which impinges upon him, man is said to be "in the form and likeness of God"—not because God has any body so as to have a shape.

MOREH NEVUKHIM I:3

One might suppose that *temunah,* "likeness," and *tavnit,* "figure," mean the same thing in Hebrew. This is not so. *Tavnit* is a noun derived from *banoh,* "to build," and it means construction or configuration. . . . That is why it is never predicated of the Deity. But *temunah* is used in three senses: of sense objects external to the mind, designating their shape and configuration . . . , of imaginary forms which exist in the fancy of an individual after sense objects are no longer present, and of the true concept grasped by the mind. In this third sense is *temunah* referred to Him: "He shall look upon the 'likeness' of the Lord" [Numbers 12:8]. Interpreted, this means, "He shall gain a conception of the Godhead."

MOREH NEVUKHIM I:4

"To see," "to look," and "to behold" are three terms denoting vision by the eyes which are used metaphorically for intellectual apprehension. In the case of "to see," this is known to the masses. . . . It is written, "My heart has seen much wisdom and knowledge" [Ecclesiastes 1:16], mentally of course. This figurative sense is found in every mention of seeing with reference to God, as when it says, "I saw the Lord" [1 Kings 22:19], . . . "God saw that it was good" [Genesis 1:10], "Pray let me see Thy glory" [Exodus 33:18]. . . . All this is intellectual, not ocular vision at all. For eyes apprehend only bodies, and these must be placed in some spatial relation to the eyes and must have certain "accidents" [*viz.,* colors, shape, etc.] of bodies. Besides, God does not perceive through an organ, as will be made clear. . . .

1. For man's thought is like God's only inasmuch as it requires no body; its essence or actual nature is totally different (see *Moreh* I:58, III:19, 20).

MOREH NEVUKHIM I:5

When Aristotle, foremost of the philosophers, undertook his inquiry into matters that were very deep and sought the guidance of argument in this regard, he made a plea to the student of his works not to attribute to him rashness or immodesty or eagerness to speak of what he knew nothing about on account of the subject matter he had chosen but rather to attribute this choice to his love of knowledge and his eagerness to discover and delineate valid beliefs, to the extent that this is humanly possible [*cf. De Caelo* II:12].

In the same spirit, we say that a man should not rush into this sublime and portentous subject without having disciplined himself in the various sciences and studies and properly refined his character and deadened the caprices and desires of his imagination. When he has arrived at true and certain premises, knows them and the rules of reasoning and inference, as well as the techniques of safeguarding against mental errors, he should advance to the study of this subject, but not by categorically affirming the first opinion that occurs to him, nor by straining and forcing his thinking toward apprehension of divinity. On the contrary, he should be modest and restrained. He should hold back and let himself rise gradually. This is referred to when it is said, "Moses hid his face, for he was afraid to look at God" [Exodus 3:6]. . . . And he was praised for this. . . . But "the nobles of the children of Israel" were overeager and strained their minds; they saw, but imperfectly. This is why it says that they "saw the God of Israel, and under His feet," etc. [Exodus 24:10], rather than simply "they saw the God of Israel": the qualifying phrase is only by way of condemning, not describing what they saw; for their vision is totally condemned to the extent that it involved corporealism, which was itself made necessary by their rushing ahead to share this cognition before they were properly perfected. . . .

MOREH NEVUKHIM I:8

Makom. The underlying denotation of this term is of place in general or a particular place, but by a broadening of linguistic usage it became as well a name for rank and status, perfection of a certain degree. Thus Scripture says . . . "He filled the place of his fathers in wisdom," or "in piety." . . . In this derived sense it is said, "Blessed be the glory of the Lord from His place" [Ezekiel 3:12], *i.e.*, according to His degree and the magnitude of His station in existence. In this manner, every mention of "place" in relation to God is intended to refer to His status in the hierarchy of being, of which there is neither like nor equal, as will be demonstrated.

You should realize that with each ambiguous term I explain in this treatise my object is not simply to inform you of the contents of that particular chapter, but to open up a theme and make you aware of a concept behind that term which will serve our purpose, distinct from the purposes of those who use this or that language.[1] Study the prophetic books and other writings by men of understanding, consider all the words used in them, and interpret every ambiguous term in a fitting sense in the context of the passage. This sentence is the key to this study, and to other things as well. . . .

MOREH NEVUKHIM I:10

. . . When we discuss one or another ambiguous term in this study our object is not to mention every sense in which that term is used. For this is not a treatise on language. We discuss only those meanings which we require for our purpose. Such is the case with *yarod* and *aloh*. These terms in Hebrew denote descending and rising: If a body moves from a higher to a lower place, the former term is applied to it; if it moves from a lower to a higher place, the latter is said of it. Beyond this, however, the two terms are applied metaphorically to indicate dignity or sublimity. When an individual was debased in rank he was said to have "descended," and when he was ennobled he was said to have "risen." Thus God says, "The stranger in your midst shall rise higher and higher over you, and you shall decline," etc. [Deuteronomy 28:43]. . . . And you know how often they say, "With holy things one may upgrade but one may not downgrade."[1]

1. Maimonides is not merely using but discussing language. The task of ordinary linguistic usage is to communicate regarding ordinary experience of the natural world; thus Maimonides is not concerned with the simple philological investigation of the "normal" usages of Biblical vocabulary. Rather his object is to discover a level of meaning which enables prophetic language to point beyond the range of ordinary experience and its confinement to the corporeal world.

1. *E.g.*, one may sell land to buy a synagogue but not vice versa; see Mishnah *Shekalim* VI:4, *Megillah* III:4.

A parallel usage is followed regarding the direction of thought: a man who directs his thought toward what is vile is said to have descended; when he turns to the lofty and sublime, he is said to have risen.

Now since we, the tribe of Adam, are the lowest of the low, not only in place, relative to the encompassing sphere, but in the hierarchy of being, and He is the highest of the high, not spatially but in majesty, sublimity, and reality, and He was pleased to shed some measure of understanding of Himself and inspiration upon certain of us, this inspiration or indwelling was expressed as "descent" and its departure as "ascent." Every ascent or descent which you find ascribed to the Creator is intended solely in such a way.

Similarly, when a disaster befalls a people or region according to His eternal plan, the prophetic books precede the description of the event by the statement that God was aware of their doings and brought down punishment upon them. This too is termed descent, since man is too insignificant for his action to be taken note of and for him to be punished—were it not for the divine will. This is made clear in the prophetic books when Scripture says, "What is man that Thou takest note of him, the son of man that Thou payest him heed" [Psalm 8:5].

MOREH NEVUKHIM I:11

Yeshivah. Originally this term denoted sitting: "Eli the priest sat in a chair" [1 Samuel 1:9]. But, since a seated person is as stable and settled as he can be, the term was applied metaphorically to any stable, established, or unchanging condition. Thus, in pledging the establishment and endurance of Jerusalem at the highest rank, Scripture says: "She will arise and sit in her place" [Zechariah 14:10], "He causes the barren woman to sit in her house" [Psalm 113:9], meaning he settles and establishes her there. In this sense it is said of Him, "Thou, O Lord, shalt sit forever" [Lamentations 5:19] . . . established and changeless in every way, invariant in identity and having no qualification to His Godhead in terms of which to vary. Nor does His connection to what is other change, for He has no connection to anything else as will be shown [*Moreh* I:52.4]. . . . "For I, the Lord, do not change" [Malachi 3:6]. . . . In this sense He is said to "sit." . . . "The Lord sits at the flood" [Psalm 29:10] means that while the earth is changed and destroyed, His relation to it does not change but remains constant, settled, and established, whether things are developing or disintegrating. For His relation is to the species of things which come to be, not to particular instances [*Moreh* III:17]. If you examine the usage of the verb "to sit" with reference to God, you will find that it is invariably applied in this sense.

MOREH NEVUKHIM I:15

Natzov ["to stand up]. . . . The term also occurs with the sense of stability or permanence, and that is the sense it has wherever it is applied to the Creator: "And there was God, standing up upon it" [Genesis 28:13]—established there permanently, *i.e.,* on the ladder one end of which is in the heavens and the other on earth. Thus whoever rises climbs by this ladder toward Him who is upon it, apprehends Him necessarily, for He is permanently established at its summit . . . How wisely is it written "ascending and descending," ascent prior to descent, for after rising and reaching a given rung on the ladder comes the descent with what has been gained, to govern and teach the people on earth [1]—which is called descent. . . .

MOREH NEVUKHIM I:16

"Rock" is an ambiguous word. . . . it refers to a stone . . . and also to the quarry from which stones are cut: "Look to the rock whence ye were hewn" [Isaiah 51:1]. From this sense a figurative usage is derived in which the term denotes the source or basis of anything. Thus after saying, "Look to the rock whence you were hewn," the text continues, "Look to Abraham, your father." . . . In this sense God is called "Rock," for He is the Ground and active cause of all things other than Himself. Thus He is called "the Rock whose work is perfect" [Deuteronomy 32:4] . . . "Rock of Eternities" [Isaiah 26:4]. . . .

MOREH NEVUKHIM I:18

"To approach," "to touch," "to come near." These three terms may signify coming close or becoming adjacent in space; they may also signify the "contact" of the act of knowing with that which is known;

---

1. *Cf. Moreh* I:54; also Plato's *Republic* VII.

for this is, as it were, an analogue of physical contact. . . .

Any reference you find in the prophetic books to any creature's approaching or coming near God (or vice versa) has this latter sense. For God is not a body, as will be demonstrated in this treatise; thus He does not "approach" or "draw nigh" anything, and nothing can "approach" or "draw nigh" Him. For transcendence of physicality implies transcendence of space, vitiating the notions of proximity and distance, contiguity, separation, contact, or sequence.

I do not see you falling into doubt or confusion over the words "The Lord is close to all who call upon him," [Psalm 145:18], "They delight in the nearness of God" [Isaiah 58:2], "God's nearness is my good"[Psalm 73:28]. All these intend an approach in terms of understanding, *i.e.*, the acquiring of an intellectual grasp, not a physical coming near. . . .

The principle you must not lose hold of is that there is no difference between a person's being at the center of the earth or the outermost sphere (if that were possible). He would be no further from God in the one place and no closer to God in the other. Nearness to Him is through apprehension of Him; distance from Him is ignorance of him. . . .

Contact . . . should be dealt with in the same way. . . .

MOREH NEVUKHIM I:19

"To fill." This is an equivocal term used to denote the penetration and repletion of one body by another: "She filled her jug" [Genesis 24:16]. . . . The term also refers to the completion or maturation of a set period of time. . . . It has also a sense referring to the reaching of perfection in virtue, the epitome of goodness: "Filled with blessedness of the Lord" [Deuteronomy 33:23]. . . . In this sense it is said, "The whole earth is filled with his glory" [Isaiah 6:3], meaning "The entire earth bears witness to His perfection," *i.e.*, it provides evidence of Him. . . . Every reference you will find to God's "filling" anything is in this sense; it does not imply the existence of some body which occupies space. However, if you wish to take "the glory of God" as a created light consistently called "glory"—and wish to believe that this is what "filled the sanctuary" [Exodus 40:34], there is no harm in doing so.[1]

MOREH NEVUKHIM I:20

"High" may mean exalted in space or in rank, *i.e.,* majesty, dignity, or worth. . . . With reference to God the latter sense is used. . . . You might ask, "How can you derive many concepts from one?" For those whose understanding is perfect, as you will soon see, God is not describable in terms of a multitude of attributes; these numerous predicates which designate majesty, worth, perfection, goodness and the rest, all reduce to one concept: His own Godhead and nothing beyond that Identity itself. . . .

MOREH NEVUKHIM I:21

"To pass." The original meaning . . . denotes the motion of a body through space; paradigmatically, the traversing of a certain distance by a living being. . . . Later the sense was extended to include the propagation of sounds in the air. . . . And it was broadened again to signify the Indwelling of the Light and the Shekhinah [the Divine Presence] beheld by prophets in the prophetic vision. . . . In this figurative sense it is said, "I shall pass through the land of Egypt" [Exodus 12:12], and so in all like cases.

Another sense is that in which a man who overdoes something is said to bypass his goal . . . or one who misses one objective makes for another. . . . In my view it is in this last figurative sense that Scripture says, "The Lord passed by His Face" [Exodus 34:6]. The antecedent of "his" is God; this is how it is taken by the Sages, although they say this in the context of narratives which have no bearing here; but it does in a way confirm our view: "His Face" refers to the Holy One Blessed be He, and the explanation, as I see it, is that Moses (peace upon him) sought a certain perception, *i.e.,* the one

---

1. The notion of the created light or glory of God may indeed be useful in eliminating troublesome anthropomorphisms in the text but it does not radically come to grips with the problem of divine immanence and transcendence but only places that problem at one remove. If what prophets behold is God's "created glory," the question remains, what is the relationship between that manifestation and the Godhead itself.

called "seeing the face" in "My Face shall not be seen" [Exodus 33:23]. He was promised a lesser perception than he sought, called "seeing the back" in "you shall see My back"[*ibid.*]. . . . What it says here is that God deprived him of that perception called "seeing the face" and passed him to something else, *i.e.,* an awareness of the acts ascribable to Him, which appear as numerous attributes, as will be explained [*Moreh* I:34]. When I say "deprived him," I mean that that perception is by its very nature concealed and impossible of access: with any perfect man, once the mind has reached that which its nature allows it to grasp, if it strives to apprehend more, over and above that knowledge with which it is already acquainted, then the perception will be either deceived or destroyed,[1] as will be made clear in a later chapter of this treatise [I:32]—unless divine protection attend him, as it is said, "I shall cover you with My hand until I pass by" [Exodus 33:22]. . . .

Do not be disturbed by the fact that this profound and abstruse subject bears several interpretations; for this is no detriment to our purpose. You may choose whatever belief you please: (1) that Moses' exalted standpoint was, as I have interpreted it, entirely a prophetic vision and that all he aspired to was intellectual perception, so that what he sought, what he was denied, and what he grasped would all be mental rather than perceptual; or (2) as Onkelos [2] interprets it, that there was visual perception along with mental apprehension, but of a created thing, through the sight of which the intellectual apprehending would be achieved—unless the visual apprehending was itself within the prophetic vision . . . or (3) that it was accompanied by an auditory perception, so that it would be the voice—doubtless created too—which "passed by His face." Choose whichever view you please.[3] The point is simply that you should not believe that "passed" here means as it does in "pass before the people." For God, exalted be He,

1. *Cf.* Exodus 33:20: "No man shall see Me and live."

2. Translator of the Hebrew Scriptures into Aramaic (or, as the Rambam calls it, Syriac) according to Jerusalem Talmud *Megillah* I:11.

3. Maimonides speaks here with a deceptive liberality. It is of course immaterial to him whether his reader surpasses the sophistication of Onkelos' gloss, so long as anthropomorphism is avoided. But the drift of the argument implicit in this chapter is that a consequence of the rejection of anthropomorphism is the realization that revelation is intellectual, not perceptual in character.

is not a body; motion is not predicable of Him; He cannot be said to pass in the original sense of the term.

MOREH NEVUKHIM I:23

"To go," the opposite of "to come," denotes departure of an animate or inanimate body from its place of rest to another. . . . In a derived sense it denotes the manifestation of things which are completely immaterial: "The command went forth from the king's mouth" [Esther 7:8]. . . . "For out of Zion the Law shall go forth" [Isaiah 2:3]. . . . In this figurative sense is every reference to God's going [and coming, as shown in I:22]: "Lo, the Lord goes forth from His place" [Isaiah 26:21], that is, His command, hidden from us until now, becomes manifest. This refers to creation of what did not yet exist, for all things which are brought into being by Him are ascribed to His word of command: "By the Lord's word the heavens were made; all their hosts, by the breath of His mouth" [Psalm 33:6]—an analogy with the acts of kings, whose instrument in executing their will is speech. But God does not require any instrumentality through which to act. He acts by will alone. . . .

Since the manifestation of a divine act is figuratively termed "going" . . . the suspension [1] of that act, according to His will, is called "return." Thus it says, "I shall go and return to my place" [Hosea 5:15], meaning that the Shekhinah would no longer remain among us. This implies the loss of Providence over us, as is shown by the warning "I shall hide My face from them and they shall be devoured" [Deuteronomy 31:17]. For the loss of Providence leaves one exposed, a butt of circumstance, whose weal and woe are left to hazard. A terrible threat indeed! [2] . . .

1. *I.e.,* its disappearance from the creature or creatures it affected: God's act as such does not cease.
2. The Existentialist concept of "forlornness" as a result of the death of God is a recognition of this consequence drawn by Maimonides. All order, rationality, design, good, wisdom, and understanding in creation are understood by Maimonides to be due to the Creator. Thus order itself, the very laws of nature, would depart from the world if God were to "withdraw" His providence from it. Nature would become the amorphous, haphazard miscellany which some claim it actually is. But such an event is hardly in keeping with God's good will (*cf. Moreh* II:27 ff.). In view of human limitations, the loss of God by individuals or by a people, however, is a common event. Nature con-

MOREH NEVUKHIM I:26

You have learned the general rule of interpretation which the Sages apply to this area: ''The Torah speaks according to human language'' [*Yevamot* 71a, *Baba Metzia* 31b]. This means that whatever mankind at large can grasp and conceive directly is what is affirmed of God. Thus He has been assigned attributes connoting materiality to indicate that He exists. For the masses cannot immediately grasp the notion of incorporeal existence. To them, what is not a body or of a body [1] does not exist. Similarly, everything that we hold to be a perfection is ascribed to Him in order to point to His being perfect in every way and completely unflawed by inadequacies. Thus whatever ordinary people take to be a deficiency or privation is not ascribed to Him. For this reason He is not described as eating or drinking, sleeping or growing sick, nor as doing wrong, or anything else of the sort. But whatever is popularly supposed to be a perfection is ascribed to Him, even though it may be such only from our point of view. For with respect to Him those things which we suppose to be perfections are extreme deficiencies.[2] But if they imagined Him as lacking such human perfections, they would think that a flaw in Him!

Motion, as you know, is a perfection for animals, necessary to the realization of their being as animals. For just as an animal must eat and drink to replace what breaks down, it must move to direct itself toward the favorable and avoid the harmful. There is no difference between describing God as eating or drinking and describing Him as moving. Nevertheless ''human language,'' *i.e.,* popular imagination, holds eating and drinking to be deficiencies for God, but does not hold motion to be a deficiency for Him—despite the fact that only dependence makes motion necessary. . . .

---

tinues in its course, but the ''abandoned'' man, having lost his bearings, becomes the victim of chance vicissitudes. For he is incapable of orienting himself among the many goods and evils which present themselves to him. Until he finds some surrogate for God (an idol—either the self or some arbitrarily selected goal or end), all values appear neutral to him, and he remains incapable of action, let alone of ordering his priorities. *Cf. Moreh Nevukhim* III:17 ff., where Maimonides equates Providence with wisdom—and the loss of wisdom with the loss of the Shekhinah.

1. *E.g.,* as whiteness is the whiteness *of* a piece of chalk.
2. Since all that finite beings can conceive as a perfection involves limitation.

MOREH NEVUKHIM I:27

Onkelos the Proselyte was quite perfect both in the Syriac [*i.e.*, Aramaic] and Hebrew languages. He made it his task to eliminate anthropomorphism by substituting appropriate glosses for any predication in Scripture which might lend itself thereto. Thus wherever he finds a term indicating one kind of motion or another, he takes it as denoting the manifestation of a "created light," *i.e.*, the Shekhinah, or providential activity. Thus he translates "God descended" [Exodus 19:11] as "God manifested Himself" . . . and so throughout his translation. But, "I shall go down with you to Egypt" [Genesis 46:4], he translates, "I shall go down with you to Egypt." [1] This is a wonderful illustration of the man's mastery and excellence of his interpretation and his general comprehension. It also opens up a whole new dimension for us regarding revelation. For at the beginning of this incident it says, "God spoke to Israel in visions of the night . . ." [46:2–3]. Since this opening places the promise within the "visions of the night," Onkelos was not abashed to convey the passage literally as he found it. And he was right. For this is a description of what was said in the vision, not of an actual event such as "the Lord descended upon Mount Sinai" [Exodus 19:20], which describes something which actually happened. [2] . . .

MOREH NEVUKHIM I:28

. . . Take the words "And under His feet was as a work of the whiteness of sapphire" [Exodus 24:10]. Onkelos, as you know, interprets this so that "throne" is the antecedent of "his." [1] . . . You must admire the extent of his rejection of anthropomorphism and anything that might lead to it even remotely. . . . But that is as far as it goes: he rejects anthropomorphism but does not explain for us what sort of thing they [2] apprehended, what sort of thing is intended by this symbolism. This is his practice throughout: he does not address himself to this subject but only to the rejection of anthropomorphism. The reason: the denial of anthropomorphism is a demonstrable fact and must

1. To wit, without eliminating the reference to physical travel.
2. *I.e.*, an actual manifestation of God.
1. Both persons and objects may be designated by the masculine pronoun in Hebrew.
2. The elders of Israel (*cf. Moreh* I:5).

be accepted as such. Certain of this, he translated accordingly. The explication of the meaning of such symbolisms, however, is a matter of interpretation; they may mean one thing or another. They are also quite esoteric, and their being understood is not credally fundamental. Nor are they easily grasped by the masses. Thus Onkelos was not concerned with this subject.

We, on the other hand, in keeping with the objective of this study, must offer some interpretation [3]. . . .

MOREH NEVUKHIM I:36

. . . If you scrutinize the entire Torah and all the prophetic writings, you will observe that the expressions "kindling of wrath," "anger," and "jealousy" are applied exclusively with reference to idolatry; only an idolator is called God's enemy or adversary, hated of God. . . . The Scriptures speak with such severity only because this false view— idolatry—relates to God. . . . For benightedness and misbelief are greater regarding a sublime subject (a being whose place in existence is immutable) than they are with respect to a lesser being. By misbelief I mean believing a thing to be other than as it is. By benightedness I mean ignorance of what it is possible to know. . . .

No idolator, as you know, ever practiced idolatry on the assumption that his idol was the one Deity. No human being of the past has ever imagined for a day (and none will imagine in the future) that the form he fashions in metal castings or stone and wood created heaven and earth and governs them. On the contrary, the idol is worshipped only as a symbol of something which mediates between us and God,[1] as it is written, "Who does not fear Thee, King of the nations," etc. [Jeremiah 10:7], and again, "Everywhere incense is offered to My name," etc. [Malachi 1:11]—meaning what they[2] take to be the First Cause. . . .

---

3. Maimonides proceeds to interpret "as a work of the whiteness of sapphire" as symbolizing "prime matter," and "under his feet" as indicating its relation to God, *i.e.*, as effect to cause (*cf. Moreh* I:37, 38).

1. This was the typical rationalistic explanation of idol-worship offered by such Greek philosophers as Porphyry.

2. The pagans. Maimonides cites his discussion in the *Mishneh Torah* at *Avodah Zarah* I; *cf.* also Part Five of this volume.

No one of our religion would dispute this. Nonetheless, despite their belief in the existence of the Deity, these misbelievers assigned to another a prerogative which was properly His, namely, the right of worship and exaltation, as it is written, "Worship the Lord," etc. [Exodus 23:25], in order that His existence may be established in the faith of the masses. This led to the erosion of faith in His existence from the creed of the masses; for the masses are aware only of the ritual act, not of its meaning or the true object of worship. It was this which made them deserving of destruction, as the text says, "Thou shalt not let one soul live" [Deuteronomy 20:16]. The reason is clearly stated to be the eradication of this false view, lest others be corrupted by it: "So that they do not teach you to do," etc. [20:18]. It then calls them enemies and adversaries, hated of God, and says that one who follows such practices provokes God's jealousy, anger, and wrath.[3]

What then would be the case with someone whose misbelief attached to God Himself, who believed that God was other than as He is, did not believe in His existence, or believed that He was dual or corporeal, passive or deficient in any way? He is, indubitably, more inadequate than a pagan who regards idols as intermediaries or claims they can bring about good or evil. Be advised, if you be such a one, that when you believe God to be a body or subject to any condition to which bodies are subject, you have "aroused His jealousy and anger," "kindled His wrath," become a much worse "enemy," and "adversary," and are much more "hated of God" than an idol-worshipper.

If it occurs to you that the anthropomorphist is excusable because he was brought up as such or because he was naïve or undiscerning, then you must hold the same regarding the idolator, for he too is such either because of his backwardness or his upbringing.[4] . . . If you say that the literal sense of the Text encourages this confusion, you must realize that the idolator too has been led into idolatry solely by distorted notions and figments of the imagination. But for one who is not able to

3. As Maimonides explains below, God has no attributes, certainly no passions: these terms indicate solely logical distance from the true conception of God.
4. But neither one's cultural heritage nor one's personal ignorance (of the truth of monotheism) may be offered as an excuse for idolatry: idolatry is forbidden by one of the seven Noahidic commandments, binding upon all mankind.

investigate for himself there is no excuse for not following those thinkers who are able to approach the truth.[5] I would not consider one who cannot prove incorporeality to be a misbeliever, but I would so consider one who did not believe in incorporeality, especially when there are the glosses of Onkelos and Jonathan ben Uzziel [6] (peace upon them), which draw one as far as possible away from anthropomorphism. This was the point of this chapter.[7]

MOREH NEVUKHIM I:37

"Face" is ambiguous mainly in its metaphorical dimension. It frequently denotes the face of any animal . . . or it denotes anger . . . frequently including that of God. It also designates the presence of or encounter with an individual. . . . It is in this sense that it is said, "The Lord spoke to Moses face to face" [Exodus 33:11], *i.e.,* He was immediately present to him.[1] . . . In this sense too is, "But My Face shall not be seen" [33:23]: My true Inbeing cannot be apprehended. . . .

MOREH NEVUKHIM I:38

"Back" is ambiguous, both a noun designating the posterior . . . or often an adverb meaning "after." It also has a sense of following or modeling one's way of life after that of a particular individual: "You

5. Such thinkers are found in all nations, Maimonides suggests.
6. Jonathan ben Uzziel, a student of Hillel, was a tanna of the first century C.E. and author of a Biblical translation, according to the Talmud, although the translation which circulated under his name in the Middle Ages is generally regarded as fourth–fifth century C.E.
7. The subject of this chapter is neither idolatry nor anthropomorphism but rather the argument that to believe God to be other than as He is is worse than idolatry. Maimonides is preparing the reader for the demonstration of the crucial facts about the logic of God which delimit the bounds of true, mature conception about the Deity. Those who fail to accept the implications of these arguments must brand themselves as enemies of God, in his view. Even if they are incapable of following the arguments, they must accept the results on authority, for Onkelos and Jonathan ben Uzziel afford sufficient evidence of the possibility of applying those results consistently to the text, and sufficient encouragement of the true interpretation to render inexcusable any succumbing to imagination ("the true evil impulse") by accepting as conclusive the literal—or literary—level of meaning.
1. See *Shemonah Perakim* 7.

shall follow at the back of the Lord your God" [Deuteronomy 13:5], *i.e.*, follow a path of obedience to Him and conformance to the effect of His acts and to His ways.[1] . . . In this sense it is said, "You shall see My back" [Exodus 33:23]: You shall apprehend what "follows Me," bears a resemblance to Me, is determined by My will, *i.e.*, all the objects of My creation. . . .

MOREH NEVUKHIM I:46

. . . There is a tremendous difference between directing someone's mind to the realization that something exists and providing a thorough understanding of the real nature of that thing. One can gain an awareness of the existence of a thing from its actions or its accidents, or even from some very nonessential relations it may have with something else. For example, if you wanted to make known the ruler of a certain region to one of the people of his land who had no knowledge of him, you might acquaint this person with the ruler and call his attention to his existence in many ways: by saying, "He is the tall, fair, white-haired person," identifying him by accidents of his; [1] or by saying, "He is the one around whom you see a great throng of people, mounted and on foot, the one with swords drawn about him, standards raised above his head, and trumpets sounding before him." Or you might say, "He is the one who lives in the palace in such-and-such a city" in that region, or, "He is the one who commanded the building of this wall" or that bridge. Or other such actions or relations to other things might be cited.

Or you might propose less tangible states of affairs as grounds for inferring his existence. If someone asked you, for example, "Has this land a ruler?" you might answer, "Yes, it certainly has." What is the evidence? You might answer, "The fact that this money-changer (who is, as you see, a puny weakling) has that great pile of money before him while this poor man, despite all his strength and all his bulk, begs for so much as a carob seed in charity—and not only does the other not give it to him, but drives him away with words. Were it not for the fear of the government, he would not have hesitated to kill the money-

---

1. *Viz.*, mercy, lovingkindness, etc.
1. *I.e.*, by referring to nonessential characteristics: accidents may distinguish the ruler from other men on a platform, even though they reveal nothing of who or what he is.

changer or push him aside and take what money he had. This is evidence of the fact that this city has a king.'' And you would have provided evidence for his existence in terms of the orderly state of the city's affairs, the cause of which is the fear of the government and anticipation of punishment by it.

Nothing in this whole illustration gives any clue as to the nature of the government or its character as a government.[2] The same problem arises in making God known to the masses in all prophetic writings including the Torah: it was necessary to guide all men together to an awareness of His existence and possession of all perfections, *i.e.,* to the fact that He does not just exist as do earth and sky, but exists, lives, knows, is powerful and active and everything else which is fittingly believed of His existence. (This will be explained later.) So minds were led to a realization of His existence by His representation as a corporeal being—of His life, by His being imagined as moving. For the masses do not regard anything as real, unquestionably certain to exist, except bodies. What is not a body but is in a body exists, but in a weaker sense than bodies do, since its existence depends upon that of a body. What neither is a body nor is in a body does not exist at all, according to man's first thought—and least of all according to imagination. In the same way, ordinary people have no conception of life apart from motion. What does not move in space is not alive for them—despite the fact that motion is not essential to the living thing but an accident belonging to it. Likewise consciousness, as we familiarly know it, comes through the senses (specifically, sight and hearing). And we neither know nor can conceive the transference of an

2. The example does not even require that the ''government'' or ruling authority be that of a person or persons: it might be a mode of organization or the internal force of conscience, although to the imagination of the mass mentality, the personal rule of a monarch who governs by constraint is immediately suggested. Maimonides has intentionally used the ambiguous word *sultân,* which may mean ruler or governing authority, so as to avoid the appearance of quarreling with popular imagination while leaving open the option of following a more sophisticated line of interpretation. The clue to this is in the fact that if *sultân* is taken to mean ''king'' (*malik*), the argument is not strictly valid: order does not prove the existence of a king but only serves as evidence for the hypothesis that there is a king who governs by constraint. Other more sophisticated hypotheses, referring to more sophisticated modes of government, might account for the same phenomena as well or better. But order does imply government.

idea from one person's mind to that of another without speech, which means sound modulated by the lips and tongue and the other speech organs. Thus, when our minds are led toward an understanding of the fact that God is aware or that ideas devolve from Him upon the prophets, so that they in turn may relate them to us, He is described to us as "hearing" and "seeing," meaning that He is conscious of things which are objects of hearing and seeing and knows them; He is described as speaking, meaning that ideas derive from Him to the prophets: this is the meaning of revelation, as will be made abundantly clear [*Moreh* II:32].

Since we know of no case in which we cause any event without performing some mechanical act, He is described as "acting." And in the same way, since the masses cannot conceive of anything as being alive unless it has a soul, He is described as having a soul. . . .

God, in short (exalted be He above all privations), is figuratively assigned bodily organs in order to allude to His acts. And those acts in turn are figuratively ascribed to Him by way of pointing toward a certain perfection which is not in fact identical with them. He is said, for example, to have eyes, ears, hands, mouth, and tongue—symbolizing sight, hearing, productive activity, and speech. But sight and hearing are figuratively assigned to Him to represent His being, in a general sense, aware. . . . And action and speech are figuratively ascribed to him to allude to the emanation which issues from Him, as will be explained [*Moreh* II:2 ff.].

Every bodily organ which you will find in all the prophetic Scriptures is either an organ of locomotion, indicating life, or an organ of perception, indicating consciousness, an organ of manipulation, indicating productive action, or organ of speech, indicating emanation of the Minds upon the prophets, as will be explained [*cf. Moreh* II:12]. The net effect of all these symbolic usages is to establish in us a belief in the existence of a Being who is alive, who is the Maker of all other things and who knows His own work. Once we have taken up the denial of attributes [*Moreh* I:53], we shall explain how all these [3] reduce to just one principle, which is His Godhead. Our purpose in this chapter is simply to make clear that all the bodily organs ascribed to

---

3. *Viz.,* God's life, action, knowledge, etc.

Him (exalted be He above all defect) symbolize the acts of those organs, which are, from our point of view, perfections: we allude to His Perfection by ascribing to Him these perfections—a fact to which the Sages awaken us by their dictum "Torah speaks according to human language." . . .

All organs, both internal and external, are really on a par, inasmuch as they are instruments through which the soul performs its diverse functions. Some, including all the internal organs, are necessary to the survival of the individual for any length of time. Others, such as the reproductive organs, are necessary to the survival of the species. Still others are advantageous to the individual in perfecting the performance of his actions. Such are the hands, feet, and eyes, which make it possible for us to move, work, and perceive efficiently. Now motion in animals serves the purpose of allowing them to pursue what is advantageous to them and avoid what is detrimental. Senses are needed to distinguish the favorable from the unfavorable. And productive work is necessary for man so that he may prepare food, clothing, and shelter for himself—for this need of providing for his own welfare is part of man's nature; and there are certain other species too which have certain crafts to fill their needs.

I know of no one who doubts that God is not in need of anything to prolong His existence or improve His condition. Thus He has no organs, for He is not a body, but acts simply through His Identity, not by an instrument. But faculties, surely, are no more than instruments. Thus He has no faculties: *i.e.,* there is nothing to Him other than His Godhead, through which to act or know or will—for attributes are no more than faculties called by another name. But that is not the point of this chapter.

The Sages, of blessed memory, made a general pronouncement rejecting all that is suggested to the imagination by any of the corporeal characteristics mentioned by the prophets. This statement of theirs shows that this usage never became an object of delusion or confusion for them. That is why throughout the Talmud and the Midrashic literature you find them still speaking in the literal usage of the prophets. They knew that this was in no danger whatever of being misunderstood. All was to be taken symbolically, as leading the mind toward a Being. Thus, when an image is used consistently, as when

He is likened to a king who ordains and forbids, punishes and rewards the people of his land, who has servants and ministers to execute his decrees and carry out his will, the Sages too sustain the conceit in every context, speaking (in accordance with the requirements of the imagery) of the acceptance and rejection of petitions, and other such acts of kings. They felt consistently secure and confident that this would cause no misconceptions or confusions.

The general pronouncement to which I allude is their dictum in *Bereshit Rabbah* [XXVII]: "How bold are the prophets who liken the creature to its Creator, as it is said, 'On the likeness of the throne was a likeness as the appearance of a man' [Ezekiel 1:26]." Thus they make it clear and explicit that all the forms perceived by all the prophets in prophetic visions are created by God—which is true, for every form in the imagination is created. But what a wonderful phrase is "How bold," as though they were overawed. For they always speak in this way when they express their awe at something said or done which is shocking on the face of it, as when they say, "Rabbi so-and-so performed *halitza*, [4] alone, with a slipper, and by night. Rabbi so-and-so said, 'How bold [5] to have done it alone!' " [*Yevamot* 104a] . . . It is as though they said, "How awesome was the thing the prophets were driven to do when they designated this Being in terms of the objects of His creation." Understand this thoroughly. They state plainly and explicitly that they are free of belief in corporealism and that all forms and configurations seen in prophetic visions are created. Yet the prophets "likened the creature to its Creator." . . .

MOREH NEVUKHIM I:47

We have stated several times that nothing which is inconceivable in God or which would be popularly regarded as implying any deficiency on His part is figuratively ascribed to Him in the prophetic writings— not even if it is something which is in principle the same as something

4. The ritual release of a man from the ancient obligation to marry his brother's widow. (*Cf.* Deuteronomy 25:5–10 and the Talmudic tractate *Yevamot*.)
5. The Hebrew and Aramaic terms discussed here would normally be understood to denote strength. It is clear from the context and from *Shemonah Perakim* 4 that Maimonides understands these terms as denoting boldness in the rabbinical lexicon, just as the term for wealth there denotes contentedness.

that is figuratively ascribed to Him. The predications which are made in His regard suggest—or make possible the envisioning of—certain perfections. It is in accordance with this finding that we should explain the reason why hearing, sight, and smelling are metaphorically assigned to Him while touch and taste are not. For His transcendence of the five senses is identical in each case, the senses all being deficient as modes of apprehension even for those who rely on them exclusively, since they are passive and subject to interference, interruption, and pain, as are the other bodily organs.

When we say, "God sees," we mean that He is aware of the objects of sight. By "God hears," we mean that He is aware of the objects of hearing. In the same way, taste and touch might have been predicated of Him, and this might have been interpreted as meaning that He is aware of the objects of taste and touch. For all His apprehensions are on a par. To eliminate one would entail the elimination of all five senses; and if one such apprehension is to be predicated of Him, then so must apprehension of all the rest of the five types of sensory objects. Yet we find our Scriptures saying, "The Lord saw," "The Lord heard," and "The Lord smelled," but not "The Lord tasted," or "The Lord felt." The reason is that it is settled in all people's imaginations that God does not come into contact with bodies in the way in which one body comes into contact with another. For they themselves have not seen Him. And these two senses, taste and touch, do not apprehend their object until they are actually in contact with it. The senses of sight, hearing, and smell, on the other hand, apprehend their objects (and the bodies which bear those characteristics) at a distance. So they were deemed appropriate by popular imagination.

Besides, the object of assigning these senses to Him metaphorically was to indicate His awareness of our actions, but sight and hearing were sufficient for that. . . . Thus the Sages preached, by way of admonition, "Know what is above you: a seeing eye and a hearing ear" [*Avot* 2:1].[1]

You know, when you think critically about it, that all the senses are on a par, and that sight, hearing, and smell are to be denied of Him on

1. These two senses were sufficient for the homiletical representation of the fact of moral accountability.

the same grounds as touch and taste. For all are physical modes of apprehension, passivities, changeable states. But with some the flaws are obvious, while others are deemed flawless. In the same way the drawbacks of imagination are apparent, while those of reflection and cogitation are not. So fantasy . . . is not metaphorically ascribed to Him, but thinking and considering . . . are. Thus it is said, "which the Lord thought" [cf. Jeremiah 49:20], and "in His understanding spread out the heavens" [Jeremiah 10:12]. The treatment of the inner apprehensions, then, parallels that of the outer, sensory apprehensions. Some are and some are not metaphorically ascribed to Him—always according to the usage of human language. What men think of as a perfection for Him is predicated of Him; what is plainly a flaw is not. But in reality He has no real, essential attributes apart from His identity, as will be demonstrated.

MOREH NEVUKHIM I:50
The reader of my study must realize that belief is not what is said but rather what is thought when a thing is affirmed to be such as it is thought to be. If you are of the sort who are satisfied with mouthing true opinions, or opinions which seem to you to be true, without conviction, without any conception of the meaning of your words—let alone seeking certainty about them—you will find this very easy. For many who are dull maintain their creeds by rote, without attaching any sort of idea to them. If, on the other hand, you are one of those whose ambition it is to rise to a higher level, at which things are thought out, if you wish to know with certainty that God is truly one, in the sense that there exists no multiplicity whatever in Him and no capability of division in any respect, then you must recognize that He has no essential attributes. Those who believe God to be one with many attributes have affirmed His oneness verbally while mentally believing Him to be many. This resembles the Christians' formula that He is "one but three" and that "the three are one," or the dictum of those who reject anthropomorphism and affirm His absolute simplicity by saying, "He is one but has many attributes, He and His attributes being one"—as though our object were simply to find out what to say rather than what to believe. We cannot believe unless we think, for belief is the affir-

mation that what is outside the mind [1] is as it is thought to be within the mind. And if belief is accompanied by the realization that what is believed cannot be otherwise in any way and the mind allows no room for an alternative, no possibility of contradiction, then there is certainty.

If you study dispassionately and without regard to prejudice or tradition the denial of attributes which I shall put forward in the following chapters, you will, if you are a person of understanding, inevitably become certain of it. You will then be among those who have a conception of divine unity rather than one of those who pay it lip service but have no conception of what it might mean. Of this latter sort it is said, "Thou art close to their mouths, but far from their kidneys" [2] [Jeremiah 12:2], whereas a man ought to be of the sort who think and understand the truth, even if they do not voice it—for that is what is demanded of the best, to whom it is said, "Speak to your hearts in your beds and be silent. Selah" [Psalm 4:5].

MOREH NEVUKHIM I:51

There are many things which are self-evident—among them, the primary objects of thought and perception.[1] Other things are nearly as obvious, sufficiently so that if man were left to himself he would need no argument in their behalf: that there is motion, for example, or that man has the capacity to act [free will], the phenomena of generation and destruction, and the properties which things manifest directly to the senses, e.g., that fire is hot and water cool. There are many other such cases. But through error or because some intentionally went counter to the facts in the service of some end, denying what is apparent to the senses or feigning the existence of things which are not real, thinkers found it necessary to prove the existence of things which are manifest and refute the reality of those supposed beings. Thus we find that Aristotle gives proof that there is motion, since it had been denied, and refutes the existence of atoms, since it had been affirmed.

The denial that God has attributes is of the same class, a primary truth of reason. For an attribute is distinct from the being of which it is

1. *I.e.,* independent of it.
2. The seat of the understanding, in Maimonides' interpretation (*cf. Moreh* I:47).
1. To wit, the axioms of reason and the uninterpreted data of the senses.

the attribute. It is a certain kind of condition of that being. Thus it is an accident. If an attribute were identical with its subject, either its predication would be redundant, as in "Man is man," or it would be an analysis of a term, as in "Man is the rational animal," for the rational animal *is* man; that is what man really is: there is no third concept, beyond rational and animal in the concept of man, and man is the one subject of whom animality and rationality are predicated. This is nothing but an analysis of the term, just as though you had said the thing called "man" is the one composed of animality and rationality.

Thus it is clear that an attribute must be one of two things: (1) It may be part of the essence of its subject and thus serve in the explication of that subject's name—a possibility with reference to God which we do not preclude on this but on other grounds, as will be made clear [see *Moreh* I:52.1]. Or (2) the attribute may be other than its subject, a principle adventitious to it—which would entail that attribute's being an accident of that identity.

To deny accidents of the Creator nominally is not to deny them in fact. For every concept adventitious to that of identity depends upon it without contributing to its reality, and that is just what "accident" means. If the attributes are plural, moreover, the implication exists of there being many eternal beings. There is no monotheism at all without belief in one simple identity, uncompounded and undifferentiated, conceptually one from any point of view and by any criteria which might be chosen, indivisible in every regard and respect—subjectively as well as objectively without plurality—as will be proved in this study [*Moreh* II:2].

Some thinkers reached the point of saying that "His attributes are neither the same as nor outside of His Identity." This is like others' saying, "Modes" (by which they mean universals) "are neither existent nor nonexistent," or like still others saying that the atom occupies a position but does not take up space, or that man cannot act but can "acquire" actions. All these formulae are mere talk; they are real verbally, but not mentally, let alone objectively. But, as you and everyone who does not deceive himself knows, these propositions are protected from attack by sheer mass of words and obfuscating illustrations and verified by shouting, name-calling, and numerous dialectical ploys and sophistries. If the person who utters and attempts to prove these things by such means stopped to consider his beliefs, he would find them nothing but confusion and inadequacy, for he is aspiring to give existence to what does not exist, to create a middle between contraries which have none. Or is there a middle between existence and nonexistence? Or between two things' being identical and their being different?

The only thing that necessitated this approach was solicitude for the objects of imagination, and the fact that all the bodies which are objects of our thought are identities each of which necessarily has attributes. For we never find the identity of a body existing alone, in isolation from its attributes. By extending this model it was supposed that God too is such, compounded of diverse principles, His identity and the principles adventitious to it. Several groups pursued this delusion to the point of believing Him to be a body with attributes. Others, holding Him to transcend this implication, denied that He was a body but preserved the attributes. All this was made necessary by their following the literal sense of the books of revelation, as I shall explain.

MOREH NEVUKHIM I:52

Every predicate affirming an attribute, in terms of which a thing is said to be thus-and-so, must be of one of the following five sorts:

(1) A thing may be described by its definition, as man is described as "the rational animal." This predicate signifies the essence or "whatness" of the thing. As I have already explained, its sole function is in the analysis of a term. Everyone agrees that this class of predicates is not to be assigned to God because He has no prior causes affecting His existence, in terms of which that existence might be defined. That is the reason for the fact, well-known to all thinkers who understand their own words, that "God" cannot be defined.

(2) A thing may be described by part of its definition, as man may have rationality or animality predicated of him. This involves the notion of implication, for if we say "man is rational" we imply that whatever has humanity has rationality. Everyone agrees that this class of predicates is not to be assigned to God, for if He had a part of an essence, His essence would be compound. This sort of predicate is ruled impossible for the same reasons as the above.

(3) A thing may be described in terms of something beyond its es-

sence and identity, so that that in terms of which the thing is described is not part of what perfects or constitutes the thing itself. In that case, that in terms of which the thing is described is some quality of it. Now quality, which is a highest genus,[1] is one kind of accident.[2] Thus, if God had an attribute of this sort, He would be the substrate of accidents—which is sufficient to show how far from His essence and nature it is that He have qualities.[3] . . .

There are four sorts of qualities, as you know. I shall illustrate each sort in order to make clear its inapplicability to God: (*a*) You may predicate, for example, mental, moral, or physiological traits of a man in virtue of his having a soul, as when you say So-and-so is a carpenter, is chaste, or is ill. It makes no difference whether you say "carpenter" or "Knowing" or "Wise." . . . It makes no difference whether you say "chaste" or "Compassionate"[4]—for every art, every science, every character trait, is a psychological set. All this will be obvious to anyone who has a passing acquaintance with logic. (*b*) You may predicate, for example, physical dispositions or incapacities of a thing, as when you say "soft" or "hard." There is no difference between saying "soft" or "hard" and saying "Powerful" or "weak": all these are physical dispositions. (*c*) You may predicate, for example, passivities or "affections" of a man, as when you say So-and-so is ill-tempered, timorous, or compassionate, in cases where the character is not firm. To the same class belong predications of color, taste, or odor, hotness or coldness, dryness or moistness. (*d*) You may predicate of a thing, for example, characters which it has in terms strictly of quantity, as when you say "long" or "short," "crooked" or "straight," etc.

If you consider all these cases of predication and the others akin to them, you will find them inapplicable to God. For He has no quantity in terms of which He might be characterized by quantity-dependent at-

1. *I.e.,* an ultimate level of classification, since it designates one of the irreducibly distinct senses of the verb "to be."

2. To wit, *f* is an accident when *f* may be said to exist not in its own right, but only as the *f* of *x*.

3. A God who served as "substrate to accidents" would be material. Thus the implication spoken of at the end of I:51: if God has accidents, then God is material. The differentiation of identity from accident corresponds to the distinction of matter from form.

4. The terms capitalized represent alleged attributes of God.

tributes. He is not passive or capable of being made the object of any act in terms of which He might be characterized by affections.[5] He has no dispositions in terms of which He might be said to have capacities, capabilities, or the like. Nor does He have a soul, that He should have a mind set or psychological traits attaching to Him, such as mildness or modesty. Nor does He have any characteristic proper to a being with a soul, such as sickness and health. It should be clear to you then that He has no attribute reducible to the highest genus of quality. Thus these three classes of predicate, those indicating essence, a part of essence, or a quality dependent on an essence, have been shown to be inapplicable in His case, since all of these imply complexity, which we shall demonstrate [*Moreh* II] to be impossible to attribute to Him.

(4) A thing may be described by its *relationship* to something else, to a time, for example, or place, or another particular, as when you describe Zayd as the father of So-and-so, or as the man who lives in such-and-such a place. This sort of predication does not imply plurality or differentiation in the identity of the subject. For the same Zayd may be the neighbor of Omar, son of Bakr . . . resident in the house in such-and-such a place, and born in such-and-such a year. The meaning of relations is that they are neither the thing itself nor dependent on it [6] as are qualities.

At first glance it appears that God may be described in this manner. But upon closer and more precise investigation, it becomes evident that this is impossible. That there is no connection between God and time or space is obvious. For time is an accident dependent upon motion . . . and motion is one of the properties of bodies. God is not a body. Thus there is no connection between God and time. By the same token there is no connection between Him and space.

What must be investigated and thought about is whether there is any real relation between Him and any object of His creation, in terms of which He might be described. That He is not the correlative of any of His creatures is obvious, for one of the distinguishing characteristics of correlatives is interdependence. But He exists necessarily, whereas all other things exist contingently, as we shall explain [*Moreh* II:1].

5. Compassion, for example, in man implies "soft-heartedness," susceptibility to being affected by others. But a Perfect Being cannot be said to be changed by others.
6. For they subsist explicitly between the thing and something else.

Thus there is no correlativity between Him and creatures.

As for there being some comparison between Him and creation, this might be deemed sound, but it is not. For it is not possible to conceive a comparison between mind and color, which share the same mode of existence, according to our doctrine. How then is it possible to conceive any comparison with something which has nothing whatever in common with anything else? For He and all other things are said to "exist" in totally different senses. There is, therefore, no comparison between Him and any object of His creation, since comparisons may be made only between two things of the same, necessarily proximate, species. If things are merely of the same genus, there is no comparison between them. That is why we do not say, this red is redder than that green . . . even though they both fall under the same genus, color.

If two things are of different genera, then there is no way of relating them whatever, not even speciously, even if the two can be brought into some common grouping: there is no way of relating, for example, "one hundred yards" and the "hotness" of peppers. For the latter is of the genus of quality, the former of quantity. There is no relation, again, between knowledge and sweetness, or between forbearance and acridity, even though all these fall under the highest genus of qualities. How then can there be a relation between Him and any of His creatures despite the enormous and unequalled gulf which separates His reality from theirs? If there were a relation between Him and them, then He would have the accident of relation attached to Him. Even though it would not be an accident of His identity, it would still be an accident in the broad sense.[7] Thus, strictly speaking, even the avenue of relations affords no way of affirming any predicate of Him. Nevertheless, relative terms are the most appropriate predicates to be indulged in designating the Deity since they do not imply a plurality of eternal beings or a differentiation of His Identity through the differentiation of the beings to which He is related.

(5) The fifth class of positive attributes are those which describe a thing by its work. By "work" I do not mean the skill of the subject, as say "carpenter" or "smith," for these traits are qualities, as I have

7. *I.e.*, it would be a qualification to (the conception of) His essence, even if it did not actually determine that essence itself in any way. As long as relations are not the essence of the thing itself, they must be accidents.

stated. Rather I mean his product or effect—as, for example, when you say, "Zayd is the one who framed this door, built such-and-such a wall, wove this robe." This sort of description is removed from the identity of the subject to which it refers,[8] and therefore it may be applied to God, once it is understood that these diverse acts, as I shall show [*Moreh* I:53], do not require differentiation in their doer as the condition of their being done. Rather, as we have shown, all His diverse acts are done by His Identity alone, and not by any adventitious principle.

To sum up this chapter: He is one in every respect. . . . The various attributes and aspects by which Scripture portrays Him reflect the diversity of His works, not any plurality in His nature—and some of them depict His perfection, in accordance with our notions of perfection, as I have explained. That a single, simplex, undifferentiated identity can perform diverse actions will now be made clear by examples.

MOREH NEVUKHIM I:53

What led those who believe that God has attributes to that belief is closely related to what led the corporealists to their belief. For the corporealist was not led to that position by reason but by following the literal sense of the Scriptures. The same is true regarding the attributes. Since the Torah and prophetic writings ascribed predicates to Him, some took this literally, believing that He actually has attributes. It is as though they had recognized His transcendence of corporeality without recognizing His transcendence of the conditions of corporeality, *viz.*, the accidents—specifically the psychological characteristics, all of which are qualities. Every attribute regarded by attributionists as an essential property of God's you will find to be a quality conceptually. Even though it may not be explicitly stated, this amounts to speaking of God in terms of the familiar conditions of any body endowed with an animal soul. It is in reference to all such attributions that it is said, "Torah speaks according to human language." The only purpose of all these predications is to ascribe perfection to Him, but not the same perfection as in a creature with a soul.

---

8. *I.e.,* implies no characterization of Him.

Mostly these predications refer to His various works. The diversity of works does not involve a diversity of real principles in their author. I shall illustrate this with an example drawn from the world around us, the fact that a single cause may give rise to a diversity of effects, even without volition. (How much the more if that cause is a voluntary agent!) Fire, for example, melts some things, hardens others, cooks, burns, bleaches, and blackens. If a man were to describe fire as that which bleaches and blackens, burns and cooks, hardens and melts, he would be right. Someone who did not understand the nature of fire would suppose it contained six different "principles," . . . that all these conflicting effects could not be produced by the same cause. But someone who understood the nature of fire would understand that it brings about all these different effects by one active quality, heat. If this occurs with things which act by nature, how much more would it be so with a voluntary agent—how much more so with Him who transcends all description.

Our grasp of Him is in terms of various conceptually different analogies because in us knowledge is different from power, and power from will. But how can we infer from this that He has in Him a plurality of elements, such that by one He knows, by one He wills, and by one He is powerful? For that is what is meant by the attributes which they uphold. . . .

I shall illustrate my point for you in terms of man's rational capability: this is a single, undifferentiated faculty by which the arts and sciences are acquired, by which again man sews, does carpentry, weaves, and builds, learns geometry, and rules the state. All these varied acts issue from the same simplex, undifferentiated faculty. These acts are very different; their number (the number of arts which reason puts forth) is all but infinite. Thus it is not to be considered unreasonable in God's case that these various acts would issue from a simple and undifferentiated identity with nothing more to it whatever. Every predicate found in the Scriptures ascribed to the Deity designates not Him but His acts or absolute Perfection. It does not imply the existence of an identity compounded of diverse elements. . . . The concept of knowledge as applied to Him is identical with that of life. . . .

MOREH NEVUKHIM 1:54

Mosheh Rabeynu (on whom be peace), the master of all who understand, made two behests, both of which were answered: he sought from God to know Him as He really is, and he sought (first) to know Him through His attributes. God acceded to the earlier request by promising Moses knowledge of all His attributes and by making him aware that His attributes are His works. He answered the other by teaching Moses that God as He really is cannot be comprehended, and awakening him to a certain theoretical consideration from which he might grasp all that any human being possibly can. What Moses comprehended has never been comprehended as well by anyone before or since.

Moses prays to know God's attributes when he says, "Cause me, pray, to know Thy ways that I may know Thee," etc. [Exodus 33:13]. Consider the wonderful implications. . . . The words indicate that God is known through His attributes . . . and the continuation, "that I might find favor in Thine eyes [*ibid.*], indicates that he who knows God—not he who merely fasts and prays—finds favor in His eyes. Everyone who knows Him pleases Him and is brought near to Him, while those who know Him not are the objects of wrath and are distanced from Him. Nearness and remoteness, favor and wrath are proportionate to knowledge and ignorance. But I digress from the point of this chapter, to which I now return. When Moses sought to know God's attributes he sought forgiveness for the nation, and this was granted.[1] He then sought to know God in Himself, saying, "Show me, pray, Thy glory" [33:18]. Whereupon his first request, "Cause me, pray, to know Thy ways," was granted [see *Moreh* I:21]: he was told, "I shall cause all My good to pass before thee" [33:19]. In answer to his second request he was told, "Thou canst not see My face," etc. [33:20]. The words "all My good" allude to the arraying of all existing things before Him, of which it is said, "God saw all that He had made—it was very good" [Genesis 1:31]. By the arraying of all existing things before him, I mean that he comprehended their nature and their interconnectedness, and thereby recognized the char-

1. The suggestion made possible by the "digression" is that Moses' favor with God, through which he was able to intercede for the children of Israel, was the direct outcome of his knowledge of God.

acter of His governance of them, both general and particular.[2] This is the idea referred to when it says, "He is firmly established [3] in all My house" [Numbers 12:7], which is to say, he has a true and well-grounded understanding of the being of My world in its entirety—for unsound opinions [4] are not firm. It follows that to comprehend these works is to "know His attributes"—through which He is known. What shows us that what was promised was grasp of His acts is the fact that that through which He is indeed encountered is a set of purely active attributes, merciful, gracious, long-suffering. Thus it is clear that the "ways," knowledge of which Moses sought and which were consequently made known to him, are the acts which issue from Him. The Sages call them characteristics [Hebrew: *midot*] and speak of "thirteen characteristics," the term current in their usage to designate ethical traits. . . . Here it does not imply that God has ethical traits but rather that He does acts analogous to those which express our ethical traits, *i.e.,* those done on account of some psychological "set"—not that He has traits. Although Moses apprehended "all His good," *i.e.,* all His works, Scripture confines itself to the mention of thirteen "characteristics" because these are the acts which issue from Him by way of giving existence to humankind and governing them. This was the ultimate object of Moses' request, for his words conclude, "and know Thee, that I may find favor in Thine eyes, and see that this nation is Thy people"—in order to govern whom I shall require ways of acting which I shall model upon Your actions in governing them.

So you see that God's ways and His "attributes" are the same; they are the acts which issue from Him in the world: [5] Whenever one of His acts is apprehended, the attribute of which such action is the manifestation is predicated of Him, and He is named by a noun

2. Through causal law; see Part Four.

3. I translate consistently with Maimonides' interpretation: *neeman* would traditionally be translated "faithful," but this seems too much to presuppose a contrast between faith and reason, which militates directly against Maimonides' point. Etymologically *neeman* means "firm" or "solidly grounded"; Maimonides resorts to this basic meaning to argue that only he who knows can be said to have firm belief.

4. To wit, those not grounded in science.

5. It was upon this proposition that Spinoza founded his famous identification of thought and extension with the attributes of God.

derived from that verb. For example, His tender care in directing the development of the embryos of living things is perceived, how He brings into being their faculties (and the faculties of those who raise them after birth) to protect them from destruction, preserve them from harm, and serve them in securing their needs. Such actions would not issue from us without our having been affected by pity. That is what "mercy" means. It is said that He is Merciful, "as a father is merciful toward his children" [Psalm 103:13] . . . not that He is affected by pity but that He treats them as would a father whose acts express pure affection, tenderness, and compassion—not because He is changed or affected. And just as, when we give something to someone who has no claim upon us to receive it, this is called "grace" in our language . . . He gives being and direction to those who have no claim upon Him to do either, and for that reason He is called Gracious.

. . . All His actions resemble those which in man proceed from psychological traits and affections, but in His case they issue from nothing other than His Identity itself. He who governs a state is obliged—if he be a prophet—to imitate these attributes: his actions must be appropriate to men's deserts, not merely the outcome of affections; he must not lose his temper nor let any passion get the best of him.[6] For the height of human virtue is to become like Him, to the extent that this is possible [7]—which means imitating His acts by our own, as the Sages made clear in commenting on "You shall be holy [for I the Lord your God am holy]" [Leviticus 19:2]. They glossed: as He is gracious, so do you be gracious; as He is compassionate, so do you be compassionate.[8] The whole point is that the attributes

6. What differentiates the effects of the action of fire is the diversity of the materials upon which it operates. What differentiates the effects of God's act are the varieties of creaturely deserts. So it should be with the just ruler, whose acts (like God's) are not the expression of his personality, whims, passions, likes and dislikes, but the impartial application of the principles of justice and mercy according to the deserts of his subjects. Such rule is required of a prophet, since he is expected to know this of God: that God's justice and mercy are not divergent personality traits or emotions but the uniform and consistent principles of His operation in the world—both express equally His identity as it manifests itself in diverse situations.

7. Cf. Plato *Theaetetus* 176, *Shemonah Perakim* 5.

8. *Sifre* to Deuteronomy 10:12; cf. *Sota* 14a, and *Midrash Va-Yikra Rabba* 24.

ascribed to Him are those associated with His acts. He does not have any qualities.

MOREH NEVUKHIM I:56

Whenever two things are of the same kind, *i.e.*, share the same essence although differing in magnitude, intensity, degree, or such, they are alike despite such differences. A grain of mustard and the sphere of the fixed stars [1] are alike in having three dimensions. . . . Thus, those who believe that the Godhead has attributes—that God is "existing," "living," "powerful," "knowing," "willing"—ought to understand that these principles are not ascribed to Him and to us in the same sense. They ought not to believe, as they do, that the difference between these attributes and ours is simply one of magnitude, fullness, duration or stability, rendering His existence more stable, His life longer, His power greater, His knowledge fuller, His will more universal than ours, while keeping the same definitions in His case and in ours. The truth is nothing like this at all. For comparison may be applied only to things to which the same notion is applied in the same sense. It implies similarity.

Those who believe that He has attributes proper to Him also believe that just as He does not resemble other beings, so His attributes, which they uphold, ought not resemble those of others [2] or share the same definition. But their belief in attributes is not consistent with this. Rather they presume a shared definition without a resemblance.[3] Anyone who understands what "resemblance" means will recognize that He and all other things are said to exist in totally different senses. Thus knowledge, power, will, and life too are predicated of Him and of all those who have knowledge, power, will, and life in totally different senses, which bear no conceptual resemblance to one another. . . .

1. Held by the Aristotelians to be the outermost bound of the universe, hence the largest physical magnitude.
2. Thus even anthropomorphists make them greater, etc.
3. An obvious self-contradiction.

MOREH NEVUKHIM I:57

On the attributes, more recondite than the preceding: it is known that existence is an accident of a being.[1] Thus existence is a principle distinct from the essence of the being. This is obviously necessary for every being whose existence has a cause.[2] In the case of a being whose existence has no cause, however (which is the case only with God, hallowed and revered be He—for this is what we mean when we say that He exists necessarily), His existence is His Inbeing and Reality; His essence is His existence, and He has not any accident by which He exists, which would render His existence distinct from Himself. For He exists necessarily, constantly. Existence is not something which He may or may not have. Thus He exists, but not through "existence." [3] In the same way He lives but not through life, is able but not through power, knows but not through understanding. Rather, all of these reduce to a single, undifferentiated principle, as will be made clear.

You must understand as well that oneness and plurality are also accidents, in terms of which what is is one or many. . . . Just as number is not the same thing as what is numbered, so oneness is not the same thing as what is one. All these are accidents of the class of discrete quantity, which apply to beings susceptible to such accidents. In the case of the Necessarily Existent, however, who is in the truest sense simplex and to whom no multiplicity whatever attaches, it is as absurd to predicate oneness of Him as it is to predicate plurality: *i.e.*, oneness is not a principle distinct from His essence; rather, He is one but not through oneness.[4]

These ideas, which are so subtle that they all but elude the mind, cannot be expressed in ordinary language (a mode of expression which

1. Avicenna had argued that since any ordinary being might either exist or not exist, existence in such cases was distinguishable from essence: for the question as to what a thing is is a different question entirely from that as to whether such a thing exists.

2. A being whose existence has a cause depends for its existence upon something other than itself. Its existence, then, does not depend on what it is.

3. In modern language: with all finite beings the judgment "*x* exists" is synthetic; with God the corresponding judgment is analytic.

4. A being who was "one through oneness" would not be one in an absolute sense. Relative oneness is possible in contingent beings such as ourselves, but not in a being who is absolutely simplex.

is one of the greatest causes of confusion), because our scope for expression in any language is so extremely narrow that we cannot conceive of such an idea without some looseness of expression. Thus when we wish to indicate the fact that the Deity is not many, there is nothing we can say but "one," even though "one" and "many" are both varieties of quantity. For this reason we give concise direction to the mind toward the truth of the matter by saying "one, but not through oneness." In the same way we say "eternal" to point at His being nontemporal. For in saying "eternal" we speak somewhat loosely, as is obvious, since "eternal" is said only of things to which time attaches. . . . Whatever the accident of time does not attach to can no more be said properly to have come to be or to be eternal than sweetness can be said to be straight or crooked, or sound to be salty or bland. . . .

All that you find in the Scriptures describing Him as "the first and the last" is comparable to His being depicted as having eyes and ears: the intention of such a description is that He is untouched by change, that in Him nothing whatever initiates. . . . All such expressions are "according to human language." When we say "one," likewise, we mean that He has no peer, not that a principle of oneness attaches to His being.

MOREH NEVUKHIM I:58

Even more recondite than the preceding: you must understand that negative predications are the correct way of describing God, since they do not involve any imprecision and do not imply any deficiency on God's part in general or in terms of specific conditions. Positive descriptions, on the other hand, bear with them connotations of polytheism and divine inadequacy,[1] as I have made clear. What I must do now is first make clear to you (1) how negations are, in a way, predications, and in what it is that they differ from affirmations; after that I shall explain (2) how it is that we have no other way of describing Him except negatively.

(1) A description, then, I would point out, does not uniquely distinguish that which is described. Rather, a description may belong to one object and be shared by another, so that it does not differentiate the

1. Since they put God on the same footing with His creatures.

one from the other. For example, if you see a man at a distance and ask, "What is that I see?" and are told, "An animal," that is a description, no doubt, of what you see, even though it does not differentiate it from all other things. It does distinguish it somewhat; it does tell you that what you see is not a vegetable or mineral body. In the same way, if there were a man in this house, and you knew that there was some body in the house but did not know what kind, assuming you asked, "What is in this house?" and received the answer "Neither a mineral nor a vegetable body," then some differentiation would have occurred: you would know that there was an animal in the house, even if you did not know what kind. In this way negative descriptions complement the positive. They must distinguish things somewhat, even if only by excluding what they negate from the universe of what we assume not to be negated.

The way negative predicates differ from positive ones is that positive predicates, even when they do not differentiate, designate some part of the object of which knowledge is sought, either a part of its substance or one of its accidents. Negative predicates acquaint us not at all with the thing in itself whose nature we wish to understand, except incidentally, as in our example.[2]

(2) Having prefaced the foregoing, I say that God, hallowed and revered be He, has been proved to be Necessarily Existent and uncompounded, as will be demonstrated. We know only His thatness, we do not know His whatness. Thus it is absurd that He be given any positive description, for He has no "that" apart from His "what" so that one or the other might be designated by a predicate. Still less is His nature compound, that a predicate might designate its two parts. Still less does He have accidents which a predicate might denote. Thus no affirmative predication whatever is possible in His regard.

It is negative predication which must be used to guide the mind to what ought to be believed of Him—the reason being that such predicates, while implying no plurality of any sort, lead the mind to the

2. Of the man in the house. "Not mineral or vegetable" implies animal only on the assumption that we know all bodies to be animal, vegetable, or mineral. Negative predicates, as we should expect, tell us nothing about what a thing is but only what it is not. Where the universe of discourse is infinite or unknown, they tell us nothing positive whatever.

highest conception of God possible for a human being. To illustrate: It has been demonstrated to us that something exists other than those things which we apprehend by sense perception and comprehend by reason. Of this being we say that it exists, meaning that it cannot not exist.[3] We later apprehend that this being is unlike the elements, say, which are lifeless bodies, so we say of it that it is alive, meaning that it is not dead. We further learn that this being is not like the heavens, which are living bodies,[4] in its mode of existence, so we say it is not a body; nor like the mind, which is deathless and immaterial, but still an object of causation, so we say that it is eternal, meaning that there is no cause of its existence. We apprehend further that its existence, which is identical with itself, suffices not only for itself but showers forth numerous beings out of itself, not as a flame sheds heat or as light flows necessarily from the sun but in a flood by which He, as we shall show, constantly sustains their existence and their order through an unswerving governance. On account of this we say that He is powerful, knowing, and willing, intending by these predicates that He is neither impotent, nor ignorant, nor oblivious, nor negligent. By "not powerless" we mean that His existence has in it sufficiency to bring into being things other than Himself.[5] By "not ignorant" we mean that He apprehends, thus that He is alive, for all things which apprehend are alive.[6] By "not oblivious or negligent" we mean that all those beings issue forth in a well-ordered and well-governed array, not in a chance or haphazard way but as do all things governed by the will and purpose of a voluntary being. Finally, we apprehend that this Being has none like Him, so we say that He is one, meaning the denial of plurality.

It should be clear to you, then, that every predicate we assign to

3. The demonstration referred to is Avicenna's argument from contingency: if there exists any contingent being, there must be a necessary being to which the former owes its existence. Yet our familiar experience presents us with no instance of a necessary being.

4. For Maimonides' understanding of this all-but-universal assumption of medieval thought, see *Moreh* II:4.

5. Without reference as to how.

6. We predicate consciousness of God in the same way that we predicate life of Him, without any reference point by which we might relate either concept to instances of them with which we are familiar.

Him either designates His act or, if intended to apply to Him rather than His work, its significance is that it denies the privation of such a character.

Even these negations are not applied to Him categorically but rather, as you know, in the manner in which what is not appropriate to a subject is denied of it, as we say of a wall that it does not see.[7] You know, dear reader, that with the heavens, which are moving bodies whose dimensions we might measure to the yard or to the inch, and for some parts of which and most of their motions we have already obtained knowledge of their measures, our minds remain totally unable to know their nature [8]—this despite the fact that we know that the heavens must have matter and form—for their matter is not the same as ours. That is why we cannot describe them in any definite or positive way, but only indefinitely: we say the heavens are neither light nor heavy,[9] impassive and therefore not receptive of effects, tasteless, odorless, etc.—all of which negations are on account of our ignorance of the material of which they are composed.

How then would it be for our minds if they aspired to apprehend Him who is free of matter, who is absolutely simple, necessarily existent, and uncaused, to whom no principle attaches beyond His perfect Selfhood, the meaning of whose perfection is its exclusion of all privations, as we have made clear? We know only His thatness, that there is a being whom no other existent resembles, that He has nothing whatever in common with all the other beings to which He gave existence, no plurality, no incapacity to give being to things other than Himself, that His relation to the world is as captain to ship, only this is

7. To wit, not as we say of a blind man that he does not see.
8. This is something of a slap in the face to the prevailing Aristotelian cosmology, which presumed to have some understanding of the "fifth substance" which made up the heavens. Given the available data, Maimonides argues, it is impossible to say much more about the heavens than that we are unable to apply to them many of our familiar physical concepts. This point has been overthrown by the advent of Newtonian physics, which can account for celestial and terrestial mechanics in the same economy. Maimonides' theological point, however, remains: if God is unique, no category of the natural world or of finite experience is applicable to Him. The difference, as Maimonides would say, between terrestial and celestial phenomena is only relative, whereas that between God and creation is absolute.
9. Since the heavenly bodies do not rise or fall.

not the real relationship, not a sound analogy, but only a means of directing the mind to the realization that He governs all that exists, meaning that He sustains all things and fittingly oversees their order— an idea which will be explained more expressly [see *Moreh* III].

Praised then be He, for when minds contemplate His Godhead, their awareness turns to incomprehension; when they consider the nexus of His acts to His will, their knowledge turns to ignorance; when tongues aspire to praise Him by ascribing attributes to Him, all their eloquence turns to tedium and vapidity.

MOREH NEVUKHIM I:59

Someone may ask, "If there is no technique of apprehending God as He really is, it being an outcome of the argument that what we grasp is only that He is, and if all positive attributes are demonstrated to be inapplicable to Him, then what makes anyone's apprehension of Him any better than anyone else's? If there is nothing to differentiate them, then what Moses or Solomon grasp is identical with what any individual student grasps—the student has nothing to learn!"

It is generally supposed, not only among adherents of revelation but also among philosophers, that there is a wide range of divergence in the quality of various such apprehensions. You should recognize that this is so. There is a very wide range, for the more predicates assigned to a subject, the more particularly that subject is distinguished and the closer he who predicates comes to an apprehension of that subject as it really is. In the same way, the more negations you add regarding Him, the closer you are to apprehension—closer than he who does not negate what you have understood must demonstrably be negated of Him. A man, therefore, may work for years to understand a certain science, to verify its premises [1] so as to hold it with certainty, with the net result that he knows demonstratively that we must deny the applicability of a certain notion to God, since it is absurd to apply that notion to Him. Another person, less insightful, might not grasp the demonstration. For him it would remain uncertain whether such a notion might be applied to God or not. Still another person, intellectually blind, will affirm of Him the same demonstrably inapplicable notion.

---

1. Many of which must be empirically discovered and confirmed.

. . . If there were a person who understood a demonstration which showed the impossibility in His regard of many things which we deem possible with regard to Him or as issuing from Him or even hold necessary for Him, then that person undoubtedly would be closer to perfection than we.

Thus it should be clear that whenever you are able to demonstrate the inapplicability of some notion to Him, you become more perfect; and whenever you affirm some additional notion of Him you are being anthropomorphic and placing yourself further from knowledge of His real nature . . . in two respects: first, whatever you have affirmed of Him is a perfection only for us; second, He is nothing but Himself (with which all His perfections are identical) as we have shown.

Now since everyone is aware that we have no way of knowing God (to the extent that it is possible for us to apprehend Him at all) except through negations, and since negations afford us no knowledge whatever of the real nature of the thing itself of which they deny something, all mankind, past and future, freely admit that God is not apprehended by minds, that none knows what He is except Himself, that to know Him at all is to be unable to know Him fully. All philosophers say, "We are overwhelmed by His beauty," "He is hidden from us by the splendor of His manifestness as is the sun from the apprehension of feeble vision." [2] The theme has been expounded at length, and it is of no benefit for us to reiterate all that has been said to this effect. The most eloquent of all such sayings is that in Psalms: "To Thee silence is praise" [Psalm 65:2], which means, "You regard silence as praise." This is awesomely expressive of this theme, for whatever we may say intended as praise and exaltation, we find applies to Him in some regard but falls short in some other. Silence is preferable to this, silence which confines itself to contemplation, as those whose understanding is most perfect say, "Speak to your heart in your bed and be silent. Selah" [Psalm 4:5].

You are familiar with the famous dictum of the Sages (I wish that all their words were like it!)—but I shall quote it for you verbatim, although you must remember it well, to point up its meaning for you: "Someone prayed in the presence of Rabbi Hanina, 'The God who is

2. *Cf*. Plato, *Republic* VII, 515–516; Aristotle, *Metaphysics* a 993b.

great, mighty and awesome, majestic and powerful, the terrible and magnificent.' 'Have you finished praising your Master?' said Rabbi Hanina. 'The first three [3] themselves could not be used by us if Moses our teacher had not pronounced them in the Law and the men of the Great Assembly had not come and established their use in the Prayer [the Amida]. And you say all this! It is as if a king of flesh and blood who had millions in gold were praised for having silver. Would this not be offensive to him?' '' [*cf. Berakhot* 33b]. Consider now this worthy man's reluctance, his aversion to the proliferation of positive predicates. Consider his explicit avowal that if it were left to reason alone not one of these predicates would have been applied or even uttered. Only the necessity of exhorting mankind in terms which would allow the formation of some conception—as the Sages say, "Torah speaks according to human language"—made it necessary for God to be described to men in terms of human perfections. We might go no further than these utterances, not name Him even by these except in reading the Torah, were it not for the fact that when the men of the Great Assembly came (they being prophets [4]), they ordained the use of these expressions in the liturgy. We can go no further, then, than to mention these words when we pray. The import of Rabbi Hanina's statement is plainly that two compelling exigencies coincide when we pray using such words: the fact that they are used in the Torah and the fact that prophets used them in composing the liturgy. Were it not for the first we should not utter them at all, and were it not for the second we could not remove them from their context for use in our prayers . . . .

He does not say that it is as though a king who had millions in gold were praised as having hundreds. For this would have suggested that His perfections differ in degree from those ascribed to Him but are of the same sort. Such is not the case, as we have demonstrated. The

3. Epithets used in the established liturgy: *ha-Gadol, ha-Gibbor, ha-Nora*—"the Great," "the Mighty," "the Awesome."

4. In their authority. (*Cf.* Maimonides' comment on *Pirkei Avot* 1:1 in the Introduction to his Commentary on the Mishnah: and his *Commentary on Pirkei Avot* 1.3: rabbinical authority is not arbitrary but divinely dictated.) The Great Assembly is credited with the establishment of Jewish liturgy and with the transfer of authority in Judaism from the priests to the scholars.

wisdom of Rabbi Hanina's illustration lies in his saying, ''who had gold and was praised for having silver,'' indicating that nothing of the sort of what for us are perfections exist in Him; all such things would be faults in Him, as he makes clear when he says in his illustration, ''would that not be offensive to Him?'' . . . Solomon has given us ample guidance to this theme when he says, ''God is in heaven and you are on earth. Therefore, let your words be few'' [Ecclesiastes 5:1].

MOREH NEVUKHIM I:60

Suppose a person has established that there is a ''ship'' but does not know to what this term applies, not even whether it denotes a substance or an accident. A second person might realize that it is not an accident, a third that it is not a mineral, a fourth that it is not an animal, a fifth that it is not a plant still growing in the ground, a sixth that it is not a single, organically connected body, a seventh that it is not flat like a board or a door, an eighth that it is not spherical, a ninth that it is not conical, a tenth that it is not round, an eleventh that it is not equilateral, a twelfth that it is not solid. This last person, obviously, would be able virtually to conceive the ship as it is, through these negations. His idea of it is comparable to that of a man who conceptualized it in terms of positive attributes, as an oblong hollow body of wood, composed of a number of boards. Each of his predecessors in our parable is further than his successor from conceiving a ship, up to the first who knows nothing but the bare word. It is in this manner that negative predications bring you closer to an awareness of God and apprehension of Him. Bend every effort therefore to increasing what you can negate of Him, by proof, not in a merely verbal way; for whenever you discover the demonstration that something which was thought to apply to Him is in fact inapplicable to Him, there is no doubt that you draw one step nearer to Him. . . .

Describing Him positively, on the other hand, is very dangerous. . . . I would not say that he who assigns positive predicates to God is deficient in his knowledge of Him, nor that he confounds Him with other things, nor that he apprehends Him differently than as He is. What I would say is that he has unwittingly disacknowledged the existence of the Deity in his creed. To explain: One is deficient in his understanding of a thing if he grasps one element of it but fails to understand another, for example, if he recognizes that the concept of "man" has all the implications of being an animal, but fails to apprehend that it has all the implications of being rational. But God has no plurality in His nature that part of it might be understood and part misunderstood. Similarly, one who confounds one thing with another understands one thing accurately and applies its concept to something else. But these attributes are not believed by those who uphold them to be the Deity but to belong to Him. Similarly again, one who understands something in a manner other than as it is must nonetheless have some understanding of it as it is. But of someone who thinks that "taste" is a quantity, I would not say that he understands taste other than as it is; I would say that he does not know that taste exists or what the word denotes. This is a rather subtle thought, so try to understand it. . . .

He who applies a positive predication to Him knowing only the word and nothing of the Being to whom this word is imagined to apply is actually ascribing predicates to something which does not exist, a spurious invention of his own imagining, just as though the being to which he wished to apply that word did not exist—for no such being as he speaks of does exist. I would illustrate such a case as follows: A man hears the word "elephant"; he knows that an elephant is an animal but wants to find out about its nature and its shape. Suppose someone who is either deceived or a deceiver says that an elephant is an animal with one leg and three wings who lives in the depths of the sea, whose body is transparent, with a broad face like that of a man, having human shape and form as well, an animal who talks and sometimes flies through the air, sometimes swims like a fish. I shall not say that this is a misconception of an elephant or a deficient apprehension of an elephant, but that this thing which is pictured in this description is a spurious figment of the imagination. No such thing exists; this is a nonexistent thing to which the name of something which does exist has been applied . . . like "horse-man." . . .

The case here is parallel: God (glorious be His praise) exists and His existence can be demonstrated to be necessary. But necessary existence implies absolute simplicity, as I shall demonstrate [*Moreh* II:1, method iii]. As for that simplex, necessarily existent being to which attributes and other such notions allegedly apply, it demonstrably does not exist at all. If we call such a being "the deity" and say that it has a plurality of elements, in terms of which it may be described, then we have applied that designation to absolutely nothing. Consider, then, how dangerous it is to apply positive predications to Him. What we must believe is that the attributes which occur in inspired writing or the books of the prophets serve solely and simply to orient us toward His perfection, unless they are characterizations of acts which issue from Him, as we have made clear.

MOREH NEVUKHIM I:61

All the names of God found anywhere in the Scriptures are derived from verbs, as is obvious on inspection—the sole exception being YHVH.[1] For this name was invented specifically for Him. That is why it is called the "explicit" name, meaning that it indicates His Godhead clearly, without any connotations. All the other revered names designate through the connotations which they have of actions the like of which we perform, as I have explained. Even the name which we pronounce instead of YHVH [Adonai, "Lord"] is derived from a verb which signifies mastery. . . . The other epithets, such as Judge, Righteous, Kindly, Compassionate, and God, are obviously used generically, and their derivation is obvious as well. But the name which is spelled YHVH has no commonly accepted etymology and is not applied to any other. This awesome name, which as you know is not to be pronounced except in the Sanctuary by "sanctified Priests of the Lord," exclusively in the priestly blessing and by the High Priest on the Day of Atonement, doubtless indicates some notion in which God does not share with any other being. Perhaps in this language (of which we today have only the merest fraction, in proportion to the spoken language) this word indicates necessity of existence. In short, the reverence in which this name is held and the restrictions on its being spoken are perhaps due to its signifying God Himself in a way in which none of His creatures may share: as the Sages have it, "My name unique to Me" [Sota 38a to Numbers 6:23–27].

The other names are all indicative of attributes, not of God's being

1. The Tetragrammaton or quadriliteral name of God found in the Scriptures. But see my note to Moreh I:62, below.

itself but of some positive character—because they are derived. They therefore suggest multiplicity; *i.e.*, they suggest the existence of attributes—an identity and various notions adventitious to it. For every derived noun signifies in this fashion. It designates a notion and, implicitly, a substratum to which that notion is linked. Once it has been proved that God is not some substrate to which various notions are attached, then it can be understood that these epithets derived from common concepts must serve either to relate an act to Him or to direct us toward His Perfection. That is why Rabbi Hanina would have been loath to say, "the Great, Mighty, and Awesome," were it not for the two aforementioned compelling exigencies—since this suggested a plurality of real attributes (perfections) existing in God. The addition of further attributes derived from verbs suggested to some people that He had a plurality of attributes. For the actions, from the designations of which these epithets were derived, are many. That is why Scripture promises that people will one day overcome this delusion, saying, "On that day the Lord will be one and His name one" [Zechariah 14:9], meaning that as He is one, so will He be known by just one name, that which designates His Godhead alone and which is not derived from any common notion.

In *Pirkei de Rabbi Eliezer* [III] the Sages say, "Before the world was created there were only the Holy One, blessed be He, and His name." Notice how this explicitly acknowledges that these derived names all came into being after the creation of the world. This is true: they are all nouns used in the conventional manner [2] to designate acts found in the world. But when you consider His Godhead in abstraction from all activity, then He will have no derived name whatever, but only the one name which has been improvised to indicate His Godhead itself. We have no other underived name than this: YHVH, *the* explicit name.

Do not suppose the case to be otherwise—do not give a thought to the ravings of the amulet writers or any of the "names" you may hear from them or find in their books,[3] names which they concocted and

2. All language, as all medieval philosophers knew, is by convention.

3. Maimonides is thinking here chiefly of the Kabbalistic type of alchemy figuring in such works as the pseudo-Abrahamic *Sefer Yetzirah,* where mystic names and Kabbalistic alphabets of number-letter elements are used in acts of theurgy by which the mystic

which do not signify anything whatever. They simply call them names and claim that they are sufficient causes of purity and holiness and that they work wonders. All this is unfit for a grown man to listen to, let alone believe! Nothing whatever is called the explicit name, but the Tetragrammaton as it is written, not as pronounced, according to the commentary of *Sifre* on the verse "Thus shall you bless the Children of Israel" [Numbers 6:23], which they gloss: " 'Thus,' *i.e.*, in these words, 'thus,' that is with the explicit name. . . ."

MOREH NEVUKHIM I:62

. . . Having observed that all the names of God are derived except the explicit name, we must now speak of that name, to wit "I am that I am." [1]

MOREH NEVUKHIM I:63

To begin with, consider Moses' words "They shall say to me, 'What is His name?' What shall I say to them?" [Exodus 3:13]. What was it in the situation which made it necessary that they would ask this question, so that he must seek some answer to it? He says, "They will not believe me or harken to my voice, but they will say, 'The Lord hath not appeared to you' " [4:1]—for it is obvious that this is just what will be said to anyone who claims to be a prophet until he offers proof. Moreover, if, as appears to be the case, the "proof" proposed is merely a name to be pronounced, then there are just two alternatives: either Israel knew that name or they had never heard it before. But if that name was known to them, then it affords no argument in Moses' behalf that he can inform them of it, for his knowledge of it would be the same as theirs. If they had never heard it before, however, then how do they know that it is God's name—if knowledge of a name is proof? [1] . . .

---

participates in the re-enactment of the divine creative act. See Gershom Scholem, *On the Kabbalah and Its Symbolism* (New York, 1965). These symbolic acts often degenerated into plain magic, and it is against such superstition that the Rambam's acerbity here is directed.

1. Hebrew: *Eheyeh asher eheyeh,* which Maimonides takes to be the full form of the Tetragrammaton. He takes *Yah* in the same vein as referring to God's eternity; and *Shaday,* to his self-sufficiency—corollaries, as it were, of necessary being.

1. The implication is that what was revealed to Moses was not a mere name.

In those days, as you know, various pagan sects were widespread. Of mankind all but a few were heathens, believers in spirits, theurgy, and talismans. Throughout that era, the purport of every religious claimant was either that his own insight and reasoning had shown him that there is a Deity of the whole world, as Abraham claimed, or else that the spirit of a star or an angel or some such had descended upon him with inspiration. But for anyone to claim prophecy in the sense that God had spoken with him and given him a mission was completely unheard of before Moses. Do not be misled by the references to God's speaking and manifesting Himself to the Patriarchs, for theirs will not be found to have been the sort of prophecy which is addressed to the people or which seeks to guide others. Neither Abraham, nor Isaac, nor Jacob, nor any of their predecessors [2] said to the people, "God said to me: you shall do this or you shall not do that" or "God sent me to you." No such claims were ever made by them. The Patriarchs were addressed only regarding what concerned them personally—that is, only regarding their own attainment of perfection, with guidance as to what they should do and annunciations as to what was in store for their descendents. Their appeal to the people was based solely on reason and instruction, as seems to us to be clear from the words, "and the souls they had made in Harran" [3] [Genesis 12:5].

Thus, when He (revered and exalted be He) manifested Himself to Moses our teacher and commanded him to address the people with God's message, Moses said, "The first thing they will ask is that I prove to them that there exists a Deity of the universe. After that I shall claim that He sent me." For of all mankind at that time only a handful were aware of the existence of the Deity. The furthest reach of their ideas did not surpass the sphere, its powers, and its effects. For they had not yet been able to separate themselves from the objects of sense perception; [4] intellectually they had not yet come of age. At this point, then, God makes Moses aware of the knowledge [5] he is to con-

2. Adam, Noah, etc., are counted as prophets inasmuch as they were addressed by God.
3. The winning of souls would not be ascribed to their action had its basis been other than their own insight and teaching.
4. Maimonides alludes to the highest reaches of pagan thought: the astronomy/astrology of the "Chaldaeans," the Physics of the pre-Socratic *physikoi,* and the pagan notion of astral influences as the ruling powers of nature.
5. Knowledge is propositional; it cannot be a "mere name."

vey to them, by which they are to comprehend the being of the Deity: "I am that I am" [Exodus 3:14]. This is a name derived from the verb "to be," signifying existence. . . . The whole secret is in the repetition of the same word, denoting existence, in the place of the predicate, for "that" calls for some characterization immediately after it, since it is a relative pronoun to which something else must be attached, the same as "who," "which," or "what" in Arabic. But here the first term, which would designate what is described, and the second, which would be the description, are identical—"I am"—as if it said explicitly: the subject and the predicate [6] are the same. This is by way of making clear the concept that He exists not through existence, which is summed up and made plain thus: "The Existent who is the Existent." For it is the necessary outcome of a demonstration which I shall make clear [*Moreh* II:1, method iii] that there is something the existence of which is necessary, something which has never not existed and never will.

Having given Moses knowledge of the arguments by which he might convince the learned of Israel (for it continues, "Go and gather the elders of Israel" [Exodus 3:16]), God promises him that they will understand and accept what He is imparting, saying, "They shall hearken to your voice" [3:18]. Whereupon Moses replied, "Once they have accepted the existence of a Deity on account of these rational demonstrations, how shall I prove that this existent Deity sent me?" It was then that He granted the miracle.[7] It is clear then that when it says, "What is His name?" it means, "Who is it that you claim has sent you?" He only says, "What is His name?" as a more reverent and more seemly mode of address, as much as to say, "Of Your Godhead and Your nature no one is ignorant, but if I am asked Your name, what manner of thing is it that is signified by that name?" He was simply ashamed to say directly to God that there are those who are ignorant of that Being, so he put it that their ignorance was of the name, not of the Being which it names. . . . There is no name for Him (exalted be He) which is not derivative, except for the four-letter

6. God's being and His mode of being, *i.e.*, what would be called His nature, character, or essence, were it proper to speak of an absolutely simplex Being as having a nature, character, or essence.

7. Of the rod and the serpent.

name, which is the "explicit" name because it signifies no attribute but unqualified existence itself. Implied in this absolute existence is invariance,[8] *i.e.*, necessary existence. Now you must understand the conclusion which we have reached. . . .

Analysis

"God," said a wag, "created man in his own image, and man returned the compliment." The charge, old as philosophy itself, that men's concept of divinity is no more than the product of human imaginings, ignorance, fears, and desires has often seemed damning to the whole religious enterprise. If man's concept of divinity is confined necessarily by his psychological, intellectual, cultural, and moral finitude, how can even a relative truth—let alone the ultimate truth—be claimed for the outcome of religious investigations?

Even the idolater at his most primitive, as Maimonides astutely points out, does not believe his god to be a mere (or ordinary) carving of wood or casting of metal. When the ritual object (ikon) is somehow identified with the god, it is vested with certain special properties quite other than the natural properties of wood or metal. This is the beginning of transcendence. When the gods are put out of the house into the sacred grove, out of the day into the night, out of the plains into the heights, elevated finally (in their last physically anthropomorphic forms) to the highest mountain peaks and the heavens, becoming invisible, immortal, and finally, after much struggle, infallible, one can see at each step the more transcendental driving out the less transcendental concept as inexorably as the gods of heaven and human justice conquer the tellurian gods of animal passion—only to be displaced in turn by the Ideals of a Plato or the absolute God of monotheism.

But human ideas of values grow and change. Thus God-concepts too will change. The guilt-merit society of the time of Hesiod finds it theologically necessary in the name of purifying the concept of divinity—thinking worthily of the divine—to replace the gods of Homer's honor-shame ethos, the gods of human passion which served the nobles of a warlike society, with gods of justice, honesty, and homely

8. Changelessness and constancy, absolute simplicity and unity.

virtues more suitable to an agrarian society. Are these men serving the gods or are the gods serving them? Have they done anything more than read their own values into theology in place of those of their predecessors? Have they, as Maimonides would put the question, come any nearer to God?

Here we find one paradox which it is the Rambam's purpose in the first part of the *Moreh* to resolve. The entire history of theological understanding may be viewed under the aspect of the constant driving out of the less transcendental by the more transcendental conception of divinity, under pressure of the logic of the concept itself—for nothing is ascribed to the divine but what is understood to be a perfection.[1] But does this not imply that "God" will be forever confined in the prisons of men's minds? That the narrowness of human values will forever prevent any human conception of divinity from claiming any degree of objectivity? It is obvious now why Maimonides makes moral rectitude a prerequisite of theological investigation—for bad values make bad gods, or to put the matter theologically, one's concept of divinity will be impious unless the values upon which it is founded are sound. But can even the stipulation of moral rectitude as a prerequisite to theology save religious understanding? To make God the reflection of our values may be nobler or more pious and edifying, but can it claim to be more accurate than to make Him the reflection of our fears?[2] Thus transcendentalism would seem to have failed its mission. For in theology, as elsewhere, man does not seem able to reach beyond the limits of his mind.

If there is something in the logic of "God" which forbids the attribution to God of anything but what we regard as a perfection, the question arises as to what sort of meaning it can have to say, "God is

1. Loki, the Norse god of mischief, may seem to be an exception, but Loki represents mischief as a perfection, a notion pre-Christian Vikings would not have found problematic in the least. What fascinated Blake in Milton's Satan and Nietzsche in Zarathustra's Ahriman was that here were deities or quasi-deities who seemed freely to have "taken evil as their good." Even here, evil (by the very fact of its appropriation by divinity) was regarded—with what logic I leave the reader to decide—as a positive value.
2. It was Freud's contention (in *The Future of an Illusion,* 1927) that religion was, in its origin and essence, a bit of both, a "wish fulfillment" expressing guilt (values) and fear, both of which attached initially to "the" father. For many of his followers this account appears to vitiate conclusively the significance of all religious utterances.

good.'' On the face of it this statement purports to make a claim about a matter of fact, God's goodness. But the way we (and others before us) have used the term "God," it does not seem permissible for us in any respect to deny that "God is good." It is not regarded as fitting or permissible to characterize God as other than good. This feature of the logic of "God" seems to be as much a consequence as a cause of transcendentalism. For it is transcendentalism which makes the term "God" behave, in some contexts at least, as though it read "the Good." Where then is the factual content of "God is good"? Does this analysis render that crucial proposition of religious discourse a tautology?

The same problem expresses itself in another way: What are the conditions of knowing that God is good? Unbelievers generally deny God's existence and believers reinterpret their entire experience before they will admit that God is evil. But if there is no conceivable evidence which can refute a given proposition, can we say that that proposition states a matter of fact? It would appear that a proposition around which we reinterpret the rest of the universe must have a kind of certainty which is denied to mere assertions of fact, that "God is good" is meant to be self-evident, merely a spelling out of what is meant by "God."

Is God, then, a being or an abstraction? A being whose imperfection is inconceivable in every regard, it can be argued, is an ideal—and ideals, it would be claimed, are surely products of the human mind. Thus to assert God's existence involves a contradiction, putting in objective terms what we implicitly assume (in other contexts, at least) to be subjective.

Often, in theistic talk about God, the divine existence is taken for granted in much the way that divine goodness is. Existence seems to become one of the perfections which God cannot lack.[3] But only an abstraction, it will be claimed, can exist in such a way that its nonexistence is undeniable. How can God be real, His existence a matter of fact (rather than wish or conception) if there is no conceivable evidence that would count against it? How, as Maimonides put it, can

3. This indeed was the explicit claim of the famous "ontological argument" by which Anselm of Canterbury (1033–1109) attempted to derive the existence of God from the concept of divine perfection.

any being have necessary existence when by having existence we mean being liable to exist or not exist?

These are some of the problems which Maimonides confronts on behalf of his reader who is perplexed. They represent the most radical difficulties every thoughtful human mind must confront in considering the question posed by the concept of God. Their resolution is necessary if there is ever to be any meaningful talk about God, let alone demonstration of His existence.

No such problems as these would arise, of course, if the religious mind were prepared to concede (as atheists and some mystics do) that God is indeed an abstraction, that "God is good" is a tautology or merely a way of voicing our inmost wishes or anxieties, that "God exists" is self-contradictory. But the transcendentalism from which such conclusions seem to arise is only one dimension of the logic of "God." The term is commonly understood to denote a real being, despite the fact that in common experience absolute perfection and actual existence do not coincide. What Job refused to concede when he refused to curse God and die was not merely the denial of a tautology or even the irrelevance of his wishes but a belief about the way the world actually runs. When theologians say that God exists necessarily, they do not mean that God is an abstraction but that God is the necessary condition of all other existence. In other words, when men affirm the existence of God, they do not believe that they are merely analyzing their own concepts but that they are making a judgment that God's existence and goodness make a difference to the character of reality at every conceivable level.

The concept of God, then, seems to be fraught with paradoxes and dilemmas arising from a tension between the logic of transcendentalism and that of belief in God as a real, active, and specifiably good force in the world. Some theologians attempt to dismiss all such paradoxes by the invention of suitable formulae. But such procedures only lend color to the charge that God is a being of reason, invented and modified to suit human convenience. What matters, as Maimonides puts it, is not what we say but what we think. The real reconciliation of the transcendent with the immanent in the logic of God can only be accomplished by careful investigation of the actual usage of religious language—of which there can be no more authoritative case than the revealed Scriptures.[4]

Maimonides' task therefore, as he sees it, is to elicit from the Torah the hints by which the dilemmas of the logic of God may be resolved. His method cannot be one of slavish repetition of the text. On the contrary, blind devotion to the apparent sense of Scripture is a chief cause of the difficulty. For the Biblical text is addressed to the people at large and must therefore employ language which stirs up the imagination—and which thus necessarily reflects, on the surface at least, the confused, uncritical, and conflicting presuppositions of the masses, who are not in the habit of testing their often-contradictory commonplaces against one another by the light of reason.

To the Aramaic translators the anthropomorphic language of Scripture is almost an embarrassment, to be glossed over in translations by way of calling attention to the impossibility of taking it literally. This is sufficient in a translation, but it does not suffice for an interpretation. To the Sages of the Talmud, the anthropomorphic language is not blasphemous but awesome (*Moreh* I:46)—they do not criticize the prophets but marvel at their daring in the use of language. Indeed, the Sages, far from being disturbed by the anthropomorphisms of the Scriptures, often echo their imagery and complete their conceits. For Maimonides too the anthropomorphisms of the Torah are less a stumbling block than a springboard. His purpose in discussing them is not to show that God is incorporeal. (That fundamental truth, like God's existence, is to be demonstrated only after the logic of "God" has been clarified.) His purpose rather is to elicit an understanding regarding the logic of "God" from the anthropomorphic texts themselves!

Thus, putting philology at the service of theology, Maimonides systematically surveys the expressions (and types of expressions) applied to the Deity by Scripture. He begins (I:1) with the word for form and points out the natural ambiguity by which the term may be applied in a

4. Maimonides does not credit the Hebrew Scriptures with exclusive possession of insight into the logic of God. He says explicitly that similar insights are to be extracted from the writings of prophets and other persons of understanding. Torah is unique, however, in its development of these themes, and the revelatory experience of Moses is not to be rivaled or superseded.

physical or intellectual/ontological sense: form as shape *vs.* form as idea. The latter sense is that which is applied to God. With the consideration of the term *temunah* (I:3) a third layer of meaning is discovered (always by reference to the text): the term may signify a physical shape, an image of the imagination,[5] or a cognitive/intellectual apprehension. Once again the highest of the three possibilities is that which is found to be applied to God. Consistently (*cf.* I:4), where the choice is to be made between the physical and the intellectual with reference to God, the latter is found to be not only possible but preferable. But the Rambam's object is not simply to show that God is an intellectual (spiritual) rather than corporeal being. That would hardly allow God to transcend human categories. Thus, in discussing *makom* (I:8), a fourth level is introduced to the hierarchy of meanings: beyond the physical, imaginative, and intellectual senses of the term, there is a sense in which *makom* denotes rank. While it is true that within various closed systems (human value systems or social systems) the term may be used in a relative way, to denote rank within the system, its use is found indeed to be sufficiently universal to allow it to be taken in a broader way to denote absolute rank as well, that is, rank in terms of goodness itself, or standing in the hierarchy of being. This, Maimonides argues, is the best way of understanding the application of the term to God. Thus the language of the prophets, despite the lack of abstract vocabulary, is capable of teaching God's supremacy in the hierarchy of value and of being.

Even the corporealists, who assimilated God to the bodies of familiar experience, did so only by way of asserting God's existence before the possibility of incorporeal existence had been conceived. Even they were sufficiently aware of the transcendentalism inherent in the concept of divinity to think of their gods' bodies as larger and more splendid than those of men, revealing that even they applied physicality to the divine only by way of signifying a perfection. The rankest anthropomorphisms of the Bible, where God is spoken of as seeing, hearing, or smelling, can easily be shown to be pictorial ways of referring (for the benefit of the masses) to God's moral and intellectual acts, *i.e.,* to the manifestations of His perfection, while at the most popular level of meaning, the baser sorts of sensations, *viz.,* taste and touch, which ob-

5. *I.e.,* a mental representation of the physical, corresponding to it part for part.

viously involve physical contact, are not ascribed to God. The language of the prophets, Maimonides concludes, is applied to God only by way of directing the mind toward a unique Being of absolute transcendence and perfection. There are no words of human language which can designate or characterize such a Being. The words which the prophets use serve only to point the way, to orient us in the direction of perfection, in which such a Being must lie, and mark out the path which we must follow if we wish to approach Him.

The Biblical text is incomprehensible, according to Maimonides, without the aid of reason. For (paradigmatically) we would not even know what was inconceivable, hence what was a conceivable interpretation of the text (let alone how one text was supported or limited by another)—we would not be able to attach any meaning to any of our formulae—without the most careful and critical rational scrutiny.

Maimonides' method, therefore, is to approach the text not with the naïveté or pretended naïveté of some fundamentalists ("We know nothing but the preaching of Scripture") nor even to approach it armed solely with the formidable interpretive literature which had grown up around the prophetic books. For these interpretations, being instances of religious language, are as much in need of interpretation as the texts they expound and often lack the clarity and authority of the latter. Rather, Maimonides approaches the text armed with certain knowledge which he takes to be apodictic regarding the logic of God. He does not state the demonstrations upon which this knowledge rests, since he knows that his reader is familiar with them. If we are to understand the impact of the Rambam's argument, however, rather than reading it as a vague and rambling diatribe on the subject of transcendentalism and anthropomorphism, we must state clearly the propositions which constitute this knowledge, note their interrelationships, and spell out the arguments upon which they rest. The cardinal doctrines which lay down the parameters of Maimonides' discussion of the logic of God are these:

(1) God is goodness (the Good, perfection, the *ens perfectissimum* or most perfect being).

(2) God is self-sufficient ("necessarily existent," requiring no cause).

From 1 it follows that

> (3) God can be known through His work or act, the manifestation of goodness in the world in the form of order, rationality, provision for the existence and survival of creatures, etc.

and

> (4) God can be "followed" by emulating the rationality (wisdom) and concern (love) evident in the governance of the world.

From 2 it follows that

> (5) God is unique (shares no characteristic with any creature). All beings with which we are familiar exist contingently, require causes, might conceivably not exist. But if God's existence is on a different basis from that of creatures, then He can have nothing in common with them, since the broadest class under which two things may be grouped is that of beings.

and

> (6) God is simplex (absolutely invariant, constant, changeless, undifferentiated in every regard). For a complex being would be contingent in that it is conceivable that its diverse aspects might not be combined as they are.

A corollary of 6 is that

> (7) God's essence is identical with His existence (*i.e.*, *what* He is is not distinct from *that* He is—for if it were, His existence would be contingent).

It follows from 6 or from 7 that

> (8) God has no "attributes." (For these would introduce complexity into His nature, and would differentiate His essence from His existence.)

It follows from 8 or from 5 that

> (9) It is impossible properly to predicate anything of God Himself. We may speak only of His undifferentiated Godhead or Identity, not

of any nature, essence (as distinct from existence), character, personality, quality, quantity, or even relation (if such reflects on God's "nature") as pertaining to Him.

From 9 it follows that

(10) Prophetic language regarding God must be taken as using "prophetic license" by way of directing the mind toward the more elevated conceptions of 1 and 2. Thus all relative and particular perfections in the world may be seen subjectively as expressions of the "attributes" of God, but objectively God has no attributes distinct from his Identity, which is absolute Perfection.

From 1 and 2 taken together it follows that

(11) God's goodness and self-sufficiency are one and the same, a result familiar to Plato, who argued that that Being who lacks nothing would stint nothing (*i.e.*, 1 follows from 2) and that Being who is most perfect must be self-sufficient (*i.e.*, 2 follows from 1).

Thus from the combined doctrine of 1 and 2 it is possible to deduce the crucial features of the logic of "God" exhibited in the context of Scripture. This does not yet show that the concept is coherent, but it does provide the unfolding of the features of that concept which will be required if that coherence is to be shown. How then are 1 and 2 derived?

The demonstration that there must exist a being that is absolute goodness was due to Plato but was refined by Aristotle and his followers. The reasoning is as follows: Some things exist which must be called good, or at least better than others. But nothing can be called good or even better unless there is some standard of goodness itself in terms of which such predications or comparisons are made.[6] This shows that there must be an ideal of goodness. It does not show that that Ideal is a real being. But many philosophers, including Plato and Aristotle and most of their followers, considered the goodness of the world to be dependent on that of such a being and identified God with that being. It is clear from the logic of "God" that God is thought of

6. The relative presupposes the absolute. To offer a mathematical analogy: there are no ratios unless there are quantities.

as such a being. Thus while the demonstration of the existence of God remains to be accomplished (see Part Two), it is clear that if there is a God, He must be goodness itself (1).

The demonstration of God's self-sufficiency, upon which Maimonides relies (*cf. Moreh* II:1.iii), is due to Avicenna: It is assumed that (*a*) Something must exist. (For regardless of what else exists, I know that I exist.) But (*b*) All existence is either necessary (self-sufficient) or contingent (in need of a cause). For these are the only two alternatives. Consider the "something" which we know (from *a*) must exist. Is it necessary or contingent? If the former, a necessary being exists. If contingent, it requires a cause, and we must ask the same question about that cause and about that cause's cause until we reach a being which requires no cause, *i.e.*, is self-sufficient—for no chain of causes can extend infinitely and yet have an actual effect (the being which *a* tells us must exist): that would be self-contradictory.[7] Ultimately, then, there must be a first cause which is self-sufficient: If anything exists at all, something must exist necessarily. But no being which exists in time or space or is in any way compounded can exist necessarily.

Where the argument for God's goodness infers from the existence of (relative or particular) goods in the world to the existence of an absolute or universal Good-in-itself, the argument for a necessary being infers the existence of a self-sufficient being from the contingency of all beings with which we are familiar. Thus both arguments involve an inference from the relative to the absolute. And it might be claimed with the contingency argument, as it was with the argument to a highest good, that the outcome of that argument is only the production of an ideal—that just as the good in the world does not imply the existence of a supremely good God, so the contingency of the world does not imply the existence of a necessary (self-sufficient) God. God, it might be claimed, is no more than the ideal which caps our hierarchy of values; His necessity is only the ideal projected from the contingency of being as we know it. This line of criticism is not as telling against the contingency argument as it is against the argument for a most perfect being (highest good). For the existence of good in the world does not logically require that a most perfect being exist as the

7. For an infinite chain cannot end.

cause of that good.[8] But the existence of any contingent being does logically require the existence of a cause; and if there cannot be an infinite series of contingent causes which has an actual effect (a finite infinity!), then there must be a necessary (self-sufficient) being. But even if this self-sufficient being is no more than an ideal against which we contrast the contingency and impermanence of existence as we know it, it remains the case that if there is a God, that God must be the necessary being whose self-sufficiency is the condition of the existence of all contingent beings, just as His goodness is cause or source of any goodness which is in them.

The question arises whether God's goodness is compatible (logically) with His self-sufficiency. For the one is known from the goodness (perfection) of the world, while the other is known from its contingency (impermanence, imperfection). The answer, as Maimonides would put it, is that the world and the creatures in it are not perfect absolutely, but perfect for what they are and in their kinds (relatively). Their relative perfection is evidence (not proof) of the existence of a Being who is absolute perfection as its cause. Their contingency requires, as its support, His self-sufficiency. Contingency is not privation but actual, if dependent, being. Thus our concept of God as a necessary and absolutely perfect being is derived from our knowledge of the world—where His self-sufficiency and perfection (which are really one and the same with Himself) are expressed, as it were, enabling us to apprehend them. It is this apprehension which is crucial. For even if the argument from contingency and the argument for a highest good do not prove the existence of a Deity, they do give us the concept by which we may recognize a Deity, and thus make it possible for us to argue from the world to the existence of God (see Part Two). They tell us what the world would be like if there is a God and what it would be like if there is not.

Having clarified the concept of God to this point, Maimonides is able to confront the radical doubts as to the coherence of the concept of God which assail the mind of his reader who is perplexed. The argument that God is a necessary being stands or falls with the coherence of the concept of "necessary existence." Can it be that there

8. That would depend on the assumption that lesser goods are caused by greater ones.

exists a being whose existence is necessary? With every being we know or the existence of which we can conceive, existence is contingent; that is, it is conceivable that a being of such sort may exist or not exist. Existence as we know it is never part of the logical concept (essence) of a being. That is why Avicenna himself, the author of the contingency argument, calls existence an "accident," *i.e.,* something separable from "essence," so that the question whether something exists can never be resolved by knowledge of what that something is. By that standard, "necessary existence" is a contradiction in terms: existence is always contingent.

So it seems when we examine existents in the world—or in our imagination. All of them might or might not exist. But God, the Torah tells us, is different, and the argument of Avicenna—which is no more than a "spelling out" of what was revealed to Moses in a single pregnant phrase—tells us why: the very assumption that all existence is contingent, which seems to undermine the concept of necessary existence, actually undermines itself. The existence of contingent beings requires that of a necessary being, for contingent beings require causes and no infinite chain of causes can ever reach to actuality. The very fact that being as we know it is contingent proves that there must be another sort of Being whose existence is not contingent but necessary (self-sufficient). It is not a contradiction to speak of such a being as a "necessary existent," only the recognition of the fact that the existence which we know (contingent existence) cannot possibly be the only kind, a truth far more eloquently expressed in the "name" (for God does not have an essence) revealed to Moses: I AM THAT I AM.

The concept of God as a most perfect being, a highest Good, from whom all other goods are regarded as depending, appeared to make of God an abstraction. Ideals, it was assumed, are abstractions, products of the human mind; and to speak of such an ideal as the highest Good as though it were a real being whose existence was a matter of fact seemed to involve a contradiction or at least an illicit inference as to the actuality of the Ideal. But the analysis of God's self-sufficiency (necessary existence) reveals the error of this attack: the fact that God's "essence" is identical with His existence explains the apparent functioning of the concept of God as an Ideal. Indeed God's goodness is identical with His existence, and with His self-sufficiency and perfection. It is true that neither in the world nor in our minds do we ever encounter an absolutely perfect Being. Our finitude could not bear it ("You shall not see My Face and live"). But the finite and relative instances of goodness which we do encounter, in the world and in ourselves, serve as evidence—as "pointers," to translate the Rambam's term more literally—to a Highest Good, from whom they derive their goodness. The fact that we do not encounter such a being in the world of our familiar experience does not imply that He is an abstraction, for the good in the world which we do encounter is not equivalent with Him (its existence is not proof of His) but only evidence of Him. Thus in speaking of His goodness, we do not speak tautologously of the goodness of our idea of the Good, but of the goodness of the absolute Good, which we infer to be the source or cause of the relative goods which surround us.

It follows from both these trains of reasoning that God is unique. For we know no other necessary being. The existence which we predicate of Him is not the same as that which we predicate of all other beings. Indeed, He, being simplex (for a complex being, as we have seen, is necessarily contingent), cannot have existence—or anything predicated of Him. And His absolute goodness too implies uniqueness, for there can be but one highest Good. Again there is nothing we can say of Him, for His perfection surpasses our powers of comprehension. How indeed can we think, let alone speak, anything of a unique being, for there are no linguistic or mental categories by which He may be classed. Even existence, the broadest possible classification, is His in a totally different sense from that with which we are familiar. Thus anyone who thinks of God in terms of any human (or humanly conceivable!) concepts is guilty not merely of anthropomorphism or even of polytheism (associating or confusing the Transcendent with immanent realities) but of absolute atheism, or rather, to be precise, of not having the faintest comprehension of or appreciation for the way the term "God" is used. To speak of God in any positive way reveals the same depths of "benightedness" and "misbelief" as to speak of an elephant with wings. This returns us where we started, to the problem of transcendence, or rather, as a result of our analysis, to its source.

It is clear from the investigation of religious language both in and out of Scripture that the God of whom the Scriptures speak transcends all human comprehension or description. How then is it possible to speak or think of God? Maimonides' answer to this apparent dilemma is as elegant as it is lucid: how do the Scriptures speak of God? The prophets employ a bold combination of poetic imagery and prophetic license, not to designate but to point the way to God—to orient man toward God. Their likening of Creator to creature, that is, their speaking of God in terms of man's corporeal, mental, or moral traits, or in terms of any finite categories serves the end of pointing toward God's absolute perfection/self-sufficiency. Thus one set of images undermines the last, allowing the mind to rise from the less transcendent to the more transcendent conception until the lesson has been learned from this rising itself, that God does not have perfections but is Perfection itself, that God does not have existence but is the Ground (cf. makom) of all existence, the Self-sufficient Being who must exist necessarily if anything at all is to exist contingently, that God does not transcend this or that human category but transcends all categories and gives being and perfection to all things which in their limited ways possess them.

If the question, then, is "How can we speak of or conceive God's infinitely transcendent perfection?" the answer is that we cannot. At best we can speak negatively, expressing no definite idea or attribute other than God's transcendence of all finite categories. Yet this mode of discourse, the *via negativa,* is not vacuous—for it involves a directionality, the directionality of perfection. Perfection is the criterion governing the adoption and discarding of all conceptions of the Divine. The marvel of prophecy is that it can orient us toward a Being before whom the wisdom of the philosophers and the songs of the poets are silenced. The Hebrew language and sacred writings themselves are repositories of insights into the logic of God which render all Israel susceptible to this message of the prophets. Thus the Rambam's epigram at the outset of this first portion of the *Moreh* makes all Israel the guardians of the divine Truth which is the core of the Biblical message. All men recognize implicitly the identity of divinity with perfection. It is for this reason that without the use of abstract or technical vocabulary, or the pretense of precise designation or characterization, the prophets are able to lead the mind to the apprehension of the divine perfection and transcendence, using "ordinary language"— *lashon benei adam*, the language by which human beings describe the perfections of the finite particulars of the world in which they live.

PART TWO

MAASEH BERESHIT /

THE ACT OF CREATION

The Existence, Unity,
and Incorporeality of God

*I*n the beginning God created heaven and earth. The earth was formless and void. Darkness covered the deep. And the spirit of God hovered over the water. Then God said, "Let there be light." And there was light. And God saw the light, that it was good. God separated the light from the darkness. And God called the light day, and the darkness He called night. Evening came, and morning came. One day.

Genesis 1:1–5

THE ARGUMENTS OF THE KALAM

Introduction

The elements of medieval theology—the principal doctrines a thinker or layman needed to know about God—were that He exists, He is one, and He is of a different order of being from the phenomena of the physical world. Given divine existence, unity, and incorporeality, the theologian could construct or derive further essential knowledge about the Deity and could rationalize, expand, and explain the vast corpus of tradition of which theology was the mere skeleton. For the common man the matter was straightforward enough. There were authorities forming a living chain going back to the sources of the tradition who were competent to inform him of its meaning and practical import and to teach by precept and practice what was essential and what was secondary. Once this was done, the choice for the common man was to accept or reject in silence. But for the uncommon man whom doubt or inquiry had opened to perplexity, for the authorities and would-be authorities capable intellectually and morally/politically of questioning their relation to tradition, a more difficult choice offered itself: either to seek some rational foundation for the elements of theology or else to sink into one kind or another of positivism. Positivism here is ac-

124

quiescence in the notion that what is given in experience or by tradition must be taken or relinquished as it is but is in itself inexplicable. In terms of their positivism, there is a marked affinity between the skeptic/agnostic and the fundamentalist/dogmatist in matters of religion, for both regard the religious datum as incomprehensible in rational terms. Thus it should not seem surprising if in times of strong social pressure against public renunciation of religious tradition we find the two sorts of positivism combined in the person of the private skeptic, public fundamentalist, the "Grand Inquisitor," who demands of others, or even of himself, that the data of tradition be accepted "on faith," that is, uncritically—*bila kayf,* as the Asharite school of Mutakallimun [1] used to say, not asking why or how.

In writing as a teacher (*moreh*) to the perplexed, Maimonides recognized implicitly the moral and intellectual untenability of the positivist option. The Rambam's belief, as his treatment of religious language clearly shows, is that there can be no commitment or appropriation without understanding, no understanding without interpretation, no interpretation without the application of rational categories. The skeptical and fundamentalist varieties of positivism are both rejected on the same grounds. For fundamentalism demands acceptance of a paradoxically incomprehensible revelation, while skepticism, by demanding the rejection of a datum it regards as incomprehensible, acts arbitrarily, leaving religious experience and tradition in particular and reality in general unexplained. It may be that reality will never respond to reason. But, if belief is intellectual acceptance or affirmation, it is self-contradictory to say that anything has been believed (or disbelieved) before it has been understood. In making any statement or judgment about anything, we affirm the rationality of being. Inquiry, then, into the groundworks of theology is necessary if any statements, pro or con, are to be made about any religious subject, or even if any statements of revelation or the larger tradition which is its setting are to be accepted or rejected or merely left alone.

Maimonides has three reasons for beginning his investigation of the foundations of theology by studying the approach of the dialectical theologians of Islam: (1) In embarking on the study of any problem a

1. The Mutakallimun (or *loquentes* in Latin; singular Mutakallim) are the practitioners of the Kalam, the tradition of dialectical theology in Islam.

thinker is obliged to consider what has already been done. This is especially true in philosophy, where fact has a way of being far richer than imagination: the philosopher must study intellectual history for the same reason that the novelist must study life. (2) Many Mutakallimun, as Maimonides remarks, had a radical way of approaching problems by which the most fundamental assumptions of a doctrine were laid bare. This was due to the Kalam method of constant debate, but it provides not only an admirable introduction to philosophical dialectic but also a preliminary exposure, in an acutely analytical context, to some of the problems the inquirer into theology must confront. (3) Finally—and decisively for Maimonides—if we are to learn from all men, then, as the rabbis tell us, we must learn also from their mistakes.

A cardinal object of the Islamic Kalam had been to establish the divine creation of the world. If it could be established that the world was produced out of nothing, then the principal doctrines of monotheism—the existence, unity, and incorporeality of God—the Mutakallimun believed, would follow by simple logical steps. But to make creation a matter of logic required a complete rethinking of the character of the world; and this, with their characteristic radicalism, the Mutakallimun undertook. To begin with, for creation to be necessary it must occur at all times. Thus the Mutakallimun transformed the Biblical (and Koranic) act of creation into a ceaseless re-creation of all that there is at every instant. Being was robbed of all inherent stability by the denial that any particle or any property endures for more than an instant. Prediction was made impossible by the rejection of the notion of dispositions and capacities. The whole of nature was fragmented into infinitesimal and instantly evanescent atoms bearing equally evanescent "accidents," properties in no way essential or relevant to any future event. Such a universe, the Mutakallimun reasoned, having no stability, coherence, or continuity of its own, could not lack an Orderer, a Determiner, a constant Provider of such order and determinacy as we may behold. The fragmentation of being into dimensionless points seemed to require the absolute dependence of existence upon the constant act of a Creator.

From *Moreh Nevukhim* I

MOREH NEVUKHIM I:73

Despite the diversity of their individual arguments and opinions, the Mutakallimun postulate twelve premises in common, which are necessary to the establishment of what they desire to prove. . . . I shall cite them here and then explain to you the meaning and consequences of each:

(1) Atomism.

(2) The existence of the void.

(3) That time is composed of instants.

(4) That substance must have certain accidents.

(5) That the accidents, which I shall describe, must subsist in the atom.

(6) That no atom endures beyond one instant.

(7) That possessions and privations are on a par: both are actual accidents, requiring a cause.

(8) That nothing exists beyond substance and accident (among created things); that natural form is also an accident.

(9) That accidents have no accidents.

(10) That the conformance of a conception to reality is no criterion of its possibility.

(11) That actual, potential, and accidental infinities are equally impossible—*i.e.,* infinities are impossible whether they exist simultaneously or are supposed to be composed of existent and nonexistent members, infinite *per accidens.*

(12) That the senses are misleading, that many sense objects elude them, and that sense judgments therefore are not to be trusted and afford no absolute grounds for demonstrations.

Having listed these premises, I shall undertake to explain the meaning and the implications of each.

(1) This means that they affirm that the entire world (*i.e.,* all bodies therein) is composed of tiny particles, too fine to be divided. A single particle, in fact, has no magnitude at all; but if several are joined together, then the aggregate has magnitude and becomes a body. . . . All these particles are alike in every way, have no differences of any sort; and no body, they say, can exist unless composed of these iden-

tical particles, aggregated by proximity. Thus generation for them is aggregation; destruction, dispersal. . . . The existence of these particles, they claim, is not secure, as Epicurus and other atomists believed; rather, God, they say, creates these substances constantly when He so wills, and their destruction too is possible. . . .

(2) *The doctrine of a vacuum.* Rigorous Mutakallimun believe further that there exists a void, that is, an expanse or expanses containing nothing whatever but voidness of all bodies and absence of all substance. This premise is a necessary consequence of their adopting 1. For if the world were full of such particles, then how would anything move? The interpenetration of bodies would be inconceivable. But the aggregation and dispersal of these particles would be impossible without motion. So they must resort to affirming the existence of a vacuum. . . .

(3) *The doctrine that time is composed of instants, i.e.,* of numerous discrete times so short in duration as to be incapable of division. This premise too is made necessary for them by 1. Obviously they had seen Aristotle's demonstrations of the parity in this regard of time, extension, and motion, to the effect that to divide any one of the three requires a corresponding division in the others. Thus they recognized that if time is continuous and infinitely divisible, it follows necessarily that so must be the particles which they had postulated to be indivisible.

Likewise, if space had been postulated to be continuous, it would follow necessarily that the temporal instant, which had been postulated as indivisible, could be divided, as Aristotle makes clear in the *Physics* [VI:4. 235^a. 13]. For this reason they assume that extension too is discontinuous and indeed composed of quanta which can no longer be divided. And time in the same way is composed of indivisible instants. The hour, for instance, is composed of sixty minutes, the minute of sixty seconds, the second of sixty "thirds," and so forth until the series ends according to them at say "tenths" or some briefer interval, which, like extension, can in no way be parted or divided.[1] Thus time

---

1. Maimonides intends to suggest a *reductio ad absurdum* here, for the Kalam instant has no duration. How, it would be argued, can time be composed of parts which have no duration; or space and bodies of parts which have no magnitude? Yet if the atom is

(on their account) acquires arrangement and position [2]—for they really do not have an adequate notion of the true character of time, which is not surprising when the most acute philosophers were baffled by time and a number of them could not understand its essence. Even Galen says that it is a divine matter whose true nature is beyond our ken—so what is to be expected of such as those who understand the nature of nothing at all.[3]

Consider some of the consequences which follow from these three premises and which therefore they accepted. They held that motion is the transference of an atom from one quantum of space to the next. It follows that no motion can be faster than any other. On this assumption they claimed that when you see two objects moving two different distances in the same time, the cause is not that one is moving faster than the other but that the motion we call slower was interrupted by a greater number of rests. . . . Faced with the objection of an arrow shot from a powerful bow, they still maintained that its motion was interrupted by intervals of rest.[4] Only the error of the senses makes one suppose that its motion is continuous, for the senses often fail to detect their objects (12). They would then be asked, "Have you seen a millstone turn full circle? Does not a part at the circumference traverse a large circle in exactly the same time it takes a part near the center to traverse a small one? The motion of the rim must be swifter than that of the interior. You cannot say that the motion of one part was interrupted more often than that of another, for the whole stone is one solid body." Their reply would be that the millstone disintegrates while revolving to allow more rests to the inner than the outer portions. How is it, they were asked, that we perceive the millstone as a monolith which even hammers cannot break? "It must break up while turning,

---

divisible even in imagination, it is extended and cannot be treated in accordance with the Kalam objective as possessing no existence of its own.

2. Characteristics classically ascribed to space.

3. The study of "the nature of things," being expressly subordinated by Kalam to the service of theology, Mutakallimun could hardly claim to present an objective picture of reality.

4. Despite the fact that the impetus of the bowshot would seem to be too strong to allow any halting in the motion of which it is the cause. The Mutakallimun, of course, did not accept the notion of force.

but knit together again when it comes to rest.'' And why do we not perceive its disintegration? Here they relied again on 12: reason, not sense perception, is the criterion.

Do not suppose that what I have told you are the most outrageous consequences of these three premises. Stranger and more grotesque implications follow from the doctrine of the void, and what I have mentioned about motion is by no means more absurd than the equality of the diagonal of a square to one of its sides [5]—which opinion led some of them to deny the existence of the square! In general I would render invalid all demonstrations in geometry in one of two ways: Some would become simply inconsistent, as, for example, those dealing specifically with the commensurability and incommensurability of lines and planes, rational and irrational lines—everything in Book X of Euclid or of a similar nature. Other demonstrations would no longer be unconditional, as when we say we want to divide a line in half—for if it were composed of an odd number of atoms this would be impossible on their assumptions. Bear in mind the well-known *Book of Machines* of the Banu Shakir, which details over a hundred mechanical devices all tested and shown to work: if there were a vacuum, not one of these would stand the test, and many types of pump would not work either. Yet lives have been spent in argument to establish these and similar premises.

To return to the aforementioned premises:

(4) *Their doctrine that accidents exist as a principle distinct from substance and that no body can be entirely free of them.* If it went no further, this would be a clear, sound, and unproblematic premise. But they say that every substance which does not have the accident of life must have that of death: for every pair of opposites, a subject must have either one or the other. Thus, they say, it must have color, taste, motion or rest, aggregation or separation. If it has life, then it must have other sorts of accident, such as knowledge or ignorance, will or its opposite, power or impotence, perception or one of its con-

5. If four dimensionless atoms are arranged in a square, the distance from top to bottom would seem to equal the distance from corner to corner. The problem results from the transition between that which has magnitude and that which has not.

traries [6]—in short, all the attributes which a living being might have or their opposites.

(5) *Their doctrine that these accidents subsist in the atom and that it cannot escape having them.* The significance of this premise is their assertion that these atoms which God creates must inevitably have certain accidents such as color, smell, motion or rest—but not magnitude, since atoms have no magnitude. (Quantity, in their view, is not considered an accident; they do not realize that quantity is an accident intrinsically.[7]) In accordance with this premise, they opine that no accident subsisting in a body may be predicated properly of that body as a whole. Rather it is in each of the atoms of which that body is composed. In this piece of snow, for example, whiteness is found not simply in the whole. Rather each atom of the snow is what is white, and only therefore does whiteness exist in the aggregate. Likewise they say of a moving body that each of its atoms is what moves and only so does the whole come into motion. Again, life, in their view, exists in each and every atom of the living body. And the same for sense: each atom of the sensing whole is what senses. For life, sense, reason, and knowledge are accidents in their view, like blackness or whiteness, as we shall make clear [see 8].

Regarding soul they disagree. Most call it the accident of one of the atoms out of which man, for instance, is composed. The whole is said to be ensouled in virtue of the fact that it has that one atom in it. Others of them say that the soul is a body composed of tiny atoms. These atoms no doubt have a certain accident which distinguishes them as a soul; and these atoms are, so they say, mingled with the atoms of the body. So they still do not avoid making of the soul some sort of accident.[8] Concerning reason, they seem to be agreed that it is an accident of an atom or of the whole of the reasoning being. As for knowledge, they are confused as to whether it is an accident of each

6. *Viz.*, blindness, deafness, etc.
7. Since it is always quantity *of* something; it cannot exist in its own right. There may be, for example, three pounds of coffee or three pounds of potatoes, but there cannot be three pounds *simpliciter*.
8. Rather than a substance. This would imply that I am the person *of* my body, rather than being an identity in my own right.

atom of the knowing being or of just one of them. But either view implies absurd consequences.[9]

Faced with the objection that most minerals and stones arc found with an intense color which they lose when finely divided (thus when we pulverize the brilliantly green emerald it turns to a white powder, indicating that the accident subsisted in the whole, not in the parts; and, more obviously still, the severed part of a living being is not itself alive, which is evidence that life is a characteristic of the whole, not of each part), they reply that accidents do not endure but are constantly created, as I shall explain in treating the next premise.

(6) *Their doctrine that no accident endures for two instants.* They claim that God creates at a stroke the atom and whatever accidents He pleases. He is not to be described (exalted be He) as being capable of creating an atom without an accident, for that is impossible. The essence of an accident, the very concept of it, is that it does not endure longer than one instant.[10] The moment one accident is created it disappears, goes out of existence, and God creates another of its kind, which disappears in turn, then a third, and so forth as long as God wills that sort of accident to endure. But if He wills to create a different sort of accident in the same atom, He does. And if He stops creating accidents, then that atom goes out of existence. . . .

What attracted them to this opinion was their notion that there is no nature which might require a given body to have certain accidents. Rather, they wanted to say that God created these accidents here and now and without nature or any other intermediary.[11] If this is said, it follows in their view that this accident cannot last. For if you said it lasted for a time and then went out of existence, it would be necessary to seek whatever had put it out of existence. If you say God did, since He so willed to do, that would be unsound in their view, as nonbeing has no cause and needs none: simply for a cause to cease its work suffices for the nonexistence of that work. This is true in a way, and it impelled them (since they wanted there to be no such thing as nature

9. *E.g.* if every atom knew, then a person might have no more knowledge in his head than in his foot; but if only certain atoms knew, *they* and not *I* would be the conscious subject of my knowledge.

10. For it is unextended in time as it is in space.

11. Contrast Maimonides' view that God acts through nature (*Moreh* II:6).

to guarantee the existence or nonexistence of anything) to hold the constant re-creation of accidents. . . .

In keeping with this premise, they say that when, as we presume, we dye a garment red, we are not really dying it at all. Rather God creates the color in the clothing *de novo* just as it comes into contact with the dye. Thus we put it that the dye impregnates the cloth; but no such thing, so they say, is the case. God is simply in the habit of creating this particular color, say black, only when a garment is in contact with indigo. The black which God creates at the moment of contact does not last, however, but disappears instantly, and He creates another; for God is also in the habit of creating not red or yellow but a similar black on the disappearance of the first.

A corollary which they draw from this premise is that the things we know now are not the things we knew yesterday—for those things no longer exist, and others have been created in their stead. They say this is so because knowledge is an accident—but so is the soul, and it follows for those who believe soul to be an accident that perhaps one hundred thousand souls must be created every minute in each being which has a soul. . . .

In accordance with this premise, they say that when a man moves a pen it is not he who moves it, for the motion in the pen is an accident created by God. Likewise the motion of the hand, which (on our account) moves the pen, is an accident created by God. The hand has no effect; God is simply in the habit of juxtaposing the motion of the hand with that of the pen. There is no causation in the moving of the pen; for accidents, they say, are confined within their subjects. . . . There is no such thing as a body which has any sort of action at all; in the last analysis the only doer is God. . . .

On the whole, then, it should not be said in any sense that this caused that. This is the view of the bulk of them. A few did uphold causality, but the majority held these in opprobrium.

Regarding human actions they disagree. The majority, including most of the Ashariyya,[12] take the position that, as this pen moves,

12. The Asharites were the more strict predestinarians of the Mutakallimun; the Mutazilites tended toward voluntarism. But, as Maimonides is careful to make clear throughout his treatment, there was a wide diversity among all schools of thought in the

God creates four accidents, no one of which is the cause of any other but each of which is simply given existence conjointly with the rest: (a) my volition to move the pen, (b) my capacity of moving it, (c) the human motion itself, i.e., the motion of my hand, (d) the motion of the pen. For they assert that when a man wills something and in his own estimation does it, the very act of willing was created in him, as well as the capacity of doing what he willed, and the action willed. He does not act through his created power of acting, nor does that power actually affect the act. The Mutazila, on the other hand, say that he acts through a created power, and certain of the Ashariyya say that the created capacity of acting does have some effect on and connection to the act. But they were abhorred for holding this view.

This created will and capacity, which they all affirm, and the created act, which some of them assert, are all accidents which cannot endure. God creates and re-creates motion in the pen as long as it is moving; and it cannot come to rest before He has created rest in it, which He does not cease to re-create again and again as long as it is at rest. Thus at every single instant, i.e., in every atom of time, God creates an accident in every individual being that exists, from angel and sphere down; and so He does at all times. This, they say, is what it really means to believe in God's creative act; and, in their view, to disbelieve that God works in this manner is to deny that He acts at all. It is of such beliefs as this, to my mind or that of any rational man, that it is said, "or as a man is mocked you mock Him" [Job 13:9]. For this is the epitome of mockery.

(7) *Their belief that privations are principles existing in a body additional to its substance—and thus are actual accidents constantly being re-created as they disappear.* To explain: they do not regard rest as the absence of motion, death as the absence of life, blindness as the absence of sight, or any other such privation as the absence of some positive characteristic which might have been possessed. Rather they put motion and rest on the same footing with heat and cold. Just as heat and cold are accidents existing in hot and cold subjects, so motion is an accident created in a moving object and rest is an accident

---

Kalam. His concern is with the general trend of such schools and the outcome of that trend.

created by God in an object at rest, enduring no longer than an instant (as posited in 6). God, in their view, has created rest in every single atom of this body and as soon as one "rest" goes out of existence He creates another, so long as that object remains at rest.

Exactly the same holds true for knowledge and ignorance in their view. Ignorance for them is something which exists, an accident, constantly going out of existence and being created so long as its subject does not know a certain thing. The same is true again of life and death; both, in their view, are accidents, and they declare that life vanishes and is re-created as long as its subject is alive. When God wills that he should die, He creates in him the accident of death on the heels of that of life, which does not last more than an instant. All this they explicitly declare.

It follows necessarily on their assumptions that the accident of death which God creates also goes out of existence in an instant and is recreated by Him. Otherwise the dead would not remain so. Just as life is constantly recreated, so too death must be. I wish I knew how long God continues to create the accident of death in the dead—as long as the shape remains? Or a single atom? For the accident of death which God creates can reside, as they would have it, only in each individual atom. Yet we find molars of dead individuals thousands of years old, which shows that God did not annihilate the substance [13] but must have been creating the accident of death in it all those thousands of years, and re-creating it anew each time it vanished. . . .

(8) *Their claim that nothing exists beyond atom and accident and that natural forms are accidents as well.* This means that in their view all bodies are composed of identical atoms, as we have set forth in introducing their premises. The only difference among atoms is with respect to accidents. Being an animal or a man, in their view, having sense or reason—all things are accidents on a par with whiteness or blackness, bitterness or sweetness. Thus the distinction among members of different species becomes no greater than that among members of the same species. . . .

(9) *Their doctrine that accidents do not bear accidents.* It is not to be said, in their view, that one accident is predicated of another,

13. Nonexistence would require no cause, but death was distinguished by the Mutakallimun from nonexistence.

which in turn is predicated of a substance. All accidents are predicated independently of substances. They avoid the opposite assertion because it implies that one accident might be the prerequisite of another. . . .

(10) *Their doctrine of what may be.* This is the linchpin of the Kalam. What it means is this: they hold that whatever can be imagined is rationally possible. For example . . . that any being in our experience should be larger or smaller than it is or have a different shape or be elsewhere than it is, such as the existence of a human being as large as a flea, or a flea the size of an elephant—all these are conceivable, they say. This sort of possibility embraces the entire world. Whatever they postulate of this sort, they can say, "It is conceivable and therefore it is possible; there is no reason why it should not be so rather than otherwise." They pay no attention to whether reality bears out their assumptions or not, for this reality, they say, with its familiar phenomena, fixed and unchanging conditions, is such only through the continuity of custom. Just as it is the custom of the sultan to pass through the city markets only on horseback and he is never seen there otherwise (although it is not inconceivable that he might walk through the city on foot but in fact altogether possible), so the tendency of earth to fall or fire to rise, of flame to burn or water to cool, are all, they say, simply matters of habit. It is not inconceivable that these habits might change—that fire cool and fall while remaining fire, or water heat and rise while remaining water.

Their entire system is built on this. Yet they all agree that for opposites to be conjoined in the same substrate at the same time is contradictory and inconceivable. In the same manner they say that a substance without an accident or (for some) an accident without a substrate is inconceivable and cannot be, likewise for an accident to turn into a substance or a substance into an accident is impossible. Again, the interpenetration of bodies not only cannot occur but in their view is conceptually impossible.[14]

That what they count as impossible is inconceivable, and what they consider possible is conceivable, is true. The Philosophers, however, say, "What you call possible or impossible is only what you can or

14. Since atoms are perfectly solid.

cannot imagine. Your notion of possibility is based not on intellect but on imagination. In this premise your criterion of possibility, necessity, and impossibility vacillates between imagination (not reason) and some of the naïve assumptions of 'common sense' [vulgar opinion]— as al-Farabi points out in discussing the meanings which the Mutakallimun give to 'reason.' " [15] What can be imagined, al-Farabi says, is considered possible by them, regardless of whether or not it is in accord with reality; what cannot be imagined they hold to be impossible. This premise becomes valid only through the nine which precede it, and it was doubtless for the sake of this one that they were adduced. Let me make this clear and lay bare the internal workings of the dialectic involved by way of the following dialogue between a Philosopher and a Mutakallim:

M: "Why is this body which is iron so hard and black while that one which is butter is so soft and light and white?"

P: "Every natural body has two sorts of accident, those which inhere in it on account of its matter, such as a man's sickness or health, and those which inhere in it on account of its form, such as a man's laughter or surprise. The matter out of which compounds are ultimately composed differs greatly in terms of the forms appropriate to it. That is how the essence of butter is different from that of iron. The different sorts of accidents which you see are consequences of their different forms; the blackness of one and whiteness of the other are accidents consequent on their being composed ultimately of different sorts of matter."

At this the Mutakallim refutes the whole reply, using his premises as follows:

M: "The forms which you claim are the basis of 'essence' and give rise to the diversity of substances do not exist at all. There are only accidents" (8).

There is no difference, the Mutakallim would continue, between the "essence" of iron and that of butter—everything is composed of identical atoms (as explained in 1, from which 2 and 3 follow necessarily as we have seen, 12 too being used to secure atomism). It is not the case, according to the Mutakallimun, that there are certain accidents

15. *Fi Aql*, ed. Bouyges (1938), pp. 11–12.

which adapt their atoms specifically to the reception of other, secondary accidents. For accidents, in their view, do not inhere in other accidents (9), and accidents do not endure (6).

The Mutakallim, then, has secured all that he desired from these premises. The result is that iron and butter are of one identical substance; every atom of them bears the same relation to any accident whatever. This atom is no more fit for this accident than that; and just as this atom is no fitter to move than to remain at rest, so no atom is more appropriate than any other to receive the accident of life or that of sense. The number of atoms makes no difference since accidents are found only in the individual atoms (5). Thus it follows from these premises that man is no more fit to think than a beetle. But their doctrine of possibility follows as well, and this was the object of the whole endeavor, for this is the kingpin from which all the rest they desire to establish is to be hung, as will be made clear.

N.B. You know already, dear inquirer, if you have studied psychology and learned the nature and function of the various faculties, that most animals, including of course all higher animals (*i.e.,* those that have hearts) possess imagination.[16] Thus it is not by imagination that man is distinguished; imagining is not the act of the intellect but its opposite. The task of intellect is to analyze and make distinctions, to form concepts and abstractions which enable us to see the true nature and causes of things, to apprehend from one thing a great many ideas which are as different to the mind in their existence as two human individuals are to the imagination. It is through intellect that universals are distinguished from particular concepts, and no demonstration can be valid except through universals.[17] Through intellect again essential predicates are distinguished from those which are accidental. The imagination cannot do any of these things; it apprehends only the particular manifold as perceived by the senses or else recombines things existing separately into an imaginary construct representing either a body or a bodily function—as when one imagines a man with wings and a horse's head and so forth. This latter case is referred to as a false figment, since nothing in reality corresponds to it. Imagination is

16. *I.e.,* the ability to "re-present" to themselves (and respond to) images of objects not physically present to them.

17. The premises of a valid demonstration must be true always and necessarily.

never able entirely to free itself from matter, even when a form is abstracted as far as possible from the material. It is for this reason that imagination does not provide a reliable criterion.

What we learn from mathematics is very much to the point. There are some things which our imagination is utterly unable to conceive, which it judges in fact to be as impossible as the union of opposites, but which nonetheless can be established by demonstration and actually turn out to exist. . . . Thus it is demonstrated in *Conic Sections* [18] II [theorem 13] that two lines between which there is a given distance at their point of origin may extend to infinity, the distance separating them constantly diminishing, without their ever meeting. This cannot be imagined, it eludes the imagination completely. . . . Thus it is demonstrated that something which cannot be imagined, something which imagination judges in fact to be impossible, can take place. In the same way it can be demonstrated that something which is necessary for the imagination is in fact impossible—*viz.*, for God to be a body or a force within a body. For to imagination nothing exists except bodies or phenomena dependent on them. Thus it becomes evident that there is something else, not imagination, by which possibility, necessity, and impossibility are to be judged—a fine and valuable thought for one who wants to break out of the trance in which imagination has held him in thrall.

Do not think for a moment that the Mutakallimun are wholly unaware of this; they do have a certain awareness of it: they term impossible imaginings, like God's being a body, fantasies or illusions, and they often declare that fantasies are false.[19] It is for this reason that they have recourse to the nine premises above, so as to be able to establish this one (10), which allows for the possibility of the sorts of imaginings they require to give them the identical atoms and identically accidental [20] accidents we have described.

Consider now what a thorny path this opens up: the concepts one

18. A geometric treatise by the Greek mathematician Apollonius of Perga (b. *ca.* 262 B.C.E.).

19. But not impossible.

20. *I.e.*, nonessential characteristics, no one of which depends on any material or formal precondition. One can always imagine any atom as having totally different accidents from those it actually has.

man claims are rational another claims are imaginary. What we need is some way of distinguishing the two. If the philosopher says that reality is his witness, and that it is through what actually exists that we judge what is necessary, possible, or impossible, the man of religion replies, "But that [21] is just the subject of the dispute. For we claim that reality is authored by an act of will and not necessarily; and this being so, it might have been made otherwise, unless rational conception determines this to be impossible as you claim." This matter of possibility is one on which I shall have more to say elsewhere in this study.[22] It is not a point to be slighted or casually shrugged off.

(11) *Their doctrine of the impossibility of any sort of infinity.* To explain: the impossibility of an infinite magnitude, or an infinite number of finite magnitudes has been demonstrated, but only on the assumption that such infinities exist simultaneously.[23] Again, the existence of an infinite chain of causes is impossible.[24] . . . But it is within a system in which natures and essences figure that the impossibility of infinity is proved. The potential infinite and the infinite *per accidens* can in some cases be demonstrated to exist, as the infinite potential divisibility of magnitude or time is demonstrated. In other cases there is more ground for speculation, such as infinite succession, called *per accidens* infinity—the existence of one thing after another has gone out of existence in infinite series. The reasoning here grows extremely abstruse: those who claim that the eternity of the world is demonstrated [the Aristotelians] say that time is infinite yet escape inconsistency because as each new time comes into being the last goes out of existence. The succession of accidents in matter, for them, occurs in the same manner, but they are not implicated in inconsistency because these accidents do not all exist simultaneously but rather successively. It is this which has not been demonstrated to be impossible.

But the Mutakallimun do not distinguish between the assertion that

21. The fundamental character of reality.

22. See *Moreh* II:17. Maimonides is acknowledging an affinity between the Kalam doctrine and his own solution.

23. Since the demonstration hinges on the logical incoherence of the notion of an actual (*i.e.*, determinate) infinite quantity.

24. Since either the first cause or the ultimate effect would never be reached, so that the causation would never take effect.

a magnitude which exists is infinite and saying that body or time is susceptible of infinite divisions; [25] nor do they distinguish between the existence of an infinite number of things arrayed simultaneously (as if you were to say that the number of human persons now existing is infinite) and your saying that an infinite number of things have come into being, although each in turn has gone out of existence (as if you were to say Zayd is the son of Omar, who is the son of Khalid, who is the son of Bakr, and so *ad infinitum*). In their view this is as absurd as the first. . . .

(12) *Their doctrine that the senses do not always afford certainty.* The Mutakallimun charge sense perception with two failings: (*a*) The senses fail to detect, they say, many objects proper to them, either because of the smallness of the objects (they cite the atoms and phenomena at the atomic level, as we have seen), or because of the distance of the object from the percipient—a man can neither see nor hear nor smell more than a few miles, nor can we detect the motion of the heavens. (*b*) The senses err regarding their objects: a man sees a large object as small at a distance, a small one as large if it is in water, a crooked thing as straight if it is partially immersed in water. To a man with jaundice everything appears yellow; to a man with yellow bile on his tongue sweet things taste bitter. They adduce many examples of this sort, saying that therefore the senses ought not to be trusted to provide grounds for argument.

Do not suppose that the Mutakallimun are not serious when they agree in affirming this premise (as most of the later Mutakallimun supposed that the ambition of their predecessors to establish atomism was unnecessary). The fact is that each of the foregoing doctrines was necessary; to eliminate any one of their premises would be to thwart their purpose completely. This last premise is most requisite. For if we perceive through our senses things which contradict what they posit, they can claim there is no turning to the senses when reason itself, as they aver, has testified and the truth is already demonstrated. . . . All these doctrines are ancient, as you know, and were used by the Sophists, as Galen relates in *On the Natural Faculties* [I:ii] where he tells of those who attempted to discredit the senses. . . .

25. Hence their atomism.

MOREH NEVUKHIM I:74

In this chapter I relate for you the arguments of the Mutakallimun in support of the world's creation. Do not ask me to present their position in their own terminology or with their prolixity. I shall simply report the object of each author and his mode of argument. . . . But when you read the voluminous tomes of their famous works you will find not one idea in their argumentation on this score beyond what you may comprehend from this discussion of mine—although you will find high-flown style and fuller verbiage, for they often use rhyme and word play or indulge in other rhetorical niceties; often they use obscure vocabulary intended to impress the hearer and overawe the novice. You will also find in their writings a good deal of redundancy, objections and their supposed solutions, and polemics against their adversaries.

Method 1. Certain of them affirm that any single event can be used as an argument for the world's creation: If you say, "Zayd, who was a drop of semen, has passed from stage to stage until reaching maturity," it is impossible for him to have brought about these changes in himself; there must have been something to change him external to himself. Thus, obviously, he requires a Maker to construct his body and bring him along from stage to stage. The same holds true for this palm tree and other things. The same holds true, they say, for the world itself. Apparently they believe that whatever holds good for a given body must hold good for all bodies.

Method 2. Again they say that the genesis of one individual capable of reproducing proves that the whole world is created. To explain: Zayd at one time did not exist. If subsequently he did exist, then it can only be on account of Omar, his father. But his father too came to be, and his existence in turn required the prior existence of Zayd's grandfather, Khalid. But Khalid himself did not exist forever— and so the series goes, *ad infinitum*. But they postulate the impossibility of this sort of infinity, as we have seen [11]. Thus when the series ends, say at a first person, Adam, who had no father, it would still be necessary to ask where he had come from. The answer might be earth, for example. So it would be necessary to ask where earth comes from; the answer might be water, say. Where then does water come from? Necessarily, they say, this series must either extend to infinity, which is impossible, or it must end at an existence which comes from nothing. This is the truth, they claim, and here the chain of inquiries comes to an end. This proves, they say, that the world came into being out of pure and absolute nothingness.

Method 3. The atoms, they argue, must be either aggregated or detached. Sometimes they are in the former state, sometimes in the latter. Plainly, then, their essence does not require them always to be one way or the other. If it did, they would never alter from the one state to the other. Thus neither state is more appropriate for them than the other. The fact that some of them are aggregated and others detached and that they do alter from the one state to the other shows that these atoms require some joining and separating agency. This, they say, shows that the world is created. You will observe now the proponent of this method relies on premise 1 with all its consequences.

Method 4. They say: "The entire world is composed of atoms and accidents. Every atom must have a certain accident or accidents, and all accidents come to be in time. It follows that the substance which bears them must also come to be in time, for everything that is bound inseparably to things that come to be in time, itself comes to be in time. Thus the whole world comes to be in time." If anyone objects that substance perhaps does not come to be in time and that accidents are what come to be in time and continuously succeed one another in a substance forever, they reply that this would entail an infinite series of events, which they postulate to be impossible. This line of argument is their most acute, and in their opinion their best. Many of them even take it as proof.

This fourth argument rests on three premises, as will not be obscure to the thinker. The first is that infinity of succession is impossible. The second is that every accident comes to be in time. But our opponent who holds the eternity of the world withholds assent regarding one accident, cyclical motion. For Aristotle claims that cyclical motion does not come into being or pass away. So there is no use in our establishing that other accidents come into being, which our opponent grants, since he claims they succeed each other cyclically in something which does not come into being. Accordingly, he claims of this accident alone, cyclical motion—*i.e.,* the motion of the sphere—that it did not come to be and that it is not of the same kind as accidents which do come into being. This accident alone then is what must be investigated and shown to have come into being. The third premise assumed by the proponent of this approach is that no sensory thing exists other than substance and accident, *i.e.,* atoms and those accidents he upholds. However, if bodies are composed of matter and form, as our opponent has proved, it should be proved that the first matter and the first form come into being and pass away, and then the proof of the genesis of the world will be sound.

Method 5. The argument from particularization. This method, greatly favored by them, devolves upon premise 10: The Mutakallim directs his mind to the whole world or to any particular part and says: "This might be as it is in size, shape, and accidents and where it is in time or place, or it might be larger or smaller, of some other shape or have some other accidents. It might have existed earlier or later or elsewhere. Its determination by this particular shape, size, time, place, or accidents, when any of these might have been otherwise, shows that there must be some Determiner and Selector who chose among these alternatives. The dependence of the world, then, as a whole, and every part of it, on a Particularizer shows that it is created. . . . All this follows necessarily if 10 is assumed. . . .

Method 6. One of the more recent Mutakallimun claimed to have discovered a very good approach, superior to all the previous methods, based on consideration of the preponderance of being over nonbeing. The world, he argued, exists contingently, as everyone admits; for if its existence were necessary then it would be the Deity, but our debate is only with those who affirm the existence of the Deity and hold the world to be eternal. Now the contingent is something which might or might not exist; it is no more prone in itself to the one state than to the other. The fact that this contingently existent thing actually does exist, while it might equally have been nonexistent, shows that there must be some cause to give preponderance to its existence over its nonexistence.

This is a very plausible argument. It is a variant of the preceding particularization argument, substituting "something to give preponderance" for "something to particularize" and existence itself for the various states of existence. The propounder of this argument, however, is either confused or attempting to confuse us regarding the meaning of the proposition "The world exists contingently." For our adversary who holds the eternity of the world applies the term "contingent" to it in a different sense from that employed by the Mutakallim, as we shall make clear.[1] Furthermore the assertion that the world requires something to give preponderance to its existence over nonexistence is a terribly suspicious notion, for the giving of preponderance and particularization occurs only to a being capable equally of one of two alternative states, or one of two different conditions, so that it can be said, "Our finding it in this state rather than the other is evidence that it must have been made so on purpose." Thus you may say, "This brass is no more suited to the form of a lamp than it is to that of a pitcher. Since we find it to be a lamp (or a pitcher) we know necessarily that someone intentionally singled out that particular alternative from among the possibilities." Plainly, the brass exists and the alternative possibilities for it do not until one is given preponderance. But with something which exists, over which there is disagreement as to whether it has always existed or come into being from nothing, this approach is untenable. It cannot be said, "Who gave preponderance to its existence over nonexistence?" until it is determined that it did come into being out of nothing—and this is the question at issue.

Taking its existence and nonexistence in a purely abstract way, we come back again to 10, which is a criterion of what may be imagined, not of what exists or may be thought; and our opponent who holds the eternity of the world considers our ability to imagine its nonexistence to be no different from our ability to imagine any other impossibility which might occur to our imagination. My purpose is not to refute these arguments but only to make clear to you that this approach, which was supposed to be different from the preceding, really is not. Rather it is on the same footing with the previous allowances of that possibility.[2]

Method 7. A certain creationist maintains that the world's coming to

1. The Aristotelian would not use the term "contingent" so as to exclude eternity. To insist on such a sense would be to beg the question.

2. *I.e.,* that reality might have been radically different from its actual state. The denial of this claim is as fundamental to Aristotelianism as is its assertion to Kalam. Maimonides qualifies his critique of the Kalam on this point since it provides the point of departure for his own argument (*Moreh* II:19).

be in time can be established from the Philosophers' doctrine of the immortality of the soul If the world were eternal, he argues, then the number of people who have died in the infinite past would be infinite; thus an infinite number of souls would exist simultaneously, but this surely has been demonstrated to be impossible. . . .

This is a marvelous approach, for it seeks to illuminate what is obscure by what is darker. To this, the proverb current among the Syrians truthfully may be applied: "Your bond requires another bond"—as though this person had already had the immortality of the soul demonstrated to him and knew in what form it survives and what sort of thing it is that is immortal so that he could adduce this in an argument.

If, however, his object was simply to implicate his adversary in the difficulties of believing both in the eternity of the world and in the immortality of the soul, these difficulties would be entailed only if the opponent granted him his own imagined version of the survival of the soul: certain modern Philosophers have resolved the dilemma by saying that the souls which survive are not bodies which would take up space and have positions and therefore cannot be infinite. Things which are disembodied, as you know, i.e., things which are neither bodies nor forces in a body, but rather minds, cannot be conceived to be pluralized in the first place, unless as cause and effect. . . . But what survives of Zayd is neither cause nor effect of what survives of Omar. All, then, would be one, as Ibn Bajja makes clear,[3] among others who were attracted to discourse about such dark subjects. But on the whole it is not from such murky areas, where intelligence itself falls short, that premises may be drawn which will shed light upon obscurity. . . .

These, then, are their main methods of establishing the genesis of the world. When they have done so through the above considerations, it follows necessarily that it has an Author who brought it into being by intention, choice, and design. They then proceed to show that He is one, using methods we shall explore in the next chapter.

3. In his treatise *On Conjunction of the Intellect with Man*. That the Rambam made resurrection an article of his creed is well known. It is less well known that he was inclined to understand "what survives of man" Platonically as having no separate individuality.

MOREH NEVUKHIM I:75

I shall explain to you in this chapter the arguments in favor of monotheism on the account of the Mutakallimun. They say, "That which existence shows to be its Maker and the Author of its being is one." They have two principal methods of establishing the unity of God: the argument from interference and the argument from differentia.

Method 1. Interference. This is the approach preferred by the majority. The Mutakallim says in essence: If there were two gods, it would be necessary for an atom which must have one or the other of two opposite characteristics either to lack both, which is impossible, or to have both together at the same time, in the same subject, which is also impossible. For example . . . if one god wanted to move this body, it is possible that the other would will it to be still. This would entail either that it neither moved nor remained still, or that it was both in motion and at rest at once.

This line of argumentation is founded on the doctrine of the atoms [1] and on the assumption that accidents are created and that privation is an actual character requiring a cause. For if someone says that matter here [1] (where coming to be and passing away alternate, in the view of the Philosophers) is demonstrably not the same as the supernal matter of the celestial spheres, and then that there are two gods, one governing the nether matter, whose act has no bearing on the spheres, and the other governing the spheres, whose activity has nothing to do with ordinary matter—as dualists in fact claim—this theory would not involve "interference" at all. Should anyone object that this would imply deficiency in one of the gods, since his control did not extend where the other's did, he might be told that this implied deficiency on the part of neither, for that on which the act of either had no bearing would be impossible for him, and there is no deficiency in a doer's incapacity to do what is impossible.

Once the Mutakallimun became aware of the weakness of this argument, despite the motives which had led them to adopt it, they had recourse to a different approach.

Method 2. If there were two gods, they argue, they would have to

1. In the sublunary world.

have something in common [2] and something which one had and the other had not, to differentiate them.[3]

This is a philosophical and apodictic approach if its premises are stated clearly and the train of argument proceeds in due order. (I shall explain it when I discuss the ideas of the Philosophers on this subject [*Moreh* II:1, *a*].) But this avenue is not open to anyone who believes in attributes, for the Eternal, in such a one's view, would have several characters which might differentiate Him: God's knowledge would be different from His power, for example; and His power, from His will, so that there would be no impossibility in each of two gods' having some characters in common and others by which they were made distinct.

* * *

Method 4. They say, "The existence of any act or work is evidence for the existence of a doer or maker, necessarily—not of several. There is no difference between positing two gods and positing three or ten or any number at random."

Obviously. But if you say, "This does not show the impossibility of plurality in the divine but only that we do not know the number; it might be one or possibly quite a few," the Mutakallim completes his proof by saying: "There is no possibility in the existence of the Deity; it is necessary. So the possibility of plurality is refuted."

The argument was set up this way. But this is a gross error, plainly, for it is the existence of God which has no contingency to it. Our knowledge of that existence is subject to possibility. For possibility in knowledge is different from possibility in being. Perhaps, just as the Christians suppose the Deity to be three and He is not, so we take Him to be one, and such is not the case. This should be clear to anyone trained in logic.

Method 5. A certain recent Mutakallim claims to have found an apodictic argument in behalf of monotheism, to wit, an argument from dependence. It runs as follows: "If one god is sufficient to make these beings, then two are redundant. But if existence cannot be ordered and complete without two gods' working together, then both of them are

2. *I.e.*, in virtue of which both were gods.
3. They would therefore each be "plural"—*i.e.*, composed or manifold and as such not capable of being self-sufficient beings (see Part One).

impotent, inasmuch as each depends on the other; neither is independent.'' This is simply a variant of the argument from interference.

The objection to such a line of argumentation is that not everyone
who does not do what is not in his nature is called impotent. For we
do not say that a human being is weak because he cannot lift two
hundred fifty tons; nor do we attribute powerlessness to God because
He cannot give Himself a body, create His like, or produce a square
with a side equal to its diagonal. . . . Thus the believer in two gods
can say, ''It is impossible for one god to act alone. This is not impotence on the part of either god, for the existence of both is a necessary
condition for the existence of either.''

These artifices became so wearisome to some of them that they said
monotheism is simply the revealed and received religion. But the
Mutakallimun held this position in great disapprobation and scorned
those who took it. For my part, I think that for one of them to have
said this he must have been a healthy-minded thinker with an aversion
to sophistries. Not hearing any real demonstrations in all they said and
dissatisfied by what they claimed to be apodictic, he declared that this
is something received by revelation.[4] For these schools had already
robbed being of any sort of stable nature on which a valid argument
might be based, and the mind of any reliable intuition by which a valid
conclusion could be drawn. All this had been done on purpose—so
that we could postulate a reality such that we might prove what cannot
be proved. This entailed that we would become unable to prove what
can be proved. We can only appeal to rational and impartial thinkers
and to God.

MOREH NEVUKHIM I:76

Incorporeality in the doctrine of the Mutakallimun. The arguments the
Mutakallimun use in disproving the corporeality of God are very
weak, weaker than their arguments in behalf of monotheism, because
incorporeality in their view is, as it were, a corollary of monotheism.
Body, they maintain, is not one.[1] If someone argued against corporeality on grounds that body is necessarily compounded of matter

4. Maimonides does not assert the validity of the religious positivism under discussion,
only that it is the sole logical outcome once Kalam has closed all other doors.
1. Because it is not simplex.

and form and that compounding is plainly impossible in God's being, to my way of thinking, he would not be a Mutakallim. For this argument is not built on the premises of the Mutakallimun. It is in fact a sound demonstration, founded upon the doctrine and conception of matter and form. This is the doctrine of the Philosophers, which I shall discuss and explain in dealing with their demonstrations of this point. But our purpose in this chapter is solely to treat the arguments of the Mutakallimun for incorporeality, in terms of their premises and modes of argumentation.

Method 1. They say, "If God were a body, His being would be constituted by all the substances (atoms) of that body, or by one of them. If by one, what use are the rest? The existence of that 'body' does not make sense. If by all, then every one of these atoms would be a god.[2] There would be not one deity, but many. But we have already seen that God is one."

In examining this argument, you will find it to be built on premises 1 and 5. What if they are told, "The body of the Deity is not composed of indivisible particles, *i.e.*, not composed of the sort of substances He creates, as you suppose, but is rather a single continuous body . . . ?"

Method 2, which in their estimation is very impressive, is based on God's uniqueness, for none of His creatures is like Him. If He were a body, however, He would resemble other bodies. (They go on at some length on this point, claiming that if you say, "a body unlike other bodies," you have contradicted yourself. For every body is like every other inasmuch as it is a body. Bodies differ only in other ways—to wit their accidents.[3]) It would also follow, in their view, that God could create His like.

There are two ways of refuting this argument: (*a*) Someone may say: "I do not concede that God has no like. What argument have you to show that the Deity cannot resemble any created being in any way—unless, by God, you tie this assertion of God's uniqueness to some prophetic text? But then the denial of divine corporeality would no longer be a matter of reason but one of revelation." If you say that

2. According to the Kalam doctrine that whatever is predicated of the whole must be predicable of the part.
3. Since atoms as such are identical.

if He resembles any created thing, then He has created His like, the disputant will reply, "It is not like Him in every way, and *I* do not deny that the Deity has different aspects and attributes"—for one who embraces God's corporeality will not flinch at that. (*b*) The second way, which is more difficult, is as follows: among students of philosophy who have gotten deeply into the systems of the Philosophers, it is regarded as solidly established that the spheres are termed bodies in a totally different sense from that applied to bodies of ordinary matter. . . . If this can be said of the spheres, all the more can those who would assign to God a body say of the Deity, "He is a body . . . but His essence is like that of no created being; the two are said to be bodies in totally different senses"—just as those who possess the truth hold "being" to be said of Him and of creation in different senses.

The proponent of corporeality does not concede that all bodies are composed of identical particles; on the contrary, he says that God created all such bodies and that they differ in substance and essence. He would no more identify the body of the "Created Light" or Shekhinah with that of the sphere of the stars than he would identify the body of the ball of the sun with dung. . . . On the contrary, he would claim that this body is the perfect, noble, never compounded, changeless and unchangeable essence—and that is why, in fact, the existence of this body is necessary forever and why it makes all other things according to its will. Ah, how I wish I knew how this sickly doctrine could be overthrown by their marvelous arguments, which I have caused you to know.

Method 3. They say: "If the Deity were a body, it would be finite." This is true. "If finite, it would have a definite size and shape." This too is a valid inference. "And whatever its size and shape," they continue, "it is possible that it might have been larger or smaller in size or different in shape, inasmuch as it is a body. Something, then, is required to have selected this particular size and shape."

This argument too I have heard them making much of, but it is less cogent than any that has gone before. For it is grounded in premise 10, and I have shown you the doubts involved there in terms of the supposition that all other beings might be different than they are. The problem in terms of God is even worse. . . . Any contingent size or shape might have been larger or smaller or otherwise shaped than as it is and therefore requires a particularizer necessarily—if it came to be. But the shape and size of the Deity (exalted be He above all inadequacy and resemblance to creation), the corporealist would argue, never came into being in the first place and therefore require no particularizer. His character is necessary—including his size and shape. . . .

Consider now, inquirer, whether you would not prefer to seek the truth and discard prejudice and caprice, reverence for authority and blind faith in what you are accustomed to hold in awe. Do not delude yourself about the achievement of these thinkers nor about the predicament they got themselves into or the outcome of their efforts. They got themselves out of the frying pan into the fire, abolishing the nature of reality and changing the character of heaven and earth, all for the sake of their claim that through these premises the creation of the world could be demonstrated. But they did not prove the world's creation, and they undermined our arguments for the existence, unity, and incorporeality of God. For the demonstrations by which all this can be shown can only be based on the stable nature of being as apprehended by the senses and conceived by the mind.

Having seen the outcome of their dialectic, we shall next discuss the premises and demonstrations of the Philosophers regarding the existence, unity, and incorporeality of the Deity. However we shall grant them one premise which we do not accept: the eternity of the world. After that I shall show you our own approach, to the extent that sound reasoning has allowed us to complete the proofs regarding these three subjects; and, having done so, I shall come back (with God's help) to take issue with the Philosophers regarding their doctrine of the eternity of the world.

Analysis

Maimonides sympathizes with the objectives of the Mutakallimun, but his profound faith in the rationality of nature compels him to reject their approach. "The purpose of all of them," he writes, "is to impose upon reality a correspondence with our own doctrines and opinions." What disturbed the Rambam most about the theology of the

Kalam was neither its inconclusive reasoning nor its *ad hoc* or false premises, but its antiempirical bias and its antiscientific outcome. The skepticism of the Kalam regarding the senses made knowledge of any sort impossible. The adoption of a world view in which the only regularities were those of divine habit eliminated the relevance of all causal inference. Science, prediction, and generalization became impossible. How then could nature be, like Scripture, a book in which the divine wisdom is seen to be inscribed? Thus, for the sake of proving what cannot be proved, the (necessary) creation of the world, the Mutakallimun had sacrificed the law-like regularity of nature, by which those who "possess the truth" are able to argue *a posteriori* for the existence, unity, and incorporeality of God.

The modern student cannot avoid being struck, as he reads Maimonides' synthesis of the views of the Mutakallimun, by the frequent material resemblances between the metaphysical underpinnings of the Kalam and those of some of the chief modern philosophers. The Kalam reduction of material objects to aggregates of infinitesimal atoms is prophetic of Leibniz's use of similar reasoning to eliminate matter altogether as the locus of substantiality. The displacement of horizontal by vertical causality, of Leibniz's pre-established harmony and the occasionalism of Malebranche. The critique of the senses parallels that found in Descartes, Locke, Berkeley, or Hume; and the treatment of causal necessity as subjective rather than objective, the result of a habit of the mind arising from repeated observations of the constant conjunction of cause with effect, foreshadows Hume.

There is no more impressive corroboration of the Rambam's claim that the theism of the Mutakallimun is not logically implied by their twelve premises. For such notions as these are put to quite different use by the moderns, just as they were put to different use in ancient times by the Stoics and the Skeptics and still earlier by the Sophists, to whom Maimonides alludes. Leibniz, Berkeley, and the French Occasionalists, to be sure, still rely upon the Deity as a kind of *deus ex machina* (in the phrase Cicero applied to the Stoics) to save the appearances of coherence in the natural world. But Hume (who lays down the boundaries within which most modern philosophers work) pressed the notion of the utter contingency of all being, the incapacity of reason to set a barrier to the fantasms of imagination, to quite the opposite effect. Contingency came to be seen as the one inalienable characteristic of being. The custom which transformed constant conjunction into causal necessity became, by a consummate act of mockery which Maimonides seems to anticipate, the habit not of the divine but of the human mind. God, therefore, became irrelevant to the argument, and theism was at last explicitly divorced from the image of a world of beings which had no inherent stability. The bond between theism and such a world view, as Maimonides (like Hume) recognized, had never been a rigorous logical nexus at all.

In rethinking our current philosophical options then, the disposition given the problem by Maimonides remains of the highest relevance. If knowledge, truth, or understanding is a goal, then the arbitrary adoption of a perspective which systematically vitiates any inferences drawn from the evidence of the senses or claims to discredit the scientific method of generalization from particulars is a poor choice. The task of the thinker who, as Maimonides puts it, would possess the truth is not the construction of a prefabricated system of postulates designed systematically to overlook any intrinsic continuity which nature might present. For to do so can no more result in the glorification of God (as the Mutakallimun supposed) than it can in the aggrandizement of man. Rather the task for the serious thinker is to open his mind as widely as possible to any sort of rationality the universe may exhibit. Only by interpretation of such rationality as experience may encounter in nature can any attempt be made at knowledge, whether scientific or theological.

The attempt to found an interpretation of nature on theoretical investigation was in Maimonides' time best represented by the Aristotelian Neoplatonists, who claimed the title of philosopher. Organized science, logic, medicine, and metaphysics were, for the time, by and large their monopoly. Thus Maimonides' next step is to assay the extent of their success. But even before he begins, he gives us cause, by mentioning their doctrine of the eternity of the world, to wonder whether they can possibly succeed.

The Philosophers, it is true, were committed in principle to the rationality of the cosmos. For the concept of science as laid down by Aristotle implied the confrontation of the subjective rationality of the mind with the objective rationality of nature. But the very commitment of the followers of Aristotle to the rationality of nature expressed itself in a faith in the world's eternity which was as *a priori* and as religious as the faith of the Kalam in creation. The world's eternity for the Philosophers was the expression of its rationality; belief in creation, for them, was tantamount to admission of the inherent irrationality of being.

The juxtaposition of these two views, the claim of the Mutakallimun that creation is necessary since being is contingent and the claim of the Philosophers that if the truths of science are eternal then creation is absurd, may give one cause at first to wonder whether true philosophy is possible, or whether it is necessary to take refuge in the positivism of the skeptic or the fundamentalist. But had Maimonides presumed such to be a viable outcome universally, he would not have written a Guide for the Perplexed.

THE ARGUMENTS OF THE PHILOSOPHERS

Introduction

"Nous n'avons pas besoin de cette hypothèse"—"We have no need of that hypothesis." Few phrases could sum up more trenchantly the nature of the abyss dividing ancient from modern physics and cosmology than the famous words in which Laplace boasted of the possibility of a comprehensive theory of the natural world which made no use of the assumption of a divine existence. Between Democritus on the one hand and Mach and Reichenbach on the other, there were, of course, always physical theorists who construed physical phenomena as primary and self-sufficing. But until the rise of Newtonian physics and the celestial physics of Copernicus and Galileo, the center stage had been dominated by the physics and the strangely aprioristic astrophysics of Aristotle, in which no change, motion, or existence were possible without the constant act of God.

No difference is evident, when the matter is stated thus abstractly, between the Aristotelian world view and that of the Mutakallimun; and, to be sure, in upholding the existence, unity, and incorporeality of a Deity upon whose act the world as we know it depends, the two positions have more in common with each other than either has with

156

the Democritean treatment of the world as independent or even with the Epicurean exiling of the divine. But existence for the Aristotelian is not an infinitesimal indeterminacy, as for the Mutakallim, but a finite determinacy with a definite, indeed inalienable, claim upon being. God's act, then, upon which the world depends, cannot be seen as a free act of creation but must be viewed as the necessary and eternal imparting of order and animation which the world cannot lack.

How then does an immaterial Deity animate material nature?

Aristotle's answer invokes all he had learned from physics, psychology, and biology: If God is immaterial, then God is unmoved. Only a goal, an idea, a value, can set things into motion without itself being moved. And God, a self-sufficing Mind living the perfect life of self-contemplation, was for Aristotle such an ideal—not an abstract value but a real Highest Good, a Thought-Thinking-Itself, upon which all determinate being depended for its determinacy, its rationality, and thus (in the special sense peculiar to followers of Aristotle) its reality. What then was the mechanism by which the nonphysical was linked with the physical?

The stars, as Aristotle conceived them, set in their spheres, composed of a "fifth element," quintessence, the empyrean, revolving ceaselessly in their endless revolutions, were the medium, the almost immaterial matter, by which the divine activity (thought) was translated into natural activity (process, motion, change). These crystalline spheres, in which divinity merged into nature, were the limbs, organs, or "principal parts" of that organism which was the Aristotelian cosmos and was, in course of time, to be adopted by many medieval Christian thinkers. These spheres were to become the target of the rising naturalistic sciences and ultimately to be shattered by Galilean astronomy and Newtonian physics, which, together, could dispense with the spheres, set the planets (including earth) in orbit about the sun, and account for all the observed phenomena of the heavens by the same laws of motion and gravitation which were observed and analyzed on earth.

But long before Galileo lashed out against the Simplicius of his *Dialogues,* an earlier battle was under way against the divine heavens and the eternal earth. John Philoponus, a Christian theologian and physical theorist of the sixth century, had undertaken to refute the eternity of the cosmos and tear down the edifice of the Aristotelian heavens. His opponent, the historical Simplicius, was one of the last members of the ancient Academy, founded by Plato at Athens nine hundred years before and closed by Justinian in 529, in large part on account of the Neoplatonists' dogged defense of the Aristotelian cosmology. The Christians did not soon forget the ardor or the arguments of Philoponus (some of which were original and some of which were as old as Philo of Alexandria or older). With the coming of Islam, those arguments, translated into Arabic, were to be revived, first by Kindi in the ninth century and more forcefully by al-Ghazali in the eleventh.

A ware of these arguments, Maimonides knew that it was not necessary unquestioningly to accept the Aristotelian claims which made of nature a divinely animated machine and seemed to make of God the immaterial power cell of nature. Many Christian thinkers came so much under the Aristotelian-Neoplatonic spell that they could comprehend creation only in terms of the Greek doctrine of eternal emanation, and thus felt compelled to admit the world's eternity and treat creationism as mere allegory or revealed (but rationally incomprehensible) dogma. This led in the end to a radical breakdown of communications between natural science and Christian theology, the effects of which are still very visible today. Jewish philosophy, however, as represented by the achievement of Maimonides, was never wedded to the divine heavens of the Neoplatonic Aristotelians. For Maimonides remained consistently critical of the eternal empyrean of the Greek Philosophers, and it never became intellectually necessary for Jewish thinkers to succumb to the eternalist dogma of the irrationality of creation. Thus the discovery, with the rise of modern science, of the natural character of the forces governing bodies in the world did not *necessitate* in Jewish thinking a painful divorce between science and theology. Maimonides' theology already allowed for a subtler relationship between God and the world than was contemplated in either Falsafa [1] or Kalam. [2] But Maimonides believed it is not possi-

1. Philosophy (*Falsafa* in Arabic) was generally regarded in the age prior to Maimonides as having a more or less fixed set of results. The Philosophers (*Falasifa*) were followers of the fused tradition of Plato, Aristotle, and Plotinus (see the general introduction).
2. See Part Four.

ble for us to grasp that subtler relationship before we have profited from the wisdom and errors of the Philosophers.

Here then are the opening pages of part II of the *Moreh Nevukhim*.

From *Moreh Nevukhim* II

AUTHOR'S INTRODUCTION

In the name of the Lord, God of the universe [1]

Twenty-five premises are necessary to establish the existence of God and prove that He (glory be to His name) is neither a body nor a force in a body. All of these have been proved beyond doubt by Aristotle and other Peripatetics after him. One further premise we shall grant for the sake of the argument: the eternity of the world.

(1) The existence of an infinite magnitude is impossible.

(2) The simultaneous existence of an infinite number of finite magnitudes is impossible.

(3) An infinite series of causes and effects, even if they have no magnitude (for example, this mind's causing a second, the second a third, the third a fourth, and so *ad infinitum*) is also clearly impossible.

(4) Change takes place in four categories: in substance as coming-to-be and passing away, in quantity as growth and diminution, in quality as transformation (alteration), and in place as translocation. It is change of place which is called motion in a strict sense.

(5) Every motion is a change, a progress from potency to act.

(6) Motion may be essential (proper) or accidental, constrained, or partial—the latter being a special case of accidental motion. Essential motion is, for example, the motion of a body from one place to another. Accidental motion is found when, for example, it is said that the black of his body moved from one place to another.[2] Constrained motion is, for example, the upward motion of a rock impelled by some

1. Or God of eternity— The Hebrew *olam* means this as well. For Maimonides this invocation (Genesis 21:33) connotes the absolute universality or infinity of God derived in part I, a universality which terms like Eternal or Omnipresent suggest but cannot adequately convey.

2. ''Black'' as such may not be said not to move; but the black of this body may—not that motion is proper to it but on account of the motion of the body in which it subsists.

force; partial motion, the motion of a nail in a ship. For, when the ship moves, the nail too is said to be in motion.[3] Thus, when any composite is in motion as a whole, its parts are said to be in motion.[4]

(7) Whatever changes is divisible, and whatever moves, therefore, is divisible and necessarily a body. Whatever is indivisible does not move and, therefore, cannot be a body.

(8) Whatever moves *per accidens* must necessarily come to rest, for its motion is not its own (essential). Thus, accidental motion cannot continue forever.

(9) Every body which moves another body does so only by being itself in motion at the same time.

(10) Everything which is said to be in a body is either such that it subsists through the body, as accidents do, or such that the body subsists through it, as is the case with natural forms. Both of these are forces in a body.

(11) Certain things, which subsist through a body, are divided when the body is divided. They are divided *per accidens*—for example, colors and other characters which are spread throughout a body. Other things, which give substance to a body, are in no way divisible—soul, for example, or mind.

(12) Any force distributed through a body is finite, because the body is finite.

(13) No kind of change can be continuous except translocation of the cyclical type.[5]

(14) Translocation is objectively the primary and fundamental sort of motion. For coming-to-be and passing away presuppose transformation, and transformation presupposes the approach of the cause of alteration to the object altered—there being no growth and diminution before there has been coming-to-be and passing away.

(15) Time is an accident dependent upon motion and implying it. Neither can exist without the other. Motion takes place only in time,

3. It does not move by itself; relative to the ship it is at rest, but it moves through the motion of the ship.

4. *Per accidens,* since properly it is the whole which is in motion.

5. Linear motion must break continuity when it reaches the bounds of a finite universe (see premise 1). Thus it is argued that only cyclical motion can continue indefinitely without interruption.

and time is unintelligible without motion. Whatever is not subject to motion does not exist in time.

(16) Nothing which is not a body can be subject intelligibly to enumeration, unless it is a force in a body, such forces being enumerable through the arithmetic of their matter or substrates. Disembodied things, then, being neither bodies nor forces in bodies, can in no way be thought of as having number, unless as cause and effect.

(17) All things in motion necessarily have some mover, either external, as a stone which is moved by a hand, or internal, as an animal's body composed of that which animates and that which is animated. Thus, when it dies and its mover, the soul, no longer exists in it, that which was animated, the body, for a while remains as it was, only it no longer moves as it did. It is because the mover is hidden and not evident to the senses that animals are presumed to move without a mover; and everything moved by an internal mover is said to move "automatically." This means that the force moving that in it which moves essentially is found throughout it.[6]

(18) Whatever proceeds from potency to act has something necessarily other than and external to itself to cause it so to proceed. For if this cause were internal, there would be nothing to hold back what was potential for any length of time—it would be actual already. If the cause of actualization were internal and something had been restraining it and was removed, then surely what removed this restraint would be the actualizing cause. You must understand this.

(19) Whatever has a cause for its existence exists contingently in terms of its own nature. For if its causes are present, it exists; if they are not present, do not exist, or are not in the proper relation to bring about its existence, it does not.

(20) Whatever exists necessarily, in and through itself, has no cause of any sort for its existence.

(21) Anything composed of two principles necessarily has that composition as a cause of its existence as it is. It is not existent necessarily, in and through itself, for its existence depends upon that of its two elements and upon their being conjoined.

(22) Every body is compounded of two principles necessarily and

6. Not that it has none.

necessarily bears accidents. The two principles through which it sub-sists are matter and form; the accidents adventitious to it are quantity, shape, and position.

(23) Whatever is potential or has any contingency in its being might, at some particular time, not exist.

(24) Whatever is potentially a certain thing must have matter, for potentiality is always in matter.

(25) The individual substance is compounded of matter and form and must have a maker, *i.e.*, some mover to prepare the substrate to receive the form. This is the proximate cause which predisposes the matter of a particular individual. Here an investigation of motion, mover, and that which is in motion is called for, but what needs to be cleared up is fully cleared up.[7] In Aristotle's words: "Matter does not move itself" [*Metaphysics* lambda 6. 1071^b. 29]. This, then, is the key premise leading to the search for a Prime Mover.

. . . To the foregoing premises, I shall add one more, affirming that the world must be eternal. Aristotle held this to be true and to be the view most worthy of belief; so we may grant it to him stipulatively in order to make clear the point we have set out to clarify. Aristotle's claim is that:

(26) Time and motion always have been and always will be actually existent. It follows necessarily, in his view, that there must exist a body forever actually in motion.[8] This is the "fifth body," on account of which he says that the heavens are subject neither to genesis nor to corruption, since motion in his view neither comes to be nor passes away. For, he argues, every motion is preceded by another motion necessarily, either of its own kind or of some other kind. Someone who supposes that the local motion of animals is preceded by no other motion is mistaken, for the causes of such motion can be traced back to the factors which called it forth, whether (*a*) a shift in biochemical equilibrium [9] giving rise to a desire to seek something agreeable or

7. See *Physics* VIII:4. Aristotle argues that even the falling of heavy objects could not be due to themselves unless they were somehow alive. It is far from certain that every-thing in this regard which requires to be cleared up is cleared up. Aristotle's argument rests on the necessity of a conceptual differentiation between the subject and the cause of motion.

8. And motion to be continuous must be cyclical (premise 13).

9. Such as that which induces hunger or discomfort.

avoid something disagreeable, or (b) the presentation of some image to the imagination, or (c) perception. It must be moved by one of these three causes, each of which presupposes prior motions. In the same way he argues that whatever happens presupposes time as a condition of its occurrence. This corroborates his premise in several ways.[10] In accordance with this premise, a finite moving object will traverse a finite course an infinite number of times, returning again and again over the same ground. This is impossible except by cyclical motion (as demonstrated in premise 13). It follows, accordingly, that there must be a successive [rather than simultaneous] infinity.[11]

This [26] is the premise Aristotle constantly endeavors to establish. But, as far as I can see, he never states categorically that his arguments in its behalf amount to proof; rather it seems to him to be the most credible, the most probable hypothesis. His followers and commentators, on the other hand, do claim it to be necessary rather than contingent and affirm it to have been demonstrated.

The ambition of every Mutakallim is to prove this is impossible. They say, "It is inconceivable how an infinite succession of events might occur." Their argument rests on what they take to be rational, a priori.[12] To me, it seems that this premise [26] is possible—neither necessary as the Aristotelian commentators claim, nor impossible as the Mutakallimun purport.[13] . . . Having stated these premises and granted them for the sake of the argument, I shall undertake to explain what follows from them.

MOREH NEVUKHIM II:1
(i) It follows according to 25 that there is a mover which moves the matter of this object which is subject to coming-to-be and passing away, allowing it to accept forms. When it is asked what sets in motion this proximate cause of motion, it follows necessarily that it must have some further mover, either of the same kind or of some other.

10. For example, if time presupposes a system of bodies in motion (premise 15), then the eternity of time implies the eternity of such a system.
11. Namely, the infinity of the revolutions of the spheres.
12. The impossibility of any sort of infinity (Kalam premise 11).
13. Its contradictory then, the doctrine of creation, would also be neither necessary nor impossible—and hence neither demonstrably true nor demonstrably false.

(For motion takes place with respect to four categories, all four sorts being called motion in the broad sense, as stated in 4.) This series cannot extend forever (as we remarked in 3). Thus we discover that every motion must be traced back to that of the fifth body and no further.[1] From this motion that of every mover or predisposer stems and derives.

The sphere's motion is one of translocation, which is the primary sort of motion, as stated in 14. Every other translocation may be traced back to the motion of the sphere. Say, for example, that this rock was set in motion by a stick, the stick by a hand, the hand by tendons, the tendons by muscles, the muscles by nerves, and the nerves by the innate body heat. Now this body heat was set in motion by the form within it, which is, no doubt, its "prime mover." What causes this original cause of motion to move is, for example, a notion, perhaps of positioning the rock with the stick into a hole to plug it up and prevent the wind from blowing through onto the hand's owner. What sets the wind in motion and causes it to blow is the motion of the sphere. In like manner, you will find, every cause of coming-to-be and passing away leads ultimately to the motion of the sphere. Arriving finally at this sphere in motion, we find its motion too must have a cause (as posited in 17) either internal to it or outside it—a necessary disjunction. If external, it must be either a body or not a body. But were it not a body, it could not be said to be "external"; rather, it would be called disembodied, for things other than bodies can only loosely be said to be "outside" a body. But if its mover (i.e., the sphere's) is in it, it must be either a force diffused throughout its whole body and divisible when it is divided, as heat in flame, or a force indivisible within it, like a soul or mind (as premised in 10). Thus, the mover of the sphere must be one of the following: (a) another body external to it, (b) something disembodied, (c) a force diffused through it, or (d) an indivisible force. But a—that it be moved by another body external to it—is impossible, as I shall outline: a body would move at the same time as that which it moves (as stated in 9).

1. Contemporary readers might be aided if they think of the role of the celestial motion as analogous to the motion in the orbits of a Bohr atom, all natural processes being traceable in theory to this primary motion. The pre-Einsteinian atom was a quantitative *and causal* ultimate in much the way that the pre-Newtonian spheres were.

This "sixth" body too then would have to be in motion to impart motion, and would, therefore, require a seventh body to move it, and this too would be in motion. The existence of an infinite number of bodies would thus be implied, and only then would the sphere come into motion. But this is impossible, as 2 sets forth.

But *c* too—that it be moved by a force diffused through it—is impossible. For the sphere is a body and hence finite necessarily (as stated in 1). Any force diffused within it, then, must be finite as well (12), for such a force would be divided when its body was divided (11).[2] Thus, it could not remain in motion to infinity (as posited in 26).

And *d*—that the sphere be moved by a force within it which is indivisible like the soul of a man within him—is impossible as well, if this mover alone is to be the cause of ceaseless motion, even if it is indivisible. To explain: if this were the first mover, it would be moved *per accidens* (as stated in 6). Here I shall add an explanation: when a man, for example, is moved by his soul (*i.e.,* his form) to go upstairs, his body is what is moved properly or essentially; his soul is the prime mover essentially, but accidentally, it too is moved, for with the motion of the body upstairs, the soul which is in the body moves upstairs as well. When the soul stops causing motion, the body, which is moved, comes to rest, but when the body comes to rest, the accidental motion which had affected the soul too must end. But everything which is in motion *per accidens* must necessarily come to rest (8); and if it does, so will that which it moves. Thus, even this "prime" mover must have some cause of its motion beyond the whole complex of mover and moved, such that when it is present to originate motion, prime movers within this complex set in motion those things they move and when it is not, they do not. This is the reason why the bodies of animals are not ceaselessly in motion, even though every one of them contains an indivisible prime mover—because their movers are not constantly in motion of themselves (essentially), but rather the stimuli which set them in motion are things external to them, either seeking the agreeable or avoiding the disagreeable, or picturing (or conceiving, for those which have conception) and then being set in

2. And any quantity proportionate to a finite quantity is itself finite.

motion. What sets them in motion [3] is moved *per accidens* itself and therefore necessarily comes to rest, as we have seen. If the mover of the sphere were within it in this manner, then it could not possibly remain in motion eternally. Whereas, if this motion is constant and eternal, as our opponent claims (and this is possible as stated in 13), it follows necessarily, by process of elimination according to this theory, that the first cause of the motion of the sphere must be of type *b*—*i.e.,* disembodied and not dependent on the sphere.

In this way it is demonstrated that if the motion of the first sphere is eternal and everlasting, then its mover cannot be a body nor any sort of force in a body. Thus, this mover is not in motion, essentially or *per accidens*. It is, therefore, not subject to division or change (premises 7 and 5). This is the Deity,[4] glory be to His name, *i.e.,* the First Cause of the motion of the sphere. He cannot be two or more since the notion of plurality is inapplicable to disembodied beings except inasmuch as one is cause of another (premise 16). It is clear already that He is not subject to time because of the impossibility of motion on His part (premise 15).

This line of reasoning, then, has led to demonstrations that it is impossible for the sphere to move everlastingly of its own accord, that the ultimate cause of its motion is neither a body nor a force in a body, and that He is one and invariant, since His existence is not timebound. These are the three conclusions which were demonstrated by the best of the Philosophers.

* * *

(iii) A third avenue of the Philosophers' reasoning on this subject is derivable from discussions Aristotle undertook with another end in view. The argument proceeds as follows: Indubitably, some things must exist, *viz.,* the objects of sense perception. Now either nothing is subject to coming-to-be and passing away, or everything is, or some things are and others are not; this is a necessary disjunction. The first alternative is plainly impossible, for we observe many things subject to generation and decay. The second is impossible as well, for the reason that if everything were subject to coming-to-be and passing

---

3. To wit, the soul.
4. For, not being subject to division or change, the Prime Mover is a Necessary Being, and therefore divine, as we learned in part I.

away, then all beings, each and every one of them, might possibly be destroyed. But what is possible for a species, as you have learned, must necessarily occur.[5] It follows that all existence must necessarily be destroyed. But if this had happened, nothing would exist, for nothing would remain of existence. Hence, nothing would exist at all. But we observe that things do exist—we exist. It follows necessarily, then, according to this line of reasoning, that there are existents subject to coming-to-be and passing away, such as we observe, and that there is some existent as well which is not subject to coming-to-be and passing away. Now this being which is subject neither to generation nor to destruction cannot possibly not exist. Its existence is necessary, not contingent. Regarding its necessary existence, there are two possibilities, he says: it might exist necessarily either on its own account (essentially) or on account of its cause—such that its existence or nonexistence was contingent in terms of its own nature but necessary with reference to its cause. In that case, its cause would be what exists necessarily (premise 19). Thus, it is demonstrated that there must be a being which exists necessarily in and through itself and without which nothing (whether subject to coming-to-be and passing away or not) would exist at all—if anything at all exists in the manner Aristotle alleges, *i.e.,* anything subject neither to coming-to-be nor to passing away on account of its being the effect of a necessarily existent cause.

This demonstration is indubitable, irrefutable, and irrefragable to anyone not ignorant of the apodictic method.[6] We continue. Whatever exists necessarily through itself must have no cause of its existence (premise 20) and will have in it no plurality of elements whatever (premise 21). It therefore cannot be a body nor a force in a body (premise 22). Thus, following this line of reasoning, it is demonstrated that there is a being which exists necessarily, of itself; that its existence is uncaused; that it uncompounded; that it is, therefore, not a body or a force in a body. This is the Deity, glory be to His name.

It can easily be proved, likewise, that such necessary, self-sufficient

5. Aristotle assumes that if what is possible for a species never occurs, something must have prevented it—*i.e.,* it must have been impossible. This assumption cannot be true unless 26 is true as well.
6. That is, if its premises be granted.

existence cannot belong to two beings. For the species "necessary existent" would be a separate principle over and above the being of either. Thus, neither of the two would be necessarily existent through itself alone—either would be necessarily existent through that principle, the species-concept of necessary existents, represented by both. It may be shown in a number of ways that no sort of duality—no isomorphism and no oppositeness—can be applied validly to a necessarily existent being, on account of its absolute simplicity and perfection (which leaves over nothing to its kind beyond what it comprehends in its own being) and its having no cause of any sort. It therefore has no peer whatever.

(iv) A fourth line of argument, also belonging to the Philosophers, is this: We constantly see things proceeding from potency to realization, as is well known. But whatever so proceeds from potency to act must have some cause external to it to make it do so (premise 18). This cause itself, obviously, was such a cause originally only *in potentia;* subsequently, it became such actually. The cause of its having been only potential at the start might be either that something within it restrained it or that it was not yet in the proper relation to that which it was to bring to realization. In either case, there must be some cause of the progress from potency to act or of the removal of the obstacle; and the same must be said regarding this cause as well. This cannot go on *ad infinitum;* the series must end at a cause of the realization of potential existing forever in the same state, having no potency whatever, *i.e.,* such that nothing within it, in its being, is potential. For if there were any contingency in its being, then it might not exist (premise 23). It cannot possibly have matter, but must be disembodied (premise 24). The disembodied being which has no potentiality whatever in its essence but exists through itself is the Deity. It has been demonstrated that He is not a body; thus He is one (premise 16).

All of these are their methods of demonstrating the existence of one God who is neither a body nor a force in a body while accepting the eternity of the world.

(*a*) There is another proof of incorporeality and unity as follows: If there were two gods, it would follow necessarily that they must have something in common, in virtue of which both are gods; and both necessarily would have to have some other aspect to distinguish them as two.[7] But if each has some character which the other lacks, then both are composite beings, and neither can be a first cause nor an existent necessary through itself; both would require causes (as premise 19 makes clear). But if the distinguishing characteristic is found in only one of them, then the "god" composed of two principles is not an existent necessary of itself.

(b) Another argument in behalf of monotheism: It has been demonstrated that all existence is like one individual with parts articulated one to the next, and that the energies transmitted from the sphere pervade the matter below and work it into form. It is not consistent with these facts that there be one God isolated in one part of reality and a second isolated in another. For the two parts are joined together. The only alternative would be for one god to work at one time and the other at another, unless they always worked together, so that nothing could be done except by both of them. But for them to act at different times is impossible for several reasons: For if the time when one operated were open to the other, what would be the cause of one's working then and the other's not? But if the time of one's action were not available to the other, there would have to be a cause governing these possibilities and impossibilities. Time itself is indifferent in this regard, and the object of the activity would be the same in either case, a single integrated being, as we have seen. Moreover, both these "gods" would thus become subject to time, for their world would be time-bound; and each of them, further, would proceed from potency to act in the course of acting, and would thus require some actualizing cause. Finally, each would have some contingency in its being.[8]

On the other hand, their doing everything always together, neither acting without the other, would be absurd as well, as I shall relate: for any whole which cannot act without the cooperation of its entirety cannot be said to have any part which acts of its own accord, and none of its parts can be a first cause of anything; the first cause would be the whole ensemble. It has been demonstrated that a necessary existent necessarily has no cause and also that when a composite whole acts, it

7. Maimonides' philosophers assume the identity of indiscernibles.
8. Although superficially resembling the Kalam "interference" argument, (method 2), this argument is strengthened by the initial assumption of the organic unity and continuity of the cosmos, which is of course unavailable to the Mutakallimun.

requires some further cause to unify it. If this unifying cause, without which it cannot act, is one, then that, of course, is God, whereas if it is a composite itself, then it requires yet another unifying cause. Ultimately, the series must end at a being who is one, the cause of this reality which is one, whether He creates it out of nothing or renders it necessary.[9]

This should make it clear to you, then, that the unity of existence argues the unity of God.

(c) A final argument for incorporeality: Every body is composite (premise 22), and every compound must have a maker to bring about the presence of its form in its matter. Obviously, any body is divisible and has dimensions; that is, of course, how it may serve as a substrate for accidents. Thus, a body is not one in terms of divisibility nor in terms of compositeness—for it is spoken of as two, since any body becomes a particular body only on account of some character superadded to its mere being a body.[10] Thus, it has two aspects, necessarily. But it has been demonstrated that a necessary existent cannot be composite in any way.

Having set out these proofs, I shall now undertake to summarize our own approach, as promised.

Analysis

There is a notable change in Maimonides' style when he turns from the arguments of the Mutakallimun to those of the Philosophers. The propositions are no longer hypothetical but categorical. The terms are governed by universal quantifiers and given technical definitions to which appeal is made when inferences are drawn. The arguments are no longer dialectical but syllogistic. This difference is not merely one of style or even of level of rigor; rather it reflects a difference of content and attitude. The Kalam is a hypothetical, dialectical philosophy;

9. *I.e.*, Maimonides accepts this demonstration as valid both on creationist and eternalist assumptions.

10. *I.e.*, one can always distinguish the particularity of a body (its matter) from its specific character (its form).

it does not deal with the nature of the world as it really is but with what may be said to follow on the basis of a given set of assumptions. The hypothetical form of argument was well suited to Kalam in that it affords ample scope to the imaginative method of Kalam-style thinking. Terms were made opaque to analysis by the propositional calculus (which takes sentences rather than words as the ultimate logical counters). There was no proposition which could not be entertained, no conclusion which could not be questioned. Thus philosophy was transformed by the conceptual radicals of the Kalam into a ceaseless dialectic in which no given was secure, no outcome established.

Syllogistic was equally well suited to the method and outlook of the Philosophers. Their premises were to be unquestionable; their arguments, as Maimonides remarks, indubitable; their conclusions, irrefragable. Thus, they required syllogistic. For Falsafa took as its scope the entire universe—"being as such," as Aristotle put it. Premises must be categorical and universal if categorical and universal conclusions are to be drawn. A propositional calculus opened far too wide a realm of possibility. For not everything which could be imagined was admissible to the realm of possibility; and the syllogism, in conjunction with empirical science, was to be a powerful instrument in defining the limits of that realm far more stringently than the *a priori* imagination could do. Thus, the difference in methods between Falsafa and Kalam reflects far more than a difference in argumentative approach; it reflects a difference in world views as well.

Falsafa is a rigorous philosophy, apodictic, as Maimonides puts it. Given its premises, its conclusions follow with all the force and clarity of logic itself. It is not, like Kalam, a radical philosophy. The Aristotelian, unlike the Mutakallim, does not conceive as a philosophical desideratum the attempt to rethink to the very foundations the entire character of being. Perhaps this difference reflects a fundamental conservatism on the part of the Aristotelians vis-à-vis the Mutakallimun. It certainly does express a profound difference in metaphysical outlook, a watershed between two divergent views with respect to which Maimonides and his perplexed reader are endeavoring to situate themselves. For the Mutakallim's view (reflected in his logic, which is hypothetical) is of the world's utter contingency. The Muslim

Aristotelian's view (reflected in his logic, which is categorical) is of the world's eternity—the fundamental givenness, the inalienability of being.[1]

Were it possible for Maimonides or his reader to presume that the Kalam view was *the* religious view and that the Aristotelian view was somehow irreligious, then perhaps Aristotelianism, like Epicureanism, might somehow have been brushed aside. But the Aristotelian Neoplatonists had never let their monotheist opponents forget that eternalism was as seriously religious an option as creationism—more serious, if the Philosophers be taken at their word, and more fitting to be believed, as Proclus put it, in words which Maimonides echoes, not only of the world, but also of the Deity. Indeed (and this is the source of all the difficulty), for the Greeks the world was a deity. The unity, the stability, above all the eternity of Aristotelian being were reflections of its essential divinity. So, too, was the inherent rationality of being which made possible the Aristotelian faith in reason.[2] And rationality, stability, unity, and eternity were inextricably bound up, in the minds of Aristotelians, with divinity. A universe which came into being would have been a manifest breach of the cosmic rhythm of natural law, an affront to the ceaseless continuity of process and time which were expressions of the divine nature of the world. How then were Maimonides and his reader who was perplexed to respond to the challenge—above all the religious challenge—of Aristotelian philosophy, especially when they, too, had been infected with the love of reason and accepted the Greek notion (which was not only Greek) that order, stability, and rationality were the marks of the divine in the world.

The answer was clear to Maimonides even as he stated the problem. The crux of the Philosophers' arguments for the existence, unity, and

1. It is interesting to observe that the revival of tentative philosophy and a contingency-oriented worldview in modern times has not only fostered a return to the imaginative criterion but also rendered the syllogism once again unfashionable.

2. To understand, for Aristotle, is to discover rationality; and this, in turn, very often is to uncover the grounds of necessity in things. To understand in the sciences is to discover the patterns, materials, purposes, and effective causes which make it necessary for things to be the way they are; the implication seems to be that to understand in metaphysics (the science of being as such) is to discover what makes being such that it must be.

incorporeality of God (and thus the crux of their theology) was premise 26, the eternity of the world. All their arguments pivot around this premise just as all the arguments of the Mutakallimun pivot around the utter contingency of finite being. For what the Philosophers are saying, in abstraction from the rigorously syllogistic language in which Maimonides articulates their argument, is simply this: the world is constantly changing and is inadequate in itself to cause the changes which occur within it. For constant change is continuous and continuous change is eternal—since any first change must have a "from which," and therefore must be preceded by some prior change. But to bring about eternal change requires an eternal mover who transcends the entire system of change (and thus transcends time and matter as well), since no physical thing could originate a motion without itself being moved either properly (e.g., if it were a body) or accidentally (e.g., if it were a soul). But proper motion would require a prior cause of motion, and accidental motion cannot go on forever. Thus, the entire argument, the entire Aristotelian theology, which conceives of God as a supreme good, fountainhead of an inherent rationality which animates being in a nonphysical way (functioning not as a motor but as a goal), depends upon the assumption of the eternity of motion in a moving world.

Now clearly the universe has either existed forever or it has come into being. This, as the Philosophers would say, is a necessary disjunction. But it does not follow that Maimonides or his disciple must choose between the God of Aristotle and the God of the Kalam. For it was not the necessary disjunction between eternity and genesis upon which the polarity between the Falasifa and the Mutakallimun was founded. Rather, the utter dependence of the world upon God presumed in the theology of the Kalam required the necessary contingency of finite being. Likewise, the ever-presentness of the Aristotelian God as a rational principle, an inalienable goal, ceaselessly animating all reality, required of the world necessary eternity.

The avenue of Maimonides' response to the apparent dilemma between eternalism and creationism, then, lies open: neither position is necessary; both are possible. It follows that no merely deductive argument can convey any conclusive outcome regarding the issue which separates the eternalists from the creationists. But this, in turn, has the welcome effect of opening a more empirical approach to theology than either the Mutakallimun or the Philosophers had been accustomed to use. Maimonides makes the question of creation contingent and subject to probabilistic speculation, but he does not thereby render God somehow a contingent being, as many ancient and some modern authors would have supposed. For, as Maimonides points out, contingency in our knowledge is quite a different matter from contingency in reality.

GOD, CREATION, AND ETERNITY
—THE POSITION OF MAIMONIDES

Introduction

The existence of God is demonstrable, Maimonides believes, whether or not the world has come to be. Thus it is possible for Maimonides at this point to demonstrate the existence of God. But it is the nature, not the existence, of God which is problematic for Maimonides and his reader. All thinkers but the last few exponents of the Epicurean position recognized that there was a plan in nature—hence that there was a deity. The issue was what sort of deity, what sort of plan? Was God free or was He bound by the law of His own nature? Was He an active and originative reality or merely a kind of concrete principle? In resolving these questions the issue between creation and eternity was critical.

Hence it is not surprising that Maimonides hastens past his demonstration of the existence of God (in *Moreh* II:2) to consider what was for him the far more problematic issue of creation versus eternity, upon which, in Maimonides' view, the possibility of Mosaic theism itself depended. It is natural too that, in introducing his argument for the existence of God, he should set out from the disjunction between creation and eternity—not of the world as a whole, for the Philoso-

175

phers were prepared to concede that the elements of sublunary nature, since they are subject to constant alteration, are not capable of eternal (*i.e.*, continuous) motion—but rather of the "fifth substance," that of the heavens, which according to Aristotle does not undergo alteration and which the Aristotelians claimed their master had proved ungenerated and indestructible.

There is perhaps no issue in the entire Peripatetic repertoire on which modern thinkers find Aristotle more disappointing than they do on that of "celestial mechanics." Awed by the heavenly array, Aristotle postulated that here surely the eternal rationality of the divine plan had been made visible. In the heavenly bodies, giant crystalline spheres, as he conceived them, revolving ceaselessly through their courses, he found the eternal clock which his analysis of motion "required" to exist.

It was not, of course, the apriorism of Aristotle's celestial mechanics which disturbed the monotheists. Nor did it trouble them that Aristotle had mingled science with theology. What they reacted to, rather, was the character of the theology which Aristotle read into his celestial physics. For they conceived the world to be dependent not merely upon the divine thought for its perfection but upon divine will for its existence and determinacy. Al-Ghazali had gone so far as to deny that theism was possible at all on the eternalist assumptions, arguing that if God had made no difference to the world it cannot be inferred that He exists.

This extreme conclusion, that eternalism and theism are incompatible, is, as we have just seen, explicitly rejected by Maimonides. The Greek notion of God as the Prime Mover of a never-ending process is not inconceivable in Maimonides' view, but the deity whose existence can be demonstrated on the assumption that the world is eternal is not the God of Abraham, of Isaac, and of Jacob. It is not the Philosophers' claim to theism which is to be rejected, but rather the outcome of their theology.

For the existence of God (this time the Jewish God) can be demonstrated on creationist assumptions. It is not the case, as Aristotle had represented, that the genesis of the universe is irrational or absurd. And the God of Genesis—that is, the God of Creation (of *bereshit*)—

will make a difference to the existence and character of the world.
Maimonides' object is to show that only through creation can sense
be made of the theological notions of the divine act and the divine determination. But to do so he must restore creation as a live option to
the monotheist overawed by the arguments of the Philosophers against
it. First he must demonstrate that creation is not impossible, that eternity is not established. Then he must show the probability (not necessity—for that position would be to fall into the error of the Mutakallimun) of the Mosaic hypothesis, "In the beginning God created heaven
and earth. . . ."

From *Moreh Nevukhim* II

MOREH NEVUKHIM II:2
This "fifth body," [1] the sphere, must either be subject to genesis and
destruction or not so subject. Its motion too must either be subject or
(as our opponent claims) not subject to coming-to-be and passing
away. Now if the sphere is such that it did come into being, then what
brought it into being is the Deity (glory to His name). This is obvious
a priori, since anything which comes into being out of nothing must
have something to bring it into being: it is logically impossible for it to
bring itself into being. [2] If, on the other hand, the sphere always has
been and always will be as it is, moving continuously, everlastingly,
then the premises already stated imply that the cause of its everlasting
motion be neither a body nor a force in a body, *i.e.,* that it be God
(glory to His name).

Thus you may recognize that the existence of the Deity (an uncaused, necessarily existent being with no contingency in His being) is
demonstrable conclusively and with certainty, whether the world came
into being out of nothing or not. His unity and incorporeality are
equally demonstrable, as already set forth. For the proof of His unity
and incorporeality holds whether the world came into being *de novo* or
not, as we made clear in discussing method iii of the Philosophers

1. See *Moreh* II, introduction, premise 26.
2. But only an incorporeal being can have existed prior to the entire natural order.

and in explaining their arguments in favor of incorporeality and unity.[3] . . .

MOREH NEVUKHIM II:13

Among those who believe that God exists, there are three views regarding the eternity of the world as opposed to its genesis:

(1) The view of all who believe in the Torah of Moses our Teacher, peace upon him, is that the entire universe—*i.e.,* all that exists except God—was brought into being by God out of absolute and utter nothingness; that God alone existed and no other thing, neither angel nor sphere nor what the sphere contains, whereupon God gave existence to all these beings, with the natures that they have, by an act of will, not making them out of anything else; that time itself was one of the things created, since time is dependent upon motion and motion is an accident of that which moves, the last itself having been created and originally not having existed. Thus they interpret one's saying that God existed before He created the world, where the word "existed" seems to indicate a time, and all such suggestions of God's having existed before the creation for an infinite duration, as mental or imaginative superpositions of the concept of time where there was in fact no time. . . .

This is one view, a principle of the Mosaic religion second only to monotheism in its importance—may you entertain no other. Our forefather Abraham, peace upon him, first proclaimed this view, to which he had been led by reason, when he issued his call in the name of the Lord, God of the universe.[1] He stated this view explicitly when he said, "Creator of heaven and earth" [Genesis 14:22].

(2) The view of all the philosophers whose words I have seen or of whom I have heard report is that God's bringing something into being from nothing is absurd.[2] Nor do they hold it possible for God to reduce something to nothing. . . . The purport of their suasion here is that just as there is no impotence on God's part in His being unable to bring about impossibilities (impossibility having a fixed nature and not

3. See arguments *a, b, c* at the end of II:1.
1. Genesis 21:33, the invocation chosen by Maimonides for each of the three parts of the *Moreh.*
2. Of the principal Muslim Falasifa, Kindi (d. *ca.* 866) was alone in denying this view.

being the work of any maker or outcome of any cause and being therefore immutable), so there is no weakness on His part in being unable to bring into being something out of nothing. For this is just another impossibility.

They believe, therefore, that there is a certain matter which exists eternally, like the Deity, neither capable of existing without the other. They do not believe that it is at His level of existence; rather He is the cause of its existence.[3] To Him it is, as it were, a potter's clay or a smith's iron, and He creates in it what He pleases—now a heaven and earth, now something else.

Proponents of this view believe that the heavens are subject to generation and corruption, but not out of or into nothing. Rather, just as individual animals come to be from (and pass away into) matter which already (or still) exists, so the heavens come to be and pass away like any sublunary being. . . . Plato himself held this belief, as Aristotle reports in *Physics* [VIII:1. 251^b. 17ff.]: he, Plato, believed the heavens were subject to genesis and destruction. You will find this plainly stated in *Timaeus*. But he did not believe as we do (as some suppose who do not think critically or analyze ideas carefully . . .) for we believe that the heavens came into being not out of anything but out of nothing at all, while he believes that they developed out of something. This then is the second view.

(3) The view of Aristotle (and his followers and commentators) is the same as the above: nothing material can be brought into existence except from the matter proper to it. But to this he adds that the heavens are not subject to genesis or destruction at all.

His view in a nutshell is that being always has been and always will be as it is. What is stable and not subject to coming-to-be and passing away, *i.e.,* the heavens, will ever remain so; time and motion are constant and eternal, neither coming into being nor passing away. What does come to be and pass away, *i.e.,* what is beneath the sphere of the moon, will always do so. Thus prime matter *per se* does not come to be or pass away but merely exchanges forms, putting off one and putting on another. The entire system, celestial and subcelestial, cannot be subverted or destroyed; nothing new can be created which is not in

3. Inasmuch as He gives it its specific determination as a this or a that.

accordance with the established pattern and precedent of nature.

Although he does not state it in his text, the implication is that it is impossible in his view for God to alter His will or originate a volition.[4] All that exists is given such being as it has by God's will, but not made out of nothing. It is as impossible for God to change His will or originate a volition, according to this notion, as it is for Him to change His essence or go out of existence. It follows that all being always was and always will be as it is now.

This, then, in brief is the substance of the views on this subject of those for whom the existence of a deity of this world is demonstrated. As for those who do not know that God exists (glory and majesty to Him) but suppose that things come into being and pass away by chance conjoinings and disjoinings without any Provider of order or control (*viz.*, Epicurus and his followers and others of like mind cited by Alexander of Aphrodisias), there is no value in our discussing these schools, for the existence of the Deity has already been proved [*Moreh* II:2], and there is no benefit in discussing the views of those who founded their thought on opinions the contradictory of which has been demonstrated. There is likewise no benefit to be gained by our attempting to verify the second view, the doctrine of those who hold the generation and destructibility of the heavens, for they too are eternalists. From our point of view there is no difference between holding that the heavens came into being, necessarily out of something, and may pass away, necessarily into something, and Aristotle's belief that they are ungenerated and indestructible. For the intent of all followers of the religion of Moses and Abraham and those who live in their tradition is exclusively the belief that nothing is eternal in any way besides God,[5] that belief in divine creation of being out of nothing is not impossible, but may indeed be compelling as some thinkers have maintained. . . .

MOREH NEVUKHIM II:14

. . . I shall consider no discussions, therefore, but those of Aristotle. His are the ideas which merit study, and if a sound rebuttal or critique

4. An implication pressed by the Neoplatonic commentators.
5. Maimonides thus rejects attempts by certain monotheistic thinkers to "compromise" by reinterpreting creation as a fashioning of the world out of pre-existent matter.

of them can be made on any point, that rebuttal or critique will be all the more effective against other opponents of the cornerstones of the Law.

I say, then:

(a) Aristotle claims that motion neither comes to be nor passes away, i.e., motion in an absolute sense.[1] He argues: assuming motion came into being, any such event is preceded by motion, progress from potency to act and realization, which would imply that motion already existed, the motion is eternal or the chain extends to infinity. Arguing on the same basis, he claims that time does not come to be or pass away. Time is dependent on motion and thus requires it. There is no motion without time; and time is unintelligible without motion, as is demonstrated. This is one of the ways in which he proves the eternity of the world.[2]

(b) A second approach of his is to say that the prime matter common to the four elements does not come to be or pass away, since if it did there would have to be some matter in which it might be realized. But this would imply that prime matter would have form, for that is what "realization" means. But prime matter, ex hypothesi, has no form. Necessarily, then, it cannot come to be from anything. It must be everlasting. This too implies the eternity of the world.

(c) A third approach of his is to assert that there is no contrariety whatever in the matter of the sphere, since rotation has no opposite,[3] as has been made apparent, and only rectilinear motion is subject to opposition, as has been demonstrated. Whatever corrupts does so only on account of contrariety; and since the sphere has none within it, it cannot be destroyed. But what cannot be destroyed cannot have been generated.[4] This too implies the eternity of the world, Q.E.D.

1. Particular motions may begin and cease, but some form of motion must always take place.
2. Time must be eternal, Aristotle argues, because the notions of a time before or after time are self-contradictory. But, as we have seen, time, as a function of motion, presupposes a system of (eternally) moving bodies—the cosmos.
3. The monotheist proponents of creation were not slow to note that rotation may occur in two senses; and Philoponus argued at length on empirical grounds against the homogeneity of the heavens.
4. The inference, for the Aristotelian, was a natural one: either, being was such that it must exist or it was not.

(d) A fourth approach: Aristotle says that whatever comes about or changes might have done so previously. . . . His recent followers support the eternity of the world with this premise. They argue that the coming-to-be of the world, prior to its occurrence must have been either possible, necessary, or impossible. If necessary, it would have to exist already; if impossible, it would never come to exist; if possible, what was the substrate of this possibility? [5] For surely, the possibility must subsist in some real subject. . . .

There are other methods too, stated by those who came after Aristotle but derived from his philosophy, in which the eternity of the world is established from the point of view of the Deity (glory to His name).

(e) One of these is that they say that if God created the world *ex nihilo*, then prior to creation God was active only potentially; on creating He became active in fact. Thus God progressed from potency to act. He must then contain some contingency and have, moreover, some cause to advance Him from potency to act.

Like the previous objection, this problem is fraught with difficulties. Its resolution and the discovery of the mystery it conceals merit the serious thought of every intelligent mind.

(f) In another approach, they say that a doer acts or fails to act at a given time solely on account of obstacles or motives affecting him either internally or externally: impediments may prevent the accomplishment of his wishes, and his own drives may arouse in him volitions he would not otherwise have had. But the Creator [6] has no drives to alter His will and no obstacles or impediments to interfere or disappear. Thus there is no basis for His being active at one time and not another. His work rather is continuous, and always actual, like His existence.

(g) They argue furthermore that His works (exalted be He) are consummately perfect, containing no excess, deficiency, or waste. This is an idea to which Aristotle constantly returns.[7] He says that Nature is wise and does nothing in vain and that she does everything in the most perfect way possible. So they say, drawing upon this, that this exis-

---

5. *Matter,* the approved Aristotelian answer, would imply an eternal universe.

6. Muslim philosophers continue to call God the Creator, but they consider creation to be an eternal, continuous act.

7. *E.g., De Caelo* I:4 241^a. 33; *De Partibus Animalium* IV:13. 695^b. 18.

tence is the most perfect possible and none better is possible. It must, therefore, exist always.[8] For His wisdom, like His essence, is constant. Indeed, His essence is the wisdom by which the existence of this reality is decreed.

All the arguments you may find advanced by eternalists are variants of these, reducible to one or another of these types—or to attempts to embarrass the opposition by saying, "How could the Deity have remained idle, doing nothing at all, creating nothing since eternity . . . and then originate being only yesterday? . . ." or to attempts to prove the point by appealing to its popularity among all nations from time immemorial. For such unanimity would suggest that eternalism is a natural rather than a conventional belief. Aristotle claims that all men confess the permanence of the heavens: "Sensing they are ungenerated and indestructible, they made them the dwelling place of God. . . ." [9] And he introduces other material in the same vein, as if to bolster by claims as to its general acceptance the view he deems himself to have shown to be true by reason.

MOREH NEVUKHIM II:15

My object in this chapter is to make it clear that Aristotle affords no proof of the eternity of the world as he understands it and that he was not deceived on this point but knew he had no such demonstration. The attempts he makes to offer an argument and the evidence he proposes are simply those which appeal to his sentiment. They are those which he favors; and, according to Alexander of Aphrodisias, they are those which involve the fewest difficulties. But one ought not to suppose of Aristotle that he believed these arguments to be demonstrations. For it was Aristotle himself who taught mankind the methods, laws, and conditions of demonstration.

The reason I must state this is that the later followers of Aristotle assert that he demonstrated the eternity of the world, and most people who claim to do philosophy slavishly accept Aristotle's authority on this subject and suppose that everything he says is a conclusive, irrefragable demonstration. They think it shameful to disagree with him

8. Its nonexistence, the Aristotelians presume, would only be in favor of a better world, which contradicts the assumption of the perfectness of God's work.
9. Cf. De Caelo I:3, 270^b. 5ff., Metaphysics lambda 8. 1074^b. 1ff.

or admit that any point may have baffled or eluded him. For this reason I thought I had best challenge their thinking by explaining to them that Aristotle himself does not pretend to offer a demonstration on this point. He says in the *Physics* [VIII:1], ''All investigators of the physical world prior to myself believed that motion neither came to be nor passed away, except Plato. . . .'' These are his words. Had the matter been demonstrated by proof positive, Aristotle would certainly not have needed to seek support from the like-mindedness of his predecessors, nor would he have had to say so much about how shocking and repugnant he found his opponent's point of view, for when something has been proved it cannot be made more true, its certainty cannot be strengthened by the common consent of all the knowledgeable; nor can its truth be diminished or its certainty weakened by the concerted rejection of it by all the people of the earth. Again in *De Caelo* [I:10] you find Aristotle . . . wants to cite the arguments of those who favored the generation of the heavens. I quote verbatim: ''If we do this our arguments will be more attractive to sound thinkers, especially if they hear the proofs of the other side first. For if we simply stated our own view and not the arguments of those who disagree, ours might appear too weak to command acceptance. . . .''

. . . His whole purpose is to show that his view is sounder than that of his opponents . . . which is doubtless true: his view is closer to the truth than theirs, inasmuch as his arguments are based on nature [1]—even so, we do not accept them. Enthusiasms may get the better of any sect, even philosophers. . . . They want to say that Aristotle proved this point, and perhaps they think he did so without realizing it, so that it had to be pointed out after him. For my part, I have no doubt that the views which he states on these subjects—*viz.,* the eternity of the world . . . and the hierarchy of intellects—were not proved by him, and he did not delude himself for a moment that these arguments were proofs. He believed rather, as he says, that argumentation reaches a dead end in these areas: we have not a clue where to begin. You have studied his words in the text: ''In areas where we have no proof or which are too big for us, it is hard to ask,

---

1. Whereas the older views seemed to be based largely on intuitive insight and imagination.

'Why?' as for example when we say, 'Is the world eternal or not?' ''
[*Topics* 104^b. 15] . . .

MOREH NEVUKHIM II:16

In this chapter my object is to make clear what I believe on this question. Having done so I shall advance arguments in support of the position we hope to establish. But first let me state that I find unsatisfactory all of the arguments which the Mutakallimun call demonstrations. I do not intend to deceive myself by labeling as demonstrations such misleading approaches. To prove a point sophistically only weakens it and renders it more vulnerable. For as soon as the fallacies are discovered, the soul's assent in the doctrine to be proved grows weaker. Thus if something cannot be proved one way or the other it is better to leave the question open or simply to take one side or the other.[1]

I have stated the arguments of the Mutakallimun for creation and shown you where they are open to attack. In just the same way, in my opinion, none of what Aristotle and his followers adduce in support of the world's eternity is a conclusive demonstration. Rather there are grave doubts surrounding their proofs, as you shall shortly hear.

What I hope to establish is that the world's coming into being, the doctrine of our Law, which I have explained, is not impossible, and that all the Philosophers' arguments to the effect can be refuted and shown not to imply the falsity of our view. If I can accomplish this and show that both creation and eternity are possible, then it will be possible, I believe, with the question reopened, to receive an answer from revelation, which makes clear things which thinking alone has not the power to reach.[2] . . .

Once I have made it clear that what we believe is possible, I shall undertake to show that it is the most probable of the contending views as well, using arguments based on reason—*i.e.,* I shall endeavor to

1. As an hypothesis (see *Moreh* II:22).
2. Maimonides does not here claim that creation can be known on the authority of Scripture; for, as he points out (*Moreh* II:25), the Scriptural statements about creation might as easily be allegorized as those about God's corporeality. The intention rather is that reason will make possible refutation of the Philosophers' doctrine of the necessity of the world's eternity and thus render possible retention of the apparent meaning of Scripture. The weight of revelation may then be added to whatever reason is able to advance in favor of creation.

show the preferability of the doctrine of the world's having come to be over that of the world's eternity. Just as there are embarrassing consequences to our doctrine of the world's creation, I shall show that even more embarrassing consequences follow from the doctrine of the world's eternity. Here and now I shall advance an original argument refuting all arguments in favor of the eternity of the world.

MOREH NEVUKHIM II:17

All things which come to be (even those whose matter already exists, which simply put off one form and put on another) have a different nature after they are fully developed and settled from that which they had while developing or realizing their potential, and different again from that which they had prior to the inception of that process. The female gamete, for instance, as blood in the blood vessels, has a different nature from that which it has in pregnancy after encountering the male sperm, different too from its nature as a maturing animal after birth. To draw inferences from the nature of a thing which has developed to full maturity about the character it had while developing or from its developmental character as to its state prior to the inception of that process is not always possible. When you err in this regard, pressing attempts to infer from the character of the realized thing to its character while yet potential, you involve yourself in serious difficulties: necessities will seem to you impossible; and impossibilities, necessary.

Suppose, by way of example, that a man of very perfect nature were born and his mother died after nursing him for several months,[1] leaving only men to complete his upbringing on an isolated island until he reached the age of reason and understanding, never having seen a woman or any female animal. If he asked one of the men with him how he had come to be and what he had been like while developing, the reply would be, "All of us can develop only in the belly of another member of our own species, like ourselves only 'female,' having such and such a form. Each of us was alive but very small inside the womb, moving, feeding, gradually growing until a certain size was reached; then a portal was opened for him on the under side of the body,

1. Maimonides' example echoes the opening of Ibn Tufayl, *Hayy ibn Yaqzan*, tr. L. E. Goodman (New York, 1972).

whence he issued. He continued to grow thereafter until he came to be as you see we are.'' The orphan would then have to ask, ''In the womb, then, when we were small, being alive, moving, and growing, did each of us eat, drink, breathe, and produce feces?'' He would be told no, and of course he would immediately assume this was a lie. Inferring from the mature and self-sufficient being, he would construct proofs of the impossibility of all these things, despite the fact that they had actually occurred. ''Any of us,'' he would argue, ''would die if deprived of air for a few moments; all his motions then would cease. How can it be conceived that any of us survives and moves while enclosed in a dense vessel inside the body for a period of months . . . without eating or drinking . . . or producing feces . . . or opening his eyes or his hands, or stretching his legs . . . ?'' And all such analogies would be pressed, to show that a man cannot possibly come to be in this way.

Consider this illustration critically, dear thinker; you will see that we are in just this position with Aristotle. For we, the folk who follow our Teacher Moses and our Father Abraham (peace upon them), believe that the world came to be in a certain way, developed from this point to that, and was created first so and then so. But Aristotle undertakes to dispute with us, taking as evidence against us the mature and settled nature of being after its potential had been realized—which we deny to be anything like what it was at its developmental stage. We declare that it was brought into being out of utter nothingness. What argument, then, can have force against us in all he says? Such proofs have force only against those [*e.g.*, the Mutakallimun] who claim that the stable nature of the finished product, being, is evidence of its having come to be. But I have already informed you that I do not claim this.

Here I shall restate the grounds of his arguments to show you how none of them affects us in any way, since our claim is that God brought the entire world into being out of nothing and caused it to evolve to the completed state which you now observe.

He says (*b*) prime matter cannot come to be or pass away, adducing evidence from things which do come to be and pass away to illustrate the impossibility. He is right, of course, but we do not claim that matter developed as a man does from semen or passes away as a man does, into dust. What we claim, on the contrary, is that God brought it into being out of nothing. . . .

We say the same of motion: He infers (*a*) from the nature of motion that it neither comes to be nor passes away, quite correctly. Once motion exists with its fixed and settled nature, its coming to be or passing away absolutely (as do particular motions) is unimaginable.[2] The same reasoning applies to everything dependent on the nature of motion.[3] . . . We say the same regarding the possibility which supposedly must precede any process (*d*): this is necessary only in the settled order we know, where whatever develops does so only from a fixed, pre-existing starting point. But with something created for the first time, *ex nihilo,* there is nothing for sense or reason to lay hold of to require such a prior possibility. . . .

The crucial point, as I said, is that being, in its mature and finished state, affords no evidence about its state prior to completion. We are not embarrassed if someone says that the heavens existed before the earth or the earth before the heavens, or the heavens without the stars, or one species of animal without another, for all this was when this universe was developing, just as an animal in development may have its heart before its testes (as may be observed empirically) or its blood vessels before its bones, although after it has matured no organ will be found without the rest, upon which the survival of the organism depends.[4] . . .

Aristotle, or rather an Aristotelian, may counter, "If being as we know it gives us no evidence, how do you know that this world came into being and that there is another nature which gave being to it?" We reply that this is not to the point. We wish at present not to establish that the world came to be but only that this is possible. Nature

2. By showing that the Philosophers have used imagination as a criterion, albeit based on the scientific study of nature rather than *a priori* caprice, Maimonides has reduced them to the level of the Mutakallimun.

3. Time; *cf. c.*

4. Thus the evolution of species is anything but inconsistent with Maimonides' creationism. The present interdependent relations of living things are no evidence against evolution, for the developmental state may have involved quite different relationships. The initial creation, being out of nothing, was totally unconstrained by (what was to be) the established order of nature.

provides no evidence of the impossibility of the world's coming to be, but we do not think nature is to be ignored. Once we have established the possibility of our claims, we shall return, as we have made clear, to argue the probability of creation.

The Aristotelian now has open to him only the theological rather than the natural arguments for the impossibility of the world's genesis, *i.e.*, those which begin not from the nature of being but from the dictates of reason regarding the Deity: *viz.*, the three arguments cited (*e, f,* and *g*). In the next chapter, therefore, I shall show you that these involve so many difficulties that they cannot provide any basis whatever for sound reasoning.

MOREH NEVUKHIM II:18
The first such argument put forward by the Aristotelians (*e*) is the one in which they claim to show that it follows from our position that God proceeded from potency to act if He acted at one time and not at another.

The way to dispose of this difficulty is obvious indeed. The argument holds only for compounds of matter (which bears potentiality) and form. . . . The noncorporeal, which has no matter, has no potentiality in it whatever. It is always actual in every way. For such beings, this argument does not hold. It is not impossible for them to act at one time and not at another without there having been any change on the part of the disembodied being or any progress in it from potency to act. . . . It is not our purpose to provide information as to the cause of God's acting at one time rather than another. . . . What we believe is that He is neither a body nor a force in a body; hence it does not follow that He changes if He acts after not acting.

The second argument (*f*) is the one in which the world's eternity is deduced from God's transcendence of impulses, incentives, and impediments. The dissolution of this difficulty is itself difficult and rather subtle, so concentrate:

Every voluntary agent which acts on account of something is constrained necessarily to act at one time rather than another by various impediments and incentives. A man, for instance, wants to have a house but does not build it because of impediments such as lack of materials at hand; or, given materials, for want of tools to prepare those materials for building purposes. Or perhaps he has the materials and the tools but does not build because he does not want to, because he thinks he can do without shelter. But when incentives such as heat or cold require him to seek shelter, then he wants to build. Incentives may cause a change of will, or impediments may hamper its execution—if the action is done for the sake of something other than itself. But when the action has no aim whatever ulterior to the fact that it is an expression of the will, then that will requires no incentives, and the willer need not act constantly, even if there are no impediments. . . .

"All this is true," someone may say, "but is there not a change in His willing at one time and not another?" "No," we reply; "to want and not want is the very essence of will. If the will in question belonged to a material being, so that external objects were sought through it, then it would change according to the impediments and incentives it confronted. But an immaterial will, which seeks no ulterior object whatever, does not change. Its willing one thing now and another later does not involve a change in it." [1] . . .

In the third method (g) the eternity of the world is deduced from the immediate issuance of whatever wisdom determines. God's wisdom, like His being, is eternal; so what it entails must be eternal as well. This is a very shaky inference, for . . . we are ignorant of God's wisdom in giving being to the universe so short a while ago. The universe is an expression of His eternal and immutable wisdom, but we do not know in the least what the rule [2] and sentence of that wisdom are. The will, indeed, in our view, is implicit in the wisdom; the whole is one thing—*i.e.,* His being and His wisdom—for we do not believe in attributes. . . .

When we take this approach the embarrassments abate. . . . Having made clear to you now that our claims are tenable, not impossible as the eternalists aver, I shall return to showing that they are more reasonable than the alternative, exposing its unwelcome consequences in the coming chapters.

1. A perfect will, while not influenced by whimsies or by obstacles or enticements, might still choose to express itself now one way, now another, now not at all. The program of these self-expressions might well be changeless or eternal.
2. *E.g.,* vis-à-vis times appropriate to creation.

MOREH NEVUKHIM II:19

You will have observed that the school of Aristotle and all who hold the eternity of the world take the position that the issuance of being from the Creator is a matter of necessity, that God is the cause and existence the effect, and therefore that the world's existence is necessary. One can no more ask why the world exists or why it is the way it is than one can inquire why God exists or is the way He is [1] (*i.e.*, one and incorporeal). All existence is thus made necessary—cause and effect alike. Nothing can fail to exist or be anything other than as it is. But this implies that everything must retain the nature it has forever, that nothing can diverge in any way whatever from the nature which it has. According to this view it is impossible for anything which exists to change its nature. It cannot be the case, then, that all things are intended to be a certain way by the will and choice of a Purposer. For if they were, they would have been otherwise prior to having been so purposed.

Our view, however, is that it is manifest that things are intended to be the way they are and are not so simply by necessity. He who purposed this can cause them to change and take some other purpose—but not just any purpose, for the bounds of impossibility are fixed and cannot be overstepped, as I shall explain [*Moreh* III:15].

My object in this chapter is to make clear to you, using arguments of nearly demonstrative force, that the present reality, with which we are familiar, provides us with conclusive evidence of its having been intended to be the way it is by a Purposer—without stooping to the Mutakallimun's denial of nature or their doctrine of atoms and the continuous creation of accidents and all their other postulates which I have explained to you and which they introduced solely to pave the way for their doctrine of determination.

Do not suppose they too said what I shall say. What they hoped to establish was, of course, the same, and for that reason they cited the same facts I shall cite and observed determination in them. But for them there was no difference between the determination that a plant be

1. There is no why or wherefore regarding God for the Philosophers since God is the ultimate principle in terms of which all else is explained. Maimonides' criticism of the Aristotelian view is that the rest of existence seems to acquire a similar inexplicability in virtue of its "necessary implication" by God.

red rather than white . . . and that the heavens have the form which they have rather than being composed of squares or triangles. They established the doctrine of determination, as you know, by those premises of theirs you have studied. I shall establish it properly, using philosophical premises based upon the nature of reality.

I shall set forth this approach after putting forward the following premise:

Whenever two things of the same matter are in any way differentiated from each other, there must be some cause (or as many causes as differences) other than and beyond that matter, responsible for the fact that one has the character it has and the other has another.

This premise is agreed upon by both eternalists and creationists. Having stated it, I shall make my intent clear by a series of questions and answers regarding Aristotle's view:

We inquire of Aristotle as follows: "You have demonstrated to us that the matter of all things below the sphere of the moon is one, common to all. What then is the cause of the differentiation of species and of their members?"

He replies, "The cause of the differentiation is the difference of chemical composition. . . ."

We reply, "If the chemistry of the elements is the cause of the predispositions of various matters to take on particular forms, what predisposed the primary matter to take on the forms of water and air, when all matter was the same and common to all things? What made the matter of earth more fit for the form of earth or that of fire more fit for the form of fire?" [2]

Aristotle replies, "That was made necessary by the difference of their locations. . . . The matter closest to the periphery was imprinted with fineness and swiftness of motion. . . . The further from the periphery and the closer to the center the matter was, the denser, darker, and grosser it became. . . ."

"This periphery itself," we must then ask, "*i.e.*, the heavens—is their matter the same as that of the elements?"

"No," he replies; "that is different matter; its forms are different. It is said to be 'body' in a different sense from that applied to the

2. Water, air, earth, fire—the elements, in the Aristotelian account.

bodies which we have among us." [3]

One must then ask, ". . . Is there any other thing beyond the sphere [4] to which this differentiation may be attributed if not God?"

Here let me point out to you how profoundly perceptive Aristotle was. He felt the force of this objection, of course (although he does not state it), and tried to escape it in several ways, but without the support of the facts. For it is plain from what he does say that he hopes to provide us with a system for the heavens as he does for the subcelestial world, so that all will be accounted for in terms of natural necessity—not in terms of purpose or voluntary intention or the freely selective choice of a determining agent. This Aristotle did not achieve; it will never be achieved. For he hoped to give the cause of the sphere's moving from east to west rather than west to east, of some spheres' moving swiftly and others' moving slowly [5] . . . but he did not accomplish any such thing. His explanations of the subcelestial world fall into a system which conforms to reality, a system in which the causes in operation are manifest and which it is possible to regard as necessitated by the motions and influences of the sphere. But in all that he says of celestial matters, he gives no clear cause of such things' being as they are, and the reality does not correspond to the account in such a way as to make possible a claim that any necessity is operative. . . .

It was no doubt because Aristotle recognized the weakness of his hypotheses regarding the causes of such things that he prefaced his embarkation upon these investigations with the following words: "We wish now to examine two problems satisfactorily, for these are problems which we must examine and speak about to the extent of our knowledge, our opinion, and our understanding. But no one must

3. Dialectically, Aristotle cannot answer yes, since he has used the periphery as the explanatory basis for the differentiation of the elements. Philosophically, any absolute difference will serve the purposes of Maimonides' argument.

4. Beyond the material universe.

5. *I.e.*, having traced the system of nature to its ultimate natural foundations, the heavens (we should say, to the atomic level), Aristotle aspired to discover even there an underlying fabric of natural necessity. This is the task Maimonides is certain can never be rewarded with success—for beyond the ultimate natural principles it is contradictory to seek yet further natural principles. Nature at such a level must be given—either by pure chance (which is impossible, *cf. Moreh* II:20) or by a divine plan.

ascribe this to any rashness on our part. What should impress him, rather, is our love of and devotion to philosophy. When we pursue problems which are both noble and important and are able to resolve them satisfactorily in the slightest, then the hearer should be delighted.'' These are his words verbatim.[6] You see he undoubtedly is aware of the weakness of those pronouncements. . . . When he speaks of ''our opinion,'' he must mean the theory of necessity, which is tantamount to the doctrine of the world's eternity; when he speaks of ''our knowledge,'' he must refer to the plain and agreed truth that every such thing [7] must have a cause and does not occur merely by chance; when he says ''our understanding,'' he must be referring to our inadequacy in assigning causes for such things in any full and comprehensive way.

All he claims to provide is some slight insight as to the nature of these causes, and that is what he does . . . but astronomy in his time was not what it is today.

The problems which Aristotle's approach cannot solve are readily resolved by our view (the creationist view), and the evidence fits well with our assumptions. For we say that there exists a Being who determined each sphere as He pleased with respect to the sense of its motion, but we are ignorant of the manner in which there is wisdom in things' being brought to be just so.[8] . . . What is the cause which singles out one tract of heaven to have ten stars while giving none to

6. Maimonides' text is a free translation of *De Caelo* II:12. 291^b. 24ff.

7. Every celestial determination.

8. Rather than otherwise. The later Aristotelians such as Averroës believed that causes could be discovered by the human mind for the ''rotation of the heavens'' from east to west (rather than west to east), the relative speeds of the planets, etc., in which causes the excellence and rationality of the divine wisdom would be manifested. Maimonides shares with these Aristotelians the assumption of the dependence of all such determinations upon the Divine and therefore concedes that they will express the divine wisdom. He does not accept the assumption that such wisdom necessarily will be transparent to man. He therefore rejects the Peripatetic project of discovering a rationale for necessity in all things: in some cases no natural necessity can be discovered. If a determinant is required to account for all differentiations, then some must be assigned to what human beings would see as will rather than what they would recognize as mind; although, of course, in God, mind and will are one, and neither corresponds (by way of limitation) to what human beings might understand by the familiar sense of the terms.

another? . . . Everything of the sort would be very improbable, nearly impossible on the assumption that all such things were somehow logically necessitated on God's part, as Aristotle presumes. On the assumption, however, that all such determinations are in accordance with the purpose of a Being who made things so, there would be nothing improbable and no bewilderment would ensue. No further inquiry is required, unless, perhaps, you ask, "What is the cause of this purpose?" [9]

In a nutshell, all we know is that all this [the placement of the stars, etc.] serves some end we do not understand. But it is not done for nothing or at hazard. For even the veins and nerves of an ass or bitch, as you know, did not just fall into being. Their size, the thickness of some veins and thinness of others, the branching of some nerves and not others, the straightness of some and the crookedness of others did not come about by chance. No such thing occurred without affording some benefit whose necessity is known. How then can anyone who is intelligent imagine that the places, sizes, and number of the stars, the diverse motions of the heavens in which they are set, occur without an object or at hazard? Of course all such things are necessitated—in accordance with the design of a purposing Being. The very idea that such an order could be the automatic outcome of some blind, undirected necessity is terribly, terribly farfetched.

No evidence of purpose is stronger, in my view, than the differentiation of the motions of the spheres and the setting of the stars in the spheres. That is why you find all prophets take the stars and the heavens as evidences of the necessary existence of the Deity. Thus there is the well-known story in the tradition of Abraham's contemplation of the stars [Baba Batra 16:2, Yoma 28:2]. And Isaiah, making known what may be inferred from such contemplation, says, "Raise up your eyes on high, and see Who created these" [Isaiah 40:26]. . . .

Despite the common matter, any differentiation below the heavens can be explained as due to the influences of the heavens or the placement of such matter relative to the heavens, as Aristotle taught us. But

---

9. An otiose question, since the divine purpose requires no causes.

of the differentiation within the heavens and among the stars—who could be responsible for that except God? [10]. . .

Our investigation, then, has brought us to the point where we must inquire into two questions:

(1) "Is there or is there not a necessity that in these differences a purposive rather than an automatic mode of differentiation is entailed?"

(2) "If all this is due to the purpose of a purposing Being who is responsible for this differentiation, is it necessary that this came to be in the first place; or is it not so necessary, and is such differentiating activity always going on?" (Some eternalists make this claim [see *Moreh* II:21].)

Now I shall take up these two questions and explain what ought to be made clear about them in following chapters.

MOREH NEVUKHIM II:20

Aristotle demonstrates for all natural things that they do not come about by chance. His proof, as he states it [*Physics* II:5. 196[b]. 10ff.], is that matters of chance do not hold always or for the most part, whereas natural things do. . . . Now if the particulars which make up nature do not come about by chance, how can the whole be due to chance? This is his proof that being is not due to chance. Attacking those of his predecessors who held that the world was due to chance and came to be spontaneously, without a cause, Aristotle writes: "Others made spontaneity the cause of the heavens, and indeed of the entire universe. They said the motion and revolution which sustain and differentiate the whole cosmic order simply occurred by themselves. This surely is most remarkable. They hold that animals and plants do not come to be and develop by chance but have a cause (nature, mind, or some such thing) since all seeds and semen breed not at hazard, but from this seed only olives come, and from that semen only men. Yet of the heavens—the bodies which alone among visible things are divine—they say they came into being by mere spontaneity, without any

---

10. *Cf.* the Maariv liturgy, "*u-mesader et ha-kokhavim bemishmeroteihem ba-rakiah ki-retzono*"—"who orders the stars in their watches in the sky, according to His will."

cause at all, such as animals and plants must have." [1] Having said this he goes on to expose more fully the fallacy involved in this misconception.

So, as you see, Aristotle believes and proves that none of these beings exists by accident. The alternative is that they exist in accordance with their essences—*i.e.,* that there is a cause of their being such as they are, having the forms they have. This is what he believes and proves. But it is not clear to me that Aristotle concludes from the world's not being spontaneous that it exists on account of the will and purpose of a voluntary and purposive being. For to combine necessary being and intentional creation into one notion [2] seems to me to be almost tantamount to combining opposites. For "necessity," as upheld by Aristotle, means that each being here which is not artificial has a cause which requires it to develop such as it is. This cause has a cause of its own; the second, a third, and so on until the series ends at a first cause, by which all is made necessary, since an infinite series is impossible. Still, Aristotle does not believe that the Creator—or rather the First Cause—makes necessary the existence of the world as a shadow is made necessary by a body, or heat by flame, or light by the sun, as those who misunderstand him claim. Rather he believes this necessity to be like the necessitation of an idea by the mind, where mind is the author of the thought, to the extent that it is thought. For the First Cause, in his view, is a mind, which although it is at the highest level of existence and perfection and although (he says) it wills what it makes necessary and enjoys and delights in it, still cannot will anything else. Now such action cannot be called intentional or purposive. For man wills to have two eyes and two hands, enjoys and delights in them, and is unable to will his being any other way. It is not he who chose this form for himself; it was not his intention which made him the way he is. The notions of "purpose" and "determination" make sense only in terms of what originally was not (but might

---

1. *Physics* II:4. 196ᵃ. 25ff. Aristotle pillories the inconsistency of those who insist upon causality in nature but assign the universe at large to chance, uncaused, or "spontaneous" events.

2. As the Muslim Philosophers al-Farabi and Avicenna seem to have wished to do.

or might not have become) such as it was intended or determined to
be.[3] . . .

MOREH NEVUKHIM II:21

Now some modern eternalist philosophers say that God is the "Author" of the world—that He is the Intender and Purposer, the Chooser
of its existence [over nonexistence], and Determiner of its being such
as it is, but that it is inconceivable that this occur at one particular
time. Rather it always has been and always will be so. The only thing
which makes it impossible for us to imagine something being done
without the prior existence of the doer in time, they claim, is the fact
that this is impossible with our own action, since every doer of whom
this is true is somehow imperfect, a doer first only potentially, moving
to the status of actual doer only upon execution of the act. But the
Deity is in no way imperfect and has no potentiality in Him whatever.
Thus His act has nothing prior to it but is eternal. The difference between God's relation to His act and man's relation to his is as great as
that between God and man themselves—quite a difference! They apply
the same reasoning to will and determination. . . .

By now the student will have realized that these philosophers (desirous, perhaps, of using more attractive expressions and avoiding a
certain amount of opprobrium) have substituted different terms for
"necessity" but retained the concept. For the idea upheld by Aristotle
that this reality is entailed necessarily by its cause and eternal through
the eternity of that cause (*i.e.*, the Deity) is identical with their doctrine that the world is the work of the Deity, existing through His
choice, will, determination, and intention—but eternally so, in past
and future, in just the way that the rising of the sun is indubitably the
author of daylight although neither event is temporally prior to the
other. But this is not what is meant by purpose or intention as we understand it. What we mean by this is that it (*i.e.*, the world) is not
made necessary by Him as an effect is made necessary by its cause,
where the effect is inseparable from the cause and cannot be different
unless the cause (or some facet of the situation) is different. If you un-

---

3. Thus (in answer to questions 1 and 2) the world is incomprehensible except in terms
of purpose, and purpose is incomprehensible except in terms of creation.

derstand the concept in this way it will be obvious that it is contradictory to say both that the world is made necessary by God as an effect is made necessary by its cause, and at the same time that it is the object of God's work, or authorship, or determination.

In the last analysis then, the matter devolves upon an investigation of the differentiation of being in the heavens, which has been proved to require a cause. Is this cause such in the sense that its very existence necessitates that particular mode of differentiation? Or is it a cause in the sense of being its author, and the selector of its modes of differentiation—as we, the followers of Moses, believe it to be?

We must address ourselves to that question as soon as one preparatory remark has been made. I must clarify the concept of necessitation as understood by Aristotle so that you may have some conception of it. Then I shall be ready to explain to you my preference for the doctrine of the world's creation, using rational, philosophical arguments free from any obfuscation. The claim that the First Intellect is necessitated by God, the Second by the First, the Third by the Second, and so forth, and likewise the belief that the spheres are made necessary by the Intellects—the whole famous hierarchy which you have studied in their texts and of which I have set down some highlights here [*Moreh* II:4]—is obviously not intended to mean that first the prior existed and then the subsequent was made necessary by it, for the assertion is not that anything was created by its antecedent but only that there is a causal necessitation . . . without there being any temporal precedence or separate existence for the causal factor. For example, someone may say, "Roughness, smoothness, hardness, softness, density, or thinness, depend on the primary qualities, which no one doubts are heat, cold, moistness and dryness . . ." although no body can be found which has the primary but lacks the secondary qualities. This is just the sort of thing Aristotle maintains regarding being at large: that this depends on that, and so until the series ends at the First Cause as he calls it, or the First Mind, or whatever you wish to call it. We are all aiming at the same objective, but he believes all other than Him is necessitated by Him, as I have explained, while we say that all these things are His work which He did on purpose and by willing this particular reality which originally did not exist but came into existence at His will.

Now I shall state the grounds of my preference, my arguments in behalf of our doctrine of the creation of the world.

MOREH NEVUKHIM II:22

A postulate agreed upon by all philosophers including Aristotle is that from the simplex only one simplex effect can emerge, whereas complex things may require as many effects as they have simple elements. Flame, for example, in which two qualities are combined, the hot and the dry, makes necessary both a heating effect and a drying effect. . . . In keeping with this postulate Aristotle says that one simplex Intellect and only one emerged from God directly.

Secondly: Not just anything may emerge from anything at random. There must always be a certain relation between cause and effect, necessarily, such that accidents do not give rise to each other at random, quality engendering quantity or vice versa. By the same token, matter does not give rise to form, nor form to matter.

Thirdly: Every doer who acts with will and purpose (rather than at the dictate of nature) may perform many different acts.

Fourthly: A whole composed of heterogeneous elements juxtaposed is more properly a compound than one whose diverse elements are blended together: bone, flesh, vein, or nerve are simpler than the whole hand or foot which is made up of these. This is too obvious to be discussed further.

Given these premises, I argue that Aristotle's account of the First Intellect's being the cause of the Second, the Second of the Third, and so forth, even if expanded to thousands of steps, would still without a doubt leave the last Intellect simple. Whence, then, is the compositeness (necessary, as Aristotle would have it) of reality as we know it? Granting all Aristotle's claims as to the proliferation of complex ideas in these intellects as their remoteness increases (for the objects of their thought [1] are many)—even granting him this conjecture, how can these minds become causes of the necessary emergence from themselves of the spheres? What sort of relation is there between matter and the disembodied, which has no matter whatever? Suppose we grant that each sphere has an intellect as its cause as suggested. Ad-

---

1. The intellects above them.

mitting some compositeness in that intellect in virtue of the fact that it contemplates itself and something else, so that it might give rise to two things—the next intellect beneath it and (from its other aspect) the sphere—it would still remain to be asked, "In respect of this one simplex aspect by which the sphere was made necessary, how could the sphere be its product when the sphere is compounded of two matters and two forms, those of the sphere and those of the star which is set therein?" If the cause of the heavens actually works in this mechanical manner, then this complex effect must have a complex cause, with one aspect to necessitate the character of the body of the sphere; and another, that of the star—that is, if the matter of all the stars is the same. But it might well be that the substance of the bright stars is not the same as that of the dim ones.[2] And every body, of course, is compounded of matter and form.

By now it is clear to you that the procession of beings [3] does not take place in this mechanical and automatic fashion. . . . If, on the other hand, we believe all this is determined purposely by a wisdom we do not comprehend, then none of these questions need assail us. They affect only those who claim that all this is a matter of necessary entailment and not one of will. But such a view is at odds with the order of being, unfounded in experience and ungrounded in argument, bearing in its train, withal, the most monstrous implications—for it robs the Deity (whom all thoughtful men confess to be possessed of all perfections [4]) of all creative power, rendering Him incapable if He so chose of having made a fly's wing any longer or a grub's foot any shorter than He did. Aristotle would say that God would not so choose, holding it impossible for God to have chosen other than as He did. But this does not augment God's perfection; rather, in a way, it demeans it.

In summing up, I shall say to you that even though I know that many partisan spirits will attack me for what I have said, either for distorting or inadequately understanding their words, I shall not be deterred by that from saying what in my weak way I have grasped and understood. This is, in sum, that all that Aristotle says about the

2. As Philoponus proposed in the sixth century.
3. From its monadic Source.
4. *Cf.* Part One above.

sublunary world is doubtless true. No one would turn his back on it unless he misunderstood it or had some prejudice to defend at the expense of experience.[5] But, with a few exceptions, everything Aristotle says about the lunar sphere and beyond is more or less conjectural. All the more so is this true of his opinions about the hierarchy of Intellects; for some of his views on such theological subjects contain glaring fallacies plain to all nations—absurd and dangerous doctrines for which no proof is given.

Do not take me to task for exposing the difficulties which follow from his view. "Do difficulties refute a position or establish its denial?" you may ask. Of course not. But we must treat this philosopher as his followers enjoin us to do. Alexander of Aphrodisias is quite clear in recommending that whenever a point is not subject to proof one way or the other, both alternatives should be assumed as hypotheses, so that it may be seen what difficulties follow from each. The one involving the fewest difficulties is the one which is to be believed. . . . We have shown you that the doctrine of the eternity of the world involves more difficulties and is more damaging to what one ought to believe about the Deity—over and above the fact that creation was the belief of Abraham and Moses (peace upon them). . . .

Analysis

To one of his assistants Einstein is reported to have said, "What really interests me is whether God had any choice in the creation of the world." [1] This precisely is the question which concerns Maimonides. Like Aristotle before him and Einstein many centuries after, Maimonides was convinced that the natural world was constructed according to the rational order of a plan, and this for him (as in their different ways for them) was sufficient evidence of the existence of a deity. But was the deity discovered by philosophy identifiable with the God of Moses and Abraham? The real question in Maimonides' mind was whether the plan or order of nature was such as to allow inference not merely

5. Maimonides' concession refers, obviously, to Aristotle's general approach to nature, not the precise jot and tittle of what the Philosopher believed.
1. G. Holton, *New York Times Book Review,* September 5, 1971

to a divine rationality, but to a divine purpose, intention, or (in the eighteenth-century sense of the term) design. That question in turn hinged upon the resolution of the problem of creation. For only if the world was created a finite time ago—*i.e.*, only if the Genesis account could be taken seriously and preserved from the allegorization that had mythologized Plato's version of the fashioning of the world in *Timaeus*—only then, in Maimonides' view, could sense be made of the monotheistic conception of God as the Determinant of the character of the world. The rationality of Mosaic theology (and, as Philo had recognized long before, the authority of Mosaic law) rested on the truth, if not the literal exactitude, of the Biblical account of *maaseh bereshit*, the act of creation.

The Philosophers' objections to the concept of creation are demonstrated by Maimonides to arise not in any weakness in their concept itself but in their own inability to think themselves clear of Greek physical and theological categories. Specifically, all of the Aristotelian naturalistic arguments presuppose the Aristotelian analysis of time, motion, and change, while the theological arguments of the later Greek philosophers presume that the conception of the divine in terms of an arbitrary will is demeaning to the absolute transcendence which they and their monotheist opponents agree is critical in man's conception of divinity. Thus in both cases the Philosophers beg the question at issue: A world with a settled nature cannot, in terms of that nature, be conceived to have come to be. But that does not prove the world did not come to be. A God whose will is always in principle explicable by human intelligence cannot arbitrarily select one moment for creation over another. But that does not establish that no such selection has occurred. The order of nature is evidence of a divine plan, and there are aspects of that order which are explicable to us only on the assumption of some arbitrariness in the divine will/wisdom. Nature, as the Philosophers themselves insisted, is replete with purpose. But the concept of purpose is incompatible with the assumption that all things must eternally have been as they necessarily were to be.

The world, as conceived by Maimonides, is not such as to demand the constant creative interference of the Deity. It has a certain stable existence and independence—a mature and settled order of its own, as Maimonides calls it. This implies that science will be possible, and allows inference to the rationality of a divine plan. The Deity, as conceived by Maimonides, is not, however, bound, as it were, by the rationality of His own will. He exercises His will upon the world, not haphazardly at every temporal instant, but once for all at the moment of creation, bestowing upon existence a character it would not otherwise have had. Maimonides thus avoids the extremes of Kalam occasionalism and Philosophical determinism. And so it might be claimed that theologically his scheme is preferable. This preferable outcome, surely, was part of what Maimonides was seeking when he set out to argue in behalf of the possibility and probability of creation. But it is clear as well that Maimonides would have considered it a worthless preferability had he not succeeded in establishing coherent, well-grounded arguments in behalf of that possibility and probability. Having set forth such arguments, in vindication of his prephilosophical ideals, he has done as much as any of the greatest philosophers can claim to have done.

PART THREE

Human Action and Values

It has been told you, O man, what the Lord requires of you: only this, to do what is right, to love compassion, and thoughtfully to walk with your God.

Micah 6:8

VALUES AND VALUE JUDGMENTS

Introduction

Somewhat less than one hundred years ago, Friedrich Nietzsche claimed to have penetrated to the core of the human value-postulating process and to have discovered the very workshops where gods as well as men were forged. Gods, Nietzsche found, were no more than projections of human values; and human value systems themselves (notably those of Christians and Jews) were no more than the offspring of a vengeance mentality attributed to the oppressed and downtrodden. No wonder gods appeared so often in the roles of legislator or redeemer.

Nietzsche's "discovery" enabled him to reaffirm the ancient Sophists' claim that all that is valuative in values is the mere result of their having been espoused—that their worth, indeed, is proportional to the intensity of their espousal. Man, then, had within him the largely unrealized capacity of creating values. Indeed, the transhuman being, whom Nietzsche called the *Übermensch* or superman, would overcome all human values; his every act would be beyond conscience and contrition (beyond good and evil), and he would thus accept to the fullest—this is the normative program of Existentialism, which Nietzsche inaugurated—his role as creator of his own values rather

208

than remaining their creature any longer.

In light of this background, it is with a somewhat poignant shock of recognition, if not outright dismay, that the modern reader first encounters Maimonides' treatment of the origin of human values and the capacity for making value judgments. For just as Maimonides' account of religious language may at first seem dangerously close to the Nietzschean notion that gods are mere projections of our moral ideals, so Maimonides' account of valuation will appear at first sight to be an anticipation of Nietzsche's moral notions, and some care is required to distinguish the two positions and get to the bottom of Maimonides' intention.

Maimonides was asked by an admittedly knowledgeable acquaintance to explain how it is that Adam can be understood to have been punished by being granted a knowledge of good and evil. Is not reason man's highest attainment? The Rambam's reply may seem at first *ad hominem* and abusive, for it presumes the questioner to be both a hedonist and a dilettante, and before addressing the question itself, Maimonides pauses to inveigh against the shallowness of those who read "the Bible as literature." Torah is not an all-time best-seller but a way of life. Those who merely dip into it will, of course, emerge only with superficialities, textual vagaries, and petty conundrums. To be rewarded with a deeper understanding, one must undertake a deeper commitment to its message and method. Only by living into the Torah can one grow to an understanding of the intention behind its words. The petty puzzles will then vanish and the truth begin to emerge.

In keeping with his confidence in the ultimate wisdom and rationality of the Torah, then, Maimonides undertakes his inquiry within the framework of what he takes to be the Torah's premise. But when, at length, Maimonides' answer does emerge, it is couched in language as radical as that of Nietzsche. Reason, Maimonides asserts, was man's from the beginning, *i.e.,* by nature. It was the capacity for making value judgments which man acquired—and this gain, the inauguration of human moral consciousness, in Maimonides' view (as in Nietzsche's), was in truth a loss. Value judgments, Maimonides writes, seemingly echoing the Sophists, are matters not of reason but of repute. Reason deals with facts. Man's valuative capacities, far from making him akin to God or the angels, place him, in a way, on all fours with the beasts. It is this strange pronouncement by the great rabbi which we must now endeavor to understand.

From *Moreh Nevukhim* I

MOREH NEVUKHIM I:2

Several years ago, a learned man confronted me with an unusual difficulty which bears some consideration, as does the response by which I resolved it. Before stating the difficulty and the solution I proposed, I should point out that, as every Hebrew knew, the term *elohim* may designate the deity, the angels, or temporal rulers. Thus Onkelos glossed correctly in translating "You shall be as *elohim* knowing good and evil" [Genesis 3:5], where the third sense is intended, by "You shall be as rulers. . . ."

Now to state the objection: The original intention in creating man, as the literal text seems to show, was that he would be an animal, like the rest, without thought or understanding or the capacity to distinguish between good and evil. Then, when he sinned, his disobedience earned him his great distinction, the capacity to differentiate good from evil, which is our highest attainment and the basis of our humanity. What seems incredible is that as a punishment for disobedience, man should be given reason, a perfection he did not yet have. The incongruity is reminiscent of stories told of men whose sins and crimes were so great they were transformed into stars in the heavens.[1] This was the essence of the difficulty, although I have not cited it verbatim.

The substance of my answer is as follows: Do you think you can reason from the first notions that strike your fancy and presume you can comprehend a book which is the guide of all men, from the earliest to the last, after a few hours' leisure reading between having a drink and making love, as you would glance through some history or book of poems? Bring your thoughts into focus and consider. The case is not as you supposed at first glance, but rather, in accordance with the following account, as will become clear when you think it over: Reason, which God gave man and which is man's highest attainment,

---

1. In the Greek myths of metamorphosis.

was Adam's before his fall. It was on account of this that he was said to be in the image and likeness of God; and it was this which made possible God's exhortations and prescriptions to him, as it is written, "The Lord God commanded" [Genesis 2:16]. For prescriptions are not given to beasts or to any being without understanding.

Reason makes possible discrimination between what is true and what is false. This Adam had to the fullest. But right and wrong are matters not of reason but of repute. For we do not say, "That the heavens are spherical is good and that the earth is flat is bad," but rather "true" and "false." [2] . . . Thus, while primeval man was at his most perfect and already had an intellect in terms of which he was said to be but little lower than *elohim* [the angels—Psalm 8:6], he had so little understanding of or concern for what is done that he found nothing wrong even in what was most manifestly unseemly, his own nakedness. But when he disobeyed, succumbing to his lusts and fancies (as it is written "that the tree was good to eat and a delight to the eyes" [Genesis 3:6]), he was punished by being stripped of the rational apprehension he had enjoyed. Thus, by disobeying the command which he had been given on account of his intellect, he acquired a sense of acceptability and sank to the level of value judgments. Only then did he realize what he had become and the worth of what he had lost. It is in this regard that it was said, "you shall be as *elohim* [3] knowing good and evil" [3:5], not "knowing true and false." For good and evil are not at all necessary, as are true and false. Consider the sentence, "Their eyes were opened and they knew that they were naked" [3:7]. It does not say, ". . . and they saw that they were naked," for what they saw was unchanged. No covering had been removed from their eyes; rather man himself had changed. What had not appeared wrong now did appear so. . . .

What is said of Adam [of man], "He changes his face and Thou sendest him away" [Job 14:20], is to be interpreted as meaning that he is driven out when he changes his orientation, for the noun "face"

2. The roundness of the earth was known to scholars since antiquity: Eratosthenes (d. *ca.* 194 B.C.E.) devised a method of calculating the size of the earth assuming the earth to be a sphere. His method was put into practice under the Caliph Mamun in 829 C.E., giving a value only fifty miles less than the true measure.

3. Temporal rulers, according to the gloss at the beginning of this chapter.

here connotes purpose, since a man faces his objective. Thus, what is said is, "When he changed his orientation and pursued what he had been forbidden, he was driven out of the Garden of Eden." That was the punishment fitting to his offense, measure for measure. For he had been allowed to eat and enjoy in security and repose. But when his appetites grew unruly and he began, as I said, to cater to his lusts and caprices, when he ate what he had been forbidden to eat, he was deprived of all this and had to eat (and then only after great trouble and labor) inferior foods, which previously he had not eaten, as it is written, "Thorns and thistles shall it bear you" etc. [Genesis 3:18], and, "By the sweat of your brow" etc. [3:18–19], and, as explanation, "The Lord God sent him out of the Garden of Eden to work the soil" [3:23]. In regard to food and most of his living conditions, God reduced him to the level of the animals, as it is written, "You shall eat the grass of the field" [3:18]; and, explaining this story, "Man unable to live in dignity is like a beast which cannot speak" [Psalm 49:13].

Praised be He the wisdom and the end of whose will is beyond our understanding.

Analysis

I believe we cannot come to terms with Maimonides' response to the dilemma posed by his learned acquaintance before we recognize that it never occurred to the rabbi to doubt that there are facts about values. The Sophist position that values are purely the creation of men, such that what is right and what is wrong are merely matters of what is thought to be right and what is thought to be wrong, had been roundly refuted by Aristotle, as Maimonides well knew. For Aristotle had demonstrated (*Metaphysics* gamma 5–6) that to deny there are facts about values, as to deny there are facts about anything else, is not only to make war against reality (what is the case) but also to deny the principle of contradiction, to assert that it is possible for things both to be and not to be as they are affirmed to be at a given time and in a given respect. For he who claims that values are as they are affirmed to be affirms both sides of all value disagreements. Maimonides was well aware of the untenability of such a position. Thus Maimonides does not claim that there are no facts about values but rather that our values are not matters of fact, and hence our value judgments are not matters of reason but matters of repute. Thus his linguistic argument gains its force. It may well be that it is good that the heavens are spherical and the earth not flat, but such judgments are beyond our ken (cf. *Moreh* II:22); we are capable of using value terms only with reference to our own desires and needs or something very like them—we cannot use such terms in an absolute way.

Maimonides' position regarding the relativity of human values arises not out of the decadent romanticism of post-Kantian continental thinking which places man in the Promethean role of value-creator (and destroyer), but rather out of an old Hellenistic controversy over the question for whose sake the world exists. The Stoics had claimed that all existence is for the sake of man. Why else, they argued, had pigs been given souls if not as preservative? The Platonists (many of whom were vegetarians in any case) countered that there is a good in everything; and, if so, then each thing that exists must exist (at least in the first instance) for its own good. The particular goods of all things subserve the greater (divine) good of the all, of which they are the expressions.

Maimonides sides unequivocally with the Platonists, rejecting the arbitrarily anthropocentric view that human goods are ultimate goods. God's goodness and wisdom are manifest in the design by which He has made one facet of creation serve the needs of another, but all goods—all ends—are means to the supreme good or ultimate end, which is God's will, an end and a good complete within itself (*Moreh* III:13) and, therefore, utterly beyond comparison with the limited ends and relative goods of creatures known to us, utterly beyond the comprehension of finite beings. Thus, in existing for its own sake, all creation mirrors and particularizes the self-containment of God and so exists for God, who cannot be said to have a "sake," unless it is Himself (*Moreh* III:25). It follows that values found within creation are all relative; even if perceived with the utmost objectivity, they can never be absolute.

Maimonides has taken the Platonic schema of the relation of the One to the many as the model for his conception of the relation of creation to Creator: nature is but an imperfect copy of its ideal, being, as we know it, is but an imperfect representation of absolute Being. Just as each creature's being is only a relative being alongside the being of Perfection, so each creature's good is only a relative good alongside the absolute good of God, which is the Good itself. Each created being shares, to the extent of its capacity, in the absolute goodness of its source. But the very logic of finitude forbids that this participation be absolute. Since all good within creation will be particularized, it cannot but be relative.

Moreover, our apprehensions are not perfect. Not only does finite being force upon us the limited perspective of finitude, but even our perceptions of that perspective are often clouded by our inadequacy (*a fortiori* for creatures less generously endowed with consciousness). For us, then, value judgments will be necessarily relativistic—*i.e.,* at best, they will be made necessarily with reference to the sort of being we are; and, at worst, they will be made through the clouds of our ignorance as well. In the latter case they will fail adequately to represent our own best interests. In neither case will they adequately represent the Good as it really is.

Now perhaps we are in a better position to compare Maimonides with Nietzsche. What Adam lost when he tasted the fruit was innocence; what he gained was subjectivity, the very gift which Nietzsche promises the superman. Adam's innocence was not the innocence of ignorance, the lack of conscience or of consciousness as Nietzscheans might be tempted to suppose. On the contrary, according to Maimonides, Adam already possessed reason, an intellect which was the measure of his likeness to the divine (*Moreh* I:1). Facts were within his domain, for he could already distinguish truth from falsity. Walking in the cool of the evening in intimate communion with God, he knew the facts about values as well. Thus, Adam was subject to the divine command, for he knew—he had been told—the truth about values. But as a result of disobedience, willful dissent from the divine command, he was alienated from the very source of rationality which had made that command accessible to him. Only then did he realize the worth of what he had lost—for only then did he become liable to a subjective perspective of value. His reason was now confined to a descriptive function; and the prescriptive role was taken over by subjective consciousness, which was faced with the task of constructing an artificial value system out of biological exigencies and subjective apprehensions—a set of values which could hardly be better than a faint, if not distorted, copy of the true good.[1]

This, Maimonides claims, is the true meaning of the story of Adam's fall. The story represents the alienation of man from the divine sources of knowledge of the absolute Good. Reason might make this knowledge available to him, but man's wilful disobedience separates him from what he might otherwise have known, and finitude obscures the truths of reason, making the supreme end, the good as known to God, as identical with Him, a mystery beyond our ken. Two differences, then, separate Maimonides' man from Nietzsche's superman: for man, as Maimonides conceives him, the transition from value-creature to value-creator already has taken place; and, for Maimonides, the change is not for the better but for the worse.

---

1. And yet man had the opportunity of maintaining the true knowledge which, apart from human willfullness, was his. He might indeed have gained thereby eternal life (*Shemonah Perakim* 8), since there is no death without sin. (See *Moreh* III:17.) And if so, it seems to follow, since man still has reason and free will (and the story of Adam is an allegory of the human condition), that the opportunity is in principle still open—as Maimonides suggests in *Shemonah Perakim* 4–5 and of course in his affirmation of human immortality.

THE ETHICS OF MAIMONIDES

Introduction

A common claim of antireligious dialectic is that there is little practical difference between the life of the believer and that of the unbeliever. God, being transcendent, it is said, will be unknown. The human mind will have no access to His decrees, and whatever moral codes or legal systems may be fathered on His name have only the arbitrary authority of human caprice to back them up. They are, at best, the products of human fancy; but delusions as to their divine origins may foster fanaticism, and the deceptions with which they are invariably presented will necessarily engender hypocrisy, which is, therefore, the inevitable concomitant of all religious notions of morality and law. Hawthorne's sanctimonious Judge Pyncheon in *The House of the Seven Gables* and the cowardly reverend Arthur Dimmesdale of *The Scarlet Letter,* Dostoevsky's Grand Inquisitor, and Lucretius's Agamemnon, stretching out his hand to cut his daughter Iphigenia's throat, are all literary symbols of the same familiar theme: religion is at best irrelevant, at worst a source of deep impiety.

No one can gainsay the evidence; nothing can outweigh the crimes and crusades, the atrocities which have been committed in the name of religious zeal, except the lives of the sincerely religious, who find in their understanding of the Holy an inner peace and joy which infuse their lives and the lives of all they touch. Sincerity alone is not the key, for the fanatic is sincere. Rather, there is a kind of genuineness to the contact of the truly religious, the *hasid* or the *tzaddik* or the saint— every language has a name for him—the true measure of whose saintliness is in the fulness of his love. It is no accident that (as Spinoza observed without comment) the Hebrew word for piety (*hesed*) means love.

There is a family of qualities known by many names in many cultures. The Greeks called them virtues (*aretai*) and mentioned courage, wisdom, justice, self-control, and generosity of spirit as prominent among them. The Christians valued charity especially, and humility; the Hindus, *ahimsa* or reverence for life; the Arabs, patience and forbearance; the Hebrew prophets, uprightness and lovingkindness. Are such qualities the fruit of an awareness of or propinquity to God? Can they be? This last, at least, is a question which our study of Maimonides' theology enables us to answer.

The world depends for its existence, according to the argument of Maimonides, upon the act of God, a necessary being of absolute simplicity who totally transcends that to which He has given being. Despite transcendence, it is possible for this Being to be known—for the determination of the world's finitude is the expression of what we, from our perspective, would call God's will or mind. We can give no absolute sense to such attributions, we can only identify such attributes of Divinity with their very expression in the world. But we are cognizant of that expression itself in the order and array of animate and inanimate nature, in the immanent rationality of the cosmos, and in the reason principle immanent in the mind of man.

Human wisdom necessarily is finite, for the same reason that the stars necessarily cannot all be placed everywhere in the cosmos. For finitude to exist at all, there must be determinacy. And it is self-evident that the determinate can never be coequal with or even proportional to its absolute Determinant. But this does not imply, somehow, that the determined is any the less an expression of the Determiner.

Man, like the world, does not exhaust the Divine Nature or even live up to it, but this does not imply that he does not reflect it. There are perfections in reality, the positive characters of being, which make something better than nothing and the higher in the chain of being or evolution better than the lower. The fact that these perfections are not absolute does not render them any the less objective. Inability to perceive them must be due to the very worst of sicknesses, that which inverts life and death, being and nothingness, consciousness and nullity, in the scale of perfections. Unwillingness to acknowledge them must be ascribed to the most unwholesome of perversities, that which takes sickness for good health. What is true of nature at large will be true of human nature as well. Here too perfections will be found.

If it is true, then, of human nature and nature at large, that objective perfections are to be found at every level, then we already have the key to the relation between God and nature and, hence, to that of God and human ethics. The perfections found in nature will be relative to the being of that in which they are found; as perfections they are nonetheless benchmarks of the Creator. It is not the case that theists are to argue from the Divine Perfection to the virtues of man. Rather, the argument is empirical. Discovering the finite particulars of perfection in nature and man, the theist is led to the postulation of an Absolute Perfection as their source, a Source who is, Himself, far transcendent of the particularities of perfection which point the way to Him without ever truly reaching Him. Ethics, then, is not to be derived from theology; quite the contrary, as Maimonides writes, a sound moral sense is the prime prerequisite for the initiation of any theological investigation. Valid theological concepts are built upon valid moral concepts. It is precisely because we know that all our moral concepts are necessarily confined within the purview of human perspectives, limited at best by the limits of human moral sensibility, if not actually perverted or suborned through the weaknesses to which all "children of Adam" are prone, and precisely because our moral concepts, although they may be perfect in their kind, cannot be perfect absolutely, that we know with certainty that we shall never comprehend in its entirety the Wholeness of Divinity.

It should be clear by now that the fact of moral relativity, *i.e.,* the fact that human ethical notions will never be more than human, or even the fact of man's ethical independence, the fact that man himself and he alone must make his own ethical decisions, unguided as Adam may once have been by the reassuring certainty of divine authority, the fact as simply stated by the Rabbis that man must stand as his own moral authority: "All is in the hands of Heaven except the fear of Heaven"—none of these facts in any way diminishes the burden of moral responsibility or renders ethical choice an arbitrary matter, a matter in which it is impossible to err or in which the very fact of choice becomes somehow its own justification.

It has been fashionable since the time of Nietzsche for some writers and philosophers in the name of Existentialism to represent the inaccessability of moral absolutes to man as logically implying or actually being equivalent to the death of God. Existentialists thereupon divide into two camps: those who joyfully celebrate the death of God and loss of value absolutes as though it conferred upon man a new kind of freedom never previously enjoyed, and those who deeply mourn the same event as though man were now confronted by a new kind of dilemma (the agony of ethical choice without absolute standards). The aura of modernity cast over this Existentialist dilemma is illusory. It is part of the human condition—as the story of man's loss of Eden endeavors to make clear—that man is forced to choose, for better or worse, in the realm of ethics, guided by no better lights than his own. The fact that these lights are necessarily his own, necessarily human, and subject to human limitations, does not make ethical choice any the less a human responsibility and does not make valid choice, within those limitations, any the less possible. If the concept of choice has any meaning at all (and Existentialist philosophy in particular is predicated on the assumption that it has), valid choice must be neither necessary nor impossible, but simply possible, contingent on the decision of the will itself.

What difference, then, is there between a purely humanistic ethic and the ethic of the theist? There is a kind of coherence added to the ethical experience of the theist by his belief that in their Source all goods are one. The virtues are united, not in conflict, by dint of the fact that they all serve the same goal. All goods are united. There is no truly tragic clash of values, no absolutely irreconcilable conflict; there is a level at which all conflicts are resolved, all particularities overcome. All there is has a place in the general scheme. Sin is not positive evil but the preference of a lesser good. The good man's life is bound together by the threads of a common theme which runs through all his endeavors: the striving for perfection. In reaching out for wealth or life, health or pleasure, the good man knows the limits of the reasonable; these limits are set by his own objective or goal, which is the cultivation of virtue, the refinement and development of his character to the point where ethical choice is not an agony but second nature. What is this goal if not the emulation of the attributes of God as these manifest themselves in the world, in terms which human beings can comprehend and emulate: compassion, patience, lovingkindness? What is it if not the discovery of wisdom, through which an understanding of divine Goodness as the unique Source of all natural (or relative) perfections may be made to shine through one's every act—the reaching out for, the attainment of divine goodness, insofar as this is humanly possible?

The ethical dimension of religion is for the Rambam the least problematic. Regarding ethics, he writes with a clarity and simplicity which clearly reflect the moral certitude of Micah or Hillel. Man's goal is the perfection of his humanity. One who fails to perceive such a truth fails in the first instance not in theology but in morals. He will inevitably fail in theology as well.

This, perhaps, will be sufficient to make clear how it is possible for the Rambam to write a systematic and objective ethic on the heels of his remarks as to the necessary subjectivity of all human ethical perceptions. It may explain as well why that ethic is grounded humanistically in the particularities of human nature and experience. If we comprehend the links binding the Rambam's ethics to his theology, then it will not be difficult to understand how he can propose the endeavor to know and become like God as the unifying feature of all ethical endeavor, despite his belief that man can never absolutely comprehend God—how it is possible for Maimonides to say that every moral act of man, despite the fact that neither God nor the Good is perfectly known to us, brings us closer to God, closer to perfection.

Shemonah Perakim

AUTHOR'S PREFACE

. . . You should realize that what I have to say in these chapters . . . is not original . . . but is simply garnered from the discussions of the Sages in the Midrash and the Talmud and other writings of theirs, from the discussions of the Philosophers, ancient and modern, and from numerous other authors: we must heed truth whoever speaks it. . . .

1. THE HUMAN SOUL AND ITS FACULTIES

Man's soul, you must recognize, is one, but it has various differentiated functions . . . called faculties or parts, as in "the parts of the soul." This is a designation frequently used by the Philosophers. In speaking of parts, they do not intend, however, to suggest a division like that to which bodies are subject, but rather simply to enumerate its diverse actions, which are to the soul at large as parts are to a complex whole.

To improve the character is, as you know, to treat the soul and its faculties. Just as the physician . . . must understand the body he treats as a whole and must know its parts, just as he must know what things make it sick that they may be guarded against and what things make it well that he may seek to secure them, so he who would treat the soul, who wishes to improve his character, must understand the soul as a whole and know its parts, what makes it sick and what cures it.

In this sense I say that the parts of the soul are five: the nutritive (also called the vegetative), the sensitive, the representational,[1] the faculty of arousal, and the rational. As already stated, we speak only of the human soul. For the nutritive faculty, for example, by which man is sustained is not that of a horse or an ass, but that of a man.[2] . . . In the same way, men and all animals are said to be sensitive purely homonymously, not that sensation in man and in other animals is the same. . . . For each species has its own soul quite distinct from

1. Or in the classic sense, imaginative.
2. For what sustains an ass or a horse will not sustain a man.

that of every other. . . . The situation might be represented by three dark places illumined—one by sunshine, one by moonlight, one by candlelight. . . . Note this point well, for it is quite different from what one might expect; and many would-be philosophers founder on it, and thus fall prey to various absurd consequences and false beliefs.

Returning to our subject, the anatomy of the soul, I say that the nutritive part comprises the faculties of gathering, retaining, digesting, expelling waste, growing, reproducing, and separating necessary from refuse fluids. The discussion of these seven functions . . . belongs to the art of medicine and is not requisite here.

The sensitive part comprises the five senses commonly known to the masses: sight, hearing, smell, taste, and touch—the last being located throughout the body's surface and having no particular organ as do the other four.

The representational part is the faculty of recalling the impressions of sense objects after they have ceased to affect the senses which perceived them. This faculty can also combine and separate various components of impressions derived from perception to construct likenesses of things perception never actually beheld, and which are, in fact, impossible to behold. Thus, a man may represent to himself the image, for example, of an iron ship flying through the air, or of a man with his head in the heavens and his feet on the ground, or a beast with a thousand eyes, and many other impossibilities which his powers of representation may concoct and endow with imaginary existence. It was on this account that the Mutakallimun made the great and grievous blunder which forms the cornerstone of their sophistry. In classifying the necessary, the possible, and the impossible, they thought or caused people to think that anything which can be imagined is possible, not realizing that this faculty can represent to itself constructs whose existence is impossible, as we have remarked [see *Moreh* I:73, premise 10].

The arousal function is that by which a man desires or dislikes a thing. From this faculty, the following sorts of action stem: pursuit and flight, inclination and avoidance, anger and gratification, timidity and boldness, cruelty and compassion, love and hate, and many other characteristics of the soul. All the bodily organs are instruments of these faculties: the ability of the hand to grasp and touch, the foot to walk, the eye to see, the heart to stir up courage or fear, and the rest of the bodily organs, internal and external alike. They and their powers are subservient to this faculty of arousal.

The rational part, found in man, is what enables him to think, understand, master the sciences, and discriminate fair actions from foul. Its functions are either practical or theoretical. The practical is divisible into the mechanical and the deliberative. The theoretical is that by which man knows changeless things as they really are—in short, the sciences. The mechanical aspect of the mind is that which is able to learn the arts—construction, agriculture, medicine, navigation, and the like. The deliberative aspect of the practical mind is that by which one examines what he desires to do at the time he desires to do it to determine whether or not it is possible to do it and, if so, how it ought to be done.

This is as much as it is necessary to state here regarding psychology. You ought to know, however, that the single soul whose parts or faculties have just been enumerated is analogous to matter: reason is what gives it form. When it does not attain this form, its capability of acquiring it is wasted and in vain. . . .

2. *HOW THE FACULTIES OF THE SOUL*
TRANSGRESS; DESIGNATION OF THOSE IN WHICH
GOOD AND BAD CHARACTER TRAITS ARE FOUND
Now, to observe or transgress the commandments of the Law belongs only to the sensitive and arousal aspects of the soul. . . . The nutritive and representational parts are not subject to commandments and thus do not transgress.[1] For in neither case is their action in the least voluntary or conscious, nor can a man consciously suspend or abate any of their operations. This is plain, since these two faculties, the nutritive and imaginative, unlike any others, operate during sleep. Regarding reason, there is some question, but I say this faculty too has an obligation regarding belief of what is true . . . but it is not prop-

---

1. Yet the Rambam calls imagination the evil inclination—as a source of error, not as a source of sin: sin requires the action of the will.

erly the subject of actions which are obligatory or infractions of obligations.[2] . . .

The virtues are of two sorts, moral and intellectual; and there are two corresponding sorts of faults. The intellectual virtues belong to the rational part of the soul. They include (1) *wisdom*,[3] *i.e.,* knowledge of the immediate and ultimate means to ends (which presupposes an awareness of the ends which are to be sought [4]); (2) *reason,* which consists of (*a*) speculative reasoning, which is ours by nature (that is, the primary conceptual elements are), (*b*) the acquired intellect,[5] which it is not requisite to discuss here, and (*c*) cleverness, the ability to understand things immediately or in a brief time. The opposites of each of these are the intellectual faults.

Moral virtues, for their part, are found only in the arousal portion— the sensitive is merely its support in this regard. There are a great many such virtues specific to this part of the soul, *e.g.,* temperateness, liberality, uprightness, modesty, humility, contentedness, courage, faithfulness, etc. The vices of this portion of the soul involve either excess or deficiency in these regards.

But the nutritive and imaginative are not said to be virtuous or vicious; the nutritive is said only to function properly or improperly, as it is said, "So-and-so's digestion is functioning properly" or "is upset"; and the imagination is said to be clear or confused, without reference to virtue and vice. . . .

3. THE ILLNESSES OF THE SOUL
The Ancients say that the soul, like the body, may be sick or well. Health in the soul means that the soul and its parts are properly adjusted for the constant performance of good or appropriate acts. For the soul to be sick is for it to be so maladjusted as constantly to

---

2. Since belief contains a volitional as well as a cognitive aspect. Only the latter belongs to the rational faculty properly speaking.
3. The *phronesis* of Aristotle.
4. Ethically, wisdom involves knowing how to get what we want, which presupposes knowing what to want. The true object of all rational endeavor, as the wise man knows, is the good (see chapter 5, below).
5. The seat of revelation. For Maimonides' account of prophecy, see Part Five of this volume.

produce bad or improper actions. The health and illness of the body are seen to by the art of medicine. Now, just as those who are physically ill may (because their sensibility is impaired) mistake sweet for bitter or bitter for sweet or may take what is good for them to be bad for them and develop a strong predilection not only for things a healthy person would not like or would reject with disgust but even for things which might be harmful, such as dust or coal or strongly acidic or very sour foods, so those whose souls are ill, *i.e.,* those who are bad or of vicious character, take bad for good and good for bad. A bad man has an abiding preference for excesses which in fact are bad but which, through the illness of his soul, appear to him to be good.

When sick people who do not know the art of medicine realize they are sick, they consult physicians, who inform them of what they ought to do, prohibiting what seemed pleasant and prescribing various bitter and unpleasant substances in order to restore their bodies' health and their ability to choose what is good and reject what is bad. In the same way, those whose souls are ill ought to consult the wise, who are healers of souls, and they will prohibit those bad things which were thought to be good and cure them, using a kind of psychiatry for the treatment of the virtues of the soul, which I shall discuss in the next chapter. But those whose souls are sick but are unaware of their illness, imagining themselves to be well, or who are aware that they are ill but do not seek help, will end as does the man who is physically ill but continues to indulge himself, neglects to seek a cure and dies before his time.

Those who persist in following what they know to be unwholesome inclinations are portrayed by the truthful Torah in their own words: "Though I walk in the stubbornness of my heart [to increase thirst by drinking]" [1] [Deuteronomy 29:18]. This means they intend to slake their thirst but only make themselves more thirsty. Those who are unaware of their moral illness are spoken of frequently by Solomon: "The fool's way is straight in his own eyes, but he who listens to

1. Maimonides does not complete the quotation but, as is his common practice, just writes "etc." in place of the bracketed words. I translate the omitted words in accordance with the Rambam's gloss. "As often in Scripture, the consequences of the idolator's self-congratulation are here represented ironically as his purpose," J. H. Hertz, *Pentateuch Commentary, ad loc.*

counsel is wise" [Proverbs 12:15]. Which is to say that he who listens
to the counsel of the wise is wise, because the latter shows the former
the way that is really straight, not just the way he thinks is
straight. . . .

4. THE CURES OF THE ILLNESSES OF THE SOUL

Good actions are those which are balanced between two extremes,
excess and deficiency, both of which are bad. The virtues are acquired
traits, dispositions of the soul poised between two bad sorts of disposition (one involving excess and the other deficiency) so as to produce
good actions. Temperateness, for example, is a character trait which
can be located between overindulgence and insensibility to pleasure.
To be temperate, then, is to act well; and the mental set from which
such action follows is an ethical virtue. But overindulgence at the one
extreme and total insensibility to pleasure at the other are both completely bad, and the two corresponding states of character . . . are
faults.

In the same way, liberality may be located between niggardliness
and prodigality; courage, between recklessness and cowardice; dignity, between superciliousness and churlishness; humility, between
conceit and self-deprecation; contentedness, between avarice and leth-
argy; goodheartedness, between meanness (or being a wretch) and excessive "goodheartedness." Forbearance is situated between irascibility and insensitivity to scorn and contempt; modesty, between
impudence and bashfulness—and so forth. One need not use the conventional terms, so long as the concepts are clear.

Often men err regarding these actions, supposing that one of the extremes is good and virtuous. Sometimes, they mistake excess for a
good, as in thinking recklessness is a virtue and calling those who are
oblivious of the risks they take with themselves courageous. When
they see a man who is totally reckless, who throws himself into danger
and deliberately ignores the risk of death, escaping perhaps only by
chance, they sing his praises and call him a hero. Sometimes, on the
other hand, they suppose the deficient extreme to be the good and call
lack of spirit forbearance or say of the lazy man that he is contented
with his lot; or the man who is too dull-natured to enjoy any pleasure,
they call temperate or abstemious. They err in the same way when

they suppose that extravagance and excessive goodheartedness are good ways of acting. This is entirely mistaken. What is really praiseworthy is the middle course; that is what a man must aim for, striving always to weigh what he does to find this middle ground.

You must understand that these virtues and vices of character are acquired and ingrained in the soul solely by repeated performance of the actions they bring about over a long period of time until they become habitual. If those actions are good, we acquire a virtue; if bad, a vice. Since men are not by their innate nature virtuous or vicious (as we shall explain in chapter 8 [1]) and since, from infancy, they doubtless will habitually perform the sorts of actions customary in their families and among their countrymen, which may be oriented toward the mean or may be, as we have seen, excessive or defective, their souls may become ill and may require treatment just as their bodies do. When the body's equilibrium is upset, we observe in which direction the balance has shifted and force it back in the opposite direction, until the equilibrium is restored. Once the balance is restored, we cease this and do only what will maintain the proper equilibrium. The same thing is done with moral attributes. For example, if a man appears to have developed the personality trait of depriving himself of anything good (because of niggardliness)—this being a fault of the soul, responsible for bad actions as we have made clear in this chapter—and we wish to cure him of this illness, we must not order him merely to be more generous. That would be like treating a man who had a high fever with some mild dose which would not break his fever. No, what we must do is have him spend extravagantly, over and over again, so many times that his propensity to be stingy disappears and he is nearly a spendthrift. But we do not let him become one; we order him to keep up his generous actions but guard against both excess and deficiency.

If, on the other hand, the man appears to be extravagant, we order him to act in a more niggardly fashion and to do so repeatedly. But he should not do so quite as repeatedly as the niggardly man must perform prodigal acts. This rather fine distinction is based on one of the subtle guidelines the therapist employs, for it is easier and simpler for a spendthrift than for a miser to come back to the mean of liberality.

1. *Q.v.* Contrast the Christian concept of original sin.

Similarly, it is easier and simpler for a man insensitive to pleasure to reform than it is for an overindulgent man. That is why we impose more ascetic actions on the sensuous man than we do sensuous actions on the insensitive man. In the same way, the coward must be required to expose himself to danger more than we require the rash man to commit cowardly acts; the wretch requires more habituation to benevolent actions than does the excessively goodhearted man to meanness. This is a guiding principle in the therapy of ethical character,[2] so bear it in mind.

In keeping with this principle, saintly persons did not hew strictly to the mean in establishing their customary dispositions, but tended a bit to the excessive or to the deficient as the case may be, providing a margin [3] and precaution. Regarding pleasure, for instance, they tended away from temperance, slightly toward insensitivity to pleasure; away from courage, slightly toward recklessness; away from goodheartedness, slightly toward excessive goodheartedness; from modesty, slightly toward lack of spirit; and so forth. This is what they are getting at when they speak of "going further than the strict sentence of the Law" [Baba Metzia 35a].

Some saintly persons at certain times inclined to the extreme—fasting, vigils, abstinence from meat and wine, celibacy, wearing clothes of wool or hair, living in the mountains or living as hermits in the deserts. None of this was done for any other reason than as therapy such as we have discussed—or on account of the corruption of the people of the society. For when the pious saw the corruption of such men and feared that they themselves might become corrupted by associating with them and seeing their doings, they fled to wilderness lands and to places where no evil man lived, as the prophet Jeremiah says (peace upon him), "Let someone but give me a lodging house in the wilderness and I will leave my people and be done with them, for they are all adulterers and a band of renegades" [Jeremiah 9:1].

When the unenlightened saw pious persons doing these things, not

2. As a consequence of the fact that the mean is not necessarily at an arithmetic middle, but that one extreme or the other may be closer to the good, as well as the psychological fact that certain habits exert a stronger hold on the mind than do others.

3. Maimonides echoes the famous dictum of Pirkei Avot (1:1)—allow a margin, literally, make a fence (seyag) around the Law.

understanding their intentions, they thought such behavior good in itself and purposed, as they thought, to become like these saintly persons. They mortified their bodies with every sort of torture, thinking
they were thereby acquiring virtue and merit and doing good and by
this means bringing man closer to God—as though God hated the body
and wanted to destroy it! They did not understand that these actions
are bad and productive of the gravest character faults. There is nothing
to which one can compare such ignorant men but to a man who,
knowing nothing of the art of medicine, sees expert physicians treating
critically ill patients with such purgatives as colocynth, scammony, or
aloe and cutting off their food, with the result that they are cured fully
and saved from death. Foolishly he concludes that if such treatments
cure the sick, they must be all the better for keeping the well in health
or augmenting their health, so he proceeds to take those medicaments
regularly and to follow the regime of a sick man. Such a fool will
doubtless become ill; and just as surely will they become psychologically disturbed who take psychiatric treatment when they are well.

That perfect Torah, which makes us perfect—as is attested by one
who knew it well: ''The Lord's Torah is perfect, restoring the soul; the
Lord's testimony is sure, making wise the simple'' [Psalm 19:9]—
mentions not a word in support of such prescriptions. The intention of
the Law is that man should live naturally and moderately, eating and
drinking what he pleases in moderation, enjoying sexual unions as permitted, in moderation, living in society, uprightly and in good faith—
not that he should live in mountain or desert wastes, wear hair shirts,
or afflict his body. The admonition against such practices, according
to the tradition, is in the statement that the Nazirite [4] ''shall make
atonement for himself for sinning against the soul'' [Numbers 6:11].
What soul did he sin against? ask the Rabbis, of blessed memory.
Against his own, by depriving himself of wine.[5] Does it not follow *a
fortiori* that if one who abstains from wine must make atonement, then
one who deprives himself of all comfort and enjoyment must all the
more so? From the words of our prophets and the Sages of our Law,
we find that these men have moderation as their object, the preservation of body and soul as prescribed by the Torah. God, through His

4. One who took upon himself a voluntary oath of asceticism; see Numbers 6.
5. *Nazir* 19a, 22a; *Taanit* 11a; *Baba Kamma* 91b; *Nedarim* 10a.

prophet, answered those who asked whether or not the annual fast was to be perpetual. They asked Zechariah, "Shall I weep in the fifth month, a *Nazir,* as I have these many years?" [Zechariah 7.3]; and He replied [through the prophet], "When you fasted and mourned in the fifth month and the seventh these seventy years, was it for me? When you ate and drank, was it not you who ate and drank!" [6] Thereupon He commanded them simply to be upright and virtuous, not to fast, saying, "Thus says the Lord of Hosts: Judge truthfully and act kindly and compassionately toward one another." And then He said, "Thus says the Lord of Hosts: The fasts of the fourth, fifth, seventh, and tenth months shall be joyous, happy holidays for the House of Judah. Peace and truth must you love." Understand that "truth" here means the intellectual virtues, since they are changelessly truthful (as stated in chapter 2). "Peace" here refers to the moral virtues, by which peace is made real in the world.

To return to my purpose. If those of our coreligionists (for it is only of our coreligionists that I speak) who imitate the Gentiles [7] claim they practice self-mortification and abstinence from all pleasures solely to discipline their psychological powers, to train their souls to incline slightly in a given direction, in accordance with the principle we have explained in this chapter that a man ought to do so, then they are mistaken, as I shall explain: the Torah forbids and ordains what it forbids and ordains for no other reason than this: that we should, by habitual practice, keep our distance from a given extreme. That is the reason for all the dietary prohibitions and for the restrictions on forbidden unions. That is the reason for the prohibition of fornication and for the strict legal requirements regarding marriage and wedlock. Even all this does not permit love-making at all times. It is still forbidden during the menstrual period [8] and after childbirth. And with all this, the Sages of our Law decreed a diminution of sexual intercourse by forbidding it in the daytime (as we have explained in *Sanhedrin*). All this was commanded by God solely to keep us well away from the extreme

6. Zechariah 8:9; fasting, like eating, is for man's benefit, not for God's; its purpose was the reform of character.
7. In the adoption of quasi-monastic ascetic practices.
8. As rather strictly defined by the Law, the menstrual period is not confined to the actual days of menstrual flow.

of overindulgence and cause us even to depart slightly from the mean in the direction of insensibility to pleasure in order that the disposition of temperateness would be firmly entrenched and ingrained in our souls.

In the same way, all the Law contains regarding giving of tithes, gleanings, forgotten sheaves, the corner of the field, the single grapes and the small bunches,[9] the law of *Shemittah* and Jubilee,[10] and the law that justice in charity is according to need—all this is close to excessive goodheartedness, so that we may keep well away from the extreme of meanness. . . .

Test most of the commandments by this criterion and you will find they serve to train and habituate our psychological dispositions: thus vengeance, bearing a grudge, and blood retaliation are forbidden by the words, "You shall not avenge, you shall not bear a grudge" [Leviticus 19:18], "You assuredly shall help him lift it up" [Deuteronomy 22:4]—to weaken the force of anger and spite.[11] The same holds for "You shall surely return them" [a strayed ox or lamb, etc. Deuteronomy 22:1], which serves to purge the tendency to avarice. Similarly, "You shall rise before a hoary head and show respect to the old," etc. [Leviticus 19:32], "Honor your father and your mother," etc. [Exodus 20:12], "You shall not diverge from what they tell you" [Deuteronomy 17:11], serve to purge one of pride and produce a disposition toward modesty. Thereupon, to preserve the distance from the opposite extreme of shamefacedness, it says, "You shall surely

9. Illustrating the refusal of the Law to set any strict upper limit to the fair share of the poor.

10. Land is to be left fallow in the Sabbatical year (*Shemittah*) and its produce is to be used in common; debts are remitted at the end of the year. In the fiftieth or Jubilee year, the laws of *Shemittah* are observed and all slaves are to be freed, all land to revert to the original (hereditary) owner. This law was designed to prevent the establishment of a permanently impoverished (or enslaved) class, and thus in Maimonides' terms to prevent the permanent institution of modes of economic relation which fostered an exploitative mentality as a trait of character and social policy; *cf.* the Rambam's account (in chapter 8) of Pharaoh's inability to extricate himself from his policy vis-à-vis the Israelites.

11. The Torah commands helping one's enemy unload his ass or lift it when it has fallen, not by way of forcing us to "love" our enemies—which may become a form of spite—but, according to Maimonides, as a moral exercise in self-control. If we can control our wrath, even with our enemies, enough to help them right an accident, the passionate force of anger in the personality gradually will be abated.

rebuke your neighbor," etc. [Leviticus 19:17], "You shall not fear him" [a false prophet], etc.—to eliminate excessive modesty [12] so that we may remain within the middle way.

If anyone foolishly tried to add to what is already given, further restricting eating or drinking, for example, or further restricting sexual unions, or if anyone should give away all his worldly goods to the poor, or should consecrate more to charity or sacred use, or estimate the value of consecrated property beyond what is assessed by the Torah,[13] unwittingly he would be doing what is bad, departing from the mean completely, and going over to the opposite extreme. Never have I heard a more wonderful remark than what the Sages have to say on this subject. In the Palestinian Talmud, *Nedarim,* chapter 9, speaking against those who impose vows and oaths upon themselves to the point that they are bound like prisoners, they say, "Rabbi Iddai said in the name of Rabbi Isaac: 'Are not the restrictions of the Torah enough for you, that you bind yourself with further restrictions!' " That is what we mean by moderation, which is neither excessive nor deficient.

It becomes apparent from the discussion in this chapter that one should aim for moderation in one's actions and not go to any extreme except by way of therapy to counter the opposite tendency. . . . The perfect man must keep his character constantly in review, constantly weigh his actions, and daily test his psychological cast. Whatever tendencies he observes in himself toward any extreme, he must swiftly treat, not leaving a bad set to be hardened, as we have shown, by repeated performance of the bad action to which it gives rise. He must pay attention to his faults, therefore, and constantly endeavor to cure them in the manner we have prescribed. For it is impossible for a man to be without some deficiency.[14] The Philosophers said long ago that it is a hard thing and a rare one to find one whose nature contains all vir-

12. *I.e.,* excessive concern for what others might think.
13. Leviticus 25:27 and Mishnah *Arakhin* set forth the proper means of estimating the fair value of property consecrated to the use or maintenance of the Sanctuary. It is as much a transgression of the Law to overestimate as to underestimate one's obligation.
14. The perfect man is humanly perfect, not divine: he has faults but is as perfect as a man can be in that he constantly battles to overcome them.

tues,[15] the moral as well as the intellectual. . . . As Solomon (peace upon him) said categorically: "There is no man on earth so righteous as to do good and never sin" [Ecclesiastes 7:20].

Moses himself, as you know, the master not only of Antiquity but also of Posterity (peace upon him), was told by God, "because you did not trust in Me to sanctify Me" [Numbers 20:12], "because you disobeyed Me at Meribah Water" [Numbers 20:24].[16] . . . All this! And his sin—that he inclined slightly away from the mean with respect to one particular virtue of character, namely, patience,[17] and toward spiteful anger when he exclaimed, "Hear me, rebels," etc. [Numbers 20:10].

God was strict with him because for a man like him to be angry before the whole congregation of Israel in a situation which did not call for anger was, relative to such a man, tantamount to blasphemy. For they all modeled their actions upon his and studied his every word in hopes thereby of finding fulfillment in this world and the next. How, then, could anger be seemly in him, when it is, as we have made clear, a bad mode of behavior and has only bad psychological effects? . . . Moses was not addressing a nation of fools nor a nation which lacked virtue but a people the least woman of which, as the Sages put it, was on a par with Ezekiel.[18] Everything Moses said and did was scrutinized by them. Thus, when they saw him angry, they said: "He has no faults of character; unless he knew that God is angry at us for asking for water and that we have angered Him by so doing, he would not have gotten angry." But we do not find that God

15. Cf. Plato, *Republic* 487D, *Phaedo* 69C.

16. Therefore, you will not be suffered to enter into the Promised Land.

17. Muslims traditionally claim infallibility for Muhammad. Maimonides not only explicitly denies such a claim with respect to Moses but imputes to him a character fault as well in regard to his impatience: it was not for losing his temper that Moses was punished, but for allowing his character to reach such a state that the passion of anger was able to get the best of him. See also *Moreh* I:54.

18. *Mekilta* to Exodus 15:2. For the people as a whole experienced a "vision" of God on a par with that which the prophet Ezekiel was vouchsafed: theologically, they were not on a level with Moses (*cf. Moreh* I:54, 63); and thus their vision (*cf. Moreh* III:6), like Ezekiel's, was not entirely incorporeal. But they were not without virtue or discernment or they would have been incapable of any such awakening.

(blessed be He) was angry in speaking to Moses about this matter. He simply said, ''Take the staff . . . and give water to the congregation and their cattle'' [Numbers 20:8].

Well, we have digressed from the theme of the chapter, but resolved one of the difficult problems in the Torah, about which a great deal has been said. It is often asked, what was the sin of Moses? Consider the answers usually given and what I have said, and the truth will work its way out.[19]

To return to my purpose: if a man weighs his actions at all times and sees to it that they are directed to the mean, he will rank with the highest rank of mankind and thus draw nigh to God, sharing in His goodness. . . .

5. THE SUBORDINATION OF MAN'S POWERS TO THE SERVICE OF A SINGLE GOAL

A man ought to subordinate all the powers of his psyche to reason, in accordance with the principles set forth in the previous chapter. He ought always to hold out before himself a single goal: to come as close to God as humanly possible.[1] That means to know God and to put all one's words and deeds—both what one does and refrains from doing—at the service of this goal, so that nothing he does will be futile in the sense of not contributing to the attainment of that goal. His intention, for example, in eating, drinking, making love, sleeping, waking, moving, resting, should be directed solely to the well-being of his body. His object in preserving bodily health should be that the soul might find her instruments [2] in a sound and healthy state so that

---

19. The truth Maimonides intends is that which is suggested by his remark that only with reference to idolatry does Scripture refer to God as angry (cf. Moreh I:10, 18, 23, 36). As long as man is not totally and willfully alienated from the Source and Standard of all good, he is not to be thought of as unalterably lost. Moses' task as a leader was to minister to the needs which had caused the people to despair, not to deepen their despair by blasphemously suggesting that their lack of moral fortitude had caused God capriciously to withdraw His favor from them.

1. The true goal of the philosopher, according to Plato (Theaetetus 176).

2. The bodily organs, according to the analysis of chapter 1, are instruments of the soul in the sense that they are the means by which the organism's functions are carried out.

she might acquire wisdom and moral and intellectual virtues by which this goal of fulfillment is reached.

By this standard, pleasure is not the sole object, as though a man chooses for food and drink only that which tastes good (and so forth in every other area of behavior). Rather, one's object should be the wholesome and beneficial, regardless of whether or not it happens to be pleasurable. When pleasure is sought, it should be as prescribed by medical science, to arouse a flagging appetite with tasty, well-seasoned foods . . . to dispel melancholy by listening to various sorts of music and melody, or by strolling through lovely gardens or buildings, or by looking at beautiful forms. . . . The purpose of all such activities is to restore the body's health,[3] and the object of the effort to restore bodily health is to enable man to acquire wisdom. The same is true with the business of earning money. The purpose of acquiring money is to be able to spend it worthily and well to sustain the body and preserve one's life until one is able to attain to and learn what it is possible for man to know of God.

The art of medicine, then, considered in these terms, has a major role to play regarding the virtues and knowledge of God, and thus in the attainment of true fulfillment. The study of medicine, therefore, and the development of medical knowledge are tasks of the greatest moment, not at all on a par with weaving and carpentry. For through medicine our actions may be refined and made human and conducive to the acquisition of true virtue. When a man eats whatever tastes good and smells appetizing, although it may be bad for him and might make him seriously ill or even cause his sudden death—as far as I am concerned, such a person is no better than an animal. For this is not properly human behavior,[4] rather, this behavior is man's inasmuch as man is an animal, "like unto beasts that perish" [Psalm 49:13]. Man acts in a properly human manner when he eats what is wholesome, at times avoiding the pleasurable and eating what is unpleasant but good for him. This is action in accordance with reason, and that is what demar-

3. Depression (melancholia) has been regarded since the time of Hippocrates as an effect of a biochemical imbalance.
4. An animal must be guided by appetite and instinct; man, in ignoring what reason and science (which is the fruit of reason) teach, descends to the animal level.

cates man in his actions from all other living things. Similarly, when a man's sexual activity is directed by pleasure, without regard to the good or harm it may bring about, he acts not as a man but as an animal.

It is possible that all a person's activity might be directed to the good, as we have stated, but that he would have made bodily health and freedom from illness his sole objectives. Such a person is not a truly virtuous person.[5] He has simply chosen the pleasure of good health where another might have chosen that of eating or sex. None of these is the true goal. But it is valid to make our bodily health and continued well-being a goal in order that the instruments of our soul's faculties, that is, the bodily organs, may remain unimpaired and that the soul, unhampered, may concern itself with the moral and intellectual virtues.

The same is true of every form of knowledge or science a man may learn. With those studies which provide a direct avenue to our goal, there is no question that this is the case. As for those which do not directly serve this goal, such as the fields of arithmetic, conic sections, mechanics, many of the areas of geometry, hydraulics, and numerous others of the sort, the object of their study should be to sharpen the intellect and train our mental faculties in the methods of argumentation, so that one may become capable of discerning demonstrative from nondemonstrative arguments. This, then, will become his means of attaining knowledge of the truth of the existence of God.

The same is true of all a man's conversation: one need not say anything but what will be beneficial to the soul or avert harm from body or soul—one should speak either of some form of knowledge or virtue, or praise virtue or a good man, or censure vice or a bad man. For to censure and deprecate evil-doers is a virtue and an obligation, if the intention is to diminish them in men's eyes in order to alienate men from them and cause others not to do as they do. . . .

When a man makes this way of living his object, he will find very

5. Or not truly pious. Piety and virtue for Maimonides are inseparable. True virtue cannot be confined to the sphere of material self-interest or even to the wider sphere of social utility. Rather, true morality reaches its peak in the *hasid*'s special relationship with God, which, in turn, infuses his attitude toward others and himself with a rectitude and spirituality whose Source is transcendent.

many of his former sayings and doings futile; he will not trouble to decorate his walls in gold or to have gold embroidery on his clothes, unless with the object of raising his spirits so that his soul may be healthy and well-removed from any morbidity, so that it will be clear and ready to learn. Thus, the Sages said, "A pleasant house, a comely wife, and a comfortable bed for the scholar" [Shabbat 25b]. For the soul is fatigued by constant concentration upon difficult problems. Just as the body grows tired from hard labor to the point that rest and relaxation are required to restore its vigor, so the soul too must relax and refresh itself by contemplating works of art and other beautiful things. Thus, it is said that when the Rabbis grew tired, they would talk in a lighter vein [Shabbat 30b]. Used in this way, such things as pictures and decorative work on buildings, utensils, and clothing are not in the least to be thought of as frivolous or bad [see also *Moreh* III:25].

You should realize this level of morality is extremely elevated, and so difficult that only a few, after enormous efforts at self-discipline, are able to reach it. If one were fortunate enough to discover a man who lived at this level—*i.e.,* who exerted all his powers for the sake of knowing God and who did nothing, great or small, and said no word unless it raised him higher or was conducive to raising him higher, who examined every act and move he made before making it to see whether or not it would bring him closer to his sole objective— then I would rank such a one no lower than a prophet.

It is toward this that the Holy One, blessed be He, calls upon us to strive [6] when He says, "You shall love the Lord your God with all your heart, and with all your soul, and with all your might" [Deuteronomy 6:5], *i.e.,* with every part of your soul.[7] . . . The Sages (peace upon them) sum up the whole matter so concisely . . . that you can tell they must have spoken with divine help—for others have written whole books on this subject without fully handling it. They said, among their injunctions, "and all that you do, for the sake of Heaven" [*Avot* 2:12]. . . .

---

6. The imperative is supererogatory: there is virtue in striving toward this goal, but no blame in failing to achieve it.

7. Maimonides identifies the powers or faculties of the soul with the might spoken of here.

6. *THE DIFFERENCE BETWEEN A VIRTUOUS OR*
PIOUS MAN AND ONE WHO "OVERCOMES HIS
IMPULSE" AND CONTROLS HIMSELF

The Philosophers say that he who restrains himself does what is right
and good but does so yearning to do what is bad. He overcomes his inclination; and, by resisting the promptings of his appetites, his faculties, and the natural bent of his character, he regretfully and reluc-
tantly does what he should. The virtuous man, however, acts in
accordance with the promptings of his desires and the bent of his character. He performs good actions desiring and deeply wanting to do so.
The consensus of the Philosophers is that a virtuous man is worthier and
more perfect than one who merely controls himself. While they admit
it is possible for the self-controlled man to be like the virtuous in many
ways, they still regard him as, on the whole, inferior. For he desires to
do what is bad, even if he does not actually do it, and this inclination
toward evil is a character flaw. Solomon expressed this long
ago . . . : "A joy to the righteous is the doing of justice, an agony
to evil doers" [Proverbs 21:25]. Thus, we see that the Prophets are in
accord with what the Philosophers state.

Consulting the words of the Sages on this subject, however, we find
that they hold one who longs to commit transgressions to be worthier
and more perfect than one who does not feel such desires and does not
regret abstention from them. Thus, they say that the worthier and more
perfect a man is, the greater his desire to sin and his regret at not so
doing. This they express as follows: "Whoever is greater than another
has also a greater inclination" [1] [*Sukkah* 52a]. This was not enough
for them. They went on to say that the reward of him who controls
himself is proportionate to his distress in so doing: "According to the
trouble is the wage" [*Avot* 5:23]. Beyond this, they enjoined that a
man ought to yearn to transgress! They forbid one to say, "I am naturally not inclined to this transgression," even though the Torah does
not forbid this. Rabbi Simeon ben Gamaliel says, "A man should not
say, 'I have no desire to eat milk with meat, to wear *shaatnez*, [2] to
enter a forbidden union,' but rather, 'I do desire it, but shall not do it,

1. A stronger evil inclination to overcome.
2. Clothing containing both wool and linen fiber, wearing of which is prohibited in the
Torah: Deuteronomy 22:11, *cf.* Leviticus 19:19.

for my Father in heaven has so commanded me.' " [3]

Taken simplistically, the two doctrines seem at first sight to contradict one another. Such is not the case. Both doctrines are true, and there is no contradiction between them at all. The evils spoken of by Philosophers as those which it is worthier not to desire are those all men recognize as evils, such as shedding blood, robbing, stealing, defrauding, injuring those who have done one no wrong, returning evil for good, scorning one's father and mother, etc. These are mitzvot [commandments] of which the Sages said, "Had they not been written, it would have been proper to write them" [4] [*Yoma* 67b]. Some of our more recent rabbis, infected by the Mutakallimun, called them the rational commandments. [5] The soul which longs to do any such thing as these or feels a yearning in that direction is defective indeed. The worthy soul will not be inclined to any such evils at all and will not regret refraining from committing such acts. But the things of which the Sages said that it is worthier and more to be rewarded to overcome one's inclination toward them than to feel no such inclination are the revealed laws. [6] And this is true. For were it not for the Torah, such things would not be evils at all. That is why they said that a man ought to allow himself to continue to love such things and allow nothing to restrain him from them but the Torah itself. Thus the wisdom of their example. They did not say, "A man should not say, 'I do not desire to kill, steal, or lie . . .' but all the things that they cite are revealed: milk with meat, wearing *shaatnez,* illicit unions. These and others like them are the mitzvot which God called "My statutes," as the Sages say, "The statutes [*hukkim*] I have ordained for you, you have not leave to cavil at, though the nations of the world revile them and Satan himself denounce them, for instance, that of the red heifer, that of the scapegoat, etc." [*Yoma* 67b]. . . .

3. *Sifra* to Leviticus 20:26 and Midrash *Yalkut ad loc.* (but with attribution to Eleazar ben Azariah). Unless a man regards the ordinances in this light, he will not feel their force as divinely imposed obligations. He may act in accordance with the Law, but he will do so *per accidens,* not in full awareness of intentional fulfillment of a mitzvah. *Cf.* Kant's distinction between acting in accordance with the (moral) law and acting out of reverence for it.

4. *I.e.,* as supplements to the Torah.

5. As though the rest were irrational! See Part Five of this volume.

6. *I.e.,* those the human mind could not have specified by its own authority.

Thus, it is clear from what we have said which transgressions are more worthily not desired . . . and which the opposite. Remarkably, the two doctrines both stand; and their language [7] reveals the truth of our interpretation. . . .

7. THE BARRIER—WHAT IT MEANS

Frequent reference is found in the Midrashic [1] and Aggadic [2] literature, including the Talmud, to the fact that certain prophets see God through numerous veils or barriers, while others see Him through just a few, depending on their nearness to God and the level of their attainment as prophets. Thus Moses, they say, beheld God through a single clear partition, *i.e.*, a transparent one. In their words: "He looked through a pellucid lens" [*Yevamot* 49b].[3]

The purport of this reference to partitions is what I am about to tell you. As we made clear in chapter 2, the virtues may be moral or intellectual. Similarly with the vices: some are intellectual, such as foolishness, witlessness, and stupidity; others are moral, such as overindulgence, arrogance, irascibility, proneness to anger, impudence, avarice, and so forth—for there are a great many. (We have already stated the system by which they are known in chapter 4.) All these character faults are the barriers which separate men from God. The prophet's words make this clear: "For it is your iniquities which have divided you from your God" [Isaiah 59:2]. . . .

You must understand, then, that no prophet has ever been able to prophesy until he possessed all the intellectual virtues and most of the moral ones, including all the most important moral virtues. They say, "Prophecy falls only on the wise, the brave, and the rich" [*Nedarim* 38a; *cf. Shabbat* 92a]. The "wise" is doubtless he who combines all the intellectual virtues. "Rich" denotes a moral virtue, contentment,

7. The fact that the Sages refer to "transgressions" rather than evils.
1. The homiletical commentaries on Scripture.
2. The fabric of legend and allegory by which Jewish tradition is enriched.
3. I translate in accordance with Maimonides' interpretation here and at *Kelim* XXX, 2, to which he here refers: the sole barrier between God and Moses is called a lens, the Rambam explains, because while it is transparent, *i.e.*, conceals nothing, it does not show things in their true magnitude and position. Thus, Moses' experience of God was undistorted by any flaw of his mind or character but still necessarily reduced to finite scale and set in finite perspective by the very fact of the prophet's finitude.

inasmuch as they call the contented man rich, when they define "rich" as follows: "Who is rich? He who is happy with his lot" [*Avot* 4.1], meaning that he is content with what opportunity brings him and does not pine for what it does not. "Brave" too denotes a moral virtue, *i.e.*, self-control in accordance with reason, as we have explained in chapter 5. For they say, "Who is brave? He who subdues his inclination" [*Avot* 4:1].[4]

It is not requisite that a prophet should have all the moral virtues and no faults whatsoever. For Solomon was a prophet, as is testified by Scripture: "In Gibeon did the Lord appear to Solomon" [1 Kings 3:5]. But we find he had vices, to wit, his excessive sexual appetite, shown by the excessive number of his wives. . . . It plainly says, "For Solomon had sinned in these things" [Nehemiah 13:26]. David too (peace upon him) was a prophet, for it says, "To me spoke the Rock of Israel" [2 Samuel 23:3], but we find him to have been ruthless. . . . It says plainly in Chronicles that God did not permit him to build the Temple, finding him unworthy because of the multitude he had slain: "You shall not build a house unto My name, for you have spilled much blood" [1 Chronicles 22:8]. In Elijah, of blessed memory, we find a trait of wrathfulness. And, although it was exercised only against deniers of God, and it was against them His anger was directed,[5] nonetheless the Sages declare that God took him from the world, telling him, "No one is fit to govern men who has as much zeal as you, for he will be the death of them" [*Sanhedrin* 113a]. Samuel too we find to have feared Saul; and Jacob feared to meet Esau. These traits and others like them are the partitions or barriers of the prophets. . . .

It is not improbable, then, that a few moral deficiencies diminish the level of prophecy, for certain character faults, we find, such as anger, prevent it altogether. . . .

Once Moses understood that he had removed every barrier between himself and God, once he had perfected within himself all the moral and intellectual virtues, he sought to apprehend God as He really is, since nothing any longer stood in the way. He said, "Show me, pray, Thy Glory." Then God caused him to understand this was impossible

4. *Cf.* also the Rambam's remarks on prophetic boldness, *Moreh* I:46.
5. *Cf.* the end of chapter 4, above.

as long as he was form in matter,[6] *i.e.,* as long as he was a man. Thus He said, "For a man shall not see Me and live." One barrier, then, and one only remained between Moses and the apprehension of God as He really is, the transparent barrier of human reason, from which he could not separate himself. . . .

8. ON HUMAN NATURE AND CHARACTER

It is impossible for a man to be born naturally and innately virtuous or vicious, just as it is impossible for a man to be born naturally possessing any particular sort of skill.[1] It is possible, however, for him to be born naturally receptive to a virtue or a vice on account of a proclivity toward one sort of action rather than another. A man, for example, whose fluid balance is slightly on the dry side, whose brain is clear of excess fluids, will learn, recall, and understand things more easily than a phlegmatic man, whose brain is clogged with fluids. Even so, if the biochemically receptive man is left completely undeveloped and uninstructed, then his potential will remain unaroused, and he will doubtless remain a dolt. Contrariwise, by instruction and explanation the naturally dull-natured, phlegmatic type can be made to know and understand, but with difficulty.

In just this way, the man whose blood is a bit hotter than normal is found to be bolder, *i.e.,* naturally fitted to become courageous. If taught courage, he will readily become courageous. Another's blood may be cooler than it should be, and he will be liable to cowardice and timidity. Training and habituation in cowardice will readily make it a part of his character. Any endeavor to make him brave will succeed only with great difficulty. But he will doubtless develop as habit trains him.

My object in setting forth this point for you here is simply that you should not regard as true the insane sophistries of the astrologers who think a man's nativity makes him either virtuous or vicious and he is forcibly compelled to act accordingly. I know our Torah and the Greek Philosophers are in clear agreement on the fact, which they well attest

6. As long as he was a finite particular. See also *Moreh* I:21, 61, 63.
1. For virtue as understood by the Rambam is very like skill; it is a knack for the art of living—and thus is necessarily acquired rather than innate. Vice too, being a habit of the mind, is acquired; *cf.* chapter 4.

by argument, that all a man's actions are up to him and not at all subject to compulsion. Thus nothing whatever other than a man himself can turn him toward virtue or toward vice, with the sole exception, already elucidated, of the biochemical basis. And that only makes a given course easier or more difficult. By no means does it compel or prevent absolutely.

If it were the case that man is compelled to act as he does, then all the commands and admonitions of the Law would be voided and the whole Torah totally false, since man would have no choice regarding what he does. Likewise, if human action is subject to compulsion, that would put an end to teaching, studying, and training in the arts. All such efforts would be futile or in vain, since it would be impossible, in any case, for one not to perform the foreordained act, resist understanding the preselected science, or avoid acquiring the predestined characteristic, because of the compelling force of external causes, according to this view. Reward and punishment, too, would be perfectly unjust, not only between man and man but also between God and man on this view. For if Simeon slew Reuben, how could we punish him, seeing he was predestined to do so and Reuben predestined to be slain? How, indeed, could a just and righteous God, who is to punish him, pass sentence on him when he only did what it was impossible for him not to do and what he could not have prevented himself from doing even if he had tried? All preparations and precautions, too, would be wasted effort, from building houses and obtaining food to fleeing when frightened and every other sort of precautionary measure. For that which is predestined to occur could not possibly not take place.

But all this is totally false, unreasonable, and counterintuitive, undermining the authority of Torah and blasphemously attributing injustice to God. The indubitable truth is that all a man's actions are his responsibility, to do or not do as he wills, without compulsion. For this reason it was proper for man to be addressed in the imperative: "Behold, I set before you this day life and good, death and evil . . . therefore, choose life" [Deuteronomy 30:15, 19]. He gave us free choice between the two, and therefore there is punishment for those who disobey and reward for those who obey: "if you hearken," and "if you do not hearken" [11:27–28]. Therefore, too, there can be an obligation to learn and to teach: "You shall teach them to your children" [11:19], "You shall learn them and observe them" [5:1]. . . . Precautions, too, can be made obligatory, as it is written in the Torah, "Make a railing on your roof lest you bring blood upon your house" [2] [22:8], "lest he die in battle" [3] [20:5–7]], "No man shall take as security the upper or the nether millstone" [4] [24:6]. And there are many more examples like these in the Torah and the Prophets.

The saying of the Sages that "all is in the hands of Heaven except the fear of Heaven" [*Berakhot* 33b, etc.] is true and in concord with what we have stated. But often men err by supposing certain of their voluntary actions to have been involuntary, such as their marrying a particular person or having a certain sum of money. This is not true. If the woman was duly and lawfully married, and she was one whom the man was permitted to marry, and he did so with the object of being fruitful and multiplying, then he has fulfilled the commandment to be fruitful and multiply [Genesis 1:28, 9:1]. But God did not predestine the performance of commandments.[5] Likewise, if a man marries a woman unlawfully, that is a transgression. God does not predestine a transgression. The same is true of one who robs another, or steals or cheats another of his money and perjuriously denies it. If we say that God foreordained this money would come into his hands and leave the possession of the other, then God will have ordained a crime. Such is not the case. Rather, among all a man's actions which are clearly brought about by his own free choice are those subject to divine commands and prohibitions. For we have already shown in chapter 2 that the commandments and prohibitions of the Torah are only as regards those actions a man may choose to do or not to do. And in this aspect of the soul [the will] is found the fear of Heaven, which is, accordingly, not "in the hands of Heaven." Rather, it is entrusted to human

2. *I.e.,* do not be guilty of manslaughter for failure to take proper precautions.
3. A man who has just been married, planted a vineyard, or built a house is exempt from military service as a precaution against tragedy.
4. A precaution against the debtor's being left unable to make a living.
5. The divine decree ordains what shall take place, but the giving of a commandment implies the possibility of obedience and disobedience, *i.e.,* of free choice and voluntary action, not the necessary fulfillment of the commandment in a predetermined manner.

choice, as we have explained. When they say "all," therefore, they must intend natural [6] phenomena, regarding which a man has no choice, such as whether he is tall or short, whether it rains . . . etc.— all things in the world apart from man's motion and rest.

This theme of the Sages, that the fulfillment and transgression of divine commandments are not up to God or dependent on His will but rather on the will of man, is an extension of the words of Jeremiah: "From the mouth of the On-high comes neither evil nor good" [Lamentations 3:38], for by "evil" Jeremiah meant evil deeds, and by "good," good deeds. Thus, he is saying that God did not foreordain man's doing of either good or evil. That is what makes it appropriate for a man to weep and mourn over his sins and transgressions, since he has sinned by his own free will: [7] "What shall a man mourn who lives? Let him mourn over his sins" [3:39]. Then he goes on to say that the cure of this malady is in our hands, for just as we did wrong by our own free choice, so it is in our power to turn back from our evil ways. Thus, he says immediately thereafter, "Let us search and examine our ways and return to the Lord, lift up our hearts on our hands to God in heaven" [3:40–41].

The widely held popular doctrine, however, found not only in the words of the Sages but also in those of the Prophets, is that for a man to sit or stand—all his movements—are according to the will of God and at His pleasure. This doctrine is true, in a sense. For when a stone is tossed into the air and falls, we say correctly that it fell in accordance with God's will. For God willed all earth to be at the center. Therefore, whenever a part of the earth is thrown upward, it comes down again.[8] . . . But it is not the case that God wills this bit of earth to fall at the time it falls, as the Mutakallimun would have it. . . . We do not believe this, but that the willing took place during the six days

6. Human nature may appear to be predetermined in the same way; but, as Maimonides has already made clear, the basic constitution of human nature does not determine the course of human action but only renders more or less difficult the development of certain strains of character. Human action is determined not by nature but by character, and the development of our character is (as shown by the story of Pharaoh below) very much in our hands.

7. Regret and repentance would be entirely inappropriate in cases of involuntary action.

8. *I.e.*, God willed this stone to fall inasmuch as He willed the laws of nature to hold.

of creation [9] and that all things continue forever in accordance with their natures, as it is said: "What has been is what shall be, what has been done is what shall be done, and there is nothing new under the sun" [Ecclesiastes 1:9]. For this reason, the Sages were compelled to say that all the wonders which go beyond the course of nature, both those which have occurred and those boded for the future, were foreordained during the six days of creation, nature being constituted at that time so that these exceptions to its usual course would occur at the appropriate junctures and appear to be spontaneous violations, although in fact they were not.

This subject is discussed at length in Midrash *Kohelet* and elsewhere, and one of the doctrines stated in this regard is, "The world follows its accustomed course." The Sages, you will observe, invariably avoid attaching the divine Will to particular things or particular times. Thus, when it is said that a man's sitting or standing is at the will of God, it must mean man's nature was made such at his original creation that he could sit or stand by his own free choice, not that God wills now, when he stands, that he should or should not stand—any more than God wills now when this stone falls that it should or should not fall. The whole point is that you must believe that just as God willed man to have fingers, to be broad at the chest, and to stand erect, so He willed that he should be self-moving, should come to rest of his own accord, and should act by his own free choice and not be absolutely compelled or restricted to a particular choice.

The truthful Torah makes this clear when it says, "Lo, the man has become as one in it [10] to know good and evil," etc. [Genesis 3:22]. The Targum [11] interprets the words "one in it to know good and evil" as intending that man was now unique in the world, *i.e., sui generis,* possessing a characteristic he had in common with no other species. What was it? That by himself and of his own accord he knew good and evil and could do whichever of them he wished to do, unhindered

9. *I.e.,* at the beginning of time, when the laws of nature as we know it were themselves framed.

10. The correct translation is generally understood to be "as one of us," but I translate according to Maimonides' interpretation.

11. The Aramaic translation of the Pentateuch ascribed to Onkelos.

[*cf. Moreh* I:2]. Thus, it was possible for him to reach out his arm and take [fruit from the tree of life] and eat and live forever.

Because it is part of the existential condition of man that he do good and evil actions by his own free choice, it becomes obligatory for man to be taught the ways that are good, to be subject to commandments and prohibitions, to be punished and rewarded; and all this is entirely just. For the same reason, it is appropriate for man to train himself in the commission of good actions to the point that these become habituated in him as virtues and to shun evil actions so as to remove from himself any vices he might have. He must never say his character is such that it cannot change, for every man's character can change for the better or the worse, entirely according to his choices. . . .

Now, one topic on this subject remains for us to explain. There are certain passages on account of which some suppose that God predestines human disobedience [wrongdoing]. This is false. We must, therefore, explain these passages, since many people have been misled by them. One such passage is God's saying to Abraham, "They shall enslave them and afflict them for four hundred years" [Genesis 15:13]. "Do you not see," they say, "that God decreed that the Egyptians were to oppress the seed of Abraham? Why then did He punish them, when it was by compulsion and predestination that they enslaved them?" The answer is this: the case is just as though God had said that of those who were to be born in the future, some would be good, some evil. And this is true. Nothing in these words in any way requires any evil person to be evil or any good person to be good. Every person who is evil is so by his own choice. Had he wanted to be good, he would be able to do so; nothing stops him. Every good person, likewise, if he wanted to be bad, could become so; nothing stops him. For the words in question were not spoken regarding any particular person, such that he might say that he is already predestined. Rather, the words are of purely general application. Every person remains free, as the very essence of his nature requires. Thus, every man of the Egyptians who persecuted or oppressed the Israelites might have chosen not to do so had he so desired. For it was not decreed that a given individual would persecute them.

The same answer may be given regarding God's words, "Lo, when you lie with your fathers, this people shall arise and go whoring [after the gods of the foreign of the land]," etc.[12] [Deuteronomy 31:16 ff.]. There would be no difference between God's having said this and His having said, "Whoever transgresses so, I shall deal with in such-and-such a fashion"—such that if no one ever does transgress in this way, the threat of punishment and all the curses become null and void. The same is true of all the penalties stipulated in the Torah. We cannot conclude, simply because we find the statutory penalty of stoning in the Torah, that he who incurs this penalty by desecrating the Sabbath was compelled to do so. Neither, then, can we conclude because certain curses occur in the Torah that those who commit idolatry and, consequently, come under the curse were compelled to be idolators.[13] On the contrary, whoever becomes an idolator does so voluntarily and is punished accordingly: "They have made a choice of their ways . . . so will I make a choice of their sufferings," etc. [Isaiah 66:3–4 ff.].

As for God's words, "I shall harden Pharaoh's heart," etc. [Exodus 14:4], and His subsequent punishment and slaying of Pharaoh, this affords the occasion for an observation out of which we may draw a major principle. . . . If Pharaoh and his counselors had committed no other sin than that they would not release Israel, this verse would represent a serious difficulty from any point of view. For Pharaoh was prevented from releasing them, as God says, "For I have hardened his heart and the heart of his servants" [Exodus 10:1], and then he was asked to release them while under compulsion not to do so. To punish him, then, and slay him with all his counselors because he did not release them would certainly be unjust and contrary to all we have said thus far. The alternative remains, however, that such was not the case. Rather, Pharaoh and his counselors had already rebelled by their own free will and without compulsion in oppressing the strangers in their

12. The passage continues by promising that if the people of Israel break the covenant, God will forsake them.

13. For the transgression is the hypothesis; the retribution, whether curse or penalty, the conclusion of a conditional statement. But no conditional proposition implies the truth of its antecedent clause. Should the antecedent prove false, the consequent (curse or penalty) is without application. The foundation of Maimonides' confidence in this claim is his belief that divine retribution occurs not by God's intervention in the particularities of temporal existence but as a natural consequence of the crime itself.

midst and persecuting them systematically, as it plainly stated in the text: "He said to his people: Behold the people of Israel are more and mightier than we. Let us deal wisely with them," etc. [Exodus 1:9–10]. This act of systematic oppression [14] was done by them of their own free will and with malice aforethought and not under any external constraint. The manner in which God punished them for this was that He prevented them from turning back, so that their justly deserved retribution would befall them.[15] The Egyptians were prevented from repenting in that they did not release them.[16] God had already made it obvious [17] that, had He wished simply to liberate Israel, He would have destroyed Pharaoh and his aides and brought Israel out of Egypt. What He willed, however, in addition to freeing Israel, was the punishment of Pharaoh for his prior oppression, as He said at the outset,[18] "And also the nation whom they serve shall I judge" [Genesis 15:14]. . . .

We thus remain unmoved from our original principle, that a man has it in his power to fulfill or transgress the imperative, that it is he who freely chooses his acts and does what he wills to do and does not do what he does not will to do. Only in punishing him for some sin he has committed does God annul the power of his will, as we have explained. But the acquisition of virtues and vices [19] is in his own hands. That is why there is an obligation to acquire the virtues for oneself, for no one else can do it for one. As they observe in the sayings collected in the present treatise: [20] "If I am not for myself, who will be?" [Avot 1:14].

14. *I.e.,* the attempted genocide of the Hebrew race through the execution of the male infants.

15. As a consequence of their stubbornness, which was itself no more than the hardening of their intended wise dealings into habits, policies, traits of character, an entrenched position from which it was psychologically and politically impossible for them to withdraw.

16. Even when it was manifestly in their interest to do so.

17. By the signs and wonders.

18. In the previously cited foretelling to Abraham of the entire Egyptian interlude (Genesis 15:14).

19. *I.e.,* the habits of character through which the will may be weakened, reinforced, or annulled.

20. *Avot,* to which the *Shemonah Perakim* is Maimonides' introduction.

Analysis

The Rambam's ethics is a compressed conspectus of Aristotle's ethics, artfully set into the context of Talmudic ethical concepts and terminology. As is necessitated by Maimonides' theology, his ethics is man-based, deriving its perception not from the divine but the human perspective and resting firmly, therefore, on human psychology.

The soul (or psyche, *nafs*) of the Philosophers was fundamentally conceived as a functional unit. In just what manner souls existed was a highly problematic and delicate question at the interface between theology and physics. But, functionally speaking, it was clear that soul was that which differentiated living from nonliving, sensitive from nonsensitive things. (Hence our word animal, from the Latin *anima*, soul.) Although phenomenologically self-consciousness manifests itself as a unity, in functional terms the actions of the human soul were differentiable into five quite distinct functions: nutrition, sensation, representation, arousal, and ratiocination.

The nutritive or, as Aristotle called it, vegetative soul comprised the various automatic and quasi-automatic functions common to all living organisms, animal and plant alike—the basic functions necessary for life.

At a higher level of integration comes sensation, present only in animals. At its fullest stage of development, sensation requires the integration (by what we would call a central nervous system) of inputs from various specialized organs. The medievals, following Aristotle, distinguished this integrative function from the individual perceptions of the particular senses. They called it the common sense (Greek: *koine aesthesis*) or representation (*phantasia* in Greek), the lineal ancestor of our concept of imagination. What was imagined or represented was literally a picture or postsensory reconstruction of sensory data, either as experienced or perhaps as recombined to form some novel image or echo of sense experience.

Volition was a fourth conceptually distinct psyche function for which analogies were traced in all animals and even in plants in the fundamental responses of pursuit/avoidance or arousal. Refined, these become love and hate, anger and desire, etc., and, most fundamentally, willing and not willing. All human emotions could be traced to one or the other of these two elemental drives, and so, therefore, could all values.[1]

Rationality, finally, as a phase in the integration of living being, is unique to man. It is at this point that the being becomes conscious of himself, and thereby acquires individual identity, subjecthood,[2] and judgment, and, therefore (following Maimonides' treatment of the "eye-opening" of Adam), moral responsibility as well.

While moral responsibility is the necessary concomitant of human rationality, it is clearly not the cognitive but the volitional to which morality applies. This is plain on two grounds: (1) It is only for actions men might have done otherwise than as they did (*i.e.,* those subject to choice and not compulsion) that they are reasonably held to account. Thus, as Maimonides argues (in clear contrast to the scruples of some puritans, both within Judaism and outside it), one is not responsible for the senses, nor for the ungoverned play of imagination, whether in sleep or waking, for this clearly is not something over which we exercise control. (2) It is only volition which generates values in us, as we have seen, by choosing and avoiding various objects.[3] These choices may be objectively good or bad for us; therefore, volition may be held responsible.[4]

With regard to knowledge, as Maimonides suggests, while it is best for us to know what is true, the attendant obligation attaches not to reason but to will and is binding upon us only to the extent that will is capable of choosing to learn. We cannot be obliged (as many Asharites supposed) to do the impossible. Thus, if there are obliga-

1. Fundamentally the same conceptual structure is followed in the *Ethics* of Spinoza.

2. And, therefore, subjectivity—for human rationality is just that, as we have seen; it is not the pure rationality of the Divine.

3. Although mind, sense, imagination, and the basal life functions, of course, may abet it.

4. This doctrine is a notable monotheistic departure from the letter of Plato's philosophy, which makes reason responsible for value judgments and, therefore, can only attribute human evil to impaired rationality. To Maimonides, as to Augustine and all great monotheist moralists, it is bad will, not merely mistaken judgment, which is responsible for human wrongdoing. In Plato's philosophy there is no real responsibility for evil, for wrongdoing is assumed to be done under the compulsion of (moral) ignorance and error. In making the will responsible for good and evil actions, Maimonides does not, however, fall into Kant's error of supposing the good will to be the sufficient condition of moral goodness.

tions regarding belief, they are obligations to discover what is true. They cannot be obligations to know a given thing without reference to its truth or its possibility of being learned.

The performance of a single good or bad action, a kindness, say, or a theft, does not make one *ipso facto* a kind person, or a thief. But behavior is relevant to the crucial issue of the formation of character. For ethics, as the Hebrew, Greek, and Arabic terms for it imply, is a matter of character. Repeated performance of a given sort of act gives one the corresponding character. Innocence or guilt is acquired by the individual choice of act, but virtue and vice are states of character, dispositions toward further actions of the same sort. They are habits of choosing, acquired by the repeated performance and enjoyment of good or bad actions.

The basic term for virtue (*malah* in Hebrew, *fadila* in Arabic, *arete* in Greek) denotes a strongpoint or excellence by which a thing is enabled to perform its function. Thus, every organ of the body has its excellence and, correspondingly, its weakness. The specific excellences of man, however, are those of the mind and rational will, the unique manifestations of soul in the human species. Intellectual virtues include the following:

(1) *Cleverness,* or intelligence in our sense of the term—that is, the ability to make logical connections swiftly and correctly. Aristotle identifies the criterion of intelligence as the ability to intuit the "middle term" immediately or in short order, thus to recognize the universal in the particular and the particular in the universal.

(2) *Reason,* which is responsible for all higher (*i.e.,* conceptual rather than perceptual or imaginative) cognition. This may be of two sorts: (*a*) *Speculative reason.* This comprises the immediate and innate intuition of such truths as the fundamental axioms of logic, which are conceptual elements of all thinking and the ability to deduce from them and the data of experience the propositions that make up the bulk of human knowledge. It is characteristic of speculative or theoretical knowledge that it proceeds discursively from that which is most evident to us to that which is least so. (*b*) *Acquired intellect.* This is the vehicle of revelation and all mystic states of awareness. Although Maimonides avoids discussing it here, it is clear from what he does say that he follows the Philosophers—particularly al-Farabi—in his

conception of the acquired intellect. According to al-Farabi, when one has proceeded quite far in the sciences, his mind becomes appropriate material for infusion of the fullness of a sort of comprehensive understanding emanating from the divine Active Intelligence, which is the real source of all truth and enlightenment. At this stage, thought no longer proceeds discursively but comprehends things as they really are, integrated in the true order of being.

(3) *Wisdom*—the *phronesis* or "practical wisdom" of Aristotle—which is most relevant to ethics since this is what affords knowledge not only of the means by which ends are to be pursued but also of the ends themselves which are attainable and worthy of pursuit. Intelligence may recognize means-ends relationships in their logical form (for means are a kind of middle term between our needs and their satisfaction), and reason may recognize particular and universal goods through theory as in the sciences or through a higher and more comprehensive insight as in prophecy or philosophy, but it is wisdom, *i.e.*, practical wisdom, which puts these insights to work in ordering men's affairs and priorities.

It is doubtful that Maimonides would admit that there is such a thing as too much intelligence, too much reason, or too much wisdom. Neither would he argue that there can be such a thing as too little murder or adultery or scorn of parents. But it is clear that there are other dimensions of human character, particularly those involving the emotions (volitional attitudes toward one's real or apparent self-interest, pleasure, advantage, disadvantage, etc.), where extremes, whether of excess or deficiency, are clearly detrimental to their subject. (See the table of moral virtues and vices on page 254.) Ingrained as habits of the mind, dispositions toward choice of the excessive or of the deficient are ultimately destructive of their subject, undermining his capability of achieving his goal of self-fulfillment. One characteristic which the mental dispositions toward excess and deficiency have in common is that both extremes are indiscriminate. The coward fears all dangers; the reckless man, none. Reason would choose a middle course, the famous Golden Mean, by discriminating the cases in which fear (or flight) is justified from those in which it is not. Such discrimination requires careful consideration of every relevant aspect of the situation, and, indeed, a well-developed capacity for distinguishing the

MAIMONIDES' TABLE OF MORAL VIRTUES AND VICES

Disposition of choice regarding:	Excess	Mean	Deficiency
Pleasure	Overindulgence	Temperateness	Insensitivity to pleasure
Immediate self-interest	Avarice	Contentedness ("Wealth")	Lethargy [Diffidence]
Expense	Prodigality	Liberality	Niggardliness
Self-esteem	Conceit	Humility	Self-deprecation
Shame	Impudence	Modesty	Bashfulness
Interests of others	Excessive goodheartedness	Goodheartedness	Meanness, being a wretch [Selfishness]
Honor	Superciliousness	Dignity	Churlishness [Lack of self-respect]
Anger	Irascibility	Forbearance	Insensitivity to scorn

All human emotions serve to orient man toward the favorable and the unfavorable. Guided by reason, they lead us to the proper mean between excess and deficiency. Applied indiscriminately, they subject us to precisely the damaging extremes which it is their function to enable us to avoid. The habituation of reasonable or unreasonable modes of choice forms wholesome and unwholesome traits of character (virtues and vices). The niggardly man applies his retentive instinct even where it is to his disadvantage to do so; the wretch refuses help to others even when it costs him nothing; the reckless man ignores even dangers which should be feared. Choice in accordance with the mean requires the application of judgment (reason) to determine what is best. Virtue, therefore, consists in the habitual making of choices in accordance with the standards of good judgment. The model is extendable to other moral virtues: *e.g.*, faithfulness is a mean between credulity and skepticism. But sin, of course, involves no virtue, hence no mean. And pure goods, such as love (*hesed*), charity (*tzedakah*), and justice (*mishpat*), too, although they must be modulated in certain respects, do not seem to have a maximum beyond which lies excess. Intellectual virtues follow their own model, since they are concerned with the development of reason itself (*i.e.*, to an optimum) rather than, as in practice, with reason's application in the adjustment of actions.

relevant from the irrelevant aspects; it cannot be done by a mere mechanical weighing or computation, for the object is to determine what is appropriate. This is the key to the distinction between virtue and vice. An automatic, stimulus-response, one-way reflex type of action is responsible for both the extremes of excess and deficiency. Virtue involves the modulation of the decision-making process by the habitual application of good judgment. Instruction, example, practice, and habituation in appropriate choice-making are means by which such dispositions are acquired.[5]

Moral standards, being grounded firmly in human nature and human needs, while not absolute, are hardly arbitrary. Take, for example, the classic case instanced by the Rambam of the pleasure-dialectic of those who "only increase their thirst in the attempt to slake it." With many human appetites, particularly those involving luxuries and the pleasures of certain educated tastes, the attempt to satisfy the appetite only enlarges it, a fact well known to Plato and all moralists.[6] In the words of Epicurus: Nature sets a limit to necessities, but with artificial wants there is no limit. Maimonides agrees. One might as well want dishes of diamond as of silver, he writes; desires, of itself, has no limit (see *Moreh* III:12). Reason, however, being self-conscious, recognizes the futility of allowing desire always to run just ahead of what one actually has. Satisfaction will never be attained until a limit is set to desire, until the mean of need is located (what Nature requires, as Epicurus says, is not much) and the virtue of contentedness is learned—contentedness, as the Rabbis specify, with what one has. Reason, again, in its role of self-critic, is needed to distinguish true contentedness from indolence, inertia, self-stultification.

The role of intellect, thus, is crucial. It is the will which implements

---

5. This is the celebrated *tendance* of the soul, of which Socrates spoke consistently as the proper task of man. Plato regarded the true function of all laws as the institution of mores which encourage behavioral patterns conducive to the formation of good character. It is clear from Maimonides' comment in chapter 4 on verse 9 of Psalm 19 that he regards the Torah as fulfilling precisely this function; *cf.* Part Five of this volume.
6. With certain unwholesome appetites, as we know, there may be more than mere psychological dependencies established, there may be addiction. Such irreversible spirals are, according to the Rambam's analysis, all too typical of the natural history of ungoverned self-indulgence.

the choices and inaugurates the practices which make contentedness a habit of the mind ("second nature," in Aristotle's words). But it is reason which recognizes the vanity of the dialectic of desires. It is reason as practical wisdom which tells us what we need and what can be gotten—not infinite pleasures or limitless "fun," for example. And it is reason which tells us how our real needs can be satisfied by suitably acting on and accommodating to the realities of our situation. Finally, it is reason which recognizes the danger of veering from one extreme to the other.

It is nonsense to pretend that there is anything arbitrary in such a process of determination, that practical wisdom is some sort of mystery or that the man of judgment is impossible to find or distinguish from his opposite. The man of good judgment (paradigmatically) is the one who does not involve himself in self-destructive or self-defeating patterns, but who knows his goal and how to go about working toward it. It is to him, in cases of moral doubt or difficulty, or where an exemplar is required for moral education or reform, that one will turn. As Maimonides remarks, it is not an obligation for everyone to be a philosopher, but it is an obligation for all men at least to benefit from the wisdom of those who have it. As Aristotle said, he who is so deficient in his character and upbringing as not to know right from wrong and not to be capable of learning this from others is badly off indeed.

Man's goal, given in his nature according to Maimonides, is the perfection of his humanity. Since man is created in the image of God, according to Scripture, and bears within himself the seeds of divinity, according to the Philosophers, his task of self-perfection is understood both from the prophets of Israel and the works of the wisest men of other nations as one of divine assimilation—to become, in Plato's words, as like to God as humanly possible. The pursuit of this goal unifies and harmonizes all actions in the lives of the wise. For God is absolute Perfection, and man's perfections—wisdom, rationality, human-heartedness—are those expressions of God's absolute goodness entrusted to man for development.

The unity of tone, harmony of purpose, imparted to human actions and lives by the organization of all human objectives (values) within the schema of this single comprehensive goal is no merely theoretical bit of theology. It is of the utmost practical import in the coordination (and subordination) of goals (priorities) which differentiates rational from absurd existence. Lesser goals, such as health, are valid but cannot be comprehensive. Other goals—wealth, pleasure, honor, or fame—may have their place in the value hierarchy but are illusory if pursued for their own sake and not for the sake of one's total well-being, development, and perfection. Such goals are of the sort that easily slip through one's fingers, and to suppose that any such objective is of absolute intrinsic value is to pursue futility. Fulfillment is found only in a life in which reason modulates all choices, the welfare of the body being sought for the sake of the soul, and the welfare of the soul for the sake of its own development as a source of goodness to others (in imitation of God's mercy, grace, and love) and as a fount of self-illumination, taking in the wisdom of creation (in imitation of God's Self-knowledge).

The same considerations which refute hedonism as an ethic—its futility, its failure to provide access to any absolute intrinsic good, its substitution for the good of that which is in certain circumstances a mere concomitant of what is conducive to our welfare—refute extreme asceticism as well. The body is the instrument of the soul. How can the music of the soul be harmonious when the body has been willfully impaired?

Modern geneticists sometimes view the body as an external vehicle for the conveyance and development of genetic information. This function, in terms of the Rambam's scheme, is just one small aspect of reproduction, which is itself just one of the seven phases of the vegetative life lying at the base of the soul's activity. For Maimonides, every organ and organ system is at the service of the soul, which is the mode of organization, the supervening purpose, the unifying idea, of the organism itself. The body serves the soul then, for the Rambam, in the same poetic sense that the phenotype of the geneticist serves the genotype. The fostering of the well-being of the body, its strength, its comfort, above all its health, upon which life itself depends, is an obligation in itself, for here perfection expresses itself on the animal level in a uniquely human way. But it is more importantly an obligation supportive of man's higher goal, as a being in whom reason appears.

The attainment of moral virtues is of help in man's integration of his life toward the goal of becoming God-like not only because this is conducive to bodily well-being. The virtues themselves, as human perfections, already constitute imitations of God. And the intimate acquaintance with such perfections which comes from practice of the virtues will, as we have seen, point the way to a fuller intellectual appreciation of the direction in which divine perfection lies. It is in these senses that moral vices constitute a barrier between God and man; clarity of character, a pellucid lens.

The notion that God, causality, or chance, or any combination of external forces is the absolute determinant of the morally relevant characters of human action to the exclusion of man himself, is in fundamental contradiction with the notions of God as lawgiver and of causes as determining their effects. Pharaoh's destruction, therefore, on retaining the Children of Israel, when it was known and foretold that God would harden Pharaoh's heart and not allow him to release them, seems at first a serious problem. Maimonides' resolution of it sheds light not only on human individual and political psychology but also on the ways in which God's judgment operates, through individual and political psychology. The refusal to release the Israelites was not the first of Pharaoh's sins. Indeed, it was but the expression of a long-established pattern of exploitation and persecution which had reached the pitch of pure wickedness years before when Pharaoh and his councilors first considered genocide: "Come, let us deal wisely with them. . . ." How were Pharaoh and the men who implemented this idea punished? They were punished, argues the Rambam, by the hardening of their insidious plan into a policy, by the incorporation of persecution as a part of their personalities, their concept of self-identity and purpose. As the escalation of a war makes its continuation a matter of policy from which it becomes increasingly difficult to disengage, as persecution of black men or exploitation of women may become the *raison d'être* of a state or the defining characteristic of an individual's personality, the bondage and the extirpation of Israel became, for Pharaoh and his accomplices (for Maimonides explicitly affirms their guilt, not by association but only by participation), a pattern, a habit of mind, a "way of life," in the sense that Naziism or slavery in the South were ways of life, from which the late and feeble pleas of reason were politically and psychologically powerless to extricate their creators. The compulsion which they themselves, by free acts of will, had instituted and nurtured to the force of a national obsession became by its very force the means by which their further choices in the matter were annulled and their inevitable destruction insured.

Vice is not mere wickedness of will; it is the acting out of bad will made habitual, made policy, a habit of the social or individual mind. Character is formed not by astral influences nor even by the humors or the genes but by human actions, and, to the extent that certain characters are beneficial or detrimental to their possessor in his search for fulfillment, vice is its own sure punishment; virtue, its own generous reward.

Environment, to be sure, in terms of the impact of exemplars of socially acceptable and unacceptable behavior patterns, does bring to bear important influences in the formation of character, impressions which legislation may serve to moderate or reinforce. And heredity, through the basic inclination of one's metabolism, may render a given course of action easier or more difficult for a given person. But an individual may always choose, as Noah did, to reject, or to refine upon, or to select among the value exemplars presented by his and the adjacent generations. It is neither example nor biochemistry, but choice which determines action. And it is the pattern of actions, the chosen lifestyle and system of priorities (value hierarchy) implemented in daily life which determines character. Thus, it is altogether fitting that character should be the vehicle of reward and punishment—for of all things which we make, our own character is the most personally ours.

For the alert reader, Maimonides makes abundantly clear just what is at stake in terms of rewards and punishments. Judaism had never taken excessively seriously the notion of creaturehood as a form of wage-servitude to God. "Do not be like servants who serve the master for the sake of a reward. Rather, be like servants who serve the master not for the sake of a reward," the Rabbis admonish (*Avot* 1:3). Indeed, to operate on vulgar assumptions, envisioning the afterlife (*olam ha-ba*) as literally a Persian pleasure park (*pardes*) and Hell as a Dantesque, Kafkaesque, or Sartrean torture pavilion, in which the Deity has prepared exquisite physical and mental tortures for the recusants not sufficiently forewarned by the fear of his demonic sense of retribution, would only be to reassume the hedonistic standard for the next world after successfully shedding it with regard to the present—to make pleasure and pain, in fact, the ultimate arbiters of human action! If sense was to be given to the ancient and widespread notion of human immortality, then that could only be done in terms of Plato's notion that man is deathless (and impassive to the vicissitudes of time) to the extent that his soul is an idea, a declension of the divine into matter, self-governing and free to the extent that he is not wholly compromised to matter, immortal to the extent that divine rationality still shines in him.

For the Rambam, Plato's notion of immortality was made feasible by Aristotle's reinterpretation of Plato's Ideas as mind-contents, thoughts-thinking-themselves in much the way that God is a thought-thinking-itself. This purged Plato's doctrine of immortality of the assumption that there are disembodied Ideas. Disembodied minds were quite another matter; God was such, and, as Aristotle had argued (*De Anima* III:5), human rationality itself—like all "form" or rationality—must have been of external provenance. Ibn Bajja, too, contributed to making of the Platonic/Aristotelian model of immortality a live hypothesis for Maimonides, for it was he who emphasized the fact that disembodied souls (or minds), being immaterial, have no arithmetic, *i.e.*, cannot be counted or said to be either one or many. This resolved the many classic paradoxes regarding the actual absolute number of souls which have existed and will exist and the nature of their relationship with other disembodied minds and with God.[7] But it created problems too. Having no arithmetic, man's disembodied rationality lacks personal identity as well. For this, a body would be required, or at least some analogue of a body as a point of reference. Thus, credally, Maimonides affirms some form of physical resurrection. But, philosophically, what can be established is some form of immortality for the soul not as a personal identity but as some sort of ideal dependency upon God. That this is what philosophy is capable of establishing of immortality is significant indeed, for this is continuous with what the human mind is capable of tasting of immortality, in the form of divine inspiration, beatific experience, in this life as well.

7. *Cf. Moreh* I:74, method 7.

The culminating experience of man as man, which marks the summit of human life as an assimilation of man to God and, if genuine, pervades every aspect of human practical and intellectual life, is the achievement of what Maimonides calls prophetic awareness of the Deity. Through such inspiration, which the Rambam regards not as the outcome of some magical theurgy, still less as the result of mental self-neglect and physical self-abuse, but rather as the culmination of a lengthy and arduous process of developing the moral and intellectual virtues, the human mind acquires, to the extent that it is able, God Himself as its object and thereby gains a foretaste of paradise by transcending its own individuality—overcoming, to the extent that this is possible, human limitations.

Maimonides is not alone among medieval authors in touching somewhat gingerly on this subject. The dangers of pantheistic and self-worshipping misinterpretations of these ideas were ever uppermost in his mind, and, while he may not have feared too much the condemnation of the vulgar (he would rather guide one wise man truly than have the adulation of a thousand fools),[8] he did hold an author (thus presumably himself) responsible for any misleading of others which might result from his work—even through misinterpretation, if such was due to negligent handling of ambiguities.[9]

This much he does make clear: revelation, inspiration, what the Ancients called mystic awakening, and human immortality are all experiences cut from the same fabric. If they differ in quality or in degree, that will be more a result of the fact that each must be tailored to the measure of the wearer than the result of any discontinuity in the Source.[10] For all of these, which are in sum the summit of human happiness (not pleasure) "in this world and the next," are reachable by men through human striving for perfection; and, in such a contest— quite unlike the futile race for pleasure, riches, and honor—the race is to the swift.

8. *Moreh* I, prefatory discourse, *ad fin.*
9. See his commentary on *Avot* 1:3.
10. See *Moreh* I:5 and Part Four of this volume.

THE OBJECT OF EXISTENCE

Introduction

The task of a philosopher, as many people might perceive it, is to provide a satisfactory answer to the question, "What is the meaning of life?" For many philosophers of antiquity and the Middle Ages this question expressed itself as a universal issue: "What is the object or intention of existence as a whole?" The answer most frequently given by Stoics and many adherents of the Aristotelian tradition was that man, the highest or most perfect of all natural species, must surely be the object for which all other things existed. And man himself, according to many adherents of monotheism, was created so that he might worship God.

Surveying the heritage of medieval philosophical and quasi-philosophical thinking of which he was the somewhat reluctant and critical heir, Spinoza calls it a matter of "general credence," "accepted as certain," that "God Himself directs all things to a definite goal (for it is said that God made all things for man, and man that he might worship Him)" (*Ethics* I, appendix). Even in the Middle Ages assent to this proposition was by no means so universal and unquestioning as Spinoza suggests. There were philosophers in antiquity who thought that the world has no purpose and that the whole category of

262

purpose is inapplicable to anything real in any objective sense. There were others, in the Middle Ages, who saw the world as a great accident, a cosmic disaster. These approaches have, of course, persisted to modern times, in the notion of certain Existentialists that life itself is futile or absurd, and perhaps also in the Positivists' claim that the categories of teleology, purpose, goal, object, or intent have no objective application.

To the Rambam such claims as these would appear to be patently false. His philosophy is in principle opposed to the wholesale elimination or distortion of major categories of experience simply because they fail to conform to our own *a priori* assumptions or desires. The categories of teleology are indispensable, for instance, in studying animal physiology, the relations of organs to organism, or in studying the psychology of human motivation. But this does not imply that the question of the overall purpose of existence is legitimate. For the question seems to assume too much. It assumes that there is a single, unified, ultimate purpose for all existence, over and against the purposes of particular things, and that this purpose is amenable to reduction to the terms of the human psychology of will and knowledge, indeed that it can be known and the criteria of its decisions put to critical scrutiny.

It is hardly necessary for Maimonides to go to the extreme of declaring existence to be futile, frivolous, or vain, for him to expose the inadequacies of this way of asking the question about the meaning of life. For where the positivists eliminate teleology, many traditionally minded monotheists seem to anthropomorphize or to anthropocentrize it. The Rambam's task, then, in tackling this question is to show how it is possible to believe that life is meaningful and existence worthwhile, avoiding the extremes of admitting that existence is absurd (or purposeless) on the one hand, or of debasing the notion of God's purpose by making man the be-all and end-all of existence, on the other.

From *Moreh Nevukhim* III

MOREH NEVUKHIM III:13

Often perfect minds grow perplexed inquiring after the object of existence. Here and now I shall expose the irrelevance of this question from any point of view. I argue as follows:

(a) Anything made or done by a purposive maker or doer must have some object or end for the sake of which it was made or done. Philosophically speaking, this is self-evident and requires no demonstration.

(b) It is self-evident as well that a thing which is thus made on purpose has come to be after previous nonexistence.

(c) It is self-evident and agreed by all that the necessarily existent, which has never not existed and never will, does not require a maker, as we have made clear. And, since it is not made, the question of its end or object is irrelevant. That is why one does not ask, "What is the end of the existence of God?" For He is not a created thing.

In keeping with these premises, it is clear that ends are to be sought always and only in the case of things created in accordance with the purpose of some being with a mind. Thus for that which arises from intellect, a final cause must necessarily be sought. But for a thing which did not come to be, as we have stated, no teleological investigation is to be undertaken.

With this understood, you should be prepared to recognize that there is no point in seeking the end of the entirety of existence—neither from our creationist point of view, nor from the viewpoint of Aristotle, which holds the world's eternity. To be consistent with the latter doctrine, no ultimate end can be sought for any part of the cosmos. For it is not permissible according to his view to ask what is the object of the existence of the heavens, or why they have this measure or that number, or why matter is such as it is. Nor can one ask the purpose of any species of animals or of plants. All these things, according to him, are under an eternal necessity which never has abated and never will abate.

Natural science does seek an end in every natural being, but this is not the ultimate end of which we speak in this chapter. For it is obvious in natural science that every natural being must have some end and that this final cause, which is the highest of the four causes,[1] is concealed in most species. Aristotle constantly proclaims that Nature does nothing in vain, *i.e.*, that every natural action must have some object.

---

1. *Viz.*, the formal, final, material, and efficient causes of Aristotle.

He plainly states that plants are formed for the sake of animals.[2] Likewise he clearly states that certain things exist for the sake of others, especially with respect to the organs of animals.

You must understand that the discovery of this type of final cause in natural things led the Philosophers inevitably to belief in a further principle, apart from nature, which Aristotle called an intellectual or divine principle.[3] It was this principle that made this for the sake of that. And you must understand that one of the strongest evidences in favor of the creation of the world, for one who is unbiased, is the demonstrated presence of some end in every natural thing. The fact that this is for the sake of that is evidence of a purposing agent, and purpose is inconceivable unless something is created [cf. Moreh II:21].

Returning to the object of this chapter, to discuss the final cause, I say: Aristotle made it clear that with natural things the efficient, final, and formal causes are one, i.e., they are one in species. The form of Zayd,[4] for example, is the efficient cause of the form of his son Omar's person, and what this cause does is to impart the form of his species to Omar's matter. Omar's end is to embody the form of humanity. And, according to Aristotle, the end of every member of a natural species which depends upon reproduction is similar. . . . But all this refers only to primary ends. As for there being an ultimate end for every species, all who discourse on nature assert this must be so. But it is difficult indeed to discover it—let alone to discover the object of existence at large.[5] The apparent outcome of Aristotle's discussion here is that he holds the ultimate end of all these species of things to be the continuance of coming-to-be and passing away (without which being could not continue in such matter as this, whose particulars can-

2. Although (given c) this contradicts his claim that species and nature as a whole are eternal.

3. For in finding particular final causes, the Philosophers sought their final causes, and the chain of ends (or goods) led them inevitably to an ultimate final cause (or Highest Good), since no causal chain could be infinite (Philosophers' premise 3).

4. His concept or mode of organization.

5. Everyone knows that when a being has reproduced, it has in some sense fulfilled itself, but why a being should reproduce, why a species should be maintained is a much more difficult question; and the question of the object of all existence is proportionately more difficult.

not endure) and the development of the highest thing which possibly could be developed from it. By this I mean the most perfect thing possible; for the ultimate purpose would be to reach the highest possible level of perfection. Clearly, the most perfect thing that could be composed of this matter is man. Thus he would be the last and highest of all these composite things, so that if it were to be said that all beings below the sphere of the moon exist for his sake, that would be true, *i.e.,* if things are set in motion for the sake of a developmental process to give rise to the most perfect product. But, in keeping with his doctrine of the eternity of the world, Aristotle cannot be asked, "What is the end of man?" For, according to him, the primary end of every particular thing that comes to be is the fulfillment of its own specific form, and every particular thing which does fulfill the functions of that form has achieved its end perfectly and completely. The ultimate end of the species is the continuance of that form, so that the continuity of the world of coming-to-be and passing away may be carried on and "becoming" not cease to seek the development of the most perfect level of being possible. Plainly then, according to the doctrine of the world's eternity, the question of the ultimate end of existence at large does not arise.

According to our doctrine of the creation of the entire world out of nothing, on the other hand, the asking of this question, the search for a final cause of all existence, might well seem necessary. Thus it might be supposed that the end of all existence is simply that the human species should exist to worship God and that all things done are done solely for man's sake, even the heavens turning solely for his benefit and in order to bring his needs into being. Certain texts in the prophetic books, if taken literally, lend strong support to this notion: "For habitation did He form it" [Isaiah 45:18]. . . . But if the heavens were made for the sake of man, how much more so were the other species of animals and plants!

If this view is examined critically, however, as intelligent men ought critically to examine views, the fallacy in it is exposed. For the advocate of this belief has only to be asked, "This end, the existence of man—is God able to bring this about without all these preliminaries, or is it the case that man cannot be brought into being until these things have been done?'' If he replies [6] that it is possible that God is able to give being to man without, say, creating the heavens, then he must be asked, ''What is the utility to man of all these things which were not themselves the object but which existed 'for the sake of' something that could have existed without any of them?'' Even if the universe does exist for man, and man's end, as has been said, is to serve God, the question remains: What is the object of man's serving God? For His perfection would not be augmented by the worship of all things that He created, not even if they all apprehended Him as He truly is. Nor would He lack anything if nothing but Him existed at all. If it is replied that it is not His perfection but ours which is served, for that is what is best for us, namely, our own becoming perfect, the same question is implied again: What is the end of our being perfect in this way? The argument can only end by assignment of this end: So God willed, or, So His wisdom decreed. And this [7] is true. So you find the Sages of Israel instituted it in their prayers: ''Thou didst set man apart from the start, and recognized him to stand before Thee. Yet who may say to Thee, 'What dost Thou?' and if man be righteous, what does it do for Thee?'' [Neilah service, Day of Atonement; *cf.* Ecclesiastes 8:4]. Thus they plainly state that there is no end but only the sheer Will.

This being so, given the belief in creation and its inevitable corollary, the possibility that causality might have been other than as it is, the absurd consequence would follow [8] that everything which exists apart from man has no end whatever. For the sole end which all these things were purposed to serve was man, and he might have existed just as well without any of them!

For this reason, the correct view, in my judgment, in keeping with religious belief and in consonance with the theories of reason, is that all beings should not be believed to exist for the sake of man's existence. Rather all other beings too were intended to exist for their own sakes, not for the sake of something else. The search for the common

6. As it seems he must.
7. The fact of the ultimate and irrefragable positivity of the Will/Wisdom, for which there is, in human terms, neither explanation nor justification.
8. From the assumption that man is the ultimate end of existence.

object of all species thus vanishes here too, on the assumption of our view of the world's creation. For we say that all parts of the world were brought into being by God's will, intended either for their own sake or for the sake of something else intended for its own sake. Just as God was pleased to have it that man would exist, so He was pleased to have it that these heavens and their stars exist, that the angels exist. For every being, God purposed the existence of that being. For what could not exist without some prerequisite thing, God gave being first to that thing, as perception precedes speech.

This view too is stated in the prophetic books: "The Lord made each thing for His/its sake" [Proverbs 16:4]. The antecedent of the pronoun might be the object ("thing"), but if it is the subject ("the Lord"), the sense is "for Himself," *i.e.,* His will, which is His identity, as has been made clear in this treatise [I:53]. We have explained as well [I:64] that His identity or self is also called His glory, in the words "Show me pray Thy glory." Thus His words here, "The Lord made each thing for Himself," would be like His words, "All that are called by My name and created for My glory, I created, yes and made" [Exodus 33:18]. It says that all that is ascribed to Me I made, solely for My will's sake, for no other. The words, "I created, yes and made," are to make clear to you that there are some things whose existence cannot be established without the prior existence of something else. Thus He says, "I originally created this first thing (*e.g.,* matter, for all material things) whose prior existence was requisite, then out of it or after it I made what it was My purpose to bring into being. There was no object but My will alone."

If you study the book which guides all who seek guidance toward what is true and is therefore called Torah,[9] this idea [10] will be evident to you from the outset of the account of creation to the end. For it never states in any way that any of the things mentioned [11] was for the sake of something else. Rather, of every single part of the world, it is

---

9. From a Hebrew root meaning to point out or guide.

10. That the higher species of things exist for their own sakes and in so doing serve God's will and no further purpose.

11. Heaven, earth, the species of animals and plants—all things held by Aristotle to be eternal, and conceded by eternalists and noneternalists alike to be the principal features of the universe.

said that He created it and its being agreed with His purpose. This is the meaning of its saying "God saw that it was good" [Genesis 1:4, etc.]. For you have learned what we have explained on how "Torah speaks according to human language." "Good," for us, refers to what agrees with our purpose. . . .

Do not be misled by its saying, anent the stars, "to light the earth and rule by night and by day" [Genesis 1:17–18], supposing it to mean they exist in order to do this. Rather it serves to inform one of their nature. . . . In the same way it says of man, "to rule over the fish of the sea," etc. [Genesis 1:28], which does not mean that this is the object for which he was created but serves only to inform one of the nature God gave him. Torah's assertion that plants, on the other hand, are put at the disposal of the sons of Adam and other animals [cf. Genesis1:29] is plainly made by Aristotle [12] and others. And it is clear that plants exist only for the sake of animals, for animals require food.[13] But such is not the case with the stars. They do not exist for our sake, to shed their beneficial influence on us. . . . From the perspective of the beneficiary of this constant flow of good, it is as if the recipient were the object of the existence of the source which sheds on him its benefits and bounties—just as a citizen may suppose that the object of the government is to protect his home from robbers. And in a certain sense this is true! . . . In just such a sense we must interpret all texts whose literal sense indicates a higher being has been made for the sake of a lower one: such texts must mean that this is what results from its nature.[14]

We deduce, therefore, the belief that all existence here was purposed by God according to His will, and we do not seek any motive or

12. *On Plants* I:2. 817b. 25. The treatise is not actually by Aristotle but probably by a first-century B.C.E. Aristotelian, Nicolaus of Damascus. But *cf. Politics* I:8. 125b. 16. Maimonides relies on *On Plants* because the *Politics* was the only major work of Aristotle's surviving canon not translated into Arabic.

13. The assertion that plants exist for the sake of animals does not render Maimonides uncomfortable because plants are lower in the scale of being than animals. It still seems possible to state that plants exist for their own sakes as well—but theirs is not as highly developed an identity. The Rambam's claim is based upon the facts that (1) without plants animals could not have existed, and (2) plants are lesser than animals in the scale of perfections.

14. Not that this was the object for which its existence was intended.

ultimate end of any sort. Just as we do not seek the end of His existence, so we do not seek the object of His will, in accordance with which He created all that has been created and all that will be created as it is. Thus do not be deluded about yourself by the notion that the spheres and angels were brought into being for our sake, for our worth has been made clear to us: "Lo, nations are as a drop from a bucket" [Isaiah 40:15]. . . . This is how one ought to believe. For if a man knows himself and is not deceived about himself but understands all beings for what they are, then he may have peace of mind, and his head will not be troubled with seeking an end for what does not have such an end [15] or seeking for an end in things [16] which have none beyond their own existence, as predicated upon the divine pleasure—or, if you prefer, the divine wisdom.[17]

MOREH NEVUKHIM III:25

Actions divide into four classes with regard to their ends: futile, frivolous, vain, and good/beneficial.

Vain actions are intended by their doer to achieve some end but fail to achieve it on account of hindrances. Often you hear people say, "I wore myself out in vain," *e.g.,* looking for a person without finding him or exhausting oneself on a business trip without making a profit. "Our effort with this patient was in vain," it is said, when he does not recover his health. And so with all actions which seek to accomplish some end and fail.

A *futile* (or meaningless) action is one not intended to serve a purpose—as when some people play with their hands while thinking. Such are all doings of mindless and oblivious people.

A *frivolous* (or playful) action is one intended to serve some low or trivial end, *i.e.,* an end neither necessary nor greatly beneficial—as when someone dances but not for exercise or does things just to make people laugh.

Such actions are doubtless to be called frivolous, but they differ according to the objectives—and the perfection—of their doers. For

15. God's will is its own end, not such an end as man would recognize.
16. *E.g.,* animal species.
17. Since God's sovereign will and wisdom are identical with His Godhead, it matters little objectively whether men differentiate the two.

there are many things which some consider necessary or important and which others hold to be totally unnecessary: physical exercise, for example, in all its different forms, necessary to the sustenance of proper health and vigor according to the medical experts,[1] and writing, which is highly beneficial in the view of scholars.[2] Thus, those who engage in sports in hope of building up their health—playing ball, wrestling, boxing, controlling their breath—or in actions done with a view to writing, such as cutting reed pens and making paper,[3] are thought by the ignorant to be merely playing, but those who know do not consider such actions frivolous.

A *good* or *beneficial* action is one intended by its doer to serve some higher end, to provide some necessity or some utility and which achieves that end.

This classification seems to me to be unassailable at each point. For each time someone does something, he either does intend some end or he does not. And every end intended is either higher or lower,[4] either achieved or not achieved. Thus our scheme is what is called for by the logic of the division.[5]

Having made this clear, I argue that there is no latitude for any rational person to say that any of God's actions is vain, futile, or frivolous. In our view—the view of all who follow the Law of our teacher Moses—all God's works are good and beneficial: "God saw all that

1. Galen (second century) wrote a short work on the benefits of ball-playing, possibly for his patient, the young Marcus Aurelius.
2. Play itself, or frivolity, may be recognized as beneficial or even necessary to human psychological well-being. Thus there may be a purpose even in indulging in purposeless activity. But no one would take seriously an adult all of whose time was spent in play—and who thus made play his ultimate purpose—or regard such an existence as a meaningful way of life. (See also *Shemonah Perakim* 4, 5.)
3. An Arabic writer traditionally cut his own reed pen to give it the proper angle. Papermaking was introduced to Christendom in the thirteenth century and did not become widespread until the fourteenth and fifteenth centuries, but it was brought to the Arab lands by Chinese war prisoners in 751.
4. Either significantly beneficial or not significantly beneficial.
5. The scheme is therefore complete; *i.e.,* the four categories given are mutually exclusive and jointly exhaust the possible types of action, analyzed with regard to purpose. It was Socrates who first proposed the method of division (analysis) as a means of attacking philosophical problems; some contemporary analysts, however, have mistaken the means for the end.

He had done, and indeed it was very good" [Genesis 1:31]. Thus everything God made for the sake of some other thing is either necessary to the existence of that thing which was the object of God's purpose or highly beneficial to it. Food, for example, is necessary to the sustenance of an animal, and the eyes are very beneficial to it in maintaining its existence. Food, in fact, serves no other purpose than to sustain the animal in life for a certain period; and the senses serve no other purpose than to provide the benefits which perception allows animals to obtain. The view of the Philosophers, likewise, is that in all of nature nothing is futile; *i.e.,* everything not man-made serves some end, whether we understand that end or not.

As for that party of thinkers who claim that God does not do one thing for the sake of another and deny the reality of cause and effect, claiming all His works are the immediate outcome of His will, ends therefore are not to be sought,[6] and one is not to ask, "Why was this made or done?" since He does simply as He pleases without concern for the wisdom of His work—why, such people classify God's acts as futile, or even lower! For he who commits a futile action intends no purpose out of negligence of what he is doing—but God, according to these thinkers, knows what He is doing but intends no end or benefit whatever.

That there should be anything frivolous in God's work is obviously impossible at a glance. The palaver of those who claim apes were created solely for men's amusement is beneath notice. Such claims are founded solely on ignorance of nature in the world of becoming and passing away and negligence of the fundamental principle that God's entire purpose was to bring into being all that was possible, just as you see it to be. For it to be otherwise was not in the least as His Wisdom ordained; that was impossible, inasmuch as things proceed according to the dictate of His wisdom.

Those who say none of God's acts is directed to any particular end were quite naturally led into this position. Regarding the whole of existence from their own point of view, they asked, "For what end does the world at large exist?" Naturally they said what every creationist would say: "Simply because God so willed, and for no other reason."

6. Maimonides derives the Asharites' denial of final causes in nature from their denial of (horizontal) efficient causality.

They then applied the same conclusion to the particulars in the world. The result was that they did not even grant that the piercing of the uvea of the eye and the transparency of the cornea are to allow the passage of the visual sense and thus the perception of what is to be perceived. In fact they do not even make this the cause of vision at all.[7] This tissue is perforated, and that one above it is transparent simply because He so willed it—even though vision would have been possible otherwise.[8]

Certain texts of ours may be found whose literal sense seems at first sight to suggest this idea, *e.g.*: "All the Lord desired, He did," etc. [Psalm 135:6]; "And His soul, that He does"[Job 23:13]; "And who shall say to Him: what dost Thou?" [Ecclesiastes 8:4]. What all these texts and others like them mean is simply that the things God wills are necessarily accomplished, since no obstacle exists which can prevent the execution of His will. But He wills only what is possible [*cf. Moreh* III:15], and not everything that is possible but only what His wisdom directs should be so. Thus the beneficent act on behalf of the end He wills [9] is what He does, and nothing can hinder or prevent it. This is the view of all followers of religion and of the Philosophers, and our own view as well. For, while we believe the world is created, none of our traditions, none of our learned men, holds that this was done by a sheer act of will alone; all of them say that God's wisdom (which is beyond our ken) made necessary the existence of the world at large when it came into being—the very same Wisdom, unchanged, which had required nonexistence before the world was brought into being.

This concept, you will find, is returned to again and again by the Sages in commenting on "He made each thing fair in its time" [Ecclesiastes 3:11 and Midrash *Kohelet ad loc.; cf. Bereshit Rabbah* IX]. All this to avoid what was well worth avoiding, the notion that the Author acts to no end whatever. Thus too the bulk of the scholars of our Law believe (and the Prophets bear them out) that all the particular crea-

7. The Mutakallimun in question allowed no explanations in terms of naturalistic causation; vision, like all other events, was the immediate creation of God; accompanying phenomena (*e.g.*, opening of the eyes, etc.) were merely their occasion.
8. God's perforation of the uvea and making the cornea transparent are therefore futile.
9. *I.e.*, the act which is good from the perspective of creation.

tures in nature were made in wisdom and by design, and mutually interdependent [10]—that all were causes and effects and none was made frivolously, futilely, or in vain. Rather all were works of consummate wisdom, as it is written, "How great are your works, O Lord. In wisdom have you made them all" [Psalm 104:24].

Most delusions that lead to perplexity and confusion in the search for the end of the world's existence as a whole or the end of any given part of it have as their foundation simply the human error of man's imagining everything exists for his sake alone, along with misunderstanding the nature of our inferior sort of matter [11] and the primary intention, which is that there should be brought into being all that possibly can exist—for existence is without a doubt a good. On account of this error and the misunderstanding of these two fundamental concepts, such doubts and confusions are created that it is imagined that some of God's acts are frivolous or in sport, some vain, and some futile! Those who were forced to swallow this repugnant implication,[12] by which God's acts are made tantamount to meaningless, purposeless, pointless behavior, put themselves in such a position only to avoid attributing the world to God's wisdom, lest that lead to eternalism.[13] That is why they ruled this out. But I have already taught you the view of our Law in this regard.[14] It is that this is what *ought* to be believed. For there is no incongruity in our saying that all these works are expressions of His wisdom—in terms of both their existence [now] and their [previous] nonexistence—despite the fact that we do not understand many of the aspects of wisdom in their Maker. It is on this view that the whole Torah of our Teacher Moses is founded. With this it opens: "And God saw all that He had done, and indeed it was very good" [Genesis 1:31]. And with this it closes: "The Rock whose

10. As could not be the case if there were not causality, both efficient and final.

11. *I.e.*, the limitations of subcelestial matter; *cf.* Maimonides' quotation from Galen in *Moreh* III:12.

12. *Viz.*, all who deny efficient or teleological causality.

13. For the claim of the Philosophers was that if nature was the effect of God's eternal and changeless wisdom, then nature too must be eternal and changeless.

14. And already refuted the Philosophers' claim as to the implication of eternalism by the attribution of the world to God's wisdom: *cf. Moreh* II:14, 18 *g*. For eternal wisdom may have a changeless (timeless) plan for changeable, temporal events.

work is perfect," etc. [Deuteronomy 32:4]. Now you must understand this. . . .

Analysis

Maimonides' demonstration of the irrelevance of the search for a single, overall purpose of existence answering to the principles of human rationality or interest is both swift and decisive. Whether one opts for the creationist or the eternalist alternative, the notion of a single humanlike purpose or intention for the world at large is untenable. Given eternalism, teleology is untenable. But, given teleology, the notion of a single end of all existence falls to the ground. Creationism, which is itself an outcome of teleology, requires the replacement of a monistic hierarchy of ends or goals by a pluralistic system which recognizes many things in the world as having been created for their own sakes (rather than for the sake of the whole or any of its parts). Anthropocentrism is displaced by a qualified humanism which sees the meaning of human life as lying first and foremost in the living and which is founded firmly on the conclusion that *mutatis mutandis* the same can be said of all things created by God: they exist not for man's sake, but for their own.

This does not imply there are no hierarchies of purposive subordination in existence or that there should be none. One thing indeed may be created for the sake of another if the existence of the former is necessary to that of the latter and if the former lies below the latter in the order of perfection. But this does not imply that every lower thing exists solely for the sake of the higher. Rather, as the argument shows, many even of the lower things must in the first instance exist for their own sakes. It is in this sense that all the objects of God's creation are called good by Him: in that they answer to His purpose and will, not to ours nor to any particular purpose or will, which His will and purpose, identical with Himself, far transcend. A glimmer of the direction of this transcendence can be had from this very difference. We call good what suits our purpose, and God calls good what suits His. But His purpose contains no element of lack, desire, or need—indeed, no particularity—therefore, no motivation other than its pure self-expression. The divine pleasure is that all that can exist shall exist and reach the highest possible level of perfection.

Man's place, then, in the universe is not as the be-all and end-all of creation but rather as a casual beneficiary of divine largesse. His existence is not so that He may serve God (who is in no way improved by having man as His servant) but for its own sake, for man's own perfection. Thus, while the divine perfection is the ideal toward which man strives (see *Shemonah Perakim* 5), it is not the case that man exists to worship God by becoming like Him. Rather he exists to perfect his humanity by becoming like Him. The difference is subtle, but what it means is that man's end (and the ends of all things which exist for their own sakes) are not outside but within them.

Far from restricting the scope of teleology by rejecting its application to the universe at large, Maimonides has restored the vigor to the notion of purposes by confining talk about them to the realm of lives and organisms where purposes can be seen and, as he would agree with Aristotle, must be recognized. Man's purpose is humanity (or rather the perfection of humanity) itself. There is no single overall end in terms reducible to those of the ends or goals of particular things. But the reason for this fact is that the purpose which creation serves is absolute and universal—the divine purpose that all things should exist as they do, for their own sakes.

In keeping with his dictum as to the preferability of negative to positive predications of the Deity and his claim that God can be known only through His act, Maimonides proceeds to interpret the notion of God's purpose in terms of the denial of any futility, vanity, or frivolity in any of God's works. For in all of them some aim is achieved (the existence of each thing for its own sake) which is by no means trivial or insignificant. This can be confirmed by the empirical study of nature itself. In seeing the world as God's creation, we attribute the goodness of all particular things (*i.e.,* their capacity to exist in and for themselves) to a Purpose which is absolute and thus beyond reduction to any of its finite expressions in the purposes of particular things.

There are those in every age who see things in the world as having no intended purpose, as serving worthless ends, or as failing to achieve the ends for which they are presumed to be intended. The Rambam's position is that ends in things are manifest—as the eye is designed for seeing, that no end in nature is base or trivial, and that nature never systematically fails to achieve its ends. Denial of these propositions has as its most frequent cause the manifest fact that it is not for our purposes that all of nature was created—the fact that God's will, expressed in nature, does not always answer to the principles of human rationality and interest. If we can see creation as a plurality of things, many of which exist for their own sakes, then we have approached somewhat closer (at least in thought) to the divine perspective.

PART FOUR

MAASEH MERKAVAH /

THE ACCOUNT OF THE CHARIOT

Divine Providence
and the Problem of Evil

In the thirtieth year, in the fourth month, on the fifth day of the month, while I was among the exiles on the banks of the River Kevar, the heavens opened and I saw visions of God. On the fifth day of the month, the fifth year of the exile of King Yehoyachin, the word of the Lord came indeed to Ezekiel the priest, son of Buzi, in the land of Chaldea, by the River Kevar, and upon him there was the hand of the Lord.

I looked, and, lo, a whirlwind came from the north, a great cloud, an engulfing flame, glowing all about, and from the midst of it, as amber in the midst of the fire. And from its midst, the semblance of four creatures, appearing so: They had the likeness of a man. Each had four faces, and each had four wings. Their feet were straight, but the sole of their feet was like a calf's. They gleamed like burnished brass. They had human hands under their wings. . . . Their wings were joined one to the next and did not turn as they went. But each creature went straight forward. The faces of the four were the faces of a man and a lion on the right side and the face of an ox on the left, and all four had the face of an eagle. Their faces and wings were separated at the top. Each had two wings joined together and two covering his person. And each went straight forward. Whither the Spirit was to go, they went, their wings not turning as they went.

The appearance of the creatures was like flaming brands of fire, as though flames were going back and forth amongst them, fire glowing, and as though out of the fire were coming lightning. The creatures darted to and fro like flashes of lightning.

As I beheld the creatures, behold, a single wheel, on the ground, near the creatures with their four faces. The wheels looked as though they were made of beryl. The four looked the same—fashioned, seemingly, one wheel, as it were, within another. As they went on their four sides, they turned not as they went. Their rings were high and awesome and were filled with colors about the four. As the creatures moved, so did the wheels near them; and when the creatures rose from the earth, the wheels rose. Whither the Spirit would go, they went . . . for the Spirit of the creature was in the wheels. . . . Above the heads of the creatures, the firmament had the aspect of dreadful crystal, extended over their heads from above. Beneath the firmament, their wings were straight, one next to the other. . . . I heard the sound of many waters, as the voice of the Almighty, when they moved, a voice bearing speech, as the sound of an army encamped.

When they came to a stop, they dropped their wings, and there was a voice from the firmament above their heads. . . . In the firmament above their heads it was like sapphire, with the form of a throne. And on the form of the throne there seemed to be a man above, upon it. I saw as the color of amber, as the semblance of fire about it. From the appearance of his loins upward, and from the appearance of his loins downward, I saw as the semblance of fire, gleaming about him.

As the sight of the bow which is in a cloud on a day of rain, so was the sight of the glow about him. This was the sight of the likeness of the Glory of the Lord. I saw and fell upon my face, and I heard a voice speaking.

From Ezekiel 1

INTRODUCTION

For the medieval thinker there was, in the final analysis, only one mystery, the mystery of the nexus between an infinite God and finite creation. This problem, the problem of theophany, divine Self-revelation, or epiphany, as it was called by Greek and Christian thinkers, was referred to by the Rambam in Talmudic language as the problem of the "account of the chariot," *maaseh merkavah,* for it was in Ezekiel's bold description of his vision that God was seen most concretely to have been introduced into the categories of the finite world. But referring to divine Self-revelation as *maaseh merkavah* is to employ metonymy, to take one small aspect of the manifestation of God in the world as though it were the whole. The notion of *maaseh merkavah* in fact encompasses all the problems considered in this book. The question of how it is that finite creatures may dare to speak of God (likening the Creator to the creature) is merely a special case of the mystery of the interface between God and creation. Likewise the problems (or problem) of creation are, as Maimonides clearly states, just another aspect of the problem of divine Self-revelation: the problem of *maaseh bereshit* is comprised within the problem of *maaseh merkavah*. For all the theological difficulties regarding time and eternity, motion, matter, and causality arise from the incongruity of the fi-

282

nite with the Infinite, which theists regard as its ground, source, or creator. The problems of ethics and of values too, as they express themselves to theists, are at bottom the outcome of the attempt to integrate the finite and human perspectives in the absolute perspective of the divine. We have seen in the preceding pages how profoundly aware the Rambam is of all these problems and how rigorous he is in setting forth the conditions for their solution. But behind the problems of creation, values, and the logic of "God," the problem of *maaseh merkavah*, divine Self-revelation, remains as yet by and large untouched.

If creation is understood to be the expression of Divinity, manifesting itself as will and wisdom, if the particular ends or goods of particular things are regarded as having been imparted to them from the absolute goodness of a Being who is pure perfection, if the capacity to recognize in the finite and relative goods of creation signposts pointing beyond themselves to an absolute, transcendent Good is regarded as having been implanted in the minds of the inspired, it remains to be seen how the Absolute can touch upon the relative, finite, and particular. In a word, it remains to be seen how creation, revelation, and divine governance of nature are conceivable. Above all, an account must be given of the mode in which divine Self-expression is delimited in its finite expressions. Stated in modern terms, what is required is an account of the dynamics of the divine act implicit in the creation and sustenance of the world or explicit in revelation. An explanation must be given of the apparent variation of God's Self-expression (as perfection, goodness, or grace) from one sector to another—what we call the problem of evil. This interrelated complex of problems is precisely what Maimonides refers to as *maaseh merkavah*.

For the Greeks, philosophical problems were divided into four main branches: (1) logic/epistemology—the study of knowing and the conditions of truth; (2) physics—the study of nature in all its forms, animate and inanimate (thus including certain aspects of psychology); (3) ethics—the study of conduct and character, including relevant aspects of psychology, and the theory of education, as well as politics; and (4) metaphysics—the study of being as such. Since metaphysics or First Philosophy, as Aristotle called it, dealt with the character of reality at large, it naturally embraced the other sciences. And since metaphysics led one to a knowledge of divinity, it was naturally identified with theology. Seen from a Biblical perspective, indeed, even metaphysics in the broad sense, encompassing all the sciences, became theological. Thus the Rambam identified the *maaseh bereshit* of Talmudic parlance—the account of Genesis and all it implies regarding the world's character as an expression of the divine will and wisdom—with the physics of the Philosophers. For, as Maimonides would say, the end and object of all human sciences regarding nature is the recognition of the divine wisdom and will expressed in all things in the world, contemplating the craftsmanship and the benevolence (to use human terms) God has manifested in creation, and thereby recognizing His transcendence and the absoluteness of His determining act in the founding of the first principles of nature. Likewise the Talmudic *maaseh merkavah* is identified by the Rambam with metaphysics. For just as the rubric *maaseh bereshit* sums up the principal issues of Biblical cosmology, the rubric *maaseh merkavah* epitomizes the very nub of what is philosophically problematic in Biblical theology and thus, if one may use the expression, in Biblical metaphysics—namely the notion of a nexus between a Deity of transcendent perfection and a world of finite particulars. What is problematic about this nexus, of course, is most clearly expressed by the fact that the Infinite is regarded as imparting some measure of its perfection to the finite without at the same time in any way becoming finite itself and without rendering the finite infinite. The paradox of providence (the problem of evil)—that God is regarded as governing the world without making it perfect and without Himself becoming enmeshed in the categories of finitude—is thus a direct expression of this more general problem.

Maimonides finds his key to the solution of this problem of the interface between God and creation in Plato's theory of knowledge, expanded as we shall see by Plotinus's account of emanation, appropriately modified for consistency with the doctrine of creation. It is from this base in one of the seminal concepts of the philosophical tradition that the Rambam works to build an understanding of the kindred notions of God's creation and governance of the world, His inspiration of prophets and giving of the Law, and the confinement of God's gift of light, being, or truth to those areas which actually are illumined.

THE PROBLEM OF EVIL

Introduction

Maimonides views the problem of evil through the window of Jewish tradition as that of the suffering of innocents, the problem of Job. Thus he explains the approach of the Philosophers as follows: given the fact that the innocent suffer, and assuming there is a God, then God must be either malevolent, powerless, or ignorant. None of the alternatives is acceptable; and, as we shall see, the solution commonly put forward as philosophical, which limited God's knowledge to universals, seemed to Maimonides to imply severe restrictions on divine power and benevolence as well. But an alternative approach had been opened by Plato himself and greatly developed by the Stoics. Perhaps the sufferings to which mankind seems indiscriminately to be subject are not evils at all.

Maimonides' approach to the problem of evil, founded upon a critique of the values the conventional statements of the problem traditionally assume, enables him initially to meet a more radical version of the problem than the Philosophers traditionally had confronted, Razi's assertion that there is more evil in the world than good. Maimonides draws his interpretation of Razi's position from the latter's striking

285

claim that creation itself was a dreadful mistake, the world would have been better left uncreated. Razi's principal arguments in defense of this extreme position were based upon the sufferings living beings undergo in the course of life and, above all, the sufferings of man. Maimonides rightly sensed that hedonism was at the base of Razi's objections to existence—for Razi, unique among the Muslim claimants to the title of philosopher, was deeply influenced by Epicureanism—and it is here, against Razi's hedonism and the anthropocentrism lying behind it, that Maimonides directs his attack.

Like the vulgar masses, the orators who flatter them, and the poets who appeal to their emotions, Razi adopted a value system which places the pleasure of the human individual at the center of human concern. Razi's is not a sybaritic philosophy. He conceives of pleasure not as mere sensuality but as a kind of repose. Freedom from pain ranks far higher in his felicific calculus than mere enjoyment. But even so, Razi's values remain hedonistic and anthropocentric: pleasure (defined as release from pain) is their orienting principle, and the human sense of the pleasurable has been made the arbiter of all value. Nor is it the human species whose interests are the measure, but rather the individual, to whose whim it seems to be left to accept or condemn being—his own and that of the world at large.

Without the assumptions of anthropocentrism and hedonism—arbitrary, irrational, and perverse assumptions by Maimonides' standards—complaints as to the absolute misery of the human condition would lose their force, and the problem of evil (the philosophical articulation of such complaints) would be vitiated. Whether we welcome the Rambam's conclusions or reject them, we must recognize that in exposing the logical dependence of the problem of evil upon hedonistic and anthropocentric assumptions, he has done much to clarify an area which for most human beings, whether inside or outside the religions, remains a source of grave perplexity.

From *Moreh Nevukhim* III

MOREH NEVUKHIM III:12

Common people often imagine that evils outnumber goods in the world, and much of the rhetoric and poetry of all nations bears in it this assumption: the wonder is that there is anything good in the temporal world. Evils, on the other hand, are said to be abundant and constant. This error is made not only by the masses but also by those who deem themselves to have some knowledge.

Razi wrote a well-known book which he called the *Theology*. Amidst its drivel and monstrous feats of ignorance he includes as one conclusion the proposition that evil is more abundant in reality than good, that if you placed man's peaceful pleasures and repose alongside the pains and sufferings, the hardships, diseases, misfortunes, adversities, sorrows, and afflictions which beset him, you would find that existence (he means human existence) is overwhelmingly an evil, a retribution. He attempts to verify this judgment by cataloguing these woes, opposing all that the monotheists have claimed regarding the manifest bounty and beneficence of the Deity, His being pure goodness itself, so that indubitably all which issues from Him is purely good.

The whole cause of the error is that this boor and those like him among the common people consider existence solely from the point of view of the human individual. The thoughtless man always imagines all existence is for his sake alone, as though there existed no other being but himself. So, if things go against his wishes, he comes to the conclusion that existence at large is evil. If man considered all of existence and conceived the insignificance of his part in it, then he would realize the truth. Men make no such outcries in behalf of the angels or the heavens and the stars, nor for the elements or their compounds, minerals, plants, and animals of all sorts; [1] their only thought is for certain individuals of their own species. If someone contracts leprosy from eating bad food, they are aghast that such a dreadful thing could happen, and equally dismayed when a promiscuous man goes blind, [2] and so forth.

From the perspective of reality, no member of the human species, *a fortiori* of any other animal kind, has any worth alongside the perpetuation of the whole of being, as the Scriptures make clear: "Man is as nothing" [Psalm 144:4], "Man is a worm; and humankind a maggot" [Job 25:6] . . . and all the other texts to this effect in the prophetic

---

1. Despite the fact that inanimate nature is filled with conflict, and often a given element or compound is overwhelmed.
2. From syphilis.

books which serve the vital and sublime purpose of informing man of his true worth, lest the individual slip into the error of supposing all being exists for his sake alone; whereas, in our belief, being exists because of the will of its Creator. Man is small indeed alongside the supernal beings, the heavens and the stars. Alongside the angels he does not compare at all. He is merely the highest phase of generation, the noblest thing to be compounded from the elements in this nether world. Yet, even so, his being is a great good, a splendid gift of God, in view of the unique attainments he has been vouchsafed.

Most of the evils which beset individuals of our species stem from themselves, *i.e.*, from deficient members of our own species. Or our complaints and cries for surcease are due to our own deficiencies. Or we suffer from evils we have produced of our own free will but attribute to God. . . .

To explain, there are three sorts of evil [3] which afflict man:

(1) Evils which man suffers on account of the nature of generation and corruption, *i.e.*, because he has a body. It is this which makes some men prey to infirmity and disease whether constitutionally or through the supervening influences of the environment. . . . Without the passing away of individuals the species itself could not be perpetuated. This makes clear the purity of the divine munificence. To desire to have flesh and blood not subject to the disabilities attendant upon matter is to wish unwittingly for a unity of opposites, to wish for something at once affectable and not affectable. For unless man were subject to effects he would be incapable of reproduction. His existence in that case would be as a single individual, not through many members of a species.

Galen says well in *De Usu Partium* III [chapter 10], "Do not become attached to the illusory notion that out of semen and menstrual blood an animal will be born which will not die or feel pain, or which will be radiant like the sun or capable of perpetual motion." Galen's words draw attention to a special case of the following general proposition: anything which can develop from whatever matter it may have develops as perfectly as it can from the matter proper to its species. Deficiencies attach to the members of the species corresponding to the

---

3. That is, things man calls evils because they affect him adversely.

deficiencies of the particular matter of the individual. The utmost that can develop from blood and semen is the human species as we know it, living, rational, and mortal. Thus this first sort of evil is necessary. Even so you will find it to be very much the exception. For cities may exist for thousands of years without being flooded or burnt. Likewise thousands are born in perfect health while a deformed babe is abnormal, or if that term seems objectionable, then very rare, not one per cent, not even one tenth of one per cent of normal births.[4]

(2) Evils which men do to one another, such as acts of aggression. These are more widespread than evils of the first sort, and their causes are diverse and well known.

Here too the origin is with us, although again the victim is not responsible. Nonetheless, nowhere in the world is there a city dominated by any such evils; here too we have the exception, as in the case of one individual attacking and killing or robbing another by night. Only in major wars does such violence become the general rule for a sizable number of people, and even then it cannot be said to engulf the greater part of the earth most of the time.

(3) Evils individuals suffer by their own doing. These are the majority of the cases, far more than the second kind. This is the kind of evil all men complain of bitterly, yet rarely spare themselves, the sort for which the victim is really to blame—where it can be said, "You brought this upon yourself" [Malachi 1:9], as it is written, "He who does it [commits adultery] does destroy himself" [Proverbs 6:32]. . . .

This kind of evil is a consequence of all vices, particularly improper indulgence in food, drink, or sex, either to excess or in some unwholesome way, or where the foods are spoiled. For this is the cause of all diseases, physical and psychological.[5] With bodily illnesses this is obvious. Psychological illnesses stem from an unwholesome regime in two ways: (a) from the change in the soul which necessarily accompanies a change in the body to the extent that the former is a faculty of

4. Frequency of all congenital malformations was estimated to be just over 2 per cent of all live births in 1968, but this included many infants who would not have lived to see a physician in Maimonides' day.

5. Functional disorders, however, such as heart disease, birth anomalies, organic mental disorders, etc., may be treated, in large part, under type 1.

the latter and behavior is conditioned by the bodily constitution, and
(b) from the fact that the soul becomes accustomed to certain things
and so acquires a habit of desiring them. Now these things are not necessary to the preservation of the individual or the species, and the
desire for them is insatiable. For, while all necessary things have a
definite measure, there is no limit to the superfluous.[6] If your ambition
is to have silver dishes, gold would be still better. Others have
crystal—why not emerald or diamond if you can get it! [7] People who
are ignorant and without a proper sense of values are always pining for
the luxuries others have, and will as a rule expose themselves to great
dangers such as sea travel and royal service to acquire them. But as
soon as such a man is overtaken by any of the misfortunes inherent in
the paths he has pursued, he complains bitterly against God's judgment and decree, carps at fate, and marvels at the fickleness of fortune. How can it be that he has been deprived of money enough to buy
sufficient wine to keep him always drunk and enough girls decked out
in gold and precious stones to keep him sexually excited beyond his
capacities—as though the whole object of existence were the pleasure
of such scum!

This misconception of the populace even causes them to believe that
God has no power over a creation subject to what they imagine to be
such dreadful evils—because He did not give being such a nature that
every immoral man can gratify his vice to his wicked heart's content
(which, as I have just shown, is to seek to fill an infinite demand).

Wise and good men understand the wisdom of this existence, as
David makes clear: "All God's ways are love and truth for them who
heed His covenant and His testimonies" [Psalm 25:10]. He tells us
that those who heed the nature of being and the prescription of the
Law [8] and understand their own role readily perceive God's goodness
and truth in everything. This is why they adopt as their goal the purpose for which they were intended as human beings: comprehension.
Because the body has needs, they seek to supply its wants—"bread to
eat, clothing to wear" [Genesis 28:20]—without extravagance. Con-

6. *Cf.* Epicurus, *Principal Doctrines* XV.
7. *Cf. Shemonah Perakim* 4.
8. The Rambam treats the term "covenant" here as signifying the Torah and "testimonies" as signifying the laws of nature—since they are evidence of God.

fining want to necessity, this is the easiest thing in the world to accomplish; and, if it seems difficult, that is only because it is difficult to find necessities while seeking luxuries. The more we seek for luxuries the harder our task becomes, as income and energy are expended for what is unnecessary and what is necessary is neglected.

Consider the environment in which we have our being: the more urgently a thing is needed by living beings, the more abundantly (and cheaply) it is found. The less dependent life is on anything, the rarer (and more expensive) it is. Thus the things man needs most, for instance, are air, water, and food; air above all, since no one can live without it for a moment; then water, without which one can survive for a day or two. Therefore air is of a certainty far more abundant than water. Likewise the need for water is stronger than for food, for some men can survive four to five days with no food but only water. Thus in every city you will find water in greater supply and cheaper than food. The same holds true with various foods: the more needed are commoner and cheaper than the less. Musk, ambergris, diamonds, and emeralds I do not suppose anyone of sound mind would consider necessary to man, unless perhaps medicinally, and even then there are many herbs and earths which can be substituted for these and similar precious substances.

This is a mark of God's goodness and bounty toward even so weak a creature. His justice and impartiality are most manifest as well. For nowhere in all the natural world of generation and corruption does any member of any animal species possess a faculty or a part beyond that which all the rest of his species have; rather every faculty, whether physical or psychological, and every organ which that particular creature has will be found in every other—essentially, even if some event external to its nature causes a lack. But this, as I made clear above [1], is the exception rather than the rule. There is no inferiority or superiority among normal individuals beyond what is required by the divergent capacities of the matter all members of a species must share. That this man has many sacs of musk and brocaded clothing while that man lacks these nonnecessities of life is not a crime or an injustice. He who has these luxuries has added nothing to his substance but has only acquired a toy and a fantasy. He who lacks what he does not need, need lack nothing: "He who gathered much [manna] had none left over, and he who gathered little had no lack; each gathered what he could eat" [Exodus 16:18]. At any time, in any place, this is what normally occurs, and the abnormal exceptions should not distract us from the rule.

These two considerations should make plain to you how God manifests His goodness to creation: His affording necessities in proportion to their need and His creating all members of a species equal. It was in keeping with this insight that David said . . . "God is good to all, and His mercies are upon all His works" [Psalm 145:9]. For, as I have shown, God's gift of being to us is a great and absolute good,[9] and His gift of self-direction to animals is an act of mercy.

Analysis

The value system represented by anthropocentrism and hedonism is vehemently rejected by Maimonides. Man, as we have seen, is not for Maimonides the be-all and end-all of existence. The universe does not exist for man's sake. On the contrary, the human individual, to perfect his humanity, must rise to responsibilities which transcend his individuality, obligations extending to his fellow men, his relations with his environment (to understand as well as preserve it) and his God. Even the notion of self-serving is not adequately bodied forth by hedonism. The righteous flourish like the palm tree and grow mighty like the cedars of Lebanon precisely in that their character and their works and thoughts afford the only true measure of their stature, the only true standard of lasting worth and achievement. Given an understanding of man's true role and place in the universe, as Plato had made clear, it would be manifest that the wicked cannot, in real terms, prosper from their wickedness or the innocent suffer through their goodness. The evil of the vicious is their direst punishment; the perfection open to the virtuous is their loftiest reward, which no pain can take away. For, as the Stoics argued, the evils besetting a man are no reflection on him, only the evils he does.

Thus, given an ethic that does not take personal pleasures and pains

9. Our creation is good not merely relative to us, as we might be tempted to suppose—for our relative good contributes in its way to the absolute good of the totality of being.

as moral absolutes, Maimonides is able to argue against the claim that
there is an absolute increment of evil over good in the constitution of
reality. Yet, while the formal statement of preponderance of evil over
good is thus overthrown, the fact remains that pains are evils, not absolutely but relative to the desires and interests of man. And the fact
remains as well that innocents do suffer. Thus, having shown that evil
is not predominant in existence, Maimonides must still explain why
there is evil or imperfection, privation or inadequacy at all. To justify
God's ways to man, then, the Rambam must go further than merely to
expose the dependence of Razi's statement on his anthropocentrism
and hedonism. Maimonides does not attempt to deny that to man at
least pain is an evil or that innocents do suffer. Rather he argues that
the bulk of human suffering is brought upon the individual by his own
doing. In such a case one cannot speak of the sufferings of innocents
but rather of the justice inherent in the very logic of our actions. As
for those who innocently fall victim to the irresponsibility of responsible beings or who succumb to the processes of nature, it must be
recognized that their vulnerability is the inevitable concomitant of their
having finite existence at all. To be capable of action, a thing must
also be capable of being acted upon; to be embodied in matter at all is
to be subject to change and ultimately to decline. To expect of flesh
and blood, as Galen puts it, that it will be immortal or impassive, ever
moving, or radiant like a star, is to demand of God a sort of being
much higher or lower in the scale of things than man has been vouchsafed. What is significant is that we have the sort of being we do (with
its attendant problems) and this is, in its way, a good, which is not
outweighed by its attendant disabilities. For the world would be the
less if finite creatures did not exist, and even pain and suffering (while
not the standards of the true worth of life) are rare on the whole, the
exceptions rather than the rule.

The problem of evil has been put forward at many times and in
many forms by probing minds, and answered in many ways. In affirming the goodness of existence even in terms of the somewhat tangential
standard of pleasure (and *a fortiori* in terms of more real values such
as the onward march of life and the generations of man, the humaniza-
tion of mankind and the divinization of humanity), Maimonides has no
doubt affirmed his transcendent faith in the mercy and graciousness of

God. It is instructive to observe how that faith is grounded. Maimonides does not beg the question as the Stoics do by refusing to admit that anything which can happen to a good man can in any sense be evil and declaring categorically that pains are perfectly irrelevant. For man, pains are evils, although not absolute evils (and pleasures are goods, although not absolute criteria of goodness). But pains are a condition of life, and the evidence of God's grace is in the fact that pains do not dominate life. Neither does Maimonides appeal to blind faith as the Asharite Mutakallimun had done by refusing to call evil anything which comes from God. Rather he admits that suffering is a relative evil and turns confidently to experience to bear out that much suffering is deserved and that suffering undeserved is a condition of being in the natural world although it is by far the exception rather than the rule.

God's goodness to creation is made manifest (and thus may be empirically studied and confirmed) in His provision of all creatures with all they require in proportion to the urgency of the need—if not individually, at least by species. This consideration does not lead Maimonides to fatalism or quietism, for creatures must be God's allies and agents in the task of self-preservation and self-perfection. Thus some materials which are medically necessary, for example, may require to be discovered and compounded, and intellect as well as energy may be among the "tools" through which God supplies our needs. God's justice is shown (again empirically) by the equality of all (normal) animals at birth.

Men are, as Maimonides indicates, strange creatures whose desires far outrun their needs and who may become addicted to their luxuries to the point of mistaking these for necessities. There is a remarkable revolution of expectations between the age when Maimonides could place so much faith in the goodness of life despite the suffering and early death which were a part of every person's immediate experience, and an age like our own, which has put illness and death itself on the defensive and yet can muster so little comparable faith. It is here, perhaps, that the Rambam's admonition borrowed from Galen, his fellow physician of a thousand years before, remains most valid and alive. We must not expect the impossible of flesh. He who would act must be prepared to suffer. The very forces which make life possible, those of generation and integration, require as their correlative that there be other forces at work in the same system as well, those of degeneration and disintegration. Such is the very nature of all natural processes, and most especially of metabolic processes: that there be an upward and a downward slope, a give and take. Life is inconceivable without dynamic (rather than. static) equilibrium. If nature like intellect, writes Maimonides (*Moreh* I:72), were self-conscious, then perhaps finer discrimination might be made; there would be no excesses or deficiencies, and disease and death perhaps would be impossible. But in nature equilibrium is rarely achieved in such a fashion. In general the balance struck must be worked out by the actual clash and mutual cancellation of opposing forces. This clash is the condition of all independent existence in a world of process, for without it everything would be absorbed in everything else. With man, as with all things in nature, identity is achieved only through difference.

Autonomy, as Maimonides tells us, is a gift. Freedom, as Kant says, is the condition of existence. But independence, self-reliance, is the condition of autonomy. It is finite, natural being which we must have in order to exist in our own right at all. It would be strange to say that this existence, which we have and in which we revel, is entirely negated by the necessary presence in it of sufferings that must be undergone and hardships that must be overcome.

GOD'S KNOWLEDGE

Introduction

It seemed plain to the Philosophers, and above all to Aristotle, that if God was to be understood in any way as a knowing or thinking being (and it followed from their derivation of thought as the highest good, most perfect and self-sufficient activity, that He was), then the object of His thought could not be the world. For the world was manifold; and God, to be self-sufficient, must be simplex. How could the Timeless be intellectually bound up with the temporal so that every change in the latter must be reflected in the former? Even to resolve this paradox on its logical level would not fully assuage the unease felt by those inclined to the Philosophical persuasion regarding the nexus between God and the world. For the root of this unease was in the fear that in binding God too closely to the world theists might make God somehow responsible for the inadequacies of finite being.

Nowhere was this issue more vivid than when it was posed in terms of the Stoic conception of God's governance of the world as a watchful and benevolent providence over all actions in the world. Alexander of Aphrodisias, the great Aristotelian, who felt most keenly the need to respond to Stoic claims, put the issue clearly: if God was in the

Stoic sense responsible for the world, then God was clearly responsible for evil. The only solution available seemed to be to cleave strictly to the pristine conception of Aristotle: God's thought and knowledge were of Himself; or else, if God knew things other than Himself, it was only their Ideas or Platonic Forms (universals) which He knew, for these were changeless. In either case, the individual particulars of the world are beneath God's cognizance.

In taking this position, however, the Philosophers seemed to have forgotten they themselves had within their own philosophical position the keys to the solution of the problem. The fundamental theme of Plato's thought, by no means neglected by Aristotle, was the interpretation of all reality, goodness, or perfection as the finite expression of a transcendent Cause. In attempting now to exempt that Cause of responsibility for the finite as such, the Philosophers not only had forgotten their own solution to that problem (which made finitude the condition of the gift of existence) but also had committed themselves to even more unwelcome theological assertions than those they had hoped to avoid. For in attempting to exempt the Deity from unconcern, they had committed themselves to asserting His absolute ignorance of the world of which they claimed He was the author.

From *Moreh Nevukhim* III

MOREH NEVUKHIM III:16

The Philosophers strayed grievously regarding God's knowledge of things other than Himself, stumbling in such a manner that neither they nor those who followed them in this view could recover. I shall now let you hear the misconceptions which led them into this pitfall, as well as the view of our religion on this matter and the manner in which we oppose their incredible, unworthy opinions on God's knowledge.

Most often what drew them toward and cast them into this position in the first place was what appears at first sight to be a lack of order in the affairs of individual men—the fact that certain good men live a life of pain and suffering, while certain wicked men live a life of pleasure and delight. This led them to draw up the following disjunction. One of the following must be the case: either (*a*) God knows nothing of these individual affairs and does not apprehend them, or (*b*) He does apprehend and know them. This is a necessary disjunction. Then they argued, if (*b*) God apprehends and knows these things, then one of these three alternatives must be the case: either (i) He orders and causes them to operate in the best, most perfect, and most fulfilled way; or (ii) he finds them unmanageable and is incapable of ordering them; or (iii) He knows and has power to govern things for the best, but does not care to do so, out of disdain, despite, or envy—just as we find among men a man may be able to provide some good for another person and know of his need but, through ill nature, wickedness, or envy, he may begrudge it to him and not provide it. This too is a sound and necessary disjunction, for anyone who knows of a certain thing must either care or not care about it—as a man may not care, say, to order the affairs of the cats in his house, or of other things less worthy of notice. But one who does care about the governance of a thing may find it unmanageable, even though he does want to manage it.

Having set up this division of alternatives, they concluded that two alternatives of these three (which all who understand must recognize as exhaustive) are impossible for God, namely (ii) that He is incapable, and (iii) that He is able but unconcerned. For this would introduce evil or impotence into God, both of which He transcends. No alternatives remain then except either (*a*) that He knows nothing at all of these conditions, or (i) that He does know them and orders them for the best. But we find that they are disordered, not conforming to reason, or determined to be as they ought to be. This is evidence that He does not know them by any manner or means.

It was this line of thinking which first caused them to stumble in this grievous way. You will find all the arguments I have summarized here and the ground of their error I have designated exposed clearly in Alexander of Aphrodisias's treatise on Governance.[1]

It is amazing, if you stop to think about it. The pitfall they have fallen into is worse than what they sought to avoid! They ignored the very point they were constantly calling to our attention and explaining

---

1. Probably to be identified with his book usually known as *On Providence*.

to us. They are worse off than they started out in that what they were trying to avoid was attribution of unconcern to God, but they ended by categorically attributing ignorance to Him, making everything in this nether world hidden from Him and unperceived by Him. And they ignored what they were ceaselessly pointing out to us in that they judged existence at large by the situations of individual human beings, whose ills are of their own causing or a necessary consequence of the sort of matter which they have, as they are constantly declaring and expounding. We have already explained what is relevant in this regard [*Moreh* III:12].

Having laid down this foundation, which completely destroys any good basis they had [2] and mars the beauty of every sound view they held, they tried to mitigate its repugnance by claiming that knowledge of these things is not possible for God,[3] for various reasons such as the following: Particulars are apprehended only by the senses, not by reason, but God does not apprehend through sense perception. Or particulars are infinite, knowledge embraces things, but the infinite cannot be embraced by knowledge. Or knowledge of things that come to be (which are doubtless particular) would imply some change in Him, for such knowledge is constantly changing. And because of our claim, we followers of the Law, that God knew these things prior to their coming to be, they attempted to implicate us in two absurd consequences: (1) that there can be knowledge of absolutely nothing, and (2) that the knowledge that a thing is actual and the knowledge that a thing is potential are the same.[4]

Often their notions conflicted. Thus certain of them said He knows only species and not individuals. Others said He knows nothing at all external to Himself—lest a plurality be introduced into His knowledge. Certain of the Philosophers believed as we do, that He knows all things and nothing is hidden from Him in any way. These were great men who lived in the time before Aristotle. They are mentioned by Alexander in the same treatise. But he rejects their view and says the greatest evidence against it is the observed affliction of the good by ills

2. For theodicy in the doctrine of human fallibility and the finite capabilities of matter.
3. And thus there is no incapability implied in His not knowing them.
4. Both implications would hold only on the assumption that God's knowledge, like man's, is temporal.

and attainment of goods by the evil.

In short, it should be clear to you that had they found the affairs of individual men ordered according to what seems to the masses to be a proper order, they would not have stumbled into this pitfall or held this view at all. . . .

MOREH NEVUKHIM III:19

Doubtless it is axiomatic that all things good must be affirmed of God and all imperfections denied of Him.[1] It is practically axiomatic that ignorance of anything is an imperfection, which therefore cannot be ascribed to Him. What led certain thinkers rashly to conclude that He knows in this way rather than that was, as I stated [*Moreh* III:16], what they imagined to be the lack of proper order in the affairs of individual human beings—although most such affairs are not simply conditions of nature,[2] but rather issue also from man's volitional capacity.[3]

The prophets stated long ago that the only thing that gives color to the inference of the unenlightened as to the nonexistence of divine knowledge of our doings is the sight of the wicked living in comfort and luxury. This makes a good man take it into his head that all his striving for the good and all the adversities he must face on account of the direct opposition of others are futile. Then the prophet goes on to state that his mind wandered without direction on this subject, until finally it grew clear to him that things must be looked at from the perspective of their over-all outcome, not from that of their first appearances. This is his description of the way all these ideas coalesced in his mind: "They said, 'How can God know? How can there be knowledge in the Most High?' Look at them—wicked but ever in comfort, growing richer. Ah, vainly did I purge my heart, wash hands that were already clean" [Psalm 73:11–13]. He goes on, "I pondered how to understand this. It seemed a wearisome task, until I came into the sanctuary of God, until I understood their end. Ah, in slippery places [dost Thou set them]. How they become desolate in a mo-

---

1. See Part One of this book.
2. *I.e.*, they are not entirely determined by external causes in the natural order.
3. And are, to that extent, not God's responsibility but man's.

ment!'' etc. [73:16–19].[4] The identical idea was put forward by Malachi [3:13–18]. . . . And David too makes it clear how widespread was this view [5] in his time and how it contributed to human aggression and acts of mutual wrongdoing. He then undertakes to argue to refute this view and announce that He knows all these things: ''The widow and the stranger do they slay, and orphans [6] do they murder, and they say, 'The Lord will not see, the God of Jacob will not be aware.' Beware, O you brutes among the people. Fools, when will you have sense! Will He who planted the ear not hear and He who formed the eye not see?'' [Psalm 94:6–9].

Here I shall explain to you the meaning of this argumentation—after I have mentioned how badly it is misconstrued by superficial readers of the Prophets' discourse. Some years ago certain distinguished coreligionists of ours who were physicians told me they were amazed at these words of David: ''By this standard of argument,'' they said, ''the creator of the mouth must eat, the creator of the lung must shout, and so for all the other organs.'' Consider now, you who study my treatise, how far they were from the correct understanding of this argument, and hear its real meaning.

It is plain that if anyone who makes any instrument had no conception of the task it was to perform, then he would not be able to make it. For example, if the smith had no conception or understanding of sewing, he could not make a needle in the shape required for sewing. The same holds true for all other instruments. Thus when whatever philosopher it was claimed that God does not apprehend particulars because they are apprehended by the senses and He does not have sense perception but rather intellectual apprehension, David urged against him the existence of the senses themselves, arguing: if the principle of visual perception is unknown or obscure to Him, how did He bring into being this instrument specifically designed for visual

4. The Psalmist searches for material success as his reward, and from this perspective all his striving after goodness seems futile. But when he considers from the point of view of Truth (enters into the house of God), thought allows him to recognize that the success of the wicked is vain. He observes how frail their joys are, how instantly their delight can turn to sorrow—because it is dependent on changeable externals.

5. The denial of divine cognizance of human affairs.

6. Widow, stranger, orphans—all helpless in antiquity since they had no one to protect or avenge them. The impious do not fear divine requital of their crimes.

perception? Do you think it came about by chance that a certain vitreous humor came to be, with another humor beyond it so, and beyond that a certain membrane, which just by chance was perforated by an aperture, which aperture was itself covered by a hard, transparent membrane? In short, the humors, membranes, nerves of the eye, ingeniously devised as we know them to be, and all directed to the end of serving this function—can anyone of any intelligence conceive that all this came about by chance? No. It is made necessary by the direction and design of nature, as every physician and philosopher explains. But nature does not have a mind with which to govern, all philosophers agree. Rather this creative governance issues, according to the Philosophers, from an intellectual principle; and, according to our view, it is the act of an intelligent being, He who first impressed their natures upon all things which have natural forces or powers. If that Mind does not apprehend this concept [7] and would not recognize it when it is instantiated, then how does He give being to (or allow to issue from Him, on the other view) any nature directed to an end of which He has not knowledge?

MOREH NEVUKHIM III:20

A point on which there is general agreement is that God's knowledge cannot be said to change, so that He would know now what He did not know previously. Nor is it proper to ascribe any plurality or multiplicity to His knowledge—not even according to those who believe in attributes. Since this is demonstrated, we who follow a Law [1] say that God knows a manifold plurality of things with a single knowledge, not by a diversity of acts of knowing, and without His knowledge varying as ours does in the diverse sciences and modes of knowing. In the same way, we say these ever-changing things are known to Him prior to their existence and known to Him ever after. Thus in no way does His knowledge change. For His knowledge is that so-and-so does not now exist, will exist at a certain time, for a certain period, and then will not exist. When that person does exist, as He foreknew him, nothing is added to His knowledge. And nothing comes to be that was

7. *E.g.*, sense perception.
1. Muslims, Christian, and Jews seem to be included in this designation.

not known to Him; rather, what comes to be is what He ever knew would come to be as it actually is.

Thus it does follow from this belief that knowledge can relate to what does not exist and can embrace the infinite, and we accept this belief. We say, nonexistents which He foreknows will be brought into being; those which He is able to bring into being are not impossible as objects of His knowledge. But what will not exist at all [2] is pure nonbeing to Him and can no more be an object of His knowledge than what is nonexistent for us can be an object of our knowledge.

As for embracing the infinite, this does present a problem. Certain thinkers advanced the doctrine that knowledge is of the species and extends, through a given concept, to the individual members of the species.[3] This is the view of all who hold to religion and heed the necessary requirements of thought.

The Philosophers, however, rule this out. They say that His knowledge may not attach to the nonexistent,[4] and no knowledge may embrace the infinite. If so, and if His knowledge never changes, then it is absurd that He should know anything that comes to be. He knows, therefore, only that which is permanent and invariant. A further doubt arose for certain of them: "Even if things must be permanent for Him to know them, His knowledge still is pluralized, for the knowledge must be manifold like its objects: each object known has its own act of knowing, by which it is known. Therefore He knows only Himself."

What I say is that the cause of all these difficulties they all got themselves into was that they assumed an analogy between our mode of knowing and His. For every party to the dispute had a theory of what it is impossible for us to know and assumed that the same holds

2. Or cannot exist.
3. Species as such do not exist external to the mind. But in the mind of God they may be known as concepts—and through these concepts, apprehended in particulars. Through concepts, of course, even human intelligence may embrace infinite particulars. For our understanding of a species is not confined to its actually existing members but may be extrapolated to the infinity of members which might exist. For God's knowledge such extrapolation is not required.
4. Not only because God's knowledge to be true must have its object but also because they regard God's knowledge as the means by which all that does exist is brought into being.

true for Him. . . . By rights the Philosophers are more at fault regarding this difficulty than anyone else, for it was they who proved His identity has no plurality to it and He has no attributes outside His identity but rather His knowledge is His identity and His identity is His knowledge. It was they too who proved our minds fall short of apprehending His identity as it really is, as we have shown. How then could they claim to understand His knowledge, when His knowledge is nothing other than His identity? Surely the same deficiency which makes our minds stop short of apprehending His identity makes them stop short of apprehending the mode of His knowledge of things. For His knowledge is not in the same class with ours that we should reason by analogies about it; it is something totally different.

Just as there is a necessarily existent identity by which, in their view, all being is made necessary, or by whose act, in our view, all besides it is created out of nothing, so, we say, that same identity apprehends all besides itself, nothing that exists being hidden from it in any way. There is nothing in common between knowledge for us and knowledge for Him, just as there is nothing in common between our being and His. The sole cause of confusion here is the shared use of the term "knowledge"—for only the name is in common, the realities are completely different. This is what entails such unwelcome conclusions. For we imagine that things necessary to our knowledge will also be necessary to His.

One further thing evident to me from the texts of the Torah is that His knowledge that a particular possibility will be realized does not at all remove that possibility from the realm of the possible. The possible retains its contingent character, and knowledge of which alternatives will eventuate does not make the existence of one of them necessary. This too is a fundamental assumption of the Law of Moses, indubitable and incontestable. . . .[5]

Consider how many different ways His knowledge differs from ours in the view of all who follow a religious law: (1) A simplex knowledge corresponds to numerous objects of knowledge which differ in

5. Maimonides reiterates the arguments of *Shemonah Perakim* 8 as to the conceptual dependence of the logic of imperatives in general and precautions in particular on the denial of a necessity which overrides the necessities of particular natural and volitional causes.

kind. (2) This knowledge attaches to the nonexistent. (3) It attaches to the infinite. (4) His knowledge does not vary in apprehending temporal events, despite the seeming disparity between the knowledge that a thing will exist and the knowledge that it does exist—despite the fact that in the latter case what was potential has now become actual. (5) According to the view of our Law, His knowledge does not determine one of two possibilities, even though He has known determinately which of them will eventuate.

So I wish I knew just how His knowledge is supposed by those who believe it to be an attribute [6] to resemble ours. Is there anything here but the mere shared use of a name? In our view, which holds God's knowledge not to be anything additional to His identity, it truly follows that His knowledge and ours will be as far different from one another as the substance of the heavens is from that of the earth. The prophets plainly state this: "For My thoughts are not your thoughts, and your ways are not My ways, says the Lord. As high as the heavens are above the earth, so high are My ways above your ways, and My thoughts above your thoughts" [Isaiah 55:8–9]. . . .

Any appearance of a contradiction among these propositions which have been grouped together is on account of their being regarded in terms of what knowledge is for us, when in fact there is nothing in common between our knowledge and His except the name. In the same way "purpose" is equivocally ascribed to our intentional acts and to what He is said to intend. Likewise, "providence" or "care" is ascribed equivocally to what we care for and what He is said to care for. . . .

MOREH NEVUKHIM III:21

There is a great difference between a maker's knowledge of what he has made and someone else's knowledge of it. For if the product was made in accordance with the maker's knowledge, then his making of it must have been dependent on his understanding of it. Anyone else, however, who considers the same product and comprehends it must do so in such a way that his knowledge of it is dependent on the product.

6. If God's knowledge is an attribute, there must be some concept known to us which we predicate of God when we speak of Him as knowing—a concept derived from our common human experience, to which a term can be assigned.

For example, the craftsman who made this case in which weights are set in motion by the flow of water to indicate how many hours of the day or night have passed knows and understands all the water that flows in it, every turning in its course, every thread it must pull, and every ball that must drop—but he does not know all this by studying these movements now as they take place. Rather, it is just the other way around. These movements which take place now could not have come to be unless they had been brought into being in accordance with his knowledge. Such is not the case for one who studies these mechanisms. Each time the student sees a given motion he gains a new piece of knowledge. He continues to study and augment his knowledge (which thus constantly grows and changes by degrees) until finally he understands the whole operation of the instrument. If you were to suppose the motions of this instrument were infinite, then the investigator would not be able to take in all of them. Nor would he be able to know any of these motions prior to its occurrence. For whatever he knows is derived from what has occurred.

This is just the situation with the whole of existence vis-à-vis our knowledge and God's. Whatever we know we know only through study of what exists. That is why our knowledge does not attach to the future or the infinite. Knowledge for us is constantly growing and changing, divided into a plurality of sciences and apperceptions which vary with the objects from which our knowledge is derived. He is not like this; i.e., He does not derive His knowledge a posteriori so that there should be multiplicity and change in His understanding. Rather, all the things He knows are dependent on His knowledge, which precedes them and determines them to be as they are, whether as disembodied entities or as particulars with stable matter, or as beings whose matter may vary in the particulars but whose over-all system or order is not disrupted and does not change.

For this reason He does not have a plurality of sciences, nor a growing, changing understanding. For it is through His knowledge of His own Godhead, which is changeless, that He knows all that is made necessary by all His acts. For us to aspire to understand how this is possible is the same as it would be for us to aspire to be Him. . . .

Analysis

The connection between God's knowledge and providence is an intimate one indeed. For, unless God knows particulars, how can He exercise providence over creation? Yet to the most authentic representatives of the Aristotelian tradition in philosophy, such as Alexander of Aphrodisias, it seemed plain that precisely because divine knowledge of particulars would implicate God in responsibility for the fates of particular things such knowledge must be denied. The array of the heavenly bodies and the species of things displayed the eternal uniformity and order which philosophers of the Peripatetic tradition were prepared to attribute to the divine. But the fortunes of ordinary (*i.e.,* sublunary) particulars did not.

This response of the Peripatetic philosophers to the problem of divine providence and knowledge seemed to the Rambam to illustrate a fundamental loss of nerve on their part. For it was the Philosophical school originally, guided by the insights and arguments of Plato, that had taught mankind the means of obviating the supposed incongruities between divine perfection and the world's imperfection. The particulars in the world, according to the teachings of the Philosophers themselves, were indeed perfect in their ways, and the world was not so totally subject to disorder as to preclude the hypothesis of divine governance. Where perfection did fall short of the Absolute, this was, according to the Philosophers themselves, the necessary consequence of the nature of matter, which the Philosophers in turn had explained to be the necessary condition of individuation, and indeed of all differentiation from the One. Thus the Philosophers seem to Maimonides to have lost sight of the original cogency of their position. If it is borne in mind that "knowledge" as applied to God has not at all the meaning it has when applied to contingent beings, that proper order in nature is not always and necessarily identical with what we consider as conducive to our own interests, and that the perfection of finite particulars logically cannot be absolute, the initial theological impetus behind denial of God's knowledge of particulars disappears.

The Torah itself contains not only the assertion of God's knowledge of all He created but also the key to the understanding of the mode of God's intelligence—or rather of what it is not. For when the Psalmist argues that He who made the eye must see and He who made the ear must hear, the claim is not that God will know as men do through experience of the function of these organs but rather that God possesses the unique and privileged understanding of the inventor (creator), for whom the conception precedes its expression. Thus God's knowledge, unlike man's, is *a priori*, not *a posteriori:* independent of experience. And as God's knowledge differs from human understanding, so too does God's governance of that which He has made. God governs (as a designer) through the natures He puts in things; His Will is manifest in the functioning of all natural things. If things serve purposes (and the Aristotelian philosophers are unequivocal in their assertion that they do), then it must be recognized that there is no purpose without intention, even though the ultimate basis of divine intention in the ultimate positivity of the divine will may far elude the grasp of our understanding.

The relation of God's will to nature does not entail the binding of God's will or wisdom to the finitude of time or other categories of finitude as the Philosophers feared it would. For the Philosophers themselves have spelled out in their own works the means by which concepts, minds, universals, may mediate the gap between the absolute and the particular (*cf. Moreh* II:2–12).

Even the paradoxes regarding God's knowledge of the infinite and nonexistent vanish on this basis. For if it is understood that the knowledge of the creator is *a priori* and atemporal, it becomes comprehensible that God's knowledge may attach to the infinite and the nonexistent. For, even with human beings, the theorist, who possesses concepts and not mere data, may make predictions about events which never have taken place, and the implications of scientific propositions—*i.e.,* propositions of universal scope—are of course infinite, since such propositions cover not only all actual but all potential events within their reference. How then is it impossible for God, who possesses the true concepts of all things, not as their student but as their Creator and Inventor (the terms are interchangeable in medieval Arabic writings), not to know them through the knowledge of their natures and govern them through the implanting of those natures?

DIVINE PROVIDENCE

Introduction

What divides the religious from the nonreligious is less fundamentally any difference as to the existence or nature of God or even as to the character of religious language than an intellectual divergence of attitudes with respect to God's relation to the world. The romantic may "believe in" God in the sense that he acknowledges divine existence and yet express rejection of God through acts of "Titanic" rebellion. The atheist may curse or even pray, while consecrating his wit to the refutation of the divine existence, which in his heart he fears. Epicurus was active in his observance of the usages of cult and had a well-developed concept of the nature of the gods and the logic of divinity. The gods for him existed, by all means. What made of Epicurus the archatheist of the Middle Ages was his exiling of the gods to the "intermundial" spaces, leaving the world to evolve without divine assistance, by the automatic operation of causality and chance. Strato (third century B.C.E.), who reduced God to a world principle, was not castigated as an atheist, for he left God in the world. But the name of Epicurus, who believed in gods, became synonymous with atheism, for he severed the nexus between divinity and the world, with the express objective of freeing man from God.

What distinguishes the man of religion is his belief in and acceptance of a divine plan, a government or overseeing of the world. Among the most crucial differences among religions and religious philosophies are their divergent conceptions of the nature and the workings of this plan. The models by which the nexus is conceived will make or destroy a religious outlook. For, as we have seen, God is conceivable by man only to the extent of the divine relation to the world; and the very character of human practical and intellectual response will be determined according to how that relation is conceived.

For religion at some naïve or primitive stage when metaphor and myth are as yet not fully disentangled from reality and explanation in the minds of many participants, the imagery of government or husbandry may suffice. But when it has been recognized that metaphorical language applied to God is no more than the measure of the inadequacy of our metaphysical conceptions of Him, such imagery is seen to be of value only to those capable of reading the signs, *i.e.*, only to those who already have some inkling of the way—who know what sort of metaphors are appropriate and what sort are not. The problem is not one of symbolism but one of fact: we stand, as the haunting parable of John Wisdom has it, in a garden, not knowing whether in fact there is an unseen gardener or there is not, knowing fully that there is much in the garden which would make it seem that there is and much which would make it seem that there is not. Metaphor expresses these seemings, but before we dare apply our metaphors religiously, that is, in earnest, we must know what is the case in fact. And here we must confront the conflict of the evidence for and against a plan, for and against the operation of divine reason and justice in the scheme of things. Somehow the evidence and the concepts it supports must be reconciled and integrated. For the uncritical or the dogmatic, naïve appreciation of the absolute power, justice, or disinterest of the divinity might afford an ideological resting place. But for Maimonides, seeking a level of philosophical rigor and writing for an audience whose analytical capacities had been sharpened by centuries of philosophical debate, the narrow claims of the advocates of God's absolute justice, power, or wisdom, or nature's impersonality, invariance, or randomness can no longer be resolved by the simple award of the issue to one side or another in the face of some portion of the evidence. A subtle equilibrium must be struck among the claims of science, theological rationalism, and piety.

From *Moreh Nevukhim* III

MOREH NEVUKHIM III:17

There are five basic views about providence, all ancient, in that they were current in the time of the prophets, when the true revelation was given to shed its light upon all these obscurities.

(1) The first doctrine is that there is no providence at all over anything. All that happens in heaven or elsewhere occurs either by chance or in accordance with the characters of things. There is nothing to order or govern, nor to care for anything. This is the position of Epicurus. . . . And the unbelievers of Israel expressed the same view: "They denied the Lord and said, 'It is not He' " [1] [Jeremiah 5:12].

Aristotle demonstrated the impossibility of this theory and proved that it cannot be the case that all things are brought into being by chance.[2] There must be some governing, ordering principle. . . .

(2) The second view is that some things are subject to ordering and governing by providence while others are left to chance. This is Aristotle's opinion.

I would sum up his views on providence as follows: he believes that God cares for the spheres and their contents and that is why each of them endures unchanged forever. Alexander of Aphrodisias makes this explicit when he says that in Aristotle's view divine providence extends to the sphere of the moon. This is an inference drawn from the Aristotelian principle of the eternity of the world. For Aristotle conceives of providence as being concordant with the nature of the being. Providence, then vis-à-vis the spheres, where the particulars are eternal, is their eternal changelessness. But inasmuch as their existence entails the existence of other beings (whose particulars have not continuous existence although their species have), a measure of providence is imparted through them, by which the eternity and stability of

1. Whose action we perceive—in this case in the calamities which pursue misdeeds.
2. For Aristotle's proof, see *Physics* II:5; *cf. Moreh* II:20.

the lesser species is guaranteed, although that of their individual members is not possible.

Even so, individuals of every species are not utterly neglected. For wherever matter has been refined sufficiently to accept the form of growth, powers which make possible survival for a definite span of time have been supplied—through which what is beneficial is drawn in and what is unfavorable rejected. Matter sufficiently refined to receive the form of perception is provided with further protective and preserving faculties, including the capacity of directed motion in pursuit of the beneficial or flight from the detrimental. And of course every individual is given whatever is necessary to the survival of the species. Finally, wherever matter has been refined sufficiently to receive the form of mind, the additional powers of thinking, governing, and reporting what will promote the survival of the individual and the preservation of the species are given in proportion to the individual's perfection.

All other motions which occur in the members of a species are incidental. For this, according to Aristotle, there is no orderer or governor. For example, if a wind or hurricane were to blow, it would surely cause some leaves of this tree to fall, or break a branch on that one, topple a stone off such and such a fence, blow dust upon some plant and destroy it, or whip up the waves at sea and wreck a ship which happened to be there, drowning some or all its passengers. According to Aristotle, there is no difference between the falling of the leaves or the toppling of the rock and the drowning of all those great and good men in the ship . . . no difference between a cat catching and worrying a mouse, spider, or fly and a ravening lion coming upon a prophet and tearing him to pieces.

The basis of his view in sum then is that any phenomenon which appeared to him to be stable, constant, or unceasing, as for example the courses of the stars, or anything whose course was altered only rarely, as the general course of nature, he would say was governed, by which I understand, attended by divine providence. On the other hand, whatever he did not observe to keep to a rigid order or continue in fixed stability, as for example the lives of men or individuals of any species of animals or plants, he designated as a random, ungoverned phenomenon, not attended by providence and incapable of being providentially attended. This follows from his doctrines of the eternity of the world and the impossibility of anything which exists being otherwise than as it is. Of those who have strayed from our Law, those who accepted this view were those who said, "The Lord has forsaken the earth" [Ezekiel 9:9].

(3) The third view is just the opposite of the second. It is held by those who believe that nothing occurs by chance; indeed everything is intended, willed, and controlled. Plainly, whatever is controlled is known. This is the doctrine of the Asharite party in Islam.

Their view entails a number of outrageous consequences, which they recognize and accept. Thus they agree with Aristotle as to the parity between the fall of a leaf and the death of a human being— "Just so," they say, "but the wind does not blow by chance. God causes it to move. And it is not the wind which causes leaves to fall, rather each one falls at the decree of God, and it is He who ordains when they will fall and where. That they should fall earlier or later or anywhere else is impossible, for all this is predestined from eternity."

In consequence of this opinion, they must accept the foreordainment of all animal motions (and rests) and the impotency of man to do or to refrain from doing anything. The same view entails further the obliteration of the very notion of possibility in such areas: all such events must be either necessary or impossible. They accept this consequence, claiming that what we call possible (Zayd's getting up, Omar's coming, etc.) is such only relative to us.[3] In relation to God, there are no possibilities about such things but only necessities and impossibilities.

Another consequence which follows necessarily from their view is that the message of revelation is of no use whatever, since man, for whose sake every revelation has been given, can do nothing to fulfill what he is commanded, nor to avoid what he is forbidden [cf. Shemonah Perakim 8]. The Asharites say that God was pleased to inspire prophets, command, forbid, and threaten, raise hopes and fears, while we are powerless to effect any action, that He is perfectly capable of imposing impossible tasks upon us, of punishing us after we have done as we were commanded or rewarding us after we have transgressed. Finally, it follows from their view that God's actions need have no object or purpose [cf. Moreh III:25, 26].

---

3. I.e., relative to our ignorance of the foreordained outcome.

They bear the burden of all these impossible consequences in order to save their dogma. Even when we see someone congenitally blind or leprous, of whom we cannot say that by his prior sins he deserves what has become of him, we still should say, "So it pleased God"; and when we see a good and pious man killed in the midst of worship, we should say, "So it pleased God to do." And there is no injustice in this; for it is perfectly permissible according to them for God to punish the innocent and reward the sinful. Their pronouncements on these matters are well known.

(4) The fourth view is that of those who hold that man does have a capacity of acting, whereby the legitimacy of the commands and prohibitions, rewards and punishments figuring in the revealed law is assured. All God's acts, in their view, follow from His wisdom; injustice cannot be predicated of Him, and He cannot punish a man who does what is right. The Mutazila too hold this view, although they do not believe in absolute free will. They also believe that God knows the fall of this leaf and the creeping of that ant and that His providence is over all that exists. So here too there are outrageous consequences, not to mention inconsistencies.

Among the absurd implications of this doctrine is the fact that when a human being is born congenitally deformed through no wrongdoing of his own, they can only say that for him it is better so, although we do not know just how; this is not by way of retribution but represents an actual benefit! Regarding the death of a good man, their answer is much the same, that this enlarges his reward in the hereafter. When pressed regarding on what account God should deal justly with man and not with other creatures and asked, "In what did this animal's sin consist that he should be slaughtered?" they even go so far as to take on the burden of defending the ludicrous proposition that this too was better for it—God will afford it recompense in the hereafter. Thus even when a flea or a louse is killed, it must be compensated by God in the world to come! If this mouse that is without sin has been eaten by a cat or a hawk, again they say that this was decreed by divine wisdom in order that the mouse might be requited in the world to come.

None of the advocates of the last three positions on providence are entirely to be blamed, in my view, for each of them is responding to very weighty obligations: Aristotle cleaves to the phenomena and the observed laws of nature. The Asharites shun attributing ignorance of anything to God, for it would not do to say that God knows this particular but not that; so they bear the unfortunate implications which follow. The Mutazila too wished to avoid ascribing any injustice to God, but it did not seem right to them to go against common sense and say that to bring suffering upon someone who did not sin was not unjust. Nor did they deem it right that He who sent all prophets and inspired all revelations should have done so for no intelligible purpose. So they too bore their share of unwelcome consequences—and inconsistency as well, for they believed that God knows all things and at the same time that man has freedom of action; and this leads, as will be seen with the least reflection, to a plain contradiction.

(5) The fifth doctrine is our own, by which I mean the position taken about providence in the Torah. I shall teach you what the books of our prophets say about it explicitly and what the great majority of our traditions hold. I shall also report what some of our more recent thinkers believe and inform you of my own belief on this subject. So, to begin: It is an axiom of our teacher Moses and all who follow him that man does have power of action absolutely, by which I mean that whatever he does within the compass of human action, he does through his own character and by his own free will and choice, without any sort of *ad hoc* capacity being created for him.[4] Likewise all species of animals move by their own volition. So God willed it from eternity: that all animals would move by their own free will and that man would have the power of doing whatever he chose to do, so long as he was able to do it. No denial of this axiom has ever been heard in our religion, thank God.

Another axiom of the Torah of Moses is that the notion of injustice is utterly inapplicable to God and that all misfortunes and blessings which affect men, collectively or individually, are deserved according to an impartial and absolutely fair justice. If a person's hand is stuck by a thorn and he immediately pulls it out, that will have been a punishment; if he enjoys the slightest pleasure, that will have been a

---

4. As many Mutakallimun would have it.

reward. All such things are deserved (as God says, "For all His ways are judgment" etc. [Deuteronomy 32:4]), but we do not always know for what.

To sum up: the vicissitudes of human fortune are attributed by Aristotle to pure coincidence, by the Asharites to sheer will, by the Mutazila to wisdom, and by us to an individual's deserts according to his actions. That is why the Asharite finds it acceptable to view God as punishing the good not only here but in what is alleged to be the eternal fire of the hereafter,[5] and why he says, "So it pleased Him," and why the Mutazila (as I have said) consider this to be injustice and hold that whoever is afflicted, be it an ant, will be requited, as wisdom would require. We, for our part, believe that human fortunes are reflections of men's deserts and that God is above injustice and does not punish anyone who does not deserve to be punished. The Torah of Moses says this in so many words: everything is in keeping with what is deserved; and the discussions of most of our rabbis follow this doctrine. For you find them saying literally, "There is no death without sin and no suffering without wrongdoing" [Shabbat 55a], and, "By the measure a man has used shall he be given his measure" [Mishnah Sota I:7]. Everywhere they stress that justice is necessarily essential to God, which means the obedient must be rewarded for all their pure and upright actions, even if these were not commanded through a prophet, and the individual must be punished for all his wrongdoing, even if he was not forbidden through a prophet. For this prohibition, against wrongdoing, is already made by human nature. Thus they say, "The Holy One, blessed be He, does not withhold his due from any creature" [Baba Kamma 38b, Pesahim 118a] . . . and, "There is no comparison between one who does a thing he was commanded to do and one who does it without being commanded" [cf. Kiddushin 31a, Baba Kamma 87a, Avodah Zarah 3a]. . . .

All their discussions take this principle as their point of departure. But our Sages add a further principle, not given textually in the Torah, the doctrine of "sufferings of love," which some of them hold [Berakhot 5a]. According to this view an individual may be afflicted through no fault of his own solely that his reward may be increased.

5. The attentive reader will not overlook the Rambam's skepticism on the subject of eternal hellfire as an instrument of divine providential care.

This is identical with the Mutazilite doctrine, but there is no foundation for it in the text of the Torah, for it is not to be confused with the
concept of trial [see *Moreh* III:24] as when God "tested" Abraham
[Genesis 22:1].

. . . Our revelation is concerned solely with the lives of human individuals: the story of recompense to animals was unheard of in ancient times, but some recent authorities, hearing it from the Mutazila,
found it attractive and adopted it.

My own belief about this central issue of providence, which I will
now set out for you, is not based on what proof has brought me to
believe but rather on what I take to be the intention of God's book and
the prophetic writings. This view I accept is less beset with unfortunate consequences than those I have already described and more capable of winning the assent of reason. What I believe is that divine providence in this world, below the sphere of the moon, extends to
individuals only of the human species, that only in this species are all
the fortunes of each individual and all the good and evil he receives
determined by his deserts. . . . For all other animals,[6] not to mention
plants and other things, my view is the same as Aristotle's: I do not
believe in the least that this leaf falls according to its own special
providence or that this spider ate that fly at the present decree and particular desire of God. . . . All this is purely coincidental, as Aristotle
recognized.

Divine providence in my personal view is a consequence of divine
emanation. The species which is touched by this overflowing of the intellectual and thereby becomes itself endowed with intellect, through
which it is made aware of all that intellect can reveal, that species is
the one which is attended by divine providence, and all of its actions
are accountable. If the sinking of a ship, drowning all who are in it, or
the collapse of a roof upon those who are in the house are, as he [Aris-
totle] claims, matters of pure coincidence, then the presence of these
people in that ship and those in the house, as I see it, are not; they are
due to the divine will, corresponding with what is deserved according
to judgments whose principle is beyond our understanding.

What led me to this conviction was the fact that nowhere could I

6. And thus for man *qua* animal.

find a text in any prophetic book which mentioned divine providence over animals individually—except for human beings. The prophets even seem surprised that human individuals are cared for providentially, man being too small (let alone other animals) to be worthy of concern. Thus it is said, "What is man that Thou knowest him" etc. [Psalm 144:3]. . . . But there are texts proclaiming providence over all human individuals and watchfulness over all their doings: . . . "Whose eyes are open on all men's ways to give to each according to his ways" [Jeremiah 32:19] . . . "Who sinned against Me I shall blot from my book" [Exodus 32:33]. . . . And all that is introduced of the stories of Abraham, Isaac, and Jacob is an unequivocal token of individual providence. . . .

An objection as to why human individuals are cared for by providence while members of other species are not does not apply to my position alone, for one must first ask why man and not the other animals was given reason. The answer here is, "So God willed," or "So His wisdom decreed," or "So nature determined," depending on which of the three preceding positions [7] one holds, and the same answer will do for the question as to providence.

Try to grasp my position in its full implications. I do not believe anything is hidden from God, nor do I ascribe to Him any incapacity. Rather, what I believe is that providence is a necessary consequence of intellect. For providence can flow only from a mind of consummate perfection; and all who are touched by that outpouring sufficiently to be reached by mind are reached by providence as well. This is the position which in my view is in harmony not only with reason but also with the texts of revelation. The prior doctrines either go too far or not far enough. Those which go too far lead to senseless jousting with reason and experience, while those which do not go nearly far enough—I mean those which do away with individual providence altogether, putting man on the same level with other animal species—imply beliefs about the deity which encourage vice and decadence and the erosion of all human virtues, both moral and intellectual.

7. The Asharite, Mutazilite, or Aristotelian models respectively. In the Rambam's view, of course, the three positions are equivalent and differ (like the opinions of the blind men about the elephant in the fable) only with regard to human ignorance.

MOREH NEVUKHIM III:18

Having set down the preceding on the confinement of providence exclusively to the human species, as opposed to all other sorts of animals, I continue by saying that it is known that external to the mind no such entity as a species exists. Species and all other universals are mental concepts, as you know; only a particular or particulars exist external to the mind. If this is known, then it is known as well that the divine emanation which exists coupled to the human species—*i.e.*, the human reason—is simply whatever individual intellects may exist; *i.e.*, the divine emanation is simply what emanates to Zayd, Omar, Khalid, Bakr, etc.[1] If so, it follows from what I said in the previous chapter that any individual person who partakes of a greater share of that emanation, on account of his material makeup or training, will necessarily be more closely watched over by providence—if providence is, as I have said, a consequence of intellect. Thus it is not the case that divine providence over all individual members of the human species is equal; rather, the extent of providence varies with their perfection as human beings. From this theory it follows necessarily that God's providence over prophets is very great, and proportionate to their rank as prophets. His providence over the virtuous [2] and the excellent is proportionate to their excellence and their virtue. For it is this measure of the emanation of divine reason which makes the prophets speak, which guides the actions of the virtuous and perfects the understanding of those who excel.[3] The unenlightened and vicious, however, are degraded in proportion to their lack of this emanated intellect, sinking to the level of members of other animal species: "He is like dumb beasts" [Psalm 49:13, 21]. That is why it may be a small matter to kill them,[4] or it may in fact be an obligation to do so for the common welfare. This principle, that providence over each individual

1. Thus it is their minds, reason in them.
2. Those who apply reason in establishing their way of life; *cf. Shemonah Perakim.*
3. Thus providence, whose measure is not material success but the divine intelligence active in man, is inevitably proportioned to desert. For true happiness is the outcome of a life of reason. In this proportionality is found the justice of God.
4. Criminals whose character is debased to the level of beasts. The willful murderer and other irreclaimable felons have no claim upon the mercy of humanity, since they are lost to the standards of humanity; it may become licit to exterminate them as pests.

member of the human species is according to his deserts, is one of the cornerstones of the Law.

Study the textual treatment of providence over the particular fortunes of the Patriarchs in all their doings, even in regard to material gain and the promises made to them that providence would watch over them. It is said to Abraham, "I am your shield" [Genesis 15:1], to Isaac, "I shall be with you and bless you" [26:3], to Jacob, "Indeed I am with you wherever you shall go" [28:15]. It was said to the Master of the Prophets [Moses], "Surely I will be with you" [Exodus 3:12], and to Joshua, "As I was with Moses, so shall I be with you" [Joshua 1:5]. In every case, providence is plainly stated to be with them according to the measure of their perfection.

And regarding providence over the virtuous and neglect of the unenlightened, it is said, "He will guard the feet of His goodly ones [*hasidav*], but the evil shall be silenced in darkness, for not by strength shall man prevail" [1 Samuel 2:9]. This is to say that the saving of some persons from disasters which others plunge into is not due to bodily powers and physical capacities . . . but depends upon the level of one's fulfillment or inadequacy, *i.e.*, on one's nearness to or distance from God. Thus those closest to Him are best protected— "He will guard the feet of His goodly ones"—while those remote from Him are exposed to whatever chance may befall them. There is nothing to protect them from whatever vicissitudes may occur. Like one who walks in the dark, they are sure to come to grief. . . .

The texts advancing this idea, the principle that providence over individual human beings is proportionate to their level of enlightenment and perfection, are too many to enumerate. The Philosophers state the same principle. In the introduction to his commentary on Aristotle's *Nicomachean Ethics*,[5] al-Farabi states, "Those who are capable of progressing from one state of moral character to the next are those of whom Plato said that God's providence watches over them especially."

It would not be valid for us to say that providence is specific rather than particular, as certain schools of Philosophers give out. For there

5. This commentary of al-Farabi's on Aristotle's work is not known to be extant at the present time, but the treatment of the problem throughout al-Farabi's works is congruent with this account of providence.

is nothing in existence outside the mind beyond individuals, and it is with these individuals that the divine mind is in contact. Thus it can only be over these individuals that providence extends. . . .

Analysis

In treating the problem of divine providence—that is, the problem of the nature of God's governance of the world—Maimonides must deal with five fundamentally different views not only of nature but also of the content of piety.

For the Epicurean, piety consists in the upholding the absolute unconcern of the divine with the world at large and with human doings in particular. All Epicurean science and ethics are founded upon this theological axiom which interprets divine transcendence as implying absolute noninvolvement. The results of this approach, however, are fundamentally unsatisfactory to Maimonides. For the Epicurean notion of piety leads to an ethic in which man is entirely self-directed and seeks no transcendent goal (rather like the valetudinarianism described by the Rambam in *Shemonah Perakim* 5), while in its account of nature the Epicurean system attributes all natural order and development to the blind forces of causal law and chance or spontaneity, working in tandem—notions which Aristotle's analysis of the continuity and directionality of the operation of causal law had demonstrated to be without application in the natural world.

Setting the Epicurean view aside therefore, Maimonides examines the three non-Biblical views with some sympathy. All of them respond to legitimate claims, but each accentuates the particular claim to which it is most sensitive while failing to detect the possibility of responding to all the values at stake without falling into inconsistency or excess.

The minimal claim of piety regarding God's relation to the world might appear to be the assertion that God does no wrong, no injustice to His creatures. This would seem to follow from the logic of God as a being who is Perfection. The implication, according to the Mutazilite school of the Kalam, was that many apparent evils are not really such at all but actual blessings in disguise. God's justice was unquestionable. True evils, therefore, must be seen as punishments. This explains the Mutazilites' somewhat inconsistent attempt to introduce some sort of human moral responsibility into the Kalam world of predestination. As for the suffering of innocents, whatever evil it genuinely did involve must be transitory. Concealed beneath the surface or delayed until some afterlife were goods (rewards) which more than compensated men—indeed all creatures—for any genuinely undeserved sufferings they might undergo. Yet if God desired to augment an innocent's reward, could He not have done so without causing so much suffering? This is merely a special case of the Rambam's argument that, if God, according to the Kalam, does not require the natural means to achieve His ends, is it not futile—and in this case absurd—for Him to employ those means? What is valid in the Mutazilite position and others of its ilk is the reluctance to attribute evil to God. But the responsibility of God for evil has been denied only at the cost of belying the true character of numerous events which, from the creatures' point of view at least, are genuine evils.

This was clearly recognized by the Asharites, who were successors to the Mutazilites as the foremost theologians of Islam. Ashari, founder of the school, broke away from the Mutazila when he dreamed, as tradition has it, that he heard a babe complain in heaven that his rank was not as high as that of a saint. "You did not have his good deeds," came the reply. "I did not have his days," the babe insisted. "I cut short your days," said God, "lest you turn to sin." Whereupon the soul of a wretch damned in Hell cried out, "Lord of the universe, why did you not cut short my days before I turned to sin!" To this there was no answer. The only explanation of the diversity of God's grace from one individual to the next according to Ashari must be the pure positivity of God's will. God's power was absolute, and so, as we have seen, was His control over creation. All things are predestined, including the giving of grace and reward and punishment according to divine pleasure. Man cannot criticize God's standards or apply human values to them. To do wrong is to disobey, and since God has no master, He cannot do wrong. There is no injustice to a chattel. Thus God's justice is preserved, but only at the cost of the coherence of the concepts of nature, which will now have no internal order or stability, and of justice itself, of which only the word is preserved, robbed of all its sense, even in terms of the analogy between the divine and human acts.

Piety for Aristotle consists in the recognition of the divinity evident in the rationality and perfection of the causal order in nature. No natural event occurs spontaneously or by chance, since all events in nature are such that they occur as they do "always or for the most part"; and, in the case of events which occur as they do always or for the most part, there must inevitably be some cause for the regularity. Nothing in nature, therefore, happens without cause, nothing without effect, but all natural events are linked together by the bonds of causal necessity. One event promotes another, and thus causes may serve to their effects as means to ends. Nothing in nature happens in vain. The regularity of the causal pattern and the possibility of ends being served in nature are both manifestations of divinity in the world, and to deny either of these things, causality or finality (purposiveness), not only is impious in that it denies the rationality of the cosmos but also has the effect of making science impossible by making nature in itself incomprehensible. Thus providence must not be understood as implying interference with the established laws of nature but rather a sort of guidance of them. But were the Peripatetics justified in concluding that these demands on behalf of the rationality of the cosmos implied the impossibility of special providence for human individuals?

The materials for resolving that question were contained within the Aristotelian and Platonic philosophies themselves. For the means of providence had been explained by the Philosophers as involving the emanation (see *Moreh* II:2–12) of ideas by which all things were made actual as exemplars of their kinds; and, in the case of man, the emanating form was human rationality (the mind) itself. Thus, if rationality is the vehicle of emanation, the claim that man is watched over by a special providence need not depend on the assertion that God contravenes the laws of nature. For conscious rationality is unique to the human species among all animals and is indeed the true measure of human worth as well as the true means to human fulfillment. The claim that providence can only be over species, then, is easily seen to be unneeded, and easily refuted by appeal to the arguments of the Peripatetics themselves: universals such as species are mere concepts. Apart from the existence of their members, they have no reality outside the mind. Providence then is confined to human individuals, and innate differences in human intellectual capacity are easily explained, some through the weaknesses to which the flesh is heir, some through the moral and intellectual self-perfection (or self-neglect) of which human beings are capable (*cf. Shemonah Perakim*).

It is therefore possible to sustain a belief in God's benevolent governance of the world. It is not necessary to assign the variations and vicissitudes of natural events to divine neglect or arbitrary interference but to the impartial operation of the laws of nature. It is not necessary to abandon the analogy between divine and human justice upon which both theistic ethics and the meaningful assertion of God's goodness (as the fundamental guide to the notion of God's absolute perfection) depend. For God's goodness is shown in the world by things' being given the actual natures and perfections they have—rationality in man's case, through which every human individual is watched over for his own benefit and impartially and inevitably judged by the logic of his own actions. True the gift may vary from one person to the next, as the material propensities which are the limiting factor to the penetration of rationality in man must vary. But, of those who are given a normal endowment of mental capability, only those whose own moral fault stifles the guidance of reason are necessarily (like Pharaoh in *Shemonah Perakim* 8) cut adrift entirely without support on the shifting sea of random vicissitudes which will inevitably seal their fate. And to compensate mankind for the fact that not all men see the truth as plainly as their fellows, human rationality gives men communication and tradition (civilization, in a word) by which those possessed of insight may transmit it to those who are able to see but not necessarily to see for themselves, and to pass that insight along and develop it from one generation to the next. This task indeed is the function of all human arts and sciences. But with reference to the art of living and the universal truths which describe the human condition in relation to God and the good for man, it is above all the task of prophecy.

GOD AND IMPOSSIBILITY

Introduction

Maimonides does not base his claim as to the goodness of existence on appeals from this world to the hereafter. Rather he faces squarely the question of the intrinsic merit of this life as something which is worth living in its own right, not something for which amends must be made in an afterworld. Nor does the Rambam rely on spurious appeals to the *deus ex machina* of divine interference in nature. Rather he affirms unbreachable causal laws, of which God Himself is the Author, and a level of logical necessity beyond causality which requires no author at all. Thus nature itself, in its regularity, not the violation of nature, is the vehicle of God's grace. And necessity is not in conflict with divine omnipotence.

Philosophers and theologians of all persuasions may uphold various views as to the nature of miracles and the impossible. Maimonides himself is inclined to believe that miracles are variations in the apparent regularity of natural law woven into the causal fabric by God at the very ordination of the natural pattern. Thus they only appear to be violations of the causal order. Other philosophers, such as Averroës, are disposed to treat miracles as marvelous natural occurrences. If the

325

world is God's act, then all creation is a miracle. The Asharites, on the other hand, believed that God can instantly alter the entire order of nature at His pleasure; while Ibn Hazm, like some modern empiricists, went so far as to say that even the laws of logic are no more than the outcome of the accustomed modes of human thought, which God transcends and might easily alter. Yet for all thinkers there is a level of absolute impossibility which even God does not surpass. Thus all must agree that no impotence is assigned to God by the (tautologous) assertion that even God cannot do the impossible.

From *Moreh Nevukhim* III

MOREH NEVUKHIM III:15

The nature of the impossible is stable and fixed; it is not the outcome of some process or product of some agent's act; it cannot in any way be changed. That is why the deity is not described as having power over it. On this point there is not the least disagreement among thinkers. No one is unaware of this except those who fail to understand the concepts they use. The sole ground for disagreement among thinkers of all schools regarding impossibility is the designation of a certain class of things which are imaginable but are classified by certain thinkers as impossible (so that the deity could not be described as being able to change them), while others classify them as possible and therefore subject to God's creative power *ad libitum*.

The joining of opposites, for example, at the same instant, in the same subject, or the "transmutation of identities," *i.e.*, the reduction of substance to accident or accident to substance, or the existence of a physical substance without any accidents—all such things are classified as impossible by everyone who engages in thought. God's creation of His equal, or annihilating Himself, or becoming corporeal, or changing—all these likewise are classed as impossible, and, therefore, power to accomplish any of these things is not regarded as attributable to God. But as to the existence of a bare accident not in a substance, a certain sect of thinkers (namely the Mutazila) imagined such a thing and deemed it possible, while others classed it impossible. Those who upheld the existence of accidents without substrates were led to this position not by thought alone, of course, but more from a desire to safeguard certain religious principles to which reason is diametrically opposed.[1] This doctrine provided them with a way out. Again, the bringing into being of an embodied thing out of no matter whatever is classed as possible by us, as impossible by the Philosophers. And the Philosophers say that the creation of a square whose side is commensurate with its diagonal . . . etc., is impossible; yet some, who are ignorant of mathematics and know nothing of these things beyond the words, without comprehending the concepts these words stand for, suppose such things to be possible.[2]

I wish I knew whether the whole thing is so wide open that anyone may claim of any notion he conceives that it is possible, while others say, "on the contrary it is impossible by the nature of the case." Or is there something which restricts the realm of possibility, so that a man may say with certainty that *this* is impossible by its very nature? Is the standard or criterion here imagination or reason? And by what means are imagination and reason to be distinguished? For one person may quibble with another—or with himself—about some matter he finds to be possible and of which he says it is possible by nature, while his disputant says this judgment as to its possibility is the work of imagination and has not met the test of reason. Is there then some means by which reason may be distinguished from imagination? Is this something external to them both? Or is it done by reason itself? All these might be subjects of some quite far-reaching investigations. But that is not the purpose of this chapter. It is plain that for every view and school there are things which are impossible, things whose existence is absurd.[3] God is not described as having power over such things, nor is He said to be impotent or lacking in power for not changing them. These things, then, are necessary in themselves, not because anyone

1. *E.g.*, certain Mutazilites believed that the instant evanescence of each atom was accomplished by the creation in no substrate of the accident of "destruction."
2. According to Maimonides (*Moreh* I:73) atomism implies the commensurability of the side of a square with its diagonal. But it can be proved mathematically that the diagonal is not measurable in any units or fractions of the side of its own square.
3. Even Ibn Hazm, who believed that God can do what is impossible in nature, and even what is impossible in (human) conception, distinguished a realm of absolute impossibilities such as God creating His equal, etc.

made them so. Clearly the disagreement regards things which might be classed in either way: are they possible or impossible? [4]

Analysis

Maimonides alerts his reader in his discussion of the doctrine of the Kalam to the central role which will be played in the metaphysics of theophany by the problem of the bounds of possibility. (See *Moreh* I 73:10, especially the passage beginning *N.B.*) It is nonsense to claim that God can do the impossible, for the impossible is by definition that which cannot be done. But what is it that cannot be done? How can the mind set limits to the realm of possibility? Does imagination provide a criterion? How can the determinations of imagination be distinguished from those of reason?

For the Philosophers, possibility is limited by the receptivity of matter. Those changes which matter cannot undergo are not possible. For the Mutakallimun the discontinuous character of the atoms and of time itself guarantee that any conceivable collocation of states is in principle possible. Clearly both the Philosophers and the Mutakallimun rest their conception of the bounds of possibility on their divergent notions of matter. But, as Maimonides perceives, neither of these conflicting doctrines of possibility has any real bearing on the question of the manifestation of an immaterial God in a material world. What one may learn from the Philosophers is that the action of a Perfect Being cannot be regarded as capricious. There must be some rule or pattern in the divine expression, even if the wisdom of that rule eludes our finite understanding. What one may learn from the Kalam is that the laws of nature need not be inferred to have been always and necessarily as they are today. Maimonides' cosmology here is clearly evolutionary: The world in its present settled state affords no grounds for inference as to its character in the most remote past. Neither does the nonbeing which remains when all existence is abstracted away afford any purchase to reason or imagination for deduction of the limits of its potentialities. What is required is a tentative approach to the meta-

---

4. The question is not the absurd one, whether God can do the impossible.

physical problem of the nature of the linkage, as it were, between material finitude and the Immaterial Absolute. Maimonides approaches this problem with the aid of the philosophic concept of emanation and the prophetic insight embodied in the visionary imagery of angelology.

ANGELS AND EMANATION

Introduction

The problem as to how an immaterial and transcendent being can be understood to influence (let alone govern!) material being is among the most difficult any theistic system must confront. Yet this problem is not peculiar to theistic systems, for any thinker who affirms the existence of minds must confront the same problem regarding the relationship of intelligence to material nature. The difficulties in this regard may become so abstruse as to lead the puzzled philosopher to deny altogether the existence of God on the one hand, or mind on the other—or, halting short of such a drastic step, the philosopher may attempt to short-circuit the problem by identifying mind with body, God with nature. The atheistic alternative, however, is ruled out by a philosopher such as Maimonides who finds the evidences of divine work in nature to be compelling. And the seemingly elegant expedient of pantheism fails to make clear in just which direction the identification is inclined. Is God being reduced to nature? If so, then divinity is denied. Or is nature being elevated to divinity? If so, then how can it retain the characteristics of nature? It makes no more sense to speak of God as having shape or weight or color than it does to predicate such

330

terms of the subject of the verbs "to think," "to dream," or "to remember." This being so, however, the problem of a relationship between God and the world returns. It is a problem to which Maimonides is justly sensitive.

One of the enduring achievements of the philosophy created by Plato and systematized by Aristotle and the Aristotelians was its delineation of a coherent conception of the nature of the relationship between God and the world such that the action of God in the world and the variability of finite being with respect to the extent of divine penetration into it could be rationally and acceptably accounted for. In Plato's scheme, particulars were understood to derive their being from universals, the true realities in which the former were understood to "participate," while the latter were the perfect expressions of the divine idea, the Good. In the philosophy of Plotinus "participation" was transformed into a dynamic relationship, through which the divine was envisioned as projecting finite being from the fullness of its infinitude. This was the "emanation" of the Neoplatonists. Neither classical emanation nor Platonic participation offered a satisfactory solution to the problem of the relationship between God and the world as it would be posed in the Mosaic theology within which Maimonides was at work, although the impress which both made upon his mind is evident in his writing. For Platonism involved the assumption of the self-subsistence of the ideas, a notion which Aristotle had shown to involve serious difficulties; and Neoplatonism, at least as conceived by the followers of Plotinus (that is, the Greek and Muslim thinkers we call Neoplatonists on account of their Platonic interpretation of Aristotle, but whom Maimonides called the Philosophers), assumed a necessary, almost logical correlation between the subject and the object of emanation—such that, as we have seen, the world's existence became necessary (and therefore eternal) and the divine act was robbed of its freedom.

In the philosophy of Aristotle himself, however, as interpreted by the great Hellenistic Aristotelian Alexander of Aphrodisias, Maimonides found a model for the solution of the problem of the relationship between God and the world which he believed to be consistent with Mosaic theology. And while he does not put on uncritically the whole cloth of Aristotle's view or accept unquestioningly what he calls Aristotle's unproved assertions, he does find in the Aristotelian view elaborated by Alexander a point of departure for the interpretation of Biblical theology—and indeed an attractive (if to the traditional mind somewhat startling) interpretation of the Biblical angelology as well.

From *Moreh Nevukhim* II

MOREH NEVUKHIM II:2

. . . My purpose in composing this treatise, you must understand, was neither to produce a work on natural science nor to write a textbook on the problems of metaphysics from a particular point of view, nor to demonstrate those metaphysical theories which are subject to proof. Nor was it my intention to trace the astronomy of the spheres or inform you of their number. There are enough books about all that; and, if they are wanting on any topic, then nothing I can say on that topic would be any better than all that has been said already. My sole object in this treatise, as I instructed you in the preface, is to clarify the problems of the Bible and bring to the surface the deeper meanings which lie beyond the level of the common understanding.

Thus if we seem to be discussing the doctrine of disembodied intellects, the number of these or of the spheres, the causes of the motion of the latter, the true nature of matter and form or divine emanation, etc., you must not suppose for a moment that my purpose is simply to determine the truth about these ideas of the Philosophers. For these ideas are dealt with in many books, and their soundness has been demonstrated in most cases. Rather, my sole intention is to treat what will clear up one problem or another in understanding the Bible; and many knots can be untied by a familiarity with these concepts. . . .

MOREH NEVUKHIM II:3

The views of Aristotle regarding the causes of the motion of the spheres, from which the existence of disembodied minds is deduced, are, you must realize, simply unproved assertions. But they are the least troublesome of all such doctrines, and, as Alexander says in *The*

Principles of the All, the most conducive to systematic treatment. They are also in harmony, as I shall explain, with many propositions of the Bible, especially as expounded in the well-known commentaries [1] for which there is no doubt of the authorship of the Sages. I shall therefore present his [Aristotle's, according to Alexander of Aphrodisias] views and his suasions in their behalf, with the end in view of selecting from them what is in accord with the Bible and the teachings of the Sages, of blessed memory.

MOREH NEVUKHIM II:4

"That the sphere has a soul is obvious on reflection.[1] This will sound difficult or improbable only to one who takes 'having a soul' in the sense that a man, an ass, or an ox has a soul; but this is not what is meant by the claim. Rather, what is meant is that the sphere's motion is surely evidence of the presence in it of a principle that moves it. To be sure, this principle of motion is, unquestionably, a soul.[2] To explain: it is absurd that the cyclical motion of the sphere be caused not by a soul but simply by nature as is the linear motion of a stone downward or of fire upward, for whatever moves in such a way is moved by its internal natural principle of motion only so long as it is where it does not belong. When it reaches the place where it belongs, it comes to rest. But the sphere moves by revolving in place.

"Now the fact that it has a soul does not entail that the sphere will so move. For any being with a soul moves only on account of nature or some conception. By 'nature' here I mean pursuit of the agreeable and avoidance of the disagreeable, regardless of whether the cause of this motion is externally objective (an animal's avoidance of the heat of the sun or seeking water when thirsty) or imagined—for animals move on account of imagined as well as real advantages and disadvantages. But the sphere does not move to avoid the unfavorable or seek the favorable, for it only goes back where it started and returns to each point it leaves. Besides, if its motion were natural in this way, it

---

1. *I.e.,* in the Midrashic literature.

1. *I.e.,* to an Aristotelian: a soul, in Aristotelian parlance, is a principle of motion.

2. Maimonides fills the mouth of the Aristotelian with persuasive language as a reminder to the reader that the argument is not intended to be rigorous.

follows that it would arrive where it was going and come to rest. For if its motion were to seek or to avoid and this could never be done, then its motion would be in vain.[3]

"This cyclical motion, then, must be at the dictate of some conception. But a conception requires a mind. Thus the sphere must have a mind. But not everything with a mind to conceive an idea and a soul to enable it to move does move at the thought of that conception. For thought alone does not entail motion. This is made clear in metaphysics, but it is obvious, for you will observe in your own case that you can think of many things toward which you are able to move but to which you do not make the slightest approach until a desire originates in you for the object of your thought; then you set out to get it. Thus it appears that the soul through which the motion takes place and the mind in which the idea is conceived are together not sufficient to originate this sort of motion, until desire for that object of conception is joined to them. It follows that the sphere must have a desire for the object of its conception. This is the object of yearning,[4] the single Deity, glory to His name."

In this manner, he says, the Deity moves the sphere, *i.e.*, through the desire of the sphere to become like what it apprehends, the idea it conceives of absolute simplicity, undifferentiation and changelessness, from which good ceaselessly flows. As a body, the sphere cannot accomplish this emulation except by revolving ceaselessly, for that is the extent to which a body can maintain continuity in what it does; and rotation is the simplest form of motion.[5] Its being, then, would be undifferentiated by its motion or by the attendant flowing forth of good. . . . Thus Aristotle avowed with confidence that there are as many disembodied minds as there are spheres. . . .

The recent philosophers [6] believe that . . . the tenth is the "Active Intellect," evidence for which is provided by the progress of our own

3. But nothing in nature, the Aristotelian assumes, is in vain; see *Moreh* III:20, 25.

4. The *Summum Bonum* or ultimate object of all activity, according to the Aristotelian philosophy.

5. It is presumed by the Aristotelian that cyclical motion might be exempted somehow from the natural state of ordinary motions which are compounded resultants of conflicting forces.

6. *E.g.*, al-Farabi and Avicenna.

minds from potential to actual awareness and by the appearance in things which come to be and pass away of forms previously nonexistent in their matter, except potentially. Everything which proceeds from potential to actual must have external to it something of its own kind to bring about that progress. A carpenter does not build a storehouse simply because he is a builder, but rather because (and to the extent that) he has the form of the storehouse in his mind. This form or idea of the storehouse in the mind of the carpenter is what gives reality to the form of the storehouse in the lumber. The bestower of forms, in this way, is, surely, itself a disembodied form. What gives reality to the mind [7] is itself a mind, the Active Intellect. . . .

This leads Aristotle in turn to the demonstrated fact that God, glory and majesty to Him, does not do things by direct contact. He burns things by means of fire; fire is moved by the motion of the sphere; the sphere is moved by means of a disembodied intellect, these intellects being the "angels which are near to Him," through whose mediation the spheres move.

Being disembodied, these intellects can in no way be plural on account of any differences in their natures. Since they are not bodies, it follows in his view that the Deity must be what gives being to the first intellect, which moves the first sphere as we have explained. The source and cause of the intellect which moves the second sphere must be the first intellect, and so forth. . . . This is the belief Aristotle asserts. The evidence for the credibility of these things is given at length in the books of his followers. The outcome of his whole argument is that all the spheres are living bodies with souls and minds which conceive the thought of God and apprehend as well the grounds of their own being.[8] Thus totally disembodied minds exist which emanate from God and are the intermediaries between God and all bodies here in this world. Now I shall explain to you in the next chapters what in our Torah is in concord with these beliefs and what is not.

MOREH NEVUKHIM II:5
From the point of view of the Bible too it is axiomatic that the heavens are alive and articulate (*i.e.,* conscious), that they are not lifeless bod-

7. As a mind, *i.e.,* as actually thinking.
8. *Viz.,* the prior intellect in each case.

ies like fire or earth, as the unaware might suppose, but rather that they are, as the Philosophers say, living beings, obedient to their Master, who praise and glorify Him in their way.[1] Thus it says: "The heavens tell of the glory of God," etc. [Psalm 19:2]. Those who take this as poetic personification miss the point completely. Hebrew never applies the terms "tell" and "relate" together to anything but an intelligent being. That an objective rather than a subjective description of the character of the heavens is intended is evidenced clearly by the words, "There is no speech; there are no words; their voice is unheard" [19:4]. The text plainly states that it is describing the actual character of the heavens as praising God and telling of His wonders without a word from tongue or lip. This is legitimate, for to praise with words is only to relate what is conceived of in the soul. The idea is the real praise; [2] the word only informs another or explains what one has grasped. . . .

In the judgment of all the Philosophers, as you must know, the governance of this subcelestial world is effected by forces which emanate from the sphere as discussed already [*Moreh* I:72], and the spheres are aware of and understand what they control. This is expressly stated in the Torah as well: . . . "to rule by day and by night . . ." [Genesis 1:18]. Rule means domination by way of control, an additional notion beyond that of giving light and darkness, which is the proximate cause of generation and corruption, expressed by the phrase "to divide between light and darkness" [*ibid.*]. It is absurd that what governs something would not know that which it governs—assuming that we know just what "governance" means in this context [see *Moreh* III:17]. . . .

MOREH NEVUKHIM II:6
The existence of angels requires no argument, as far as the Bible is concerned.[1] The Torah explicitly states a number of times that they do

1. As always, what is problematic here for Maimonides is not what Scripture says but what it means.
2. The idea in this case is a declension from the Highest Idea, what Plato calls the Idea of the Good—they praise Him in that they reflect, each in its own way, His absolute perfection.
1. This suggests that their mode of existence is regarded by the Torah as unproblematic.

exist. . . . It says, "He is the God of gods" [Deuteronomy 10:17]—meaning the God of angels, Lord of lords, master of the heavens and the stars, which are lords of all other bodies. . . . It cannot mean that He is the master of everything of stone or wood which is believed to be divine, for there is nothing to boast of or exalt in a god's being lord of stone or lumber or a casting of metal. It can only mean that He is the Ruler of rulers, *i.e.,* of the angels, Lord of the heavens. (A previous chapter of this treatise [*Moreh* I:49] has already explained that the angels are not bodies.) Now this is what Aristotle says, although there is a terminological difference here in that he says, "disembodied intellects" and we say "angels." But Aristotle's doctrine that these disembodied intellects serve as the nexus between God and being, by whose mediation the spheres are brought into motion, which is the cause of all becoming, is the express import of all the Scriptures. For you will never find in Scripture any activity done by God except through an angel. And "angel," as you know, means messenger. Thus anything which executes a command is an angel. So the motions of living beings, even those that are inarticulate, are said explicitly by Scripture to be due to angels if such motions occur at the behest of the Deity, who provides them with the power so to move. It says, "My God hath sent an angel and closed the lions' mouths, and they have not hurt me" [Daniel 6:23]. The movements of Balaam's ass were all brought about "by an angel," and the elements themselves are referred to as angels: "Who makes the winds His angels and the flaming fire His ministers" [Psalm 104:4].

By now you must realize that "angel" may refer to a human messenger . . . a prophet . . . the disembodied minds which manifest themselves in prophetic vision, and to the powers of animals, as we shall make clear.

Our argument here is concerned solely with those "angels" which are disembodied intellects. For our Bible is not unaware that God governs this existence through the mediation of the angels. With reference to the passages "Let us make man in our image" [Genesis 1:26] and "Let us go down" [11:7] in the plural, the Sages write, "The Holy one, as it were, does nothing without consulting the supernal host." "Consulting"—a wonderful choice of word, the same Plato used when he said that God consults the realm of intellects, whereupon existence flows forth from Him.[2] . . . In *Bereshit Rabbah* too, commenting on the *Kohelet* passage "What they have already done" [Ecclesiastes 2:12], it is said, "It does not read, 'What He has done' but 'What they have done.' He and, as it were, His court deliberated regarding each and every limb in your body and set it in position . . ." [*Bereshit Rabbah* XII].

The import in all these texts is not, as a primitive mentality would suppose, to suggest any discussion or planning or seeking of advice or opinions on God's part. How could the Creator receive aid from the object of His creation? The real import of all is to proclaim that being, including particular individuals and even the formation of the parts of animals such as they are, is brought about entirely through the mediation of angels. For all forces are angels. How blind, how perniciously blind are the naïve! If you told someone who purports to be a sage of Israel that the Deity sends an angel who enters a woman's womb and there forms the embryo, he would think this a miracle and accept it as a mark of the majesty and power of the Deity and of course of His wisdom—despite the fact that he believes an angel to be a body of flaming fire one third the size of the entire world. All this, he thinks, is possible for God. But if you tell him that God placed in the sperm the power of forming and demarcating these organs and that this is the angel, or that all forms are produced by the Active Intellect, that here is the angel, the "vice-regent of the world" constantly mentioned by the Sages, then he will recoil; for he does not understand that true majesty and power are in the bringing into being of forces which are active in a thing although they cannot be perceived by the senses.

The Sages, of blessed memory, state clearly (to those who are wise themselves) that every bodily power (not to mention forces at large in the world) is an angel and that a given power has just one effect and no more. It says in *Bereshit Rabbah*, "We are given to understand that no angel performs two missions, nor do two angels perform one mission" [L]—which is just the case with all forces. To confirm the conclusion that individual physical and psychological forces are called angels, there is the dictum of the Sages in a number of places, deriving ultimately from *Bereshit Rabbah*, "Each day the Holy One,

2. See *Timaeus* 29–30.

blessed be He, creates a band of angels who sing their song before Him and go their way" [LXXVIII]. When this text was countered with another which suggests that the angels are permanent (for it is made clear many times that they are "alive and enduring") the answer given was that some are permanent and others perish. And this is in fact the case. Particular forces come to be and pass away in constant succession; the species of such forces, however, are stable and enduring.

There it says in the story of Judah and Tamar, "Rabbi Yohanan said, 'He sought to pass, but the Holy One, blessed be He, manifested to him the angel appointed over lust' " [*Bereshit Rabbah* LXXXV], *i.e.*, the sexual drive. This force too is an angel. In this manner you always find them speaking of the angel appointed over this or that, for every force charged by God with some affair is an angel "appointed over" that thing. To quote Midrash *Kohelet,* "When a man sleeps, his soul speaks to an angel, and the angel to a cherub" [20:10]. Thus they reveal to the aware that the imaginative faculty [3] is also called an angel; and the mind, a cherub.[4] How beautiful this will appear to the sophisticated mind, and how disturbing to the primitive. All of the various forms in which angels are seen are part of the prophetic vision, as stated earlier. Some prophets, you will observe, see angels as human beings . . . others, as awesome and dread-inspiring persons . . . others, as fire. . . . The seeing of an angel occurs only in prophetic vision and varies with the capacity of the beholder.

Thus here too there is nothing in what Aristotle says which is in conflict with the Bible. Where he does contradict us consistently is in his belief that all things are eternal *a parte ante,* implied necessarily by God in this manner. What we believe is that all this is created, that God created the "disembodied intellects" and set the power of "yearning" for them in the sphere—that it is He who created the intellects and the spheres and gave them their powers of governance. In this we disagree with him. . . .

3. A power which according to the Philosophers was most active in sleep.

4. The imagination is conceived as communicating with the consciousness through dreams. Thus the mind iteslf may communicate metaphysical understanding to the imagination, which imagination clothes in symbols, a fact of great significance in the explanation of prophetic revelation. See Part Five of this book.

MOREH NEVUKHIM II:7

. . . Do not suppose that the spheres or the intellects are on the same level as other corporeal forces which are physical and not conscious. The spheres and intellects are conscious of their own acts, which are voluntary and deliberate. But their freedom of choice and deliberateness are not the same as ours, which deal entirely with temporal events. . . . Their scope for will and choice is at the level of action assigned to them, while ours is at the level assigned to us and in keeping with our capacities. We are prone to fall short in the execution, and our deliberation and action arise out of want, while the intellects and spheres show no such inadequacy but always do what is good and are not capable of anything else. . . .

MOREH NEVUKHIM II:8

One ancient view, widespread among philosophers and common folk, was that the motion of the spheres produced great and frightful sounds. . . . This view has been quite popular among our coreligionists. Surely you are familiar with the Sages' descriptions of the mighty sound of the sun. . . . Aristotle rejected this view and makes it clear that the spheres make no sound.[1] . . . Do not be disturbed that Aristotle's view contradicts that of our Sages for . . . as you know, they themselves preferred the secular view to their own in these astronomical matters. They say plainly, "The Sages of the nations of the world conquered" [*Pesahim* 94B]. This is true, for in matters of thought any discussant may proceed only where the argument leads. That is why what can validly be demonstrated must be believed.

MOREH NEVUKHIM II:10

. . . The Sages' pronouncement that the angel is one-third of the world in *Bereshit Rabbah* [X] . . . is now clear as can be.[1] . . . There are three kinds of created being: (1) Disembodied intellects, *i.e.*, the angels; (2) the bodies of the spheres; (3) prime matter, the constantly changing bodies beneath the sphere of the moon.

In this manner, one who wants to understand the enigmas of pro-

1. Maimonides cites *De Caelo* II:9. 290ᵇ. 12ff.
1. Maimonides cites his *Mishneh Torah: Hilkhot Yesodei ha-Torah,* II:3.

phetic language and arouse himself from uncritical slumber may do so, and so may be rescued from the slough of ignorance and rise to a place among the highest. But whoever enjoys wallowing in his own ignorance may sink "lower and lower" [*cf.* Deuteronomy 28:43]. He need not trouble body or spirit; let him just lie still and he will descend as low as nature allows. Try to reflect upon each thing I have said and understand it.

MOREH NEVUKHIM II:11

A man who is deductively oriented exclusively, on studying and reading about the astronomical matters touched on here,[1] might presume that what he is reading are conclusive demonstrations that the form and number of the spheres are as they are said to be. Such is not the case, nor is this the objective of astronomy. Some points in astronomy can be demonstrated—*e.g.*, that the course of the sun declines from the equator. Of this there is no doubt.[2] But as to whether the sun has an eccentric sphere or an epicycle, this has not been demonstrated—a fact which does not trouble the astronomer in the least. For the object of astronomy is to propose a configuration which allows for the uniform revolution of the stars consistent with what is observed, while minimizing the complexity of the motion and the number of spheres.
. . . That is why we prefer the eccentricity hypothesis in the case of the sun to the postulation of epicycles. . . . It is not impossible that every star have a sphere of its own. . . . In that case there would then be as many intellects as stars,[3] as it is said, "Is there any number to His troops?" [Job 25:3] . . . Even so our system would not be overthrown. . . . For our purpose, as you have understood by now, is not to give a painstaking and precise account of the intellects and the spheres as they really are, but rather to survey broadly the forces we encounter in existence. It all comes down to this: being, below the level of the Creator (exalted be He), is divided into three sorts: (1) disembodied intellects; (2) the bodies of the spheres, which are sub-

1. In the present translation most of Maimonides' discussion of astronomy has been omitted.
2. Given the evidence of the senses.
3. Or as atoms, to preserve the modern analogy!

strates of stable forms, such that forms are not interchanged among these substrates and the spheres do not change essentially; and (3) the present bodies which come to be and pass away, all of which have the same matter in common.[4] Order and governance flow forth from God to the intellects, according to their capacities. These in turn shed light and benefits (from the good they have derived) on the bodies of the spheres, which in turn radiate energies and beneficial effects upon this body, subject to generation and corruption, from the wealth of good they have received from the grounds of their being.

No source of good in this hierarchy exists for the sole aim and object of shedding its benefits. The implications of that would be sheer absurdity. For the end is nobler than the means, so the higher being would exist for the sake of the lower—a thing no rational person would imagine [see *Moreh* III:13]. Rather the case is as follows: a thing endowed with a certain perfection might be so endowed only sufficiently for itself, or it might be overabundantly endowed, such that its good suffices for itself and overflows to others. You might say, by way of analogy, that one person, perhaps, has wealth enough to provide only for his own needs, with none left over to support someone else; another person might have sufficient left over to enrich many people, giving them ample to make them rich, and leaving them enough surplus to enrich others as well. This is what happens in the case of being. The flood of being which flows forth from God to bring into being the disembodied intellects flows on from them. Each of them brings the next into being, until the Active Intellect is reached and the giving of being to disembodied intellects ceases. Each of them sheds further being in turn, until the sphere of the moon is reached. Beyond lies the present body, subject to coming-to-be and passing away—*i.e.,* matter and all that is composed of it. From every sphere forces flow. Their tide is stemmed when they reach the elements, and their power is spent in the influence they exert upon coming-to-be and passing away.[5]

These concepts, we have already made clear, are not in conflict with

4. And therefore do "interchange forms."

5. To wit, not that their energy is exhausted but simply that the matter of the elements is as low as being can reach before the level of nothingness.

anything touched upon by our prophets [6] and the upholders of our Bible. . . .

Since the ''flowing forth'' or emanation of intellects from the Deity has been mentioned repeatedly in our discussion, we ought to make clear to you exactly what this is—*i.e.*, what it is really that is given the metaphorical name emanation. . . .

MOREH NEVUKHIM II:12

Clearly everything which comes to be has necessarily a maker to bring it into being. This cause or maker must be either a body or not a body. But bodies as such do nothing; they are active only *qua* this or that sort of body,[1] *i.e.*, in virtue of their forms. . . .

This proximate cause, which brings about a temporal event or brings into being a temporal being, might itself have come into being as well. But this cannot continue *ad infinitum*. Necessarily, if anything comes to be in time, then we must reach an eternal cause of becoming, not itself subject to becoming, which is the cause of this event.

The question remains, why did this cause act now rather than before, for then too it existed. What prevented this cause from acting must have been either want of the appropriate relationship between the subject and object of the act if the cause was a body, or want of fit matter if the cause was not a body.

An examination of physical science reveals that no body affects another without either coming into contact with it or coming into contact with something else which comes into contact with it (in the case of a cause which acts only through intermediaries). This body which is now hot, for example, was heated by fire, unless the fire heated the air and the air surrounding this body heated it. In the latter case, the proximate cause of the heating of this body is the heated air. Even a magnet attracts iron at a distance by a force it propagates in the air adjacent to the iron. That is why magnets do not draw bodies at any

---

6. *N.B.* Maimonides does not assert categorically the truth of the doctrine of emanation but rather its consistency with the content of Scripture. The Philosophers and the prophets poetically express the same fundamental truth, which they are either unable or unwilling to express in more literal terms.

1. *E.g.*, lye is not caustic *qua* matter but *qua* alkaline; if it were caustic *qua* matter, all matter would be caustic; *cf.* premise 25 of the Philosophers.

distance whatever, just as flame does not heat bodies at any distance whatever but only as far as it can affect the air between it and the object to be heated. If the heated air is deflected from a candle, the wax will not melt. The same is true in the case of magnetic attraction.[2]

If something is heated which was not originally hot, some cause must have intervened. Either a fire has been generated or else a flame which was far off has altered its distance, supplying the wanting relation. The same holds true, we discover, with all causes of change. The underlying cause is the blending of the elements, bodies which affect and are affected by each other. The cause of all such events, then, is the proximity or distance between one body and another. But events we observe do not depend on mere chemistry; the appearance of the panoply of forms must also have a cause. This is the Form Giver, which is not a body since the Author of forms must itself be a form. . . .

The following may help to elucidate this: Every blending may be progressively augmented or diminished. But forms are not so. They do not come about progressively and thus are not subject to motion. They simply come to be and pass away in no time.[3] Thus they are not the work of chemistry; chemistry only predisposes matter to receive them. The Form Maker, like its products, is not susceptible to division.[4] Thus it appears that the Maker or rather the Bestower of forms must itself be a form, a disembodied form.

The preference of this immaterial cause [5] cannot possibly be due to the relation between it and its object; for, not being a body, it cannot be near to or far from a body, nor can a body be near to or far from it. There is no relation of distance between a body and a nonbody. The cause of the nonoccurrence of the effect, then, must be want of prepa-

2. The experientially observed diminishing effect of magnetism and the experimentally observed dependence of a candle upon convection indicate that heat and even magnetism, as physical forces, are subject to all the limitations of scope and transport which would be expected of functions of finite bodies.
3. Maimonides has in mind here essential characteristics, which determine the identity of a thing as a member of its species. These are either present or absent. They do not come and go.
4. If it were, forms would be produced gradually.
5. *I.e.*, for a particular moment in which to act.

ration in the matter to be affected. It appears, therefore, that the interaction of bodies with respect to their forms entails a predisposing of their matter to the reception of the influence of something which is not a body, something whose effects are forms. Since the work of this disembodied mind is manifest and plain to be seen in existence, in all that comes about that does not arise from mere chemistry, it is known necessarily that this cause does not act through direct contact or at a fixed remove, for it is not a body. Its action therefore is always labeled emanation or flowing forth, likening it to a spring which flows in all directions but has no particular direction from which it draws or toward which it directs its flow; rather it flows forth from every direction and spreads its waters constantly in every direction, near and far. By the same token, this mind cannot be reached by forces from any determinate quarter or distance. Nor is its influence on everything else confined to a particular direction or distance or time. Rather, its action is constant, so long as something has been prepared capable of benefiting from that ever-existent action termed emanation.

The Creator as well, since it is demonstrated He is not a body and all is His work and He is its cause (as we have explained and shall explain further), is said to give rise to all He brings to be by emanation. And in the same way He is said to cause knowledge which emanates to His prophets. What this means is that these effects are the work of one who is not a body, the term in this case being applied to His act.

This designation, "flowing forth," is predicated of God in Hebrew too, where God is likened to a spring of flowing water [Jeremiah 2:13], as already stated. No finer comparison will be found for the act of a disembodied being. For we are incapable of knowing the true word, corresponding with the true idea. The conception of a disembodied being's act is as difficult at least as the conception of a disembodied being. Just as imagination can conceive nothing but bodies or forces in bodies, so imagination cannot conceive the bringing about of any effect without the cause being in physical contact or at a particular distance in a particular direction. And since some vulgar minds realize that God is not a body and does not draw close to the object of His act, they imagine that He commands the angels and they in turn execute those acts by physical contact or coming into range [6] as we do. They imagine the angels too are bodies. Some even imagine that God commands a given thing in words like our own, *i.e.*, consonants and vowels, whereupon that thing is done. All this is dependence upon the imagination, which is also the true "Evil Inclination." For all ethical and intellectual deficiencies are the work of imagination or result from it. . . .

The words "For with Thee is the fountain of life" [Psalm 36:10] intend the emanation of being, and the completion of the line, "In Thy light do we see light," means exactly the same thing: through the flowing forth of mind from You, we are enabled to think, to draw conclusions and inferences, and to apprehend intelligence in turn. Try to understand this.

Analysis

Emanation, as conceived by the great Greek Neoplatonists Plotinus, Porphyry, and Proclus and adapted by their Muslim followers to the purposes of monotheism, is the ceaseless flowing forth of being, goodness, and perfection from their divine source. The imagery of an everflowing fountain (or of the flooding forth of light from the sun) to which such thinkers turned habitually in attempting to symbolize this eternal process was carefully devised so as to emphasize the inexhaustibility of the Source, the ceaselessness, and above all the immateriality of the process. The Source of being, it was thought, could not but overflow with being, and the process by which the transcendent became immanent was thought to reflect in its immateriality the immateriality of its point of origin—thus to be eternal and therefore timeless.

Despite the drawbacks which the timelessness of emanation and the apparent necessity of this flowing forth represented to Maimonides' Mosaic point of view, emanation did afford an admirable model for the relation of the divine to the world. If somehow emanation could be disentangled from the eternalistic physics and deterministic theology

---

6. *Cf.* the magnet.

with which it had been traditionally associated, then this relation might afford the avenue of a possible solution to the problem of the relation of God to the world. But could this divorce be accomplished? Maimonides believed it could. For the notion of a timeless process itself contained a tension which seemed to indicate that eternity was a condition added to the notion of emanation. In reality, perhaps, emanation was more compatible with creation than it was with eternity. By tracing the concept of emanation back to its roots in the thought of Aristotle, Maimonides, in fact, is able to divorce it from its eternalist connotations.

The Aristotelian idea from which the Neoplatonic notion of emanation is derived is that of the priority of the actual to the potential. In nature, according to Aristotle, we normally observe that things develop into what they (actually) are out of what they are potentially. But if we ask which came first, the actual or the potential, we must always, according to Aristotle, answer the actual. For the more, Aristotle would argue, cannot come from what is less, the perfect from the imperfect. But what is the actual? Actuality according to Aristotelian philosophy is the form or idea (*i.e.*, the definite specification, or perfection of a thing as such) imposed upon its matter (or potential). The precedence of the actual to the potential, then, would require the precedence of the ideal to the particular. This implication of Aristotle's thought was recognized by the Hellenistic Aristotelian Alexander of Aphrodisias, in terms of whose thought Maimonides founds his interpretation of the Biblical account of the relation of God to the world.

Since Aristotle had destroyed for all Peripatetics the credibility of the Platonic notion of the separate subsistence of Ideas, Alexander could not situate the ideas upon which particular reality depended simply in limbo. But the expedient remained of placing them within a mind, and this precisely is what Alexander did. He made the ideas, from which all actuality in the world was believed to derive, thoughts in the divine Mind, the plan or concept of the God of Aristotle, who was pure mind (and therefore pure actuality). Thus every process of realization in the world, whether the objective realization of a perfection in some being or the subjective realization of perfection as thought in a mind, could be traced to the causal agency of God. Subsequent thinkers removed this office of Form Giver or Active Intellect from the direct purview of the Deity, largely to protect His transcendental character. The function instead was generally assigned to the tenth or lowest of the incorporeal intellects which were thought by Aristotelians to govern the motions of the spheres. There was not, or at least there need not be, anything in this scheme inimical to the fundamental tenets of Biblical theology. For the conception of the world and all things in the world as dependent upon God for their development and perfection is, in Maimonides' view, the message of the Bible as well as the conclusion of the Philosophers.

The precise details of the model offered for the nexus between God and the world are, to Maimonides, profoundly unimportant. The exact number of the spheres, for example, makes little difference to the ultimate outcome of the investigation. The function of astronomy, as Maimonides tells us (*Moreh* II:24), is not the description of the precise reality of the heavens but the delineation of a model by which what is observed can be accounted for as comprehensively, satisfactorily, and economically as possible. The same may be said of theology. What is crucial in this regard is the recognition of three main classes of being: finite particulars,[1] God, and the beings which mediate between the two. What is crucial about the last is that they can be understood to exist and perform their function on the model of mediation between the absolute and the particular, as agents responsible for the importation of perfection into individual beings by differentiating perfection in general into its specific kinds and particular cases. Which is to say that the disembodied intellects of Aristotle and the ministering angels of Scripture perform precisely the same function and may be seen, in Maimonides' view, to perform it in precisely the same way.

Two qualifications must be made to this analogy of function, according to Maimonides. (1) Since matter is the condition of differentiation or particularization, the angels will require matter as the object of their act. Thus if matter is created, the angels cannot be required to act eternally but must be regarded as awaiting the provision of matter prior to the inception of their imparting of perfection to it. (2) In imparting perfection to particulars, the angels will infringe upon temporality. Their act, therefore, becomes temporal—and so, it follows,

---

1. Including, of course, the spheres.

must their being as well. Some angels, as Maimonides puts it, exist just for the moment of their act; others are eternal. This welds the nexus between the Divine and the particular elegantly indeed; for the angels which Maimonides concedes to be eternal correspond to universals, and may thus be seen as existing eternally in the mind of God. They pose, therefore, no threat to the uniqueness of divine eternity. The angels which come in contact with the world, however, are temporal, created instances of these universals, the forces in a body which are divided when bodies are divided and destroyed when bodies are destroyed—the forces whose coming and going mark all processes of realization in nature.

Thus Maimonides rejects the primitive understanding of the Biblical angelology, deriding the inconsistency of those who can believe that an angel may be one third of the world in size and yet enter into the womb of a woman or the loins or heart of a man as the Bible so often seems to require us to believe. In place of the primitive notion he substitutes the sophisticated notion of angel as force, *i.e.*, a form of energy or state of realization—a form or thought—which he shows to be consistent with the Biblical and Talmudic usage regarding the angelic function.

But Maimonides does not reduce the meaning of ''angel'' to that of ''force.'' For some angels are eternal (as Maimonides believes no mere force can be), and some indeed—those associated with the heavens, *i.e.*, the principal parts of the world—are conscious and intelligent as well. That this should be so is natural; for, as Maimonides writes, in matters of thought we must follow where the argument leads, and to accept the priority of the actual to the potential is by implication to accept as well the priority of subject to object. But the intellects or angels which exist eternally with God are in fact no real threat to Maimonides' monotheism or creationism or even to the economy of his ontology. For these ''counselors of God'' are identified with the eternal forms which Plato's God ''consulted'' when about to fashion the world: they are thought universals, the eternal idea or plan or word (*cf.* Philo's *logos*) in which or in accordance with which the world was created, and the instances of which come and go in the development of particulars—whether in the perfection of a fetus or the inspiration of a mind. They are, in other words, the principles of divine wisdom in which God created the world, and it is only natural that Maimonides should expect them to be conscious since they are the thought of God.

The operation of the world, in Maimonides' view, does not, as the Mutakallimun had supposed, require constant, direct divine intervention. Rather, God acts through intermediaries, through the delegation, as it were, of authority. Thus there is a nature by which the world is governed, although of course this cannot be a material nature. This position, which recommends itself to reason, is the stance of Scripture as well. When God wishes to burn, He burns with fire, for He created the world in accordance with a certain plan, and it is in accordance with that plan that the world operates. This, in Maimonides' view, is the way in which the inquiring mind may comprehend the divine governance of the world.

THE STORY OF JOB

Introduction

Nowhere is the question of the apparent incongruity between divine perfection and the human condition put more forcefully than by the haunting symbolic figure of Job, from whom everything was taken, wealth, children, even physical comfort—everything except the will to live and the inner sense of personal innocence. The God of Job, who whimsically gives this good man into Satan's hand and answers Job's plaintive cry with a great show of force, has often seemed a bully and cheat to the casual readers of the Book of Job, those who read the Bible as "literature." Yet the Rambam has provided, through his analysis of providence and the problem of evil, the means by which even the plight of Job may be made humanly comprehensible.

From *Moreh Nevukhim* III

MOREH NEVUKHIM III:22

The strange and wonderful story of Job is pertinent to our present concern, for it is a symbolic exposition of people's views regarding providence. You are familiar with the clear admission of certain of our

351

Sages: "Job did not exist and was not created, but was a symbol" [*Baba Batra* 15a]. Those who claimed that Job was created and did exist and that his story actually did take place did not know his period or locale. However, certain of the Sages say he lived in the time of Moses; others, that he lived in the time of David; others, that he was among those who returned from Babylon. This only confirms the view that he did not exist at all. On the whole, whether he existed or not, all thoughtful people are always perplexed about situations of the sort described in his story—so much so that things are said about God's knowledge and concern such as I have mentioned to you [see *Moreh* III:12]. By situations of this sort, I mean the affliction of a moral and upright man who was honest in his actions and scrupulously guarded against misdeeds [1] by a succession of terrible disasters befalling his fortune, his offspring, and his body, which were not brought upon him by any wrongdoing.

In either view, whether Job existed or not, the prologue [Job 1:6–12], *i.e.*, Satan's address to God, God's reply, and the giving over of Job into Satan's hand, is all of course symbolic, as any intelligent person sees. But this symbolism is not like any other; for it is symbolic of wonderful things, "things which are the mystery of the universe." [2] By it, immense obscurities are made clear and the most profound truths are brought to light. I shall state what I can and cite the passages in the Sages which alerted me to what I have understood of this magnificent allegory.

The first thing you must consider are the words, "There was a man in the land of Utz" [Job 1:1], which introduces the ambiguous word *Utz,* which may denote a person—"Utz, his firstborn" [Genesis 22:21]—or the imperative of to think or deliberate—*"Utzu etza,"* "take counsel together" [Isaiah 8:10]. It is as though it said to you, "Meditate on this parable, reflect on it, grasp its meaning, and see what the correct view is."

Next it states that "the sons of God" came "to present themselves before the Lord" and "Satan" came in their throng and number. It does not say, "The sons of God and Satan came to present themselves

---

1. Maimonides glosses Job 1:1.

2. The same expression is used in *Haggigah* 13a in connection with Ezekiel's vision: by the mystery of the universe the Rambam refers to the mystery of God's act.

before the Lord,'' which would put them all on the same level of existence. Rather, it says, "The sons of God came to present themselves
before the Lord, and also in their midst came Satan" [Job 1:6, 2:1].
This manner of speech is used not of one who comes sought for or intended for his own sake, but only of one whose presence is attendant
upon that of those whose presence was intended.[3]

Next, it states that this "Satan" roams throughout the face of the
earth and that there is no connection whatever between him and On
High; there he has no scope to roam. This is expressed in the words:
"From going up and down the earth and walking to and fro on it"
[1:7, 2:2]. Thus, he roams and circulates only on the earth.

Next, it states that this upright and moral man was given over into
the hand of "Satan" and that all the hurts he suffered in his fortune,
his offspring, and his body were caused by "Satan."

Having presupposed this situation,[4] it sets forth various theorists'
doctrines about the case. It states one view and ascribes it to Job, and
assigns others to his friends. I shall specify them quite clearly, viz.,
those views which involved conflicting interpretations of the events
whose entire cause was "Satan"—despite the fact that all of them,
Job and his friends alike, supposed that God himself acted here directly and not through Satan.

The most striking and remarkable aspect of the story is the fact that
Job is not described as a wise, discerning, intelligent, or knowledge-
able man, but only as a man of moral character and upright doings.
For, had he been a wise man, his situation would not have been an

3. Note how carefully the Rambam speaks of the presence rather than the existence of
evil. Evil is not intended for its own sake, but in the very act of unfurling the panoply of
forces (angels) upon which nature and all finite existence depend, evil is implied. Thus,
evil may be said to "accompany their throng," although it is not on a par with them in
intention or in existence. The very first turning away or alienation from God, even at the
level of the angels, marks the birth of evil (otherness). But, without this turning away,
nothing at all would come to be of what we call existence. The ambiguous standing of
evil is explained by the ambivalent status of matter, which is the principle of individuation and, in a sense, of all differentiation. Matter thus is the basis of all finite existence
and therefore, necessarily, of all privation as well.

4. The prologue is seen as stating, as a premise, the most problematic dimension of
human suffering, namely, the suffering of a good, upright, and pious man; it thus poses
the problem to which the body of the book is addressed.

enigma to him, as will be made clear.

Next, it scales his misfortunes in terms of human values. For some people are not dismayed at the loss of their fortune and take it lightly, but are awestruck at the death of their children and perish from grief. Some people, again, can bear even the loss of children without losing heart. But no being with sensation has power to bear physical torment with equanimity.

All men, *i.e.*, the masses, pay lip service to God's glory and characterize Him as just and fair when they are comfortable and successful, or even in times of bearable affliction. But when the disasters which are stated to have afflicted Job strike, then some reject their faith and believe all existence to be misgoverned when they lose their money. Others keep their faith in the justice and order of the world despite loss of their fortune; but, if tried by the loss of their children, they cannot bear it. Still others bear with patience and untroubled faith the loss of children. But bodily torment is something no one can bear patiently, without complaint or resentment, either voiced or unspoken within the heart.

As to the words, "to present themselves before the Lord," this is said of the "sons of God" both the first and second times. But of "Satan," it is said both times that he came in their throng and press; however, the first time it does not say "to present himself," but the second time, it says, "and the Satan came too in their midst to present himself before the Lord." You must understand this nuance and observe how remarkable it is. See how these ideas come to me almost like inspirations! For the meaning of "to present themselves before God" is that they exist, subject to the order of His will. . . . Thus, it is clear that the status of the sons of God in being is not the same as that of "Satan." Rather, the sons of God are more permanent and more firmly established. But "Satan," too, has a certain share of being below them.[5]

Another marvelous feature of this allegory is that when it mentions Satan's roaming (exclusively) over the earth and the things he does

5. While evil (*i.e.*, privation) is not real in the true sense, in which a thing is real only to the extent that it partakes of the divine perfection, it is nonetheless objective; it is not a figment of our imagination. Neither is matter, the condition of privation, unreal.

there, it makes clear that he is debarred from dominion over the soul. He is given power over all earthly things; but there is a barrier between him and the soul: "Only spare his soul" [Job 2:6]. I have explained already that the term "soul" is ambiguous, and may denote what remains of man after death [*Moreh* I:41]. This is what "Satan" has no power over.

Now listen to the helpful words of them who are truthfully called Sages; this makes everything clear, sheds light on all obscurities, and makes plain one of the greatest mysteries of the Torah [the problem of evil]. I am referring to their dictum in the Talmud: "Rabbi Simeon ben Lakish said, 'It is Satan, the evil inclination, and the angel of death' " [*Baba Batra* 16a]. Thus he makes clear all we have stated in a manner that will not be at all obscure to the intelligent: it should be plain to you that the same principle is given these three names, and all the actions ascribed to any one of these three are entirely the effects of one single thing. Thus, too, the ancient Sages of the Mishnah plainly stated, "It teaches: he descends, misleads, ascends, accuses,[6] obtains leave, and takes the soul" [7] [*ibid.*].

You will have realized by now that what David saw in his prophetic vision at the time of the plague, "his sword brandished in his hand outstretched over Jerusalem" [1 Chronicles 21:16], was shown to him only to symbolize that idea. The very same idea is referred to by the prophetic vision dealing with the disobedience of the sons of Joshua the High Priest: "And the Accuser [*satan*] standing to his right to accuse him" [Zechariah 3:1]. Thereupon it is made clear how far he is from Him in these words: "The Lord chastise you, Satan! The Lord who favors Jerusalem chastise you!" [3:2]. He it was whom Balaam saw, also in prophetic vision,[8] on the road, when he says, "Behold, I am come forth as an adversary [*satan*]" [Numbers 22:32]. Note that *satan* is derived from "*Steh me'alav vaavor*," "Turn away from it and pass on" [Proverbs 4:15]; *i.e.,* it denotes turning away or alienation, because it is he indubitably who turns men away from the ways of truth and causes them to perish in the ways of error. The identical

6. The verb is cognate with the noun *Satan*.
7. The deceiver, the accuser, the messenger or instrumentality of death are the same.
8. For Satan is not a person but a principle or idea personified in the imagination.

idea is expressed by "For the inclination of man's heart is evil from his youth" [Genesis 8:21]. . . . But the good inclination is found in man only after his mind has undergone a process of development. For this reason, they said, the evil inclination is called "a great angel," and the good inclination "a child, poor but wise" in the parable. . . . All these things are attested by the Sages in well-known texts.[9]

Now, if they make clear to us that the evil inclination is Satan and indubitably an angel—*i.e.,* he is called an angel, because he is in the throng of the "sons of God"—then the good inclination must really be an angel. Thus, the familiar image of the Sages: every man accompanied by two angels, one on the right, the other on the left. These are the good inclination and the evil inclination. In Gemarah *Shabbat* [119b], they clearly state that one of these two angels is good and the other evil.

Observe how many mysteries this statement has cleared up for us and how many delusions it dispels.

As I see it now, I have clarified and explained the story of Job from start to finish.[10] However, I do wish to explain the views ascribed to Job and each of his friends, using evidence I have gleaned from their speeches. . . .

9. Man is not evil by nature, but human goodness requires development (moral education). The untrained soul will naturally turn to evil since it has not learned the art of living and choosing wisely. The parable is in Ecclesiastes 9:14–15 and 4:13; its interpretation by the Sages in Midrash *Kohelet ad loc., Sanhedrin* 91b, *Bereshit Rabbah* XXXIV, *Nedarim* 32b.

10. Job's sufferings, in other words, are due to evil, either to the "evil inclination" of his own moral choices, or to the primordial "evil" of the inadequacies of his own material nature. True, the latter are not, in the moral sense, his fault; both sorts are his responsibility in the sense that it is up to him to attempt to resist them and alleviate or overcome them (by the therapy of the soul and body) to the extent that this is humanly possible. Their ontic status, too, *i.e.,* their status in being, is on a par: moral faults, like physical flaws, are privations. That is why both are symbolized by Satan, whose place in being is indicated by the text when it says he comes in the throng of the angels: there cannot be finite goodness without privation. Man's task is to approach to God as close as humanly possible. But, as long as individuation is maintained, there cannot be identification or assimilation without alienation and difference. The evil are punished not by the withholding of material rewards but by their alienation from God, their debarment from human perfection. The good are rewarded not by worldly success but by the possibility of enlightenment, knowledge of God, which virtue opens to the truly wise.

MOREH NEVUKHIM III:23

Assuming the story of Job is true, the first thing that happened was something on which all five, *viz.*, Job and his friends, agreed: All the misfortunes which befell Job, they agreed, were known to God, and it was God who brought them upon him. They all agreed as well that wrongdoing is not predicable of Him, and that injustice is not to be ascribed to Him. You will find this theme repeatedly stated in Job's speech.

Examining the speeches of the five in the course of their discussion, you might almost conclude that whatever is said by one of them is said by all. The same arguments seem to be repeated over and over again; and they seem to run together, broken up by Job's describing the intense agony of the pain and gravity of the misfortunes that had befallen him despite his rectitude, and by descriptions of his honesty, his nobility of character, and the goodness of his actions. Breaking up the discourse, likewise, are his friends' admonitions to patience, expressions of sympathy, and exhortations to resignation, urging him to be silent and not give rein to speech like a party to a dispute with another person. Rather, he should yield to the decree of God and be still. He says, however, that the agony of his pain makes it impossible for him to be patient, to show fortitude, or to speak as is seemly.

All his friends agree, moreover, that whoever does good will be rewarded and whoever does ill will be punished. Whenever you see a transgressor enjoying success, then, in the end, you may be sure his good fortune will be reversed, he will be destroyed, and disaster will befall him and his children and descendants. Whenever you see an obedient man in distress, then the hurt done him is sure to be repaired. This is a point you will find repeated in the speeches of Eliphaz, Bildad, and Tzofar. All three agree in this view. But this is not the purport of the story as a whole. Rather, that to which attention is being drawn is what makes each of them different. This is what makes us aware of each one's view about these events, *i.e.,* the falling of the harshest and direst misfortunes on the finest and most perfectly upright individual.

Job's opinion is that these events show that the good and the depraved are the same to Him, since He holds the human species in contempt and has disowned them. He says, among other things, "It is all one, therefore, I say. The innocent and the wicked He destroys. If the flood [1] slay suddenly, He will mock at the downfall of the guiltless" [Job 9:22–23]. . . . He confirms this view by saying, "One dies in his full strength, wholly at ease and quiet, his pails full of milk," etc. "Another dies with a bitter soul and has never eaten well. Together they lie down in the dust and the worm covers them over" [21:23–26]. Likewise, he argues at great length from the prosperity and success of the wicked: "As I think of it, I despair, and trembling grips my flesh: Why do the wicked live and grow ancient and powerful, their seed established in their sight?" etc. [21:6–8]. Having described the perfect success of the wicked, he goes on to say to those with whom he is speaking, Even if things are as you say, and the children of this prosperous unbeliever [2] are destroyed after his time, their traces obliterated, what harm is there to him in the misfortunes of his family after he is gone? He says, "What cares he for his house after him when the number of his months is sped?" [21:21].

Job next sets out to prove there is no hope of an afterlife, that nothing endures except the same neglect. He expresses wonder that God did not neglect to undertake to make a human being, but created him and then disdained to look after him: "Didst Thou not pour me out like milk and curdle me like cheese," etc. [10:10]. This is one of the beliefs held regarding providence. [3]

You are familiar with the verdict of the Sages that this opinion of Job's is as unsound as can be. They said, "May there be dust in Job's mouth," "Job sought to upset the plate," "Job denies the resurrection of the dead," "He began to blaspheme and complain" [Baba Batra 16a]. As for God's saying to Eliphaz, "For you did not speak rightly of Me as did my servant Job" [Job 42:7], the Sages say in defense of this, "A man is not to be blamed for his agony" [Baba Batra 16b], i.e., he is excused on account of the severity of his pain. [4] But this is

1. Translating in accordance with the Rambam's gloss.
2. The transgressor is assumed to be godless because he does not fear divine retribution.
3. That God created man but then abandoned him as being beneath His concern. In terms of the role afforded here to providence, Maimonides equates this view with that of Aristotle. See below in this chapter.
4. The Sages treat God's remonstrance with Eliphaz as excusing Job's speech, not as vindicating its truth.

not in keeping with the parable.[5] The true explanation, as we shall now make clear, is that Job retracted this view, which is the epitome of error, and demonstrated he had been mistaken. That this is the view most likely to be held naïvely, especially by one who suffers calamities and knows he is innocent, no one will deny. That is why this view [6] is attributed to Job. But Job said all he said while he still lacked understanding and did not know God except by faith, as the religious masses know Him. When he knew God with certainty, then he was sure that true happiness, which is the knowledge of God, is guaranteed to all who know Him, and no such misfortune as these has any power over man.

As long as Job knew God only by hearsay and not by way of thought, he imagined that these felicities (as they are thought to be) of health, wealth, and children are the ultimate goal. That is why he fell into such perplexity and said such things. This is the meaning of his words, "By the hearing of the ears I had heard of Thee, but now with my eyes I see Thee. Therefore do I abhor and repent of dust and ashes" [Job 42:5-6]. The words delineate the meaning: For this reason I reject all that I used to desire, and repent my being in the midst of dust and ashes—as his life was supposed to be: "He dwelt in dust and ashes" [2:8].[7] It is on account of his final statement, which points the way to the true apprehension, that it is said of Eliphaz on the heels of this, "For you did not speak rightly of Me, as did my servant Job." [8]

The view of Eliphaz on Job's reverses is also one of the previously discussed views on providence. He says that all that befell Job was deserved by him on account of sins he had committed. Thus Eliphaz says to Job, "Is not your wickedness great, and are not your sins without end?" [22:25]. He then argues with Job, this uprightness of actions, this exemplary life which you have led and to which you now

---

5. That is, the premise of the story.

6. That the fate of the innocent and guilty is the same.

7. Maimonides understands the line to refer not to Job's sitting in ashes as a sign of mourning, but to his whole former condition of life, all objects of his previous desire being dust and ashes compared to the ultimate felicity of knowledge of God.

8. For Eliphaz sought God's justice in terms of material rewards. He had not yet overcome the hedonistic value system which the enlightened Job renounced.

turn for support, do not entail that you are perfect in the eyes of God and, therefore, should not be punished: "Lo, He trusts not in His servants, and His angels does He charge with folly. How much more those who dwell in houses of clay, whose foundation is on dust" [4:18–19]. Eliphaz continues in this vein. He believes that all that befalls a man is deserved by him but that the faults by which we merit punishments are concealed from us and the respects in which these punishments are deserved are beyond our ken.

The view of Bildad the Shuhite on this question is belief in recompense. Thus he says to Job, These grievous calamities, if you are innocent and without sin, serve only to augment your reward. You will be compensated well, and all your misfortunes are for your own benefit; they have befallen you only in order that the benefit you receive in the end may be that much greater. For he says to Job: "If you are innocent and upright, surely now He will awaken to you and repay the dwelling of your righteousness; [9] and, though your start was strait, your end shall be much increased" [8:6–7]. You have already learned how widespread this view of providence is, and I have already explained it. [10]

Tzofar the Naamatite's view is that which holds all things to be determined by God's pleasure and believes one cannot seek any sort of grounds for His actions or ask why He did a thing. Thus, no sort of justice is to be sought, no dictate of wisdom to be inquired after in any of God's acts. For His Awesome Truth requires that He do as He wills, while we are debarred from the secrets of that wisdom which forces Him to do just what He wills to do without regard for any other considerations. [11] Thus he says to Job, "Would that God would speak and talk to you, tell you the secrets of wisdom, [12] for they are twice as deep. . . . Shall you find out the Almighty?" [11:5–7].

9. The body, as the seat of righteousness, will be recompensed with material rewards for its material sufferings, according to Bildad. But if bodily sufferings are no more than pretexts for enlarging bodily rewards, it remains unfair to distribute them unequally—and perverse, indeed, to rely on such a method of distributing material largesse.

10. See *Moreh* III:17, the Mutazilite view. This was the position adopted by Saadya.

11. There is a paradox in Tzofar's view as well, then: he seems to see will as compelling actions without regard to rational considerations (wisdom) rather than selecting them in accordance with rational considerations.

12. God's wisdom does not answer to the tests of human rationality.

Observe and consider how the story which has so perplexed people is constructed, how it puts forward the views on divine providence over creation which have already been explained. Each view called for by the division is stated and ascribed to a different man famous in his day for virtue or learning, if the story is a parable—or, if the story is true, to the person who actually held it. The view ascribed to Job [13] corresponds to that of Aristotle. The view of Eliphaz corresponds to that of our Law. The view of Bildad corresponds to the Mutazilite doctrine. And the view of Tzofar follows the Asharite approach. These were the ancient views on providence.

At this point, another view is interjected, the one ascribed to Elihu. He is regarded by them as a better man. It is stated he was the youngest and most learned of them. He berates Job and accuses him of rank naïveté for taking himself so seriously and being unable to fathom how misfortunes could befall him who did good deeds—for Job had gone on at length about how goodly his doings were. He likewise blasts the views of Job's three friends on providence and says a number of remarkably enigmatic things. If one studies his speech, one might be surprised and suppose he adds nothing whatever to what was said by Eliphaz, Bildad, and Tzofar but only repeats the themes of their arguments in other words and at fuller length. For Elihu does not go beyond castigating Job, ascribing justice to God, describing God's wonders throughout existence, and asserting that He does not care whether one is obedient or not. All these things had already been said by Job's friends.

On closer examination, however, the added concept becomes clear to you. This is the point of Elihu's speech, and it did not occur in any of the prior arguments. Alongside this concept, he restates everything the others had said, just as Job and his three friends had all repeated one another's ideas, as I mentioned to you. This is to conceal what is distinctive in the idea of each individual, so that it will appear to the masses that they all hold the same view and that all agree. But such is not the case. The concept added by Elihu, not mentioned by any of the others, is stated symbolically in terms of intercession by an angel. He says it is known from experience that when a man is ill, facing death,

13. Prior to the revelation of the truth to him.

and is given up, then if an angel, any angel, intercedes for him, that intercession is received and the invalid is restored to the finest condition. But this does not continue constantly. There is no continuous intercession. Rather, twice or three times [Job 33:23ff.]—as he says, "If there be an angel, intercessor in his behalf [one in a thousand to vouch for a man's uprightness]" [33:23].[14] After describing the patient's recuperation and his joy at his recovery to perfect health, he says, "Lo, all these things does God do twice or thrice with a man" [33:29]. Now this concept [15] is unique to Elihu's exposition. He adds as well, as his preface to this concept, a description of how prophecy takes place, saying, "Once will God speak, or twice, yet they will not perceive it, in a dream, a night vision, when deep sleep [16] falls upon men" [33:14–15]. He then proceeds to offer confirmation of this view and explain how this works by describing numerous natural phenomena such as thunder and lightning, wind and rain. He mixes with this many things about the lives of living things, e.g., the outbreak of plague, referred to when he says, "In a moment they die—at midnight," etc. [34:20], and the outbreak of great wars, referred to when he says, "He breaks great men without number and sets others in their stead" [34:24], and many other such phenomena.

Similarly, you will find that the revelation Job experienced, which made clear to him his mistakenness in all he had imagined, does not involve anything beyond the description of natural things—it is confined exclusively to descriptions of the elements, meteorological effects, and the natures of various species of living things. What is said there regarding the heavens and the firmament, Orion and the Pleiades [38:37, 31], is only on account of their effect on the atmosphere. For what He makes Job aware of is entirely within the sublunary world [the world of nature]. Elihu likewise takes his lesson from animal species. "He teaches us through the beasts of the land; from the fowl of the heavens does He make us wise" [17] [35:11]. The longest part of this homily is the description of the Leviathan, a hybrid of bodily properties found separately in animals that walk, swim, and fly. The

14. I translate in accordance with the Rambam's gloss.
15. That designated by the symbol of intercession in behalf of a sick man.
16. *Tardemah*, often translated "slumber," is trancelike sleep.
17. I translate according to the Rambam's interpretation.

purpose of introducing all these things is to show that our minds do not reach far enough to grasp how these natural things come to be, which exist in the world of generation and corruption, nor do they conceive how these natural powers come to exist in them. For they do not at all resemble the things we make; how then are we to expect that His governance of them should resemble our governance and care for what we take care of? Rather what we must do is stop, having gone thus far, and believe that from Him nothing is concealed, as Elihu says here, "For His eyes are on man's ways, and He sees his every step. There is no darkness nor death shadow to conceal those who do wickedness" [34:21–22].

Thus, providential care, for Him, is not what it is for us; and what it means for Him to govern the objects of His creation is not what it is for us to govern what we govern. There is no single definition common to divine and human care, as is supposed by all who are perplexed and confused on this subject. Nor is there anything in common between divine and human governance and concern beyond the bare name. Just as there is no resemblance between our works and His and they have no single common definition, just as there is a gulf that separates natural from artificial events, so there is a gulf between divine governance, divine providence and care, divine purpose and intention for these natural things, and human governance, human care, human purpose and intention for what we govern, care for, and intend. This is the message of the whole Book of Job, to lay down this fundamental basis of belief and to awaken you to this evidence from natural things, so that you will not err by seeking in your imagination to make His knowledge like ours or His purpose, providence, or governance like ours. Once a man understands this, all hardships are easily borne by him, and misfortunes do not add to his doubts about the Deity and whether He knows or does not know, whether He cares for or neglects creation. Rather, hardships will only increase his love, as is said at the close of Job's revelation: "Therefore do I abhor and repent of dust and ashes" [18] [42:5–6]. As the Sages say (of blessed memory), "The pious act out of love and rejoice in sufferings" [*Shabbat* 88b].

If you study everything I have said, as this treatise deserves to be

18. The emphasis here is on the "therefore": Job has learned from his experience; he has gained a heightened understanding of and relation to divinity.

studied, and carefully scrutinize the Book of Job, then its meaning will become clear to you, and you will find I have summed up its whole theme, omitting nothing except what is necessary for the connection of the narrative and development of the imagery, as I have explained to you several times in the course of this study.

MOREH NEVUKHIM III:24

The matter of "trial," too, is a very difficult problem, one of the weightiest in the Bible. The Torah mentions it in six places, as I shall make clear to you in this chapter. What is widely believed by the people regarding the problem of trial is that God causes injuries to descend upon a person who has not previously sinned in order to increase that person's reward. But this is a principle no text whatsoever in the Torah explicitly states. Nothing in the Torah, taken literally, even suggests this idea, except one of the six passages, which I shall explain. The Biblical principle is, in fact, diametrically opposite to this view and is stated in His words: "A God of faithfulness and without injustice" [Deuteronomy 32:4]. Neither did all the Sages adopt this vulgar view. For they said, "There is no death without sin and no suffering without guilt" [*Shabbat* 55a]. This is what every religious person of intelligence ought to believe rather than ascribing wrong to God (which He transcends) by believing that Zayd is clear of sins, perfect, and not deserving of what has befallen him.

The literal sense of "trial," which is stated in the Torah in the contexts where the notion is found, refers to the performance of a test or experiment so that the measure of this person's (or that nation's) faith or allegiance may be known. This concept [1] is the serious problem, especially in the story of the *Akeydah*, [2] which was unknown except to God and those two [Abraham and Isaac]. For it is said to Abraham, "For now I know that thou fearest God" [Genesis 22:12]. [3] . . .

Now you must know that of every "trial" that occurs in the Torah, the sole purport and meaning is to teach the people what they are

1. Not the false issue of sufferings imposed to justify augmented rewards, which is not an authentically Biblical concept at all.

2. *I.e.*, the binding of Isaac.

3. The problem is, of course, that this seems to suggest that God had not known previously, that it was for His sake that the test was performed.

obliged to do or to believe. Thus, it is as though the meaning of the trial is that a certain action is done, not for its own sake but to provide a model to be followed or emulated. Thus (1) the words "[The Lord your God puts you to proof] so that it be known whether you do love [the Lord your God with all your hearts and with all your souls]" [Deuteronomy 13:4], are not to be interpreted as meaning "so that God may learn" that. For He already knows. Rather this is on the pattern of "so that it be known that I, the Lord, do sanctify you" [Exodus 31:13], which means "so that the nations may know." Thus it says here [interpreting Deuteronomy 13:2ff.], If a claimant to prophecy arise and you see his suasions as plausible, then you should know that this is something God willed in order to make known to the Gentiles the measure of your certitude in His Law and your grasp of its authentic essence, that you are not taken in by the deceptions of a charlatan and your faith in God is not shaken.[4] . . .

So, it is clear that the meaning of "that it be known" here is that people should know. Thus (2) the words regarding the manna, "In order that He might try you and test you, that it be known what is in your heart—whether to keep His commandments or not" [Deuteronomy 8:2], mean: so that the Gentiles might know and it might be famed throughout the world that those who cleave to His service are provided for in an undreamed of way.[5]

In exactly the same sense it is said (3) of the manna when it first fell, "so that I may prove them, whether they will walk in My Torah or not" [Exodus 16:4], meaning, "so that everyone might learn from this experience and see whether cleaving to His service is beneficial and sufficient or not."

When it says a third time, again of the manna (4), "Who fed you manna in the wilderness which your fathers knew not, so as to try you and test you, that your end might be the better" [Deuteronomy 8:16], this seems to suggest God might cause suffering to a person in order to augment his reward. But, in fact, such is not the case. Rather, what this pronouncement means is either (a) the concept already twice

---

4. There is a strong suggestion here that the Rambam applies the prophetic words to the militant evangelism conducted in his time in behalf of the Islamic prophet.

5. The Rambam wishes us to understand the manna itself as a symbolic instance of divine providence.

raised in connection with the manna, in the first and second statements, *i.e.,* in order that it may be known whether or not fealty to God suffices to give one sustenance and respite from trouble and weariness; or (*b*) the meaning of ''to try you'' is ''to inure you,'' as in ''the sole of her foot is untried'' [Deuteronomy 28:56]—as though He said that first He inured you to hardship in the desert, so that your enjoyment would be the greater when you entered into the land. This is sound, for to go from weariness to ease is more pleasurable than to remain at ease.[6] And it is known too that, were it not for their hardship and weariness in the desert, they would not have been able to conquer the land and do battle. The Torah says this explicitly: ''For God said, 'lest the people repent when they see war and return to Egypt.' So God led the people by way of the Red Sea Wilderness'' [Exodus 13:17–18]. For luxury banishes valor, but a hard and restless life engenders it; and this was the ''good end'' the story speaks of.[7]

The words (5) ''For God has come to try you'' [Exodus 20:17] have the identical meaning to those of Deuteronomy regarding a pagan claimant to prophecy. . . . Here, too, at the Assembly at Mount Sinai, He said to them, Do not be afraid. This awesome experience you have beheld was only so that you would have the certainty of direct witness. Thus, if the Lord puts you to the test with a false prophet who calls upon you to repudiate what you have heard, the extent of your faith will be manifested publicly, you will stand firm and not stumble. For had I come to you through a messenger (as you preferred [8]) and related what had been told to Me without your hearing it for yourselves, then it would have been possible for you, deludedly, to have taken as true a message brought by someone else who came to

6. The ''so that,'' in this case, would represent the result rather than the rationale of God's action.

7. Not that warlike ways are good absolutely—but these were what the Israelites would require at that juncture of their history. The ''good end,'' then, may be the martial spirit engendered by long inurement of hardship, or it may be (as before) the outcome of the ''experiment'' performed before all nations; it may even be the subjectively augmented pleasure of ease after a life of hardship, so long as this is not imagined to involve a claim that the ease itself was a recompense being pleaded as justification of the hardship.

8. *Cf.* Exodus 20:16: ''They said unto Moses, 'Speak to us, and we shall hearken, but let not God speak to us lest we die.' ''

repudiate what I had told you—had you not heard it for yourselves.

Lastly (6), the story of Abraham's binding of Isaac. This contains two major themes which are among the most important in the Bible. One is to make known to us where the limit of love for God and fear of Him lie. For Abraham, in this story, was commanded to do something which cannot be compared with the laying down of money or even with the laying down of life, the most bizarre act that could possibly take place, one to which human nature cannot be imagined as giving its assent. A man was childless and yearned for a son as longingly as anything can be yearned for. He was greatly blessed with wealth and honor, and hoped that from his seed a nation would come. Finally, after he had given up hope, he had a son. How he would love him! Yet, next to his fear of God and his love of following His command, he regarded his beloved son as a trifle, threw away all his hopes for him, and made haste to sacrifice him after a journey of several days. Had he desired to do this immediately on having the command revealed to him, the act would have been done out of shock, a disturbed and inadequately considered action. Done several days after the imparting of this command to him, it is a reflective act based on a valid assessment of divine authority and on his love for and fear of God. It cannot be claimed to have been otherwise, or that he was in any way influenced by passion. For Abraham our father did not hasten to sacrifice Isaac in fear that God might kill him or make him poor but solely in obedience to the duty of all Adam's sons to love and fear Him without hope of reward or fear of punishment, as we have made clear in a number of places. For the angel says to him, "For now I know that you fear God" [Genesis 22:12], meaning, "By this act, on account of which 'God-fearing' is predicated of you, all men will know what is the ultimate limit of the fear of God." This concept, you must understand, is amplified and spelled out throughout the Torah. For the Torah states that its entire object, through all its commands and prohibitions, its promises and narratives, is just one thing: fear of Him. This is put as follows: "If you do not take heed to do all the words of this Torah written in this book to fear this awesome and revered Name," etc. [Deuteronomy 28:58]. This is one of the two themes intended by the *Akeydah*.

The second is to make known to us that prophets regard as true what reaches them from God by revelation. Thus, no one may suppose that because this takes place in a dream or vision, as we have explained (*Moreh* II:26–41], and through the mediation of the faculty of imagination, that what they hear or what is symbolized for them might be uncertain or mingled with anything illusory. It intends to teach us that whatever is seen by a prophet in a prophetic vision is certain truth for him, no part of which is in any way open to doubt. For him, it is on the same footing with anything else which is real, as apprehended through the senses or the intellect. This is shown by the fact that he hastened [9] to sacrifice "his son, his only son, whom he loved" [*cf.* Genesis 22:2] as he was commanded to do, even though this command came in a dream or vision. If the content of their revelation was problematic for prophets, or if they had any doubt or unclearness regarding what they had apprehended in a prophetic vision, then they would not hasten to do something which nature rebels against, and Abraham's soul would not have assented to this awful act.

Truly it is appropriate that this story of the binding is Abraham's and in connection with the like of Isaac. For our father Abraham was the first to recognize the truth of monotheism and to affirm prophecy, the first to perpetuate this view and draw people to it. It says, "For I [God] have known him in order that he may command his sons and his house after him, that they may keep the way of the Lord, to do righteousness and justice" [Genesis 18:19]. Thus, just as they followed his true and beneficial doctrines, which they heard from him, so ought one to follow the opinions to be derived from his actions, especially that action by which the validity of prophecy was verified and the furthest extreme to which the fear and love of God may reach was made known. [10]

In this fashion, therefore, ought one to understand the concept of trials, not in the sense that God wants to test and experiment with something to find out something He did not already know. Exalted be He, and exalted once again above the foolish imaginings and misconceptions of the unwise.

9. As is shown by Abraham's early rising to undertake the journey to Moriah.
10. Even if this may involve willingly relinquishing our grip on all we hold most dear.

Analysis

Whether the precise events described in the story of Job ever actually occurred to a particular person of that name is recognized by the Rambam to be irrelevant to the problem the story poses. Regardless of its historicity (and Maimonides, like many Talmudic Sages, notes strong reasons to doubt it), the story, like its prologue, which is purely allegorical, is obviously intended to be symbolic. It does no good to say that no such person as Job existed. The very vagueness of Scripture regarding the time and locale, which gives rise to suspicions that Job is fictional, is clear evidence that he is meant to be symbolic of an undeniable dimension of human experience. Job is the archetype of the suffering innocent, and his plight, therefore, represents a challenge to the faith of all who believe in divine providence.

The framing of the story of Job, like a drama with a prologue, sets the tone of allegory; Maimonides responds by heightening his normally acute sensitivity to the nuances and hints of language, responding to the name *Utz* as an imperative demanding from the reader the closest consideration. What we are called upon to consider, or reconsider, is the basis of our values. For clearly the issue of God's justice cannot adequately be decided until the proper measure of value is determined. In this regard, the delineation of the true scope and ontic status of evil is of the greatest relevance.

Satan, the principle of evil and death, is not spoken of in the same terms as the other angels in God's throng, a clear indication that while evil may subsist (as privation), it does not have positive existence. Yet matter does exist as the condition of finitude; and, with finitude, privation (evil) becomes inevitable. Thus evil finds its habitation in matter ("the earth"). Over the soul, a direct emanation of God, it has no dominion except to the extent that the soul through free will turns away from God and higher things and toward matter and privation. But when the soul is attached to the thought of God (*cf. Moreh* III:51), neither death nor evil has any sway over it. For evil can affect only matter. The perfection man achieves in the contemplation of God is inviolable. These are things Job would have understood had he been a wise as well as a good man.

Analyzing the speeches of Job's friends for what they have in common and in what they differ, Maimonides discovers that all agree that Job's plight must be assigned to the act of a just God. But they differ as to how to interpret the resultant paradox. The view Job expresses in his agony (but later retracts) asserts divine neglect of creation and corresponds to the Aristotelian view. Not that Aristotle believed, of course, that God first created and then abandoned the world, but Job seems to come to the same conclusion that an Aristotelian would regarding the functional role of providence in nature: the divine act gives being to all things but does not sustain them all.

Eliphaz's view, which Maimonides calls Biblical,[1] is that Job is wrong to believe himself beyond sin, that he must have hidden faults for which his afflictions by God are the just punishment. This view is distinguished from the fourth view of *Moreh* III:17 and the related doctrine of the Mutazila in three ways:

(1) The Biblical view of Eliphaz avoids the assertion that all God's acts follow necessarily from (what we conceive to be) His attribute of wisdom. It thus avoids the attempt to justify every natural event in terms of human moral standards.

(2) There is no excursion on the part of Eliphaz into the problematic notion of recompense and the question whether some other mode of existence (or more of the same) can compensate men for the sufferings of this life.

(3) No attempt is made here to maintain what Maimonides takes to be the mutually inconsistent doctrines of human free will and predestination. Rather, free will is assumed by the Torah to hold in the moral sphere, and any moral faults Job may have are thus treated by Eliphaz as his own responsibility, even if he is not, as in the pure voluntarist model, the immediate, consciously active cause of every action to which such traits of character may give rise.

But can Job's sufferings be seen as retributions? Indeed, if hindsight and cross-cultural objectivity are of any help in clarifying our moral

---

1. Eliphaz holds the Biblical view in that he affirms God's justice. But, while the Bible for the benefit of the masses represents God's justice as operating on a material plane, the revelation of Job makes it clear that matter is exposed to privation, inadequacy, and death. The true locus of God's justice is in the intellectual reward which is open to (but not necessarily grasped by) the righteous.

vision (of others, to be sure, not of ourselves), then we may say that Job's hidden faults are actually somewhat more visible to us as outsiders than they may have been to him. Thus, there seems to be a certain priggishness in Job, a certain pious self-righteousness, which Eliphaz obviously finds offensive, a certain self-deception, easily detectable to us, in Job's notion that by animal sacrifices he can vicariously atone for any sins his children may have committed in their social gatherings, rather than a shouldering of the obligation of inquiring into and attempting to reform any faults they may have acquired.[2] Thus, we see that Job is not morally perfect, as he may believe himself to be. And, if Job is meant to be a universal figure, it certainly is no trivial fact that he has faults. For while other men may not share Job's failings, all men have faults. (See the discussion of Moses' fault, *Shemonah Perakim* 4.) It is possible to concede that a just God might punish a man for hidden faults, some of which he may imbibe from the very environment in which he was raised and which would require tremendous intellectual/critical gifts to detect in the unquestioned assumptions of one's own culture, not to mention tremendous gifts of self-discipline to purge once detected in oneself. The fact remains that Job's sufferings, even if regarded as punishments for unseen moral faults, seem far too severe to be justified by such an explanation.

Bildad, like a Mutazilite, upholds belief in recompense; while Tzofar, in affirming the inscrutability of the divine decree, parallels the Asharite denial of God's accountability to human moral standards. Both these views are unsatisfactory for reasons the Rambam has already made clear. Recompense cannot justify the fact of suffering if the reward could be achieved without the undeserved pain. And the Asharite abandonment of the claim as to God's goodness in anything like the human sense severs the connection between religion and morality (as opposed to mere positive law or fiat) and also casts us adrift theologically from the one concept which can orient us toward an understanding of God, the concept of Perfection.

Elihu's contribution is on a much more profound level than the others'; he introduces the theme of inspiration as a means of grace. God's help to men, enabling them to live wisely in the midst of na-

---

2. "You shall surely rebuke him" (Leviticus 19:17), etc.; see *Shemonah Perakim* 4.

ture's conflicting elements, comes through inspiration—first to the inspired, and, through them, to mankind at large. Elihu's description of the awesome events of nature, the outbreak of wars and plagues, is meant to symbolize this aspect of the activity by which God animates and informs nature. The inspiration of prophets does not pour forth uniformly. Like a storm or earthquake, inspiration comes in fits and starts upon mankind, reflecting no inadequacy in the Source, but only in the shifting soil of the human psyche, which cannot bear the full brunt of divine self-revelation. In the revelation made to Job, as in Elihu's speech, the inherence of natural properties in things and, above all, of life in animals represents the true level of the operation of divine providence. God does not govern the universe as a king governs a city but rather through the play of natural forces, which have God Himself as their source, not the least of which is human intelligence.

Throughout the Rambam's discussion of Job, one possible line of interpretation is consistently rejected: the notion that the sufferings of innocents represent a test of moral strength—a point of view which is anything but ruled out by the prologue. Having discussed the symbolism of Job and the implications of the sufferings of innocents for our conception of the nature of God's justice and His governance of the world, Maimonides proceeds to examine the true Biblical content of the notion of trial and distinguish it from the notion of the "sufferings of love."

In every Biblical occurrence of the trial motif, as the Rambam shows, the meaning clearly is the demonstration of the measure of a person's or a nation's loyalty rather than its testing or tormenting. That is why the manna is referred to by Scripture as a trial—not because it tempts, abuses, or strains Israel's loyalty but because it is a visible sign of God's sustenance of those loyal to Him. Similarly with regard to false prophets. They are a trial, in the sense not that they are sent to deceive Israel and tempt her loyalty to God but that they afford Israel's opportunity of demonstrating her loyalty to God. So, in the binding of Isaac, God demonstrates to Israel the epitome of human devotion to God in self-sacrifice.

Thus, the notion that God may choose certain individuals He loves by singling them out for special sufferings not only is belied by science but also proves, on careful study of the text, not to be an authentically Biblical concept. For intelligence is the only vehicle of special providence to man, a providence which does not involve violation of nature's laws. Intelligence is not a guarantee of fulfillment; but it cannot be a detriment, and it can become a means to human fulfillment. Torah does not ask us to believe anything else. For the tests Abraham and all Israel are said to undergo are not selectively imposed sufferings, still less investigations by the Creator into the limitations of what He created. Rather, they are challenges to the mettle of God's creatures, through which they are enabled to demonstrate their steadfastness and loyalty in the tasks they have been assigned.

PART FIVE

DIVREI ELOHIM HAYIM /

THE WORDS OF THE LIVING GOD

*Prophecy
and the Revealed Law*

*T*he heavens express the glory of God, and the firmament bespeaks His
handiwork.
Day passes the message to day, and night conveys the knowledge to night.
Without speech or word or sound, their order extends throughout the world,
And their directions to the ends of the earth.
Among them He has made a pavilion for the sun,
Which comes forth like a bridegroom from his canopy,
Rejoicing like a champion, to run its race.
It sets out from one end of the heavens
And its course extends to the other.
Nothing is hidden from its heat.
The Law of the Lord is perfect, restoring the soul.
The testimony of the Lord is sure, assuring the simple.
The ordinances of the Lord are fair, a joy to the heart.
The command of the Lord is clear, enlightening the eyes.
The awe of the Lord is pure, enduring forever.
The laws of the Lord are truth, altogether just,
More precious than gold, than much pure gold,
Sweeter than honey, dripping liquid from the comb.
I too, Thy servant, am aroused by them.
The consequence of keeping them is immense.
Who knows his own faults?
Cleanse me of my unseen flaws,
And restrain me too from vices—
Let them not gain power over me.
Then shall I be perfect
And clear of much iniquity.
May the words of my mouth and the thought in my heart
Be acceptable before Thee, O Lord,
My Rock and my Redeemer.

Psalm 19

PROPHETIC REVELATION

Introduction

It was assumed by most medieval thinkers that prophecy took place, and the issue of what prophecy might be was not greatly beclouded, for philosophers at least, by confusion with divination or auguring about the future. Prophecy was understood to be a privileged form of knowledge by which certain individuals were apprised of important truths about reality, divinity, and the good life. Prophecy was not regarded by philosophers and certainly not by Maimonides as necessarily unnatural. The Rambam, in fact, ascribes the cessation of prophecy in Israel not to the ending of the age of miracles but to the demoralizing effects of exile. Whenever the restoration of Israel to her land (with the coming of the Messiah) allowed the restoration of national self-confidence, Maimonides was certain prophecy would be resumed.

Prophecy, of course, was and is the key to the Jewish religion. But with prophecy, as with other theological concepts, religious understanding was made much more problematic than need be by the confinement of the mind within primitive conceptions. The same deity envisioned as a person or a body might readily be imagined as

378

communicating with arbitrarily selected spokesmen by visual displays of his person or by actual voices or his own handwriting. If this seemed too crude, one might still lean upon the notion of created angels carrying messages between God and men. In terms of such primitive imaginings there is no doubt that prophecy becomes problematic. But on a conceptual level it was possible to develop much more sophisticated and much less troublesome accounts of God's communication with mankind.

There was, in medieval psychology, the crucial faculty of imagination, which mediated between sense and intellect, representing sensory data, and fleshing out abstract conceptions on the common ground of concrete symbolism. There was, as well, the theory of emanation, by which the operation of the immaterial on the material, of idea on matter, might be figured forth. And thus a philosophical theory of prophecy was possible, which rose from the common experience of dream to a higher level of prophetic vision through which truths understood acquired a symbolic status in the imagination, heightening their vividness and, thus, their transmissibility to mankind. It was thus possible to account for prophecy within the framework of the general body of human knowledge, and what remained problematic were primarily the questions as to the reach of prophetic knowledge, its relation to other forms of human knowledge, and the means by which true prophets are to be distinguished from charlatans and imposters of all sorts.

From *Moreh Nevukhim* II

MOREH NEVUKHIM II:32
People's views on prophecy correspond with their views on the eternity/creation of the world. . . . Thus there are three views on prophecy among those who believe that God exists:

(1) The view of most unenlightened people who accept prophecy as well as some common folk within our own religion is that God selects whomever He pleases for a prophetic mission, regardless of whether that person is young or old, knowledgeable or ignorant. They do, however, make a certain goodness, a certain probity of character, a condition of this happening. For those who hold this view have not

gone so far as to say that God might cause a wicked man to prophesy without first making him good.

(2) The Philosophers' view is that prophecy is a natural stage in man's development, achievable only by training, through which the human potential may be educated—unless some constitutional block or external cause prevents this. But this is the sort of hindrance which may occur at any phase of the development of a species. . . . On this view, an ignoramus cannot be made to prophesy. Nor can a man become a prophet overnight as though he had made some discovery. Rather, what happens is that an exceptional person, whose moral and intellectual capacities are fully developed, if his imagination is as perfectly developed as possible and he is primed as I shall relate, will necessarily become a prophet. . . . It is no more possible, in this view, for an individual to be fit for prophecy and not prophesy than for one in sound health to eat properly and not have healthy blood, etc.

(3) The view of our Law, and a mainstay of our religion, is exactly like the Philosophical view except in one point: we believe that one who is fit for prophecy and suitably prepared for it might not be made a prophet. That is due to the divine will, and is in my view as much a miracle as any other (and must be understood the same way). For the natural thing is that whoever is suitable, by nature, training, education, and instruction, will prophesy. If he is prevented from so doing, this can only be as Jeroboam was prevented from moving his hand [1 Kings 13:4]. . . .

For ignorant persons from the masses to prophesy is in our view no more possible than for an ass or a frog to be turned into a prophet. Our principle is that training and development are necessary. Only then does the potential arise to be touched by the divine power. . . . Even at the Assembly at Mount Sinai, although, through a miracle, all witnessed the great flame and heard the awe-inspiring and dreadful sounds, none reached the rank of prophecy who were not suitably prepared for this; and even they, in varying degrees. . . . Our judgment that the prophet requires preparation and perfection of the rational and moral qualities is certainly expressed by the Sages' saying, "Prophecy rests only on the wise, the bold, and the rich." [1] [*Shabbat* 92a, *Nedarim* 38a]. . . .

1. *Cf. Moreh* I:46, II:38, and *Shemonah Perakim* 7.

MOREH NEVUKHIM II:33

It is apparent to me that in the Assembly at Mount Sinai not everything that reached Moses reached all Israel. Rather it was Moses who was addressed. That is why the Ten Commandments are in the second person singular. He in turn (peace upon him) went to the foot of the mountain and relayed to the people what he had heard. The Torah text is, "I stood between the Lord and you at that time to tell you the word of the Lord" [Deuteronomy 5:5]. . . . They heard the awesome sound but no discrete words. . . . Only Moses heard speech, and he told it to them. This is the literal text of the Torah [1] and of most of the Sages' discussions. But they (blessed be their memory) made one statement in a number of places in the Midrash and in the Talmud too, that " 'I am' and 'You shall not have' were heard directly from the Power" [Makkot 24a, Midrash on Song of Songs], meaning that these [2] reached the people in the same manner they reached Moses, and were not conveyed to them by him. For these two principles, that God exists and that He is one, are grasped entirely by human reason; and, with everything that is known via demonstrations, a prophet is on a par with anyone else who knows it, in no way superior. Thus these two principles were not known through prophecy alone. The Torah states explicitly, "Unto you was it shown, that you might know [that the Lord is God and there is none else beside Him]" [Deuteronomy 4:35]. The remaining Commandments, however, are to be classed as common or public tradition, not as truths of reason.[3] . . .

MOREH NEVUKHIM II:35

. . . The prophecy of Moses will be dealt with in these chapters neither verbally nor by allusion, for the term "prophet" in my judgment is said of him in a different sense from that applied to others. . . . The Biblical evidence for the difference between his inspiration and that of all his predecessors is in God's words: "I appeared to Abra-

1. It thus requires interpretation.

2. Viz., the first and second of the Ten Commandments. See Exodus 20:2, 3.

3. There is no self-contradiction involved in denying (or rejecting) them, unless further propositions and values are assumed, complex connections made, etc. These Commandments could be called revealed, but they were revealed to Moses, not to Israel. Israel knows them on the authority of Moses—thus through the mediation of his intelligence.

ham," etc., "But my name YHVH I did not make known to them" [Exodus 6:3].[1] . . . And it makes clear that his apprehension was different from that of all who came after him in Israel when it says, "There arose no more in Israel any prophet like Moses whom God knew face to face." [2] [Deuteronomy 34:10]. Thus it makes clear that his apprehension is unique in the whole Congregation of Israel that succeeded him, who were "a nation of priests and a holy people" [Exodus 19:6], "in whose midst is the Lord" [Numbers 16:3]—*a fortiori* in other nations. . . .

MOREH NEVUKHIM II:36

What prophecy really is is an emanation flowing forth from God (exalted and glorified be He), through the mediation of the Active Intellect, first to the rational faculty and then to the faculty of imagination. This is the highest level a man can reach and the highest possible stage of development for the human species. This is not at all something which just any man can achieve. Perfection in the intellectual sciences and refinement of all facets of one's moral character to the finest and fairest degree possible are not enough if the highest level of perfection in the innate powers of the imagination is not conjoined with them.

As you know, the perfect development of the bodily powers (of which imagination is one) requires the optimal constitution, size, and purity of matter in the organs which perform these functions. This is not something which can be restored if deficient or supplied if lacking, by any sort of regimen. For an innately misconstituted organ can be restored by a proper regimen, at best, to a certain degree of health; it cannot be brought to the best possible condition. If its defect is in size, placement, or substance (*i.e.,* its matter) there is no remedy for it at all. . . .

You are already acquainted with the natural functions of this faculty of imagination—preserving, composing, and recalling sense images. You know as well that its highest and most portentous function takes

1. See *Moreh* I:61–63.
2. The difference between the prophecy of Moses and that of all others is that Moses did not confront God through the medium of imagination but through the "pellucid lens" of his intellect; *cf. Shemonah Perakim* 7.

place only when the senses are at rest, not performing their functions. At such times a certain emanation flows forth to this faculty, proportioned to the extent of its preparedness. This is the cause of "true dreams," and the identical phenomenon is the cause of prophecy. The difference is solely one of degree, not of kind. You are familiar with their repeated dictum: "Dreaming is one-sixtieth [1] part of prophecy" [*Berakhot* 57b]. . . . They repeat the same idea in *Bereshit Rabbah:* "Dreaming is the unripe fruit of prophecy" [XVII, XLIV]. This is a marvelous metaphor, for the unripe fruit is identical with the fruit itself except that it has fallen before its development has been perfected, before it is mature. In the same way the operation of imagination in sleep is identical with its operation in prophecy, except that it falls short of its goal.

But why do I teach you from the words of the Sages (of blessed memory) and neglect the actual texts of the Torah? "If there be a prophet among you, I the Lord do make Myself known to him in a vision and do speak to him in a dream" [Numbers 12:6]. Here He Himself tells us the true nature and essence of prophecy and teaches us it is a stage of perfection which comes through dream and vision. Vision (*mareh*) is derived from *raoh*, to see: *i.e.*, the faculty of imagination operates so perfectly that it sees its object as though it were externally present to it. The image which originated in the imagination appears as though it had come from the external senses. These two alternatives, dream and vision, include all levels of prophecy, as I shall explain [*Moreh* II:45].

It is well known that the object to which a man has turned his senses or with which he has been occupied a great deal while awake, or which he has loved or yearned for is the one with which imagination works while he is asleep and the Intellect is emanating upon him to the extent of his preparedness. . . .

Given these premises, you should understand that if (*a*) a particular person has innately the optimal equilibrium in the substance of his brain, the purity of its matter and the special constitution required in all its parts, the proper size, placement, etc., and if (*b*) no other organ

---

1. The Sages of the Talmud adopted the Babylonian system of dividing quantities into sixtieths which still survives in our scheme of time measurement. Thus they use the term "one-sixtieth" as we use the term "one per cent," to designate a small fraction.

imposes any metabolic block, then (c) that person will grow in learning and wisdom until his potential is realized, the human mind is fully
developed and perfected in him, and the moral traits of humanity are
refined and equably balanced in him. All his passion then would be to
understand the mysteries of this existence and to know the causes of
things. His thought would be directed to higher things, and his sole
concern would be to know God and study His works and what one
ought to believe about things. His thought then would become detached, his craving for animal things vitiated, specifically, preference
for the pleasures of food, drink, and sex—and in general for the sense
of touch, which, as Aristotle explained in his *Ethics* [cf. *Nico-
machaean Ethics* III:10. 1118^b.2], is a discredit to us. How fine it is
that he says this, and how right he is that this is a discredit. For we
have this sense simply inasmuch as we are animals like any other.
There is nothing distinctively human about it. The other sensory pleasures such as smell, hearing, and sight, although bodily, still involve
at some time pleasures which are peculiarly human, as Aristotle explains. (I have digressed, but it was necessary, for most of the
thoughts of those who are distinguished scholars are pre-empted by the
pleasures of this sense [2] and the craving for them. Yet they are surprised that they are not made prophets, if prophecy is natural!)

Thus it is necessary that this person be disinterested and free of the
lust for false power, *i.e.*, the quest for domination and the adulation of
the masses, the hunger for glory and obedience for their own sake.
Rather he should look upon all people in terms of their situations, either as members of the flock or as predatory animals. If the perfectly
developed man who holds himself aloof thinks at all of them, it will be
only in terms of avoiding the harm some of them may do him if he
should chance to associate with them or of benefiting from them as
necessity may require.

Thus a person of this description, who is at the highest possible
phase of perfection, will receive from the intellect emanation proportionate to his intellectual development, and will apprehend, when his
imagination functions, only divine things, and those the most remarkable. He will "see" only God and His angels and will not know or be

---

2. The sense of touch. This implies that they are as yet bound up with the physical.

aware of anything but true ideas and universal principles for the governance and reform of human relations.

It is well known that the three objectives I have summarized—perfection of the rational capacity by study, of the powers of imagination which are innate, and of the character by freeing the mind from all thought of bodily pleasures and purging the lust for every sort of primitive and vile vainglory—may be achieved to very greatly differing degrees in different persons; and, on this account, the levels attained by different prophets will differ as well.

Every bodily power may be weakened or exhausted or disrupted at times and function well at others. The faculty of imagination is certainly a bodily power,[3] and that is why you find inspiration ceases in prophets when they are in grief or anger, etc. You are familiar with the Sages' saying that "prophecy does not descend in the midst of lassitude or sadness" [*Shabbat* 30b], and you know that Jacob received no inspiration throughout the period of his mourning because his imagination was distracted by the loss of Joseph [*Pirkei de Rabbi Eliezer* 38]. Moses (peace upon him) received no revelation, as he had done, from the return of the spies until the whole desert generation had died. For the enormity of their transgression weighed upon him—even though, as I have mentioned several times, the prophecy of Moses did not involve the imagination at all but only the pure emanation of intelligence upon him, without the intervention of imagination; for he did not receive his prophecy through symbols, as other prophets do.
. . . And likewise you will find that certain prophets as well prophesied for a time and then lost the gift of prophecy,[4] the continuity being broken by some intervening event. Such, surely, was the essential proximate cause [5] of the cessation of prophecy during the Diaspora. For what situation could befall a man involving greater lassitude or sadness than being a chattel slave in bondage to barbarously ignorant criminals who combine senselessness with the fullblown passions of beasts—and "having no power in your hand" [*cf.* Deuteronomy 28:32]. This is what we were warned of, and this is what it meant by

3. For images can be presented only in some physical configuration.
4. *Cf.*, for example, Numbers 11:25.
5. Although, of course, like all events this cause may be traced back further in the causal sequence, ultimately to God.

saying, "They shall frantically seek the word of God and not find it" [Amos 8:12], and "Her king and officers are among the nations. There is no Law, and even the prophets find no vision from the Lord" [Lamentations 2:9]. And this is true. The cause is obvious. For the organ is not performing its function. And this will be the means by which prophecy is restored to us as promised,[6] in its familiar form in the days of the Messiah, speedily may he be manifested.

MOREH NEVUKHIM II:37

You ought to observe the nature of that divine emanation which enables us to think and by which some minds are made superior to others. A person may receive of this emanation sufficient for his own development alone; or he may receive, beyond what his perfection requires, sufficient for that of others—just as is the case with being in general: some receive enough perfection to govern others, while others do not.

Now you must understand that if this intellectual flowing forth touches only the rational capacity and does not at all reach the imagination, either for want of fullness in the flow or of innate imaginative gifts in the recipient, this is the level of scholars, thinkers, and scientists. If it reaches both the imagination and the reason, as we and certain Philosophers [1] have explained, and the imagination is innately at the peak of its possible development, then this is the level of prophets. Finally, if the emanation flows only to the imagination, restricted by lack of intellectual talent or training, then this is the level of statesmen, lawgivers, priests, seers, dreamers of true dreams, etc.[2] Likewise, those who do amazing things by means of strange tricks and hid-

6. *I.e.*, the imagination will resume its attention to higher things when the Diaspora has ended. The true Jewish conception of the Messianic age, as presented by Maimonides, it should be noted, is quite distinct from the transcendental, nonphysical notion of the "world to come," *i.e.*, the intellectual afterlife in which there is no physicality (and hence, no individuation). The Messianic age is a historical epoch, and the coming Messiah, like those of the past (*e.g.*, David), will be a natural man. The reforms of the Messianic age, therefore, will be political. Even the resurrection of the dead (not to be confused with the eternal life of those who attach themselves to God in meditation) will take place within the natural order.
1. Especially al-Farabi.
2. In general, those we call visionaries.

den devices, without being learned, all belong in this third class. You must recognize that certain members of this class, however, imagine very remarkable things and dream amazing dreams, even while awake, somewhat like prophetic visions. They thus suppose themselves to be prophets and grow quite excited about what they recall of their imaginings, supposing that they have gained knowledge without studying and acquired sciences without instruction. They introduce enormous confusions into the most momentous areas of thought, mingling truths with delusions in an amazing amalgam. All this is the work of imagination abetted by a weak reason which is unfulfilled, *i.e.,* unrealized as reason.

. . . Emanation to a thinker may be sufficient to make him a seeker, a person of discernment and understanding, although he is not moved to teach others than himself or to write, finding no such desires in himself, or no such abilities. Or it might be sufficient to move him necessarily to write and teach. Likewise with the second class: a prophet might receive inspiration such as to perfect him alone, or such as will require him to address a call to people, to teach them and share with them the perfection he himself has received.

Obviously, were it not for this further stage of development, the sciences would not be set forth in books, and prophets would not address their call to knowledge of the Truth to mankind. For a scholar does not write to teach himself what he already knows but rather it is the nature of intelligence to flow forth constantly and extend itself from one recipient to the next, until it finally reaches someone who can carry it no further but can only be perfected by it himself, as I put it symbolically in another chapter of this study [*Moreh* II:11].

It is the nature of this emanation to require one whom it has reached to this higher degree to address a call to men whether they are receptive to it or not, even if he is done bodily harm. Thus we find prophets who summon the people until they are killed. This divine force moves them and will not let them go or give them peace or rest even if they meet the utmost rigors. That is why Jeremiah (peace upon him) confessed that the contempt he met from the impious and sinful people of his time made him long to hide his prophecy and cease to summon them to the Truth, which they despised. But he could not: ''For the word of the Lord has become my shame and my disgrace all the day. I said, 'I will not declare it; I will no longer speak in His name.' But there it was, like a fire burning in my heart, shut up within me. I struggle to contain it, but cannot'' [Jeremiah 20:8–9]. And the same experience is expressed by another prophet: "The Lord God spoke. Who will not prophesy?'' [Amos 3:8]. Now you must understand this.

MOREH NEVUKHIM II:38

In every man there must be some capacity for boldness. Otherwise he would not be moved mentally to protect himself from harm. This capacity, in my opinion, is the psychological counterpart of the natural drive for self-protection. It varies in intensity, as do all capacities, from one person to the next. Thus you find there are people who advance boldly upon a lion while others cower from a mouse, some who go forward against an army and do battle with it while others quake with fear if a woman shouts at them. . . .

Likewise sensitivity is found in all people (although to differing degrees), especially regarding things a man is greatly concerned with and thinks about a great deal. Thus you find yourself thinking that So-and-so has said or done such-and-such in such-and-such a case and it turns out to be so. Among people you find some whose intuitions and ability to surmise are so very strong and so very right that virtually everything they imagine turning out a certain way actually does turn out as they picture it, at least in part. The factors involved in making such a judgment may be many, past, present, and future, but such a person's intuition is so sensitive it reviews all these inputs and draws its conclusion so swiftly it seems to take no time at all. This ability enables some people to give cautions against disasters.[1]

These two powers, boldness and sensitivity, must both be very strong in prophets. And when the emanation of intelligence comes to them it makes them stronger, until it finally reaches the level we

1. Maimonides is not arguing in favor of any sort of "ESP"; quite the contrary, the burden of this argument is that prophecy is natural and continuous with other more familiar forms of knowledge which come not "from the blue" but from swift, sensitive intuitive handling of complex, imponderable data. Does this imply that prophecy does not stem from God? On the contrary, the theory of emanation is founded upon the proposition that all knowledge is from God; the issue (*e.g.,* versus the Asharites) is only as to the means by which knowledge is acquired. Maimonides' thesis is that it is acquired naturally.

know: a lone person advancing boldly to the great king with nothing but his staff, to save a nation from the yoke of slavery, undaunted and undismayed because he has been told, "I surely shall be with you" [Exodus 3:12].

True prophets, you must understand, achieve a grasp of matters of reason the data for which a man certainly could not grasp by unaided reason. This parallels their awareness of things a man could not know by unaided surmise or common intuition. For the same emanation flowing forth to the imagination, perfecting its operation to the point it apprehends things which will take place as though they had been perceived by the senses and had come thence to the imagination, perfects as well the operation of the rational faculty to the point that it knows things which really exist and apprehends them as though it had deduced them from their premises.

I included the condition that this account applies to true prophets solely so as to exclude members of the third class, who have no rational ideas at all and no real knowledge or science, but only sheer figments of the imagination and conjectures. These, *i.e.,* the notions of such people, are perhaps simply ideas they had had before which left their traces etched in the imagination along with a number of other such impressions, so that when they clear their imaginations of much of what they contained, these impressions stand out and these people suppose them to be something newly introduced from without. I would compare them to a man who had thousands of animals in his house, then removed all but one that was among the rest . . . and jumped to the conclusion that that one had just come in. . . . That is why you find some people attempting to confirm their ideas by dreams they have had, imagining that what they see in sleep is something different from the ideas they have heard or believed while waking. That is why one ought not to pay attention to anyone whose powers of reasoning are not perfected and whose thinking has not reached the highest stage of development. For only such a thinker can grasp further ideas when the divine intelligence flows forth upon him. He it is who is a real prophet, as the text states explicitly: "The prophet has a heart of wisdom" [2] [Psalm 90:12]. This too ought to be understood.

---

2. The "heart" is of course the seat of understanding.

MOREH NEVUKHIM II:40

. . . Man . . . is not like other animals which do not need to band together in societies. Human individuals are much more complex . . . and therefore so much more diverse that you can scarcely find two individuals alike in any specific facet of their characters, even though their outward appearances may be identical. The cause of this is the diversity of their physical makeup.[1] They are composed of different matter, so the accidents which stem from their form [2] differ as well. (For every natural form has certain specific accidents which depend on it apart from those which depend directly on matter.) [3] No such individual diversity is found in any other species of animals. . . . For you may find two persons who are as different in every point of character as though they belonged to two different species. One man may be so hard he would slaughter his youngest son if he got angry enough, while another is so softhearted he feels compassion if a bug or other vermin is killed. The same holds true with most accidents.

Since nature makes the members of our species so diverse and since human nature requires the establishment of a society, this society can be established successfully only by an organizer who takes account of human behavior and develops the deficient, restricts the excessive, and institutes modes of behavior and strains of character which everyone observes as common and constant established practices—so as to cover over the natural disparities with a wealth of conventional consonances, to the end that the collectivity be well integrated and well ordered. That is why I say that a system of law, even if not natural in origin, must have bearing upon what is natural. It is part of the Deity's wisdom, by which our species is enabled to survive (since He so willed), that He made it part of our nature that certain persons of our species have the capability of governing. Some are themselves inspired with the means by which such governance may be achieved.

1. Form (idea) is regarded as responsible only for unity, so all diversity must be attributed to matter.
2. As human beings. Accidents in this Aristotelian context are those characteristics of things which may vary without altering the specific essence of the thing: *e.g.*, a man may be pale or sunburnt, but he is nonetheless a man. This sense is quite distinct from the Kalam sense of the term which Maimonides discusses in Part Two.
3. Man's complexity as man makes possible an immense range of characteristics (accidents) in which men differ as individuals even though they are alike as men.

These are prophets and legislators. Others have the capacity to put into practice and effectuate what a prophet or a legislator has laid down. These are rulers and those who adopt a system of legislation or who claim to be prophets but merely adopt wholly or in part the law revealed to a prophet, either because this is easier for them or because they emulously want to suggest that these things came to them via their own inspiration rather than by following someone else. . . .

If you find that the whole object and sole determining intent of a given system of law are the regulation of civic affairs, the elimination of injustice and aggression, with no regard taken for the realm of thought, no attention paid to the perfection of the rational capacity, and no concern shown for whether the ideas of the people are sound or unwholesome, but the sole intent is to organize people in some manner or other so that they may obtain what is regarded as happiness in the ruler's opinion, then you know that this is a human system of law, whose legislator is of the third sort mentioned above: perfect in imagination alone.[4]

If you find, on the other hand, a system of law whose ordinances look not only to bodily welfare (as we said) but also to the reform of belief, undertaking to impart sound views regarding God in the first place and the angels,[5] which aspire to make man aware, understanding, wise enough to comprehend all reality as it really is, then you can tell that this system of governance stems from Him, that this law is divine law. It only remains then for you to find out whether one who claims this inspiration has reached such a degree of perfection, or whether he has taken over from others the words he claims as his own. The means by which this can be tested is by examining the level of perfection that person has attained, tracking down his doings and studying his way of life. The biggest sign to look for is disdain of bodily pleasures, for that is the first step taken by persons of understanding, *a fortiori* by prophets. . . .

4. Even if he claims to be divinely inspired. The limitation of his vision is manifest in the narrowness of his goals.
5. *E.g.,* that they are not independent deities but forces subordinate to God.

MOREH NEVUKHIM II:41

There is no need to explain what a dream is, but a vision . . . *i.e.,* what is called a prophetic vision . . . is an awesome and terrible state which a prophet experiences while awake. . . . In such a state as this, as in dreaming, the senses cease to function and the emanation which flows forth to the rational faculty spills over to the imagination, fulfilling it in the performance of its function. . . .

Now when it is stated of any prophet that revelation came to him, this may be ascribed to an angel or to God, but it is in any case undoubtedly through an angel.[1] The Sages, of blessed memory, state explicitly, " 'God said to her' [Genesis 25:23], *i.e.,* through an angel" [*Bereshit Rabbah* LXIII]. Furthermore, whenever the text says of anyone that an angel spoke with him, or the word of God came to him, you must recognize that that cannot have occurred in any other way than in a dream or prophetic vision [*cf.* Numbers 12:6]. . . .

MOREH NEVUKHIM II:42

. . . When it says in the story of Jacob, "He wrestled with a man" [Genesis 32:25] . . . and likewise in the story of Balaam when the she ass spoke to him on the road [Numbers 22:22]—all this took place in a prophetic vision. . . . Do not imagine for a moment that an angel can be seen or heard to speak, except in the dreams and visions of prophecy. . . .

MOREH NEVUKHIM II:43

As I have pointed out elsewhere [*Mishneh Torah: Hilkhot Yesodei ha-Torah* VII:3], prophets may use symbols in their prophecies. The reason is the prophet may see a thing symbolically and have the meaning of the symbol explicated for him within the same prophetic vision,[1] just as a dreamer may dream he has awakened, told his dream to someone, and had it explained, although it was all a dream. This is what they call a dream interpreted within a dream. Some dreams too

---

1. Through the mind. God does not communicate directly to man (as He does to Himself) but only through the mediation of imagination and intelligence.
1. This explication is not an artificial or literary contrivance but a natural phase in the interaction of the intellect with the imagination.

are understood conceptually after waking. In the same way, the symbols of prophetic inspiration may be explicated conceptually within the prophetic vision. . . . But with many other symbols the conceptual content is not explicated within the prophetic vision, but only afterwards does the prophet understand their import. . . .

MOREH NEVUKHIM II:45

Having explained the nature of prophecy in accordance with the dictates of reason and in keeping with what is made clear by our Law, I must now list the various levels of prophecy according to these two sources. Not everyone who has reached one of what I call the degrees of prophecy is a prophet. In fact, the first two stages are rather steppingstones to prophecy, and one who has gone only thus far is not to be counted as a prophet in the same sense as those of whom I have been speaking, even if he is on some occasion called a prophet—for this is a broad manner of speaking on account of his being very close to the state of prophets. Do not be confused either by the fact that you may find in the prophetic books a prophet inspired in the manner of one of these levels, and apparently in some other as well. For these degrees I list here are such that one portion of a prophet's inspiration may come to him in one manner and another, at a different time, in a lower manner. For just as prophets do not prophesy continuously their whole lives long . . . so a prophet might prophesy at a certain time in the form characteristic of a high level of prophetic attainment and subsequently in the form characteristic of a lower prophetic level. He may well attain that higher level only once in his life and then be deprived of it and remain at a lower level until the time when his prophecy ceases—for prophecy must inevitably go out of all prophets' lives before they die. . . .

I shall now undertake to list the degrees to which I have referred:

(1) The first level of prophecy is for a person to be seconded by divine help which motivates and spurs him on to accomplish some great and beneficial action such as delivering a body of virtuous persons from a body of wicked persons, or saving a great and good man or bestowing some good upon a great many people. He finds in himself something moving and calling him to this task, and this is called

"the spirit of God." . . . This is the rank of all the Judges of Israel . . . and all the anointed [1] of Israel who are virtuous. . . .

Such a power did not depart from Moses from the time he reached manhood. It was this which moved him to slay the Egyptian . . . and the force of this drive in him was so strong that even after he had fled in fear, when he reached Midian, a stranger and a man in fear, when he saw wrongdoing, he could not help righting it; he could not tolerate it, as it says: "Moses rose and helped them" [Exodus 2:17]. David too had such a force in him from the time of his anointment. . . . That is why he advanced against the lion, the bear, and the Philistine. Now such a spirit as this never made any of these persons articulate anything. The most it does is to move the person to whom it gives strength to some deed—not just any deed, but to succoring some victim of wrongdoing. . . . Just as not everyone who has a true dream is a prophet, so not everyone who is aided in any matter whatever (such as making money or attaining some purely personal goal) can be said to be seconded by the spirit of God. . . .

(2) The second level is for the person to find that something as it were has possessed him, that some power (different from the preceding) has come over him which compels him to articulate and speak words of wisdom or praise, of useful admonition or political or theological relevance—all while he is awake and has normal use of his senses. Of such a one it is said that "he speaks through the holy spirit."

In such a holy spirit David composed the Psalms; and Solomon, Proverbs, Ecclesiastes, and the Song of Songs. Likewise Daniel, Job, Chronicles, and all the rest of the Scriptures [2] were composed through such a holy spirit. That is why they are called Scriptures,[3] meaning they were written under the influence of the holy spirit. . . .

(3) This is the first level of those who say, "The word of the Lord came to me," and who use other expressions of the same import. It consists in the prophet's seeing some symbol in a dream, with all the conditions set forth previously [*Moreh* II:36ff.] regarding the true es-

1. Messiahs, that is, anointed kings.
2. The Hebrew Bible is traditionally divided into the Law, the Prophets, and the Scriptures. Maimonides goes on to list numerous other cases of this sort of inspiration.
3. Rather than prophetic books.

sence of prophecy. The meaning of the symbol, *i.e.*, what it stands for, is made clear in the same dream, as with most of the symbols of Zechariah.

(4) The prophet clearly and distinctly hears some speech in a dream without seeing the speaker. This occurred in Samuel's first inspiration. . . .

(5) The prophet is spoken to by a man in a dream, as in certain of Ezekiel's prophecies. . . .

(6) He is spoken to by an angel in a dream. This is the situation of most prophets. . . .

(7) The prophet has a prophetic dream in which he seems to see God speaking to him, as Isaiah says, "I saw the Lord" etc. [Isaiah 6:1]. . . .

(8) Inspiration comes to the prophet in a prophetic vision and he sees symbols—like the vision of Abraham "between the sections" [Genesis 15:9–10]. . . .

(9) He hears speech in a vision. . . .

(10) He sees a man speaking to him in a prophetic vision. . . .

(11) He sees an angel speaking to him in a vision, as Abraham when he bound Isaac. This, in my judgment, is the highest rank of prophets whose status is attested by Scripture, given our assumption that the rational powers of a prophet must be perfected, as reason requires,[4] and provided that Moses is excepted from consideration.

Whether a prophet in a prophetic vision can seem to see God addressing him is improbable in my judgment. Imagination does not reach so far, and we have not found this state in any prophet. Thus the Torah says clearly, "In a vision do I make known Myself, in a dream do I speak to him" [Numbers 12:6]. . . .

You may object: "You counted as one of the degrees of prophecy a prophet's hearing speech addressed to him by God. . . . How can that be, in view of our principle that every prophet hears what is addressed to him solely through the mediation of an angel except for Moses, of whom it is said, 'I spoke to him face to face' [Numbers 12:8]?" This is so: the mediating principle here is the faculty of imagination. For a prophet can "hear" God speaking to him only in a pro-

---

4. For the Active Intelligence cannot operate directly upon the imagination (as the senses can) but must work through the intellect.

phetic dream. Moses however . . . heard Him without the intervention of imagination [5] . . . "face to face," "as one man speaks to another." . . .

MOREH NEVUKHIM II:46

. . . Just as a man may see himself in sleep as having journeyed to such-and-such a city and there married and lived for some time, having had a son born to him who was given such-and-such a name and who was in such-and-such condition and position, so too the symbols seen or presented in prophetic visions follow the requirements of the symbolism. The performance of some action or operation by the prophet, the passage of time, symbolically stated to have elapsed between one action and another, transference from one place to another—all take place only in the prophetic vision; none are real to the outward senses. Yet sometimes these are mentioned without qualification in the prophetic books—for, since it is understood that all of this took place within a prophetic vision, it is unnecessary to repeat with every detail of the imagery that this was part of a prophetic vision. In just this manner a prophet says, "God said unto me," and does not need to explain that this occurred in a dream. But the masses, consequently, suppose that those actions, transpositions, questions, and answers all took place within the purview of senses, not in a prophetic vision. . . .

MOREH NEVUKHIM II:48

Most plainly, everything that comes to be in time must have some proximate cause which brings it into being; this cause too must have a cause, and so until the series ends at the First Cause of all things, the Will and Choice of God.[1] On this account there is a tendency to skip all these mediate causes in prophetic utterances, ascribing particular, temporal effects directly to God and saying He brought them about. This is well known and is discussed by other partakers of the Truth [2] besides myself. It is the view of all adherents of our religion.

---

5. Cf. Shemonah Perakim 7: Moses did not "hear" God in this case through a vision or dream but confronted Him directly through the intellect.
1. See Part Two of this volume.
2. The designation includes monotheists and monotheistic philosophers of all faiths.

Having heard this prologue, consider what I am about to explain in this chapter more carefully than any other chapter in this study: *All proximate causes, essential/natural, voluntary, or accidental/random . . . are ascribed to God in the prophetic books and are thus expressed as things which God did, commanded, or said. . . .* This is the idea to which I wanted to awaken you in this chapter: since the Deity is understood to be the one who made this volition preferable to this inarticulate animal and made that rational choice necessary for this rational animal,[3] who makes natural things operate as they do (for chance, as has been made clear, is the outcome of a superfluity of natural causes,[4] and most of it is accounted for by nature or by choice or will [5]), it follows that what is entailed by these causes may be said to be commanded by God, to be or be done as its proximate causes require.

Let me give you some examples of each such case. Apply them to every analogous case of which I have not spoken: [6]

(*a*) Regarding natural events which are constant, such as the melting of snow when the weather grows warm and the forming of waves on the sea when the wind blows, it says, "He sends His word and melts them" [Psalm 147:18], "He spoke and a strong wind arose which lifted up its waves" [Psalm 107:25]. . . .

(*b*) Regarding things caused by human choice, such as wars of

3. Not in the sense that God has made the choice but in the sense that he has given a nature (rationality in this case) in accordance with which the choice must be made.

4. Chance is understood by Aristotelian philosophers to be identical with randomness, *i.e.*, the outcome of a near equibalance of conflicting causal factors; cf. *Moreh* II:20; Aristotle, *Physics* II:6.

5. Maimonides allows for a residue of pure chance or indeterminacy, and this he seems to ascribe to the formlessness of pure matter, hence to what we apprehend as the divine attribute of pure will. The argument of *Moreh* II:20 does not require the total elimination of chance, since only what is "always or for the most part" must be treated in accordance with the model of natural law. Room remains therefore for rare sporadic events such as those Maimonides associates with the imparting and withholding of prophetic inspiration.

6. The obvious analogy is with the attributions of speech, commands, etc., to God throughout the Law. These are to be understood as expressing propositions and imperatives voiced through the behavior of proximate causes, *i.e.*, through the laws of nature, including human nature. It is these which prophets recognize as containing divine utterances and imperatives which prophetic language ascribes directly to God.

aggression or one person's setting out to do injury to another or even to insult him, it says of the aggression of the wicked Nebuchadnezzar and his armies, . . . "I will send him forth against a hypocritical nation" [Isaiah 10:6]; and in the story of Shimei ben Gera it says, "For the Lord said unto him, 'Curse David' " [2 Samuel 16:10]. . . .

(c) Regarding events caused by the volitions of animals, moved by animal motivations, it says, "God spoke to the fish" [Jonah 2:11], for it was God who caused it to give preference to such an appetite [7]—not that He turned it into a prophet and granted it a revelation! . . .

(d) And regarding matters of pure chance, it says in the story of Rebeccah, "Let her be your master's son's wife, as the Lord has spoken" [8] [Genesis 24:51]. . . . And in the story of Joseph it says, "God sent me before you" [9] [Genesis 45:5].

Thus, plainly, whether the predisposing causes are essential or accidental, rational/voluntary or appetitive/volitional, these five expressions are used: commanding, saying, speaking, sending, and calling. If you understand this and apply this knowledge uniformly in every relevant context, many incongruities will disappear and the truth will grow plain to you. . . .

Analysis

True prophets, according to al-Farabi, were the historical exemplars of Plato's ideal of the philosopher king. In touch with the divine source of understanding, the Active Intellect, they combined the philosopher's insight into the true nature of reality and man's priorities with the practicality of the statesman, the imagination of the poet, and the verbal gifts of the orator. Thus prophets were legislators whose political sense was never shallow or misguided by false or superficial values, seers who were not stargazers but builders capable of effectuating

7. As would require it to swallow moving things in its path.
8. The outcome, although due to chance, was ascribed to God, who was its ultimate cause.
9. Although Joseph's transference to Egypt had been left to the pure chance of whatever travelers might first find him in the pit.

what they dreamed, poets whose visions represented not the idle play of imagination but true metaphysical insight into the highest reaches of reality, brought down to earth and made concrete for the sake of less far-ranging minds, persuaders whose gifts with language and the play of human emotion were put to the service not of any salesman's task but of man's good itself—the reform of society—which would in turn make possible the perfection of the individuals within it.

Does this conception of the nature of prophecy eliminate its element of the supernatural? In a sense it does, for it allows a clear distinction to be drawn between prophets and all classes of self-styled wonder-workers, soothsayers, mediums, astrologers, augurs, and so forth. Prophets are guided not by conjecture but by clear insight into the nature of the universe—and thus into the word of God. Those who operate only on the level of imagination, as Maimonides argues, are either statesmen or diviner/tricksters, depending upon the way their normal intellectual capacities and moral strengths allow them to organize their lives, *i.e.,* interpret their insights. Those who achieve intellectual insight but do not find it graphically represented in their imagination are scientists, scholars, and philosophers but are not equipped for prophecy. The prophet, however, is in touch with divinity and does have a supernormal intellectual genius and capacity for transmitting his intellectual perceptions to the representational stage, the symbol-creating theater of the imagination. The prophet does not see angels, for angels are not bodies but forces and ideas. Rather he beholds—as if by perception—symbolic forms which represent the unseen and unseeable realities lying behind the visible world. *A fortiori* the prophet does not see God. Rather, all the wonders beheld in prophetic dreams and visions are the products of a subjective state, beheld as if perceptually objective. They are not, however, pure figments of the imagination. For the imagination only works up the materials given to it, and in the case of true prophets the imagination is given not merely the disjointed elements of day-to-day sensory experience for representation but the real concepts which are, according to Platonic philosophy, the veritable substances of which material objects are mere shadows and projections. These realities are what the prophetic imagination symbolizes—the realities in principle available to the more pedestrian conception of philosophers, but which the prophets' soaring intellect, given the wings of prophetic imagination, seizes in their entirety.

Is this an adequate conception of the nature of prophecy? That depends, as Maimonides has shown, on how one understands divinity. It is possible to regard insight into nature and thus into divinity as divine inspiration if one regards divinity as in some sense the Ground of being. But such a view of prophecy as is presented by Maimonides would hardly seem adequate to one who conceived of God as a sort of superconjurer and of creation as a series of conjurer's tricks. Although he may have better access to the sources of the truth, the prophet, for Maimonides, does not have open to him a better source of knowledge than the scientist, scholar, or philosopher. He must look to nature, as they do, for it is there, in nature, that the word of God is made articulate, or so it is understood by all adherents of either of the sister concepts, creation and emanation. Thus, the prophet must be a scientist, scholar, and philosopher before he can become a prophet. For neither imagination nor the process of reasoning can add content to what a man knows; they can only organize and symbolize what is already in the mind. This indeed is the basis of the difference between true prophets and mere symbolic prestidigitators. No amount of manipulation of the common archetypes of human conscious and subliminal experience can add insight or depth to what is in itself shallow, confused, undigested data. There is only one way for man to acquire knowledge, and that is (in the broadest possible sense) through the sciences, natural and humane.[10] Even Moses, as Maimonides makes clear (*Moreh* I:54), is said to have known God "face to face" and to have spoken with Him "as one man speaks with another" only in the sense that his understanding was not impeded by the intervention of imagination (*Shemonah Perakim* 7). He did not evade the sciences but on the contrary perfected himself in them, understanding that only through creation could God's attributes, *i.e.,* His being as manifested to man, be known.

The question of whether a given law stems from God or not, then, becomes easy to resolve. A law which takes material, pragmatic goals

10. For without such preparation on man's part, the Active Intellect itself has no sphere of operation in him.

as its sole good is obviously not divine in its intention; one which reaches out toward higher goals and bids fair to achieve them is. Plato, in the *Republic,* had made clear centuries before the Rambam wrote that true justice requires attention not merely to relative and particular goods but to the absolute and universal good as well, service not merely to man's unexamined goals but to the true perfection of society, and, through society, of the individuals making it up. True justice, then, must arise from the conception of the absolute good and its application in the finite and particular affairs of men. It was for this reason that Plato had declared that the troubles and abuses so familiar in all human societies would not end until philosophers became kings (he did not mean mere dabblers with ideas, of course, but rather persons who have a profound knowledge of the good in its absolute form and the means of its application in practice), or kings somehow acquired the virtues of philosophers. Philo had recognized twelve centuries before Maimonides that Moses was the practical philosopher who actually established institutions which integrated the particular good for man with man's absolute good and the Good itself in the universe, *i.e.,* God. To Maimonides this appeared self-evident. It remained, then, in distinguishing prophets from imposters, only to verify that a truly divine law such as that of Moses had not been plagiarized in whole or part by someone who did not have the moral stamina and discipline in virtue to have acquired the sciences necessary to receiving such a law—let alone the fullness of inspiration for it.

The one exception the Rambam makes to the Philosophers' naturalistic account of prophecy as a special outcome of emanation is that he maintains the possibility (he calls this a miracle) of a person's achieving all the necessary prerequisites of prophecy without becoming a prophet. The reason is that the prophet depends not merely upon science and the perfection of his moral character, which can be acquired by training. He depends as well upon imagination; and this, according to Maimonides, has in it an element of chance, for imagination, unlike intellect, being a physical theater, depends entirely upon its physical organ, the brain, thus upon the constitution of the matter of the brain, and therefore on the chance of birth and personal history. Such chance, like all effects, may be attributed, according to the Rambam, to God. And it is clear that this is what Maimonides means by calling the withholding of prophecy a miracle. For just as form in the universe expresses the rationality, the "wisdom" of God, in the laws of nature and man's intellect, so matter in the universe expresses (what we conceive as) the arbitrary pleasure or "will" of God, in the placement of the stars in the heavens and other determinations whose rule our minds cannot fathom: the apportionment of more refined or worked-up matter to some than to others, the assignment of the brain of a prophet to one man and the brain of an imbecile to another. For if we read God's word in the book of the universe, it is not always clear that He is talking sense—at least not in our language, although He may make perfect sense (as Job saw) from a less subjective, more eternal point of view.

It is intriguing that Maimonides should call the withholding of prophetic inspiration a miracle. For it is plain that by the standards which trace all effects to the ultimate causal source in God, the giving of prophecy is a divine act as well. But the withholding of prophecy is apparently the rarer event and the causal law (as Maimonides reads Aristotle) only requires that nature keep to its accustomed course for the most part (*i.e.,* as we might say, statistically). The miracle, then, which separates the prophet's mind from the philosopher's is not unnatural but rather the chance concurrence of the mind of a philosopher with brain-matter which allows an extranormal increase in the capacity and speed of the imagination. I use the terms "capacity" and "speed" advisedly, for, on this level, the apparatus of the brain is decidedly comparable to a mechanism. Maimonides himself uses the term *âla,* which means instrument and organ interchangeably, and the modern reader cannot help but think of the comparison of different generations of computers. Indeed, imagination is envisioned by medieval writers as a kind of simulation-model display. What differentiates the mind from a machine and renders it, in some respects, independent of the matter with which it is associated is the intellect, which, of course, philosophers and prophets have in common.

The insight of the prophet, then, like that of the philosopher, is natural, although it derives, like all things natural, from a transnatural source, *i.e.,* from God, and is developed to an extraordinary degree. The mode in which God speaks to prophets is the same as that in which He speaks to all scientists, moralists, poets, statesmen, and persons of intuition: God speaks through nature, propounding His propositions in the laws of nature which express His Wisdom and in the matter of nature which expresses the full arbitrary potency of His Will, uttering His imperative to all voluntary creatures in the interplay with the environment of the motives by which their wills are governed, and His imperative to all rational, choosing beings in the logic of action and the potential of human nature for its own development and perfection. These are the truths which all who have some aspect of the truth endeavor to grasp and articulate—poets in images, statesmen in laws and institutions, scientists in theories, scholars in conceptions—but which prophets grasp entire, with the clarity of science, the force of poetic vision, the comprehensiveness of true scholarship, and the responsiveness and responsibility of statecraft of the highest order.

THE REVEALED LAW

Introduction

Nature, to the Rambam, like Scripture, and Scripture, like nature, are parallel expressions of divine intelligence. Both are to be approached with the assumption of their rationality. The faith in the implicit rationality of nature which is the inalienable characteristic of the scientist is to the Rambam equally applicable to Scripture. This indeed is the key to the rationalism of the exegetical method established by Akiba's demand for a presumption of significance in every letter and expression of the Torah. It is the key as well to an understanding of Maimonides' underlying approach to the revealed Law.

The most vital force in defining the Jewish tradition, and indeed in molding Jewish nationhood, has been the Torah, that is to say, the Law—for it is crucial to the understanding of Jewish thought and spirituality to recognize that Scripture for the Jew is not a narrative but an imperative; prophecy is not a privileged vision of the future but a spelling out of the logic of the divine word—the truth as manifested in nature, the divine command as applied to human affairs. Thus the most portentous function of the Bible is neither to record the epochs of sacred history nor to predict the climax of profane history by its trans-

404

mutation into the posthistorical, messianic epoch. History in the Bible serves only as the setting for the revelation of the Law (*cf. Moreh* III:50). And, for that very reason, the Law itself will have a history, in terms of man's progressive awakening to it.

There is of course, as we have seen, an indicative as well as an imperative subject matter to be found in the Torah. This is the vehicle of the theology which is the subject matter of the *Guide to the Perplexed*. But while the object of the *Guide* is to shed light upon the problems of that theology, that is, to explain how prophets dare to speak of God, etc., the object of the Torah in including theology at all is simply to establish the relation between the transcendent God and the Law. Thus theology in the Torah is subordinate to Law. And this is as it must be. For the sole concrete grasp we may have of a being who is absolute Perfection must be in terms of attributes such as intelligence/will or mercy/loving-kindness. Thus the positive theology of the Torah, by which God's "attributes" are revealed, can only serve to establish our conception of God's relation to the world as its Creator and the ordainer of its law, causing us thereby to recognize the authority and underlying wisdom of that aspect of God's law which applies to thinking, choosing beings.

Traditionally there were said to be 613 divine imperatives (*mitzvot*) in the Pentateuch. But, according to the Sages of the Talmud, the Law itself contained the principle of its own elaboration. This is the meaning of the notion of an oral law, transmitted side by side with the written Torah. The theaters for the elaboration of the Law were the Jewish law courts, synagogues, academies, schools, and assemblies of the Babylonian exile and of Palestine from the fifth century B.C.E. onward. The judgments of the Sages (as the Rambam calls them) were collected and codified by Rabbi Judah the Prince (*ca.* 220 B.C.E.) in the six "orders" of the authoritative code of Jewish law, the Mishnah. This in turn was greatly elaborated by the addition over the ensuing centuries of a complement (Gemarah) of uncollected opinions, minority reports, *obiter dicta,* commentary, digressions, historical and allegorical supplementation, providing a vehicle for the indirect exposure of numerous political, philosophical, mystical, ethical, and theological insights, which were not discussed directly (*cf.* the Introduction to this volume). The Mishnah and its discursive complement, the Gemarah, together form the Talmud, organized around the framework of the sixty-three tractates of the Mishnah and completed by approximately 400 C.E. in the case of the Palestinian Talmud and 500 C.E. in the case of the Babylonian.

Naturally, the Talmudic mode of presentation is far better suited to study than to reference, and it is clear that long before the Rambam's time the Talmud had become more a way of life than a law book. It was a world in which one could immerse oneself; indeed, one could not claim to be a scholar unless one had. But by the same token it could not readily function as a handbook of the Law, nor could the many volumes of the Talmud (or rather the two sets of volumes of the Babylonian and Palestinian Talmuds), with their composite authorship over the course of many centuries, possibly marshal the principles of the Law in systematic fashion or explain systematically the functions of the mitzvot. This was the task the Rambam undertook as a legal and social thinker.

If the Law was to be understood as law, it was necessary to disengage to some extent the Mishnah as a legal code from the far more comprehensive embrace of the Gemarah. Thus as a young man of twenty-three, Maimonides undertook his Commentary, not on the Talmud, of which there were several by his time, but on the Mishnah. It was in this ten-year labor that he developed the mature understanding of the rational principles of the Law which were to be his for life. For a guiding principle of the Commentary on the Mishnah was that every commandment was "given with its explanation." That is, that every imperative of the Divine to man was intrinsically amenable to reason. The overall achievement of this Commentary is that it revivifies the Torah as Law by exposing the inherent rationality of that Law as codified in the Mishnah.

To establish fully the authority of the Law, it was necessary further for Maimonides to return to Scripture to determine precisely which were the 613 commandments of the Law of Moses. This he did in his magisterial *Sefer ha-Mitzvot*, the *Book of the Commandments.* In it Maimonides lists 248 positive commandments, from belief in God to the laws of torts and inheritance, and 365 negative commandments, from the rejection of polytheism to the laws of monarchy, excluding duplications and any inferences beyond the text. Besides listing the commandments, the Rambam states the principles of his enumeration and comments briefly upon each mitzvah, explaining its import. It is then possible to see exactly how the oral law grows out of the Pentateuchal revelation.

As a final step in his systematization of the Law, the Rambam wrote his *Mishneh Torah,* or legal code. The title of this work is not to be confused with that of the Mishnah. *"Mishneh Torah"* in Maimonidean language means the Law in Review; the name in fact is the same as that commonly used for the Pentateuchal book of Deuteronomy, where the giving of the Law to Israel is reiterated by Scripture. Maimonides' objective is only slightly less ambitious: his goal is to produce a single work to serve as an exhaustive, authoritative statement of the Law, obviating the need to use the Talmud as a legal reference, by reclassifying the laws according to their legal subject matter and purpose, omitting all Talmudic material that does not represent a final, binding judgment as to law, and including the supplemental decisions of *Sifra, Sifre,* the Tosefta, and the Geonim.

In the course of writing these three books, the *Book of the Commandments,* the Commentary on the Mishnah, and the *Mishneh Torah,* then, Maimonides compiled three irreplaceable and ultimately almost canonical legal works. What he accomplished as well was to establish comprehensively the possibility of understanding the rationality of the Law as law—the dynamic of its inner logic and the intelligible meaning of its function in the governance of human life. Some of his remarks toward the close of the *Guide* deal with the relevance of the Law, not as a quarry for theological investigations or touchstone of metaphysical inquiries but as an expression of the divine imperative through which God's providential governance over Israel is made manifest.

From *Moreh Nevukhim III*

MOREH NEVUKHIM III:26

Just as religious thinkers differ as to whether God's works follow from His wisdom or His sheer will without serving any end whatever, so do they differ in exactly the same way as to the legislation they regard

Him as having laid down for us. There are those who seek no grounds whatever in his legislation, saying that all laws stem from sheer will. There are others who say that every command and prohibition of the Law expresses wisdom and is intended to serve some end, that every law is grounded in the provision of some benefit.

That all our laws have some justifying ground, although we may not know the grounds of some or not understand in just what way wisdom is expressed in them, is the doctrine of all of us,[1] the masses and the specially prepared alike. For the texts of the Bible on this are quite clear: *"hukkim u-mishpatim tzaddikim,"* "righteous statutes and laws"[Deuteronomy 4:8]; "The laws of the Lord are truth. They are altogether just" [Psalm 19:10]. Those referred to as statutes, such as *shaatnez,* milk with meat, and the scapegoat, are those of which the Sages (of blessed memory) said explicitly: "Things which I [God] have ordained as statutes for you and which you have not leave to cavil at, though Satan may denounce them and the nations of the world revile them" [*Yoma* 67b].[2] The majority of the Sages do not believe these are groundless in the least nor that ends cannot be sought for them, for this would imply God's acts might be frivolous, as we have stated [*Moreh* III:25]. Rather, the majority of the Sages believe the statutes must have grounds, *i.e.,* beneficial ends, which are, however, not plain to us, because of either the limitation of our reason or our lack of knowledge. Thus all the mitzvot, according to them, have as their justification some utility, either obvious to us, as with the prohibition of killing and stealing, or not, as with the banning of *orlah* [3] and of sowing double in the vineyard [Deuteronomy 22:9]. Those commandments whose utility is plain to the masses are called laws [*mishpatim*], while these, whose benefits are unclear to the masses, are called statutes [*hukkim*]. Regarding "for it is not an empty thing" [Deuteronomy 32:47], the Sages always say, "—and if it is empty, that is on your account" [Palestinian Talmud *Peah* I, *Ketubot* VIII], meaning that this legislation is not a vain or useless thing, and

1. Jews, as opposed to other communities based on systems of religious law.
2. *Cf. Shemonah Perakim* 6.
3. The first produce of immature trees; see Leviticus 19:23.

if it seems so to you in any of the mitzvot, the fault is in your comprehension.[4] . . .

. . . All their dicta are based on this principle,[5] and the Biblical texts confirm it. I have found one passage of the Sages, however, in *Bereshit Rabbah* [XLIV], which seems at first glance to suggest that certain mitzvot have no other ground than simply to lay down a law and do not look to any further object, utility, or good. This is where they say, "What difference does it make to the Holy One, Blessed be He, whether one slaughters animals by cutting their throats or the back of their necks? [6] One must say the mitzvot were not given except to purify mankind.[7] . . ." Although this is a very strange statement, unparalleled anywhere in their discourse, I have been able to interpret it, as you shall hear, consistently with the general pattern of their discussion and the principle, accepted by consensus, that the entire system of our Law can be treated in terms of purposes beneficial to existence, "because it is not an empty thing." . . .

What anyone of sound intellect ought to believe on this issue is that the general principles of the mitzvot have rational grounds and were laid down for the sake of the benefits they provide; but it is the precise details that are said to express a sheer imperative.[8] To kill animals as necessary for food is obviously useful. . . . As for not poleaxing them . . . this and all like commandments serve to "purify mankind." Thus, clearly, in their example . . . (I use this example only because it occurs in their text) . . . since necessity calls for the eating of animals, the easiest death for them was intended, consistent with ease of accomplishment. For decapitation would be possible only with

4. Thus the presumption of the Torah's rationality is applied specifically to its legislation, to imply that it is purposeful.

5. The Talmudic method is founded on the assumption of the rationality of the Law. On this basis the principle of the elaboration of the Law may be said to be contained within the Law.

6. The former is commanded.

7. *E.g.*, by the disciplining effects of pure obedience.

8. *I.e.*, the pure positive will. Safety on public roads is a benefit, for which reason provides by legislating that all traffic will keep to one side or the other of the road. To reason it is immaterial which side is chosen, but reason demands that the will must choose arbitrarily.

a sword or some such instrument.[9] . . . It is for the sake of easing the animal's death that a sharp knife is required.

What truly illustrates this matter of the details of the mitzvot, however, is the subject of sacrifices. The general principle of offering sacrifices has a momentous and obvious utility, as I shall explain [*Moreh* III:32]. But the fact that this offering is a lamb and that a ram, or the specific numbers of animals employed, will never be given a rational ground, and anyone who spends his time trying to find justifications for any such details of the Law is on a madman's errand, which does not serve to clear up incongruities but only to increase them. Anyone who imagines such details have rational grounds is just as far from the truth as one who imagines that the commandments, as a whole, do not exist to provide any benefit.[10]

MOREH NEVUKHIM III:27

The overall purpose of the Law is twofold: to promote the welfare of the body and to promote the welfare of the soul. The welfare of the soul is achieved inasmuch as sound views are implanted in the minds of the populace, to the extent they are capable of grasping them. For this reason, certain ideas are stated directly while others are expressed through symbols, since it is not within the natural capacity of the common populace to grasp the latter class of truths directly.[1] As for bodily welfare, this is secured by properly ordering the conditions of men's social relations with one another. This is accomplished in two ways: (*a*) the elimination of inequities, which means it will not be the case that every person is at liberty to do whatever he wills and is able to do but is restricted to actions conducive to the general welfare, and (*b*) the acquisition by every person of socially beneficial traits of character.

Of the two objectives of the Law, spiritual well-being is certainly

9. Torah does not wish to make it impossible for any individual to slaughter his own meat, as needed for food, even if this does involve not slaughtering the animal in what may be absolutely the most humane way possible.

10. For neither person seems able to distinguish the level of law capable of rational justification from that which is not capable of such justification and does not require it.

1. Thus, they require poetic language—metaphor, symbol, allegory—to aid the imagination in grasping what their understanding does not reach; *cf.* Plato's conception of the use of myth.

the higher . . . but bodily welfare is prior in time and nature. It involves the governance of the state and the promotion of the welfare of all its citizens insofar as this is possible. This, then, is the more fundamental object, and it is to the securing of this objective and all it entails that the Law devotes the greatest part of its attention—since the higher object cannot be achieved until this one has been attained. For it is a demonstrated fact that man has two levels of perfection in his development, that of the body and that of the soul. The first is that he be healthy and as well off from a bodily point of view as possible, and this cannot be realized unless he finds all his needs when, as, and if he seeks them—food and all other things necessary for the care of the body, such as shelter, bathing facilities, and so forth. All this cannot in the least be obtained by a single isolated individual. This level can be reached for each person only if all band together in a civil society, as it is well known that man is a social animal by nature.[2] Man's higher level of perfection, his becoming actually a rational being (*i.e.*, having a mind that actually thinks) and thus understanding what a man is capable of understanding regarding all things, obviously does not [in and of itself] imply actions or moral traits but only ideas, to which thought leads one and to which argument gives force. But it is equally obvious that this higher level of development cannot be achieved until the first has been attained. For a man cannot think a thought even if it is explained to him (let alone discover it for himself) if he is in pain, or greatly hungry or thirsty, or extremely hot or cold. But only after bodily well-being has been attained can he reach that further, higher sort of perfection which is the sole means to everlasting life.

The true Law, then, which we have already made clear is unique,[3] the Law of Moses our Teacher, serves solely to afford us these two sorts of perfection together: (1) provision for the commonweal of the people in their relations with one another through the elimination of inequities and the inculcation of virtuous and high-minded characters in the citizenry, so that their tenure in the land may be firmly established and they may live under a single stable system in order that

2. Maimonides echoes Aristotle's *Politics*.
3. The Rambam argues in *Moreh* II:39 on Scriptural and rational grounds that the Torah as Law is unprecedented, irreplaceable, and optimally equibalanced between excess and deficiency; *cf. Moreh* II:38, 40.

each of them may perfect himself in the higher way as well, and (2) the imparting of sound ideas to the people, through which this higher perfection is attained. . . .

MOREH NEVUKHIM III:28

. . . From the preceding, it follows that every commandment, positive or negative, which calls for the abolition of injustice among men, or incites them to nobility of character such as is conducive to the betterment of human life, or imparts true opinions which must be believed either for their own sake or because they are necessary to the abolition of men's exploitation of one another [1] or to the acquisition of noble character, plainly does have a manifest ground in the benefit it provides. Regarding these commandments, there is no question as to their end, for no one has ever been perplexed for a moment or inquired as to why the Law lays down that God is one, or wherefore we are forbidden to kill or steal or to take vengeance or exact retaliation, or why we are commanded to love one another.[2] What people are perplexed about and where they do differ is regarding the commandments which do not obviously afford one of the three aforementioned benefits: imparting some opinion, instilling nobility of character, or eliminating interpersonal wrongdoing. Some say these mitzvot serve no purpose beyond the bare command itself, while others say they do afford a benefit but it is hidden from us. These commandments seemingly cannot be classed as contributing to spiritual wellbeing through the imparting of sound beliefs, nor to material welfare through the provision

1. Maimonides cites as an example the belief that God looks upon wrongdoers with fury. This is not literally true but, like the myth of the metals in Plato's *Republic*, it is an emotionally cogent surrogate (symbol) which stands in for an abstruse truth regarding providence, which would produce a similar response in human actions if people understood it.
2. The Law lays down that God is one because this is a demonstrated truth. It forbids killing, stealing, etc., because these actions are harmful. It commands men to love one another because cooperation is the foundation of human existence and to love God because this is the summit of human perfection. It instills virtue because it is necessary to the peace of society and the perfection of each individual. The justification of these laws is immediately obvious in the benefits they provide, the belief of what is true, the elimination of mutual wrongdoing, the service of the commonweal, and the attainment of human perfection.

of laws beneficial to the ordering of the state or the home: the prohibition of *shaatnez*, for example, or of milk with meat . . . etc. But you shall hear me explain them all and on grounds demonstrably valid for all of them, but (as I said) not for their specific details nor for individual commandments. I shall make clear to you that all these and all of this sort must be classed under one of these three principles: (1) the reform of belief, and (2) the reform of political conditions, which resolves into (*a*) the elimination of interpersonal wrongdoing and (*b*) the acquisition of virtuous character. . . .

MOREH NEVUKHIM III:29

It is well known that our Father Abraham was brought up in the religion of the Sabians,[1] whose belief is that there is no deity except the stars. . . . They said, . . . "Abraham was raised in Kuta, and when he went against the community, claiming there is a cause other than the sun . . . they argued the obvious effects of the sun . . . and he replied, 'You are right. It is as the ax in a carpenter's hand!' " . . . They go on to state that the king imprisoned Abraham . . . and then, fearing the subversion of his state . . . banished him. . . . You will find this story in full in the *Nabatean Agriculture*, but they do not mention . . . Abraham's prophetic inspiration. . . . Because he bore all this . . . it was said to him, "I shall bless who blesses you, and who curses you will I curse. Through you shall all the families of the earth be blessed" [Genesis 12:3]. And it did result from his efforts that there is such unanimity throughout the world in revering him and such a sense of blessedness attached to his name that even those not his descendants link themselves to him.[2] And no one still rejects him or remains ignorant of his greatness except the last remnants of that all-but-extinct religion who survive at the extremities of the earth—the as-yet-unconverted Turkic tribes in the farthest north and Indians to

1. "Sabian" is the Rambam's term for all pagans, for he takes the pagan cult of the star-worshipping Sabians of Harran to be paradigmatic of the mature form of polytheism. He derives his knowledge of pagan myth and practice from a number of Arabic sources, including Ibn Wahshiyya's so-called *Nabatean Agriculture* (904 C.E.), purportedly based on an ancient Chaldean text.
2. For the spirit of monotheism is identified with the name of Abraham in much the way that the spirit of philosophy is identified with that of Socrates.

the far south. But these are the remnants of a paganism which once was universal throughout the earth. And the farthest progress made by the thought of any philosopher in those times was to imagine that God is the spirit of the sphere, that the sphere and stars are a body of which the Deity is the soul. . . .

When Abraham arose and it grew clear to him that there is a transcendent God who is not a body nor a force within a body, that all these stars and spheres are His works, when he saw the absurdity of their superstitions, in which he had been raised, he undertook to refute their doctrine and expose their beliefs as specious. He opposed them openly, issuing his call "in the name of the Lord, God of the universe" [Genesis 21:33], an invocation which implied the existence of God and the creation of the world by that God.[3]

In keeping with their opinions, the Sabians set up idols to the stars, gold for the sun, silver for the moon. They assigned the minerals and climatic zones to the stars, saying that such-and-such a star was the god of such-and-such a region. They built temples and consecrated statues in them, saying the influence of the stars emanated to those idols, and that, therefore, those idols could speak, comprehend, understand, and inspire people with revelations as to what was good for them. They said the same of the trees assigned to those stars. . . . All this was due to the prevalence of those beliefs,[4] the wide diffusion of ignorance, and the folly of the world in those days regarding this sort of imaginings. These opinions came to have such a hold on them that "soothsayers, sorcerers, witches, spell-casters, mediums, and necromancers" [cf. Deuteronomy 18:10–11] arose among them.[5] . . .

3. Abraham's invocation (echoed by the Rambam as the epigraph of all three parts of the *Guide*) implies the priority of God to nature, since it rejects the confinement of the divine by any finite category of time and space. Rather it expresses the conception of an absolute and universal God.

4. It is clear to the student of the history of ideas that key notions of alchemy, astrology, theurgy, and thaumaturgy—much of what we would today associate with the "occult"—originate in the pagan concepts of astral influences, affinities, etc., which were thought to explain the means by which the star-gods governed nature. It should be clear as well that such notions depend upon the conception of finite gods with limited spheres of action and are thus incompatible with monotheism, the belief in a universal God.

5. It is striking that Maimonides, in a time when superstition was widespread indeed, assigns the belief in the existence of magic powers to ignorance and superstition rather than to any special knowledge of "black arts." Maimonides was among the most

You know from the explicit statements of the Torah in a number of places that the prime intention of the Law as a whole is the elimination of pagan worship and the obliteration of all trace of it and everything connected to it, not only anything which tends toward any of its practices, but even anything reminiscent of it. . . . Thus all the mitzvot which set forth the prohibition against pagan worship and all that is related to it or resembles or is associated with it have a manifest utility. For they serve to purge us of those unsound views which distract us from all that is worthwhile in terms of our two levels of perfection. . . .

With many of the laws, their meaning has become clear to me and I have recognized their basis only through understanding the doctrine, opinions, practices, and cult of the Sabians. . . . An acquaintance with those beliefs and practices is a major gateway indeed to the discovery of the justifying grounds of the commandments. For the foundation of our Law and the axis on which it turns are the obliteration of those beliefs from men's minds and of every vestige and effect of them from existence . . . as they say, "Here you learn that anyone who professes idolatry rejects the Torah altogether, and anyone who rejects idolatry professes the Torah altogether" [*Sifre* to Numbers 15:23]. You must recognize this.

MOREH NEVUKHIM III:30

If you study these ancient beliefs, you will find the accepted view of all people was that the worship of the stars is what makes the earth habitable and the land fertile. The scholars and devout and holy men of those days exhorted the people in such terms and taught them that agriculture (upon which human survival depends) can be successful only through worshipping the sun and stars, that if you angered those celestial beings by disobedience, then the land would become barren and ruined. . . . Thus they connected their idolatry with agriculture. . . . And the pagan priests, in their homilies to the people assembled in the temples, drummed it into their heads that it was on account of those rites that rain fell, trees bore fruit, and the land became fertile

outspoken opponents of astrology and foremost among medieval philosophers in making explicit the dependence of astrology upon pagan beliefs; *cf.* his famous "Letter on Astrology."

and capable of sustaining life. . . . They came to promise even more—long life, immunity from illness and injury, and high yields of crops and fruit. . . .

Now since these beliefs were so widely held that they were regarded as certainties [1] and God in His mercy wanted to efface this error from our minds and remove the toil from our bodies of the laborious and useless tasks idolatry had imposed upon us and give us our Law through the instrumentality of Moses, Moses told us, on divine authority, that worship of these stars or idols would cause the rain to be cut off and the earth to be ruined, so that nothing would grow and the fruit would drop from the trees . . . that conditions would be bad, there would be bodily illnesses and shortening of lives, while if they abandoned such worship and accepted the worship of God, then the rain would fall, the earth would be fertile, conditions would be good, there would be bodily health and long lives [2]—just the opposite of what the pagans preached to the people . . . for the foundation of the Law is the elimination of that view and the obliteration of its effects, as we have explained. [3]

MOREH NEVUKHIM III:31

There are among mankind certain people who regard the giving of grounds for any of the laws as something dreadful. What they would like best is that no intelligible sense be found in any injunction or prohibition. What compels them to take this position is a malaise they discover in themselves but which they are unable to articulate or adequately to express. They suppose that if these laws afford any benefit in this existence of ours or were legislated for the sake of this or that purpose, then they might as well have originated from the insights and opinions of any intelligent being. Whereas, if they are something which has no intelligible significance and which is not conducive to any utility whatever, then they must certainly derive from God—for

1. Being by-and-large unquestioned.
2. See especially Leviticus 26:3–45, Deuteronomy 10:13–21.
3. This implies, of course, that Moses' promises of rain, etc., are homiletic in the same vein as the pagan promises they seek to counteract, a revelation shocking only to those who imagine that rain, etc., rather than intelligence, are the true measure of divine concern.

none of them would be the outcome of any human process of thought. It is as though for these feeble intellects man were higher than his Creator, for it is man who speaks and acts purposively while the deity does not but simply orders us to do things of no good to us and forbids us to do things of no harm to us. Exalted be He, and exalted further still above such notions! In point of fact, just the opposite is the case, as we have shown [*Moreh* III:25, 27, 28] and as is made clear by the words, "As a good for us each day, to give us life as we have today" [Deuteronomy 6:24], and "who shall hear all these statutes and say, 'Surely this great people is a wise and discerning nation' " [4:6]. It states expressly that even the statutes [*hukkim*], all of them, will manifest to all nations the wisdom and discernment in which they are conceived. If the laws have no knowable, rational ground, afford no benefit and forestall no harm, then wherefore is it said of him who professes or performs them that he is wise and discerning and so manifestly worthy that the nations will think it remarkable? Rather, as we said, each of the 613 commandments most certainly does serve either to instill a sound opinion or remove an unsound one or impart a rule of equity or eliminate inequity, inculcate good traits of character or guard against those traits of character which are vicious. . . .

MOREH NEVUKHIM III:32

If you study the divine works and acts (which is to say, the works and acts of nature), then the way God's grace operates and His wisdom is expressed in the formation of living things will become obvious to you.[1] . . . Thus God's grace subtly provided for all mammals: since they are extremely delicate at birth and cannot feed on solid food, they were provided with milk-giving breasts which yield a liquid food, easily assimilated by the young, until their organs very gradually have become sturdier and more solid. The identical sort of providential care is afforded by many of the items in our Law. For it is not possible to go from one extreme to the other all in one fell swoop. Thus, it is not open to human nature to abandon all that is familiar all at once. So, when God sent Moses our Teacher to make of us "a nation of priests

1. Maimonides gives several examples taken from Galen's *De Usu Partium* (*On the Usefulness of the Parts of the Human Body*) to show how nature proceeds progressively along a continuum rather than demanding abrupt transitions involving discontinuities.

and a holy people'' [Exodus 19:6] . . . and to cause us to cleave to
His worship . . . the accepted way of life throughout the world (as far
as what was familiar and customary then) involved that common form
of worship in which we were brought up. It consisted solely in sacri-
ficing various sorts of animals in those temples in which idols were set
up and prostrating oneself and offering incense before them. All devout and devoted people of the time were attached to service in those
temples consecrated to the stars, as I have made clear. Thus God's
wisdom and His grace (which is made manifest in all the works of His
creation) did not demand the legislation of complete abolition, nullifi-
cation, and abandonment of all acts of worship of any of these types.
For the very capability of receiving such a law in terms of human nature, which welcomes the familiar, would have been inconceivable.
This would have been the equivalent, for those times, of a prophet
coming in our times, calling people to serve God, but saying, ''God
has ordained you shall not pray nor fast nor take refuge with Him in
time of stress, but you shall serve Him solely by meditating, without
doing anything at all.'' This is the reason that these sorts of worship
are preserved and transferred from artificial and imaginary things,
which have no reality, to His name, and why we are commanded to do
them ''for Him.'' [2] Thus, He commanded us to build a temple to Him
. . . that there should be an altar to His name . . . that sacrifice be to
Him . . . prostration to Him and incense offered before Him. And He
forbade any of these things to be done for any other than Him. . . .
He set apart priests to serve in the Sanctuary, as it is said, ''to be
priests unto Me'' [Exodus 28:41]. As it was necessary to provide for
them, since they were fully occupied with the Temple, dues were set
aside for them, *viz.* those of the Levites and priests. And it was by this
subtle act of divine grace that the memory of pagan worship [3] was
erased and the true and mighty pillar of our faith, the existence and
unity of the Deity, was established without arousing the revulsion of
men's spirits and without alienating them by abolishing the forms of

2. So that He will be recognized as the proper focus of all piety, regardless whether our
conception of piety has not evolved beyond the level of sacrifices, prayer and works, or
contemplation.
3. The sense of emotional attachment to its familiar usages and hence to the false spiritual values it instilled.

worship with which they were familiar. For no other mode of worship was then known.

I realize your spirit will naturally rebel at first on confronting this idea and find it very disturbing. You will ask me, mentally, "How can commands and prohibitions involving such momentous actions, so carefully detailed and scheduled, not be intended for their own sakes but only for some other end—as though God played a trick on us to accomplish His ultimate objective? What prevented Him from legislating what He wanted in the first place and making us capable of receiving such legislation? . . ."

The answer, which will relieve your unease and reveal to you the essence of what I am drawing to your attention, is in a text of the Torah which presents a very similar situation: "God did not lead them by the way through Philistia, although it was short," etc., "God led the people by the way through the Red Sea Wilderness" [Exodus 13:17–18]. Just as God caused them to stray to a different road and away from the main one toward which they had been heading, to protect their bodies from what their nature could not bear, in order to accomplish His primary purpose, so did He impose these laws we have mentioned in order to protect their souls from what they could not psychologically accept, in order to accomplish His primary intention, which is that we should know Him and that idolatry be discarded. For just as it is not in human nature to grow up in slavery amidst clay and bricks and such, and then simply wash one's hands and straightaway do battle against the "Sons of Anak," [4] so, too, it is not in human nature to grow up with a great many forms of worship and practices which have become so familiar as to be like axioms of thought, and then suddenly to abandon them all. Just as the Deity exercised a subtle grace in causing them to wander in the desert until their spirits had grown hardy . . . and until a generation had been born which had never known the humiliation of servitude . . . so did this portion of the Law [5] stem from God's subtle grace in allowing men to maintain the sorts of practices to which they were accustomed, in order to confirm the faith which was the original object.

4. *I.e.,* the warlike inhabitants of Canaan; *cf.,* Numbers 13:28.
5. To wit, the portion in particular dealing with the Temple cult of priests, animal sacrifices, etc.

You ask a second question: What prevented God from legislating His primary intention and making us capable of living up to that intention? That implies that you should ask, "What prevented God from leading them through Philistia and making them capable of waging war without their detour? . . ." And thirdly you should ask on what grounds the entire Law is set forth with such graphic positive and negative sanctions. For it can be said to you, "Since God's ultimate object is that we believe in this Law and perform its practices, why did He not give us the power to do so constantly rather than gulling us with promises of favor in return for obedience and threats of vengeance in return for disobedience? For this, too, is a ruse by which we are tricked into accomplishing His primary objective. What prevented Him from making the inclination toward the desired sort of behavior and the disinclination toward the disapproved sort permanent features of our nature?"

The answer to these three questions and all similar ones is the same general one: even if miracles change the nature of things, God does not change the nature of man. It is because of this awe-inspiring principle that it is said, "Would that they had a heart such as this [always, to fear Me and to keep My commandments!] [6] [Deuteronomy 5:26]. That is why commandments and prohibitions, rewards and punishments, are given at all.[7] . . .

Returning to our specific point, I say that since this sort of worship, *i.e.*, sacrifices, served the object of the Law in secondary fashion, while prayer of all sorts and other such acts of worship come closer to the primary intention and are necessary to achieve it, a great distinction is made by the Torah between the two sorts of act. For, with sacrifice, even when done in His name, it is not imposed on us as it was originally,[8] *i.e.*, sacrifices being offered anywhere or at any time. Temples may not be built just anywhere, nor may just anyone offer sacrifice who so desires. . . . All this regulation serves to restrict this

6. Even God must recognize the limitations of human nature.
7. Not that God could not have made man differently; but, given God's decision to make man as he is, the Torah, with its symbols, economies, and exhortations, is appropriate. Had man been made incapable of choosing or of erring in his choice, the Torah as Law would be irrelevant to His needs.
8. In pre-Mosaic times.

sort of worship, allowing only as much of it to survive as His wisdom
does not demand be entirely abandoned. Prayer, on the other hand,
whether the organized prayer of public worship or the private prayer of
personal devotion, may be offered anywhere by anyone. Likewise,
with the tzitizit [9] and the mezuzot,[10] the tefillin,[11] and other similar
practices of worship. It is because of this conception I have just revealed to you that there is so much censure in the prophetic books of
people's zeal for the sacrifices, and why it is explained to them that
these are not primary objects intended for their own sake and that God
can do without them. Thus Samuel said, "Does the Lord delight in
burnt offerings and oblations as He does in hearkening to the voice of
the Lord?" etc. [1 Samuel 15:22]. Isaiah said, " 'Why do I need your
multitude of sacrifices?' says the Lord," etc. [Isaiah 1:11]. And Jeremiah said, "For I spoke not to your fathers when I brought them out
of Egypt commanding them regarding burnt offerings and oblations. I
commanded rather this: 'Hearken to My voice, and I shall be your
God, and you shall be My people' " [Jeremiah 7:22–23]. This statement has been difficult for everyone whose comments on it I have seen
or heard. They say, "How can Jeremiah say of God that He gave us
no charge regarding burnt offerings and oblations when the major part
of the mitzvot is concerned solely with that subject?" The point of
Jeremiah's statement, however, as I have made clear, is to declare that
the prime intent of the Law is, that you know Me and worship none
other: "I shall be your God, and you shall by My people." This
legislation regarding the sacrificial cult and the mechanics of the Temple's operation was wholly subservient to the accomplishment of that
primary end—It is only for the sake of this object that I transferred
those modes of worship to My name, so as to obliterate all trace of
paganism and establish the principle of My unity. But you undermined
the end and held fast to the means in that you doubted My being:
"They denied the Lord and said, 'It is not He' " [Jeremiah 5:12].[12]
And practiced pagan worship . . . while still turning to the Temple

9. The fringes of the garment ordained in Numbers 15:38.

10. The writing on the doorposts of the house ordained in Deuteronomy 6:9, 11:20.

11. Phylacteries, *cf.* Exodus 13:9, Deuteronomy 6:8, 11:18.

12. The use of this passage in *Moreh* III:17: the denial of God's efficacy (and hence, for
practical purposes, of His existence) is implicit in willful acts of immorality.

of the Lord and offering sacrifices, which were not intended for their own sake in the first place!

I have another perspective on the exegesis of this verse from Jeremiah, which tends to exactly the same conclusion. Text and tradition alike make it clear that in the earliest legislation we received, there was nothing concerning offerings and sacrifices. . . . For the first commandment made after the Exodus from Egypt was that given at Marah . . . and our authentic tradition has it that the Sabbath and civil ordinances . . . (that is, the elimination of inequities) were legislated at Marah. And this was the prime intent, as we have shown, *viz.,* affirmation of true belief, *i.e.,* the creation of the world (for, as I have taught you, the basis of our laws regarding Sabbath is simply to entrench this belief, as I have explained in this study [*Moreh* II:31], and besides true belief, the intention is to eliminate inequities among people. Thus, plainly, the first legislation contained nothing regarding burnt offerings or oblations, since these were secondary in intention.[13]

The identical idea expressed by Jeremiah is voiced in the Psalm as a reproach to the whole community for their negligence of the prime intention of the Law and their failure to distinguish the primary from the secondary: "Hear, O My people, and I will speak; O Israel, and I will testify against you. God I am, your God. Not with sacrifices will I reprove you, nor your constant offerings. I shall not take a bullock from your house nor any he-goats from your folds" [Psalm 50:7–9]. Wherever this theme is repeated, this is the purport.[14] Understand this well and reflect on it.

13. The Rambam's hypothesis may seem somewhat bold to those who fail to recognize that the Torah to Maimonides is not a mere document but a legislative system. It will, then, of course, have a history, and it is not surprising if priority of intention is accompanied by historical priority as well. This is not to say that the Rambam here anticipates the "Higher Criticism," for he presumes an underlying unity of purpose throughout the Hebrew Scriptures, which may allow for their stratification but not for their fragmentation into mutually conflicting or competing strains of thought. Such a presumption on his part is radically alien to the methods of Protestant literalism and Enlightenment historicism in which the Higher Criticism took root.

14. God's rebuke, in Maimonides' interpretation, and His rejection of Israel's offerings are on account of their supplanting the end by the means. Thus the assertion of God's being and relationship to Israel ("God I am, your God") coupled with the mention of the constant sacrifices and God's rejection of them.

MOREH NEVUKHIM III:33

Among the objectives of the perfect Law, further, is the restriction, depreciation, and repudiation of the passions as much as possible and their confinement to what is necessary.[1] As you know, most popular license and vice stem from an excessive appetite for food, drink, or sex. This is what vitiates man's higher development and impairs his ability to reach physical perfection as well, corrupts the citizens, and undermines home life. For by following pleasure for its own sake, as the unenlightened do, the yearning for understanding is supplanted, the body is debilitated, and thus men die before their natural lifespan is completed. Anxieties, miseries, jealousies, enmities, and conflicts over what others have increase—all because the ignorant make pleasure alone the end they seek for its own sake.[2]

For this reason, God (exalted be His name) with subtle grace legislated laws for us which would abate the force of this focus of motivation and turn our thoughts away from it as much as possible, forbidding everything conducive to vice or to pleasure viewed as an end in itself. This is a major object of the Law. . . .

Another object of the Law, by the same token, is the encouragement of a gentle, agreeable character in man, to ensure that he is not rough or coarse but responsive, compliant, helpful, and considerate. You know His command: "Circumcise, then, your hearts, and be not stiff-necked any longer" [Deuteronomy 10:16]. . . .

Another object of the Law is purity and the imparting of sanctity. . . . It states plainly that sanctity involves renunciation of sex, just as it states that sanctity involves abstinence from wine.[3] . . .

Cleanliness of clothing and cleansing of the body of grime are also objects of the Law. But first come purification of heart and act from

1. The passions as understood here are the destructive effects of psychological excess and deficiency. This specifically excludes from condemnation those actions or attitudes which express appropriately moderated emotion; *cf. Shemonah Perakim* 4.
2. They are, therefore, incapable of judging their desires by the standard of any other value.
3. Like the other paragraphs in this chapter, this serves only to explain general principles—in this case, how the law comes to regulate abstinence from wine and sex (by a Nazirite, *cf. Shemonah Perakim* 4). The Rambam does no more here than describe the connection of a certain class of laws to the end they serve. He does not here explain in detail how those laws modulate behavior to serve that end.

the pollution of thought and character. For to confine oneself to outward purity, washing and cleansing one's garments, while wallowing in lust and license, gluttony and promiscuity, is the height of impurity.

If you study these objectives, too, which I have stated in this chapter, the grounds of many laws will grow clear to you which were unknown prior to the understanding of these objectives. . . .

MOREH NEVUKHIM III:34

One thing you ought to know is that the Law is not directed to the exceptional. Legislation does not deal with what is rare. Rather all that it seeks to accomplish regarding belief, or any useful practice, is intended solely for the majority of cases, without regard to infrequent events or the detriment of an individual which may be due to its rulings and determinations. For the Law is something divine,[1] and you must bear in mind that in nature, too, general benefits may entail harm to particular individuals [cf. Moreh III:18]. . . .

On the same reasoning, you should not be surprised, moreover, that the object of the Law is not accomplished in every single person. Rather, it is necessary that individuals exist for whom the governance of the Law is not complete. For natural forms of species are not perfectly realized in every individual to which they give rise.[2] . . .

For the same reason, too, it is not possible for the laws to vary according to the situations of particular individuals and the conditions of particular times, as does medical therapy, which can be adapted to each person's present equilibrium. Rather, the governance of the Law must be absolute and universal, even if this does not suit some persons. . . . For if it were left to the individual [to determine whether the sentence of the law should apply in his own case], then everything would be undermined. . . . For this reason, matters of primary intention in the Law are not time-dependent or place-dependent but are absolute and universal principles, as He said, "For the congregation, there shall be one law" [Numbers 15:15]. But only the general welfare

---

1. To wit, in that it does not respect persons but looks upon all with complete impartiality.
2. If they were, a plurality of individuals would not be necessary as their expression.

of the majority is considered therein, as I have explained.[3] Having laid down the preceding background, I shall proceed to the explication which was our object.[4]

MOREH NEVUKHIM III:35

I have classified all the mitzvot, according to their objects, into fourteen classes: [1]

(1) Commandments involving fundamental ideas. These are the ones I surveyed in "Laws of the Foundations of the Torah." [2] They also include repentence and fasts,[3] as I shall explain. Regarding com-

---

3. The preceding is one of the most elegant and economical chapters in the *Guide*. In it, Maimonides premises that the Torah, like a law of nature, is concerned with the general rather than the exceptional. From this premise he derives: (1) the impartiality of the law, and the attendant possibility of disadvantage to particular individuals; (2) the minimalism of the Law's demands resultant from the fact that it must bind the majority and thus the insufficiency of law to perfect every individual to the fullest, and the resultant possibility that the Law may fail with a particular individual yet is not for that reason to be rejected as having failed at its overall objective, as well as the fact that the law in itself need not suffice for the perfection of exceptionally virtuous or wise individuals but may content itself with mere hints which they must follow; (3) the absoluteness and immutability of the Law. The last is a point of special contemporary relevance: the Law applies to all and (like God and nature) knows no persons. Thus, it is not open to the individual to determine that he is exempt from its sentence. The Law, therefore, does not regard external circumstances of time or place. It is not culture-dependent, nor the product of a particular mentality at a particular stage in history but absolute and universal. Drawing upon the marked confinement of the laws of Temple ritual to particular times and places, however, the Rambam emphasizes what is the outcome of the argument regarding the absoluteness and universality of the Law: it is only the matters of primary intention which are so. Matters of secondary intention, such as animal sacrifice, since they are manifestly the products of a particular historical situation and plainly express an effort to deal with the limitations of a particular cultural viewpoint, indeed may be transcended.

4. The explication of the general classes of grounds by which all mitzvot are justified.

1. The fourteen headings given here all represent sections (but not necessarily whole books) of Maimonides' *Mishneh Torah*. Each rubric is treated further in subsequent chapters of the *Guide*.

2. Laws dealing with the fundamental principles of Jewish faith, upon which all allegiance to the Torah must be founded, are dealt with in part 1 of "The Book of Knowledge," which is book I of the *Mishneh Torah*.

3. Repentance is considered in part 5 of *Mishneh Torah* I.

mandments which impart true beliefs and ideas which are supportive of adherence to the Law, one does not inquire, as I have explained [*Moreh* III:27], as to their utility.

(2) Commandments connected with the ban on pagan worship. These I have surveyed in "The Laws of Pagan Worship." [4] Note that the laws regarding garments of mixed stuffs, produce of immature trees, and double planting in a vineyard are also in this class. [5]

(3) Commandments connected with the improvement of character. These I surveyed in "The Laws of Ethics." [6] For it is well known that the life of man and human society is realized by good character, which is necessary in turn for the ordering of human life.

(4) Commandments connected with charity, loans, and gifts, and related matters such as assessments and condemnations, rules regarding loans and slaves, and all the mitzvot I surveyed in "The Book of Seeds," [7] except those dealing with mingled stuffs and vineyards and the produce of immature trees. The ground for all these is obvious, for they benefit everyone alike. For one who is rich today (or his descendants) may be poor tomorrow, and one who is poor today (or his offspring) may be rich tomorrow.

(5) Commandments relating to the prevention of wrongdoing and aggression. They are those contained in "The Book of Torts" in our work. [8] The usefulness of these is obvious.

(6) Commandments relating to penal law, as the laws on theft, robbery, and false witness—most of what I deal with in "the Book of

4. *Mishneh Torah,* book I, part 4.
5. They are dealt with, however, according to their legal subject matter in "The Book of Seeds," *Mishneh Torah,* Book VII.
6. *Mishneh Torah,* book I, part 2.
7. Maimonides deals with charity, interest-free loans, and gifts, etc., in part 10 of *Mishneh Torah,* book VII, "The Book of Seeds." Here he puts forward his famous "eight degrees of charity": morose giving, gracious giving, giving on request, giving directly, giving openly to an unknown recipient, giving anonymously to a known recipient, and, highest of all, rendering one's brother self-sufficient. The laws regarding assessments of consecrated property are dealt with in book VI of the *Mishneh Torah,* "The Book of Asseverations," Part 4.
8. "The Book of Torts" is book XI of the *Mishneh Torah.* Part 1 deals with damage caused by chattels; parts 2, 3, 4, and 5 deal with civil aspects of the crimes of theft, robbery, wounding and damaging, murder and manslaughter respectively.

Judges." [9] The utility of this class of laws is manifest and clear. For if criminals are not punished, crime will not be diminished at all, and those who contemplate wrongdoing will not be deterred. There is no more fatuous fool than those who claim that the abrogation of all penalties would be a kindness to mankind. That would be the most barbarous cruelty to men as well as the ruin of civil order. The compassionate thing, in fact, is to do as He commanded: "Establish judges and magistrates in all your precincts" [Deuteronomy 16:18].

(7) Fiscal rules, relating to transactions such as loans, wages, pledges, buying and selling, etc. Inheritance law also belongs in this grouping. These are the mitzvot I surveyed in "The Book of Acquisition" and "The Book of Judgments." [10] The usefulness of this class of commandments is obvious. For these financial dealings are necessary to people in any society, and it is therefore necessary that just laws be laid down to govern these transactions and regulate them beneficially.

(8) Commandments regarding days when work is forbidden, *viz.*, Sabbaths and holidays. [11] The Bible explains the grounds for every day of rest and states the reasons for it: to attain a certain idea, to rest the body, or to combine the two together, as we shall explain [*Moreh* III:43].

(9) Further practical acts of worship such as prayer, reading the Shema, and others I surveyed in "The Book of Devotion," [12] except for circumcision. [13] The benefit conveyed by this class is plain, for all of these are actions which strengthen the love of God and the beliefs one ought to have of Him.

(10) Commandments related to the Sanctuary, its implements, and service. These are the mitzvot I surveyed in part of "The Book of

9. Book XIV of the *Mishneh Torah*. The book embraces all aspects of the administration of law, including basic political theory—the structure of the Sanhedrin (judicial) and the basic laws of kingship (executive)—for it is as administrators of law that such officers derive their authority.

10. Books XII and XIII of the *Mishneh Torah* respectively.

11. These are dealt with in "The Book of Seasons," *Mishneh Torah,* book III.

12. Book II of the *Mishneh Torah*.

13. Circumcision is dealt with in part 7 of book II of the *Mishneh Torah*, "The Book of Devotion." According to Maimonides, this mitzvah belongs under 14.

Worship.'' [14] We have already stated the utility of this class.

(11) Commandments relating to the sacrifices. These are the greater part of the mitzvot I surveyed in ''The Book of Worship'' and ''The Book of Sacrifices.'' [15] We have already stated the utility of this legislation of sacrifices in general and its necessity in that time.

(12) Commandments relating to purity and impurity. All these intend in general to restrict entry into the Sanctuary [16] so that the soul will regard it with awe, fear, and veneration, as I shall explain [*Moreh* III:47].

(13) Commandments relating to the forbidding of certain foods and related matters. These mitzvot I surveyed in ''Laws of Forbidden Foodstuffs.'' [17] The laws of *Nazirs* and of vows [18] are also in this class, and the purpose of the entire class is to restrict license and overindulgence in pleasure-seeking and the adoption of eating and drinking as ends in themselves, as I explained in the introduction to *Avot* in my Commentary on the Mishnah [*Shemonah Perakim* 4].

(14) Commandments relating to banning certain unions. These mitzvot I surveyed in ''The Book of Women'' [19] and ''The Laws of Forbidden Unions.'' [20] Interbreeding of beasts belongs also to this class. Its purpose is to diminish the importance of sex and restrain the influence of the sexual drive where possible so that sex will not be regarded as an end in itself, as the ignorant tend to do, as I explained in my Commentary on *Avot*. Circumcision, too, belongs in this class.

As you know, all the mitzvot may be divided into two classes: transgressions between man and man and those between man and God [*Yoma* 85b]. The former class includes 5, 6, 7, and part of 3. The rest are in the latter class. For every command and prohibition whose pur-

14. Book VIII of the *Mishneh Torah*.
15. Book IX of the *Mishneh Torah*.
16. Entry into the Sanctuary is dealt with in part 3 of book VIII of the *Mishneh Torah*, but the laws of purity and impurity are discussed at length in book X, ''The Book of Purity.''
17. The laws of forbidden foods and the related laws of ritual slaughter are treated in parts 2 and 3 respectively of book V of the *Mishneh Torah*, ''The Book of Holiness.''
18. The laws of vows and oaths as well as the special vows of the *Nazir* are treated in book VI of the *Mishneh Torah*, ''The Book of Asseverations.''
19. Book IV of the *Mishneh Torah*.
20. Part 1 of ''The Book of Holiness,'' *Mishneh Torah*, book V.

pose is to inculcate a certain moral trait, instill an idea, or improve behavior exclusively with reference to the individual's personal development is classed as between man and God by the Sages,[21] even it it
actually does affect relations between man and man—for this may
result only after numerous intermediate stages. . . .

Analysis

Since the function of the *Guide* is to shed light on the obscurities of
the Torah, and since the ultimate function of the Torah is legislative,
Maimonides could hardly complete it without a summary of the underlying rational purposes expressed in the revealed commandments,
which he had studied so exhaustively in his three greatest legal works.
This, in a way, sums up his philosophy of the Law. Law, like nature,
is an expression of the divine imperative. Just as the laws of nature at
large express God's will and wisdom, so God's laws for man express
those "attributes" under the form and character appropriate to rational
beings capable of choice and error, governed by reason, capable of
wisdom, individuated by bodies which require physical sustenance,
capable of emotions which may be spent in the creative tasks of self-
perfection or exhausted in the self-frustrating and self-destructive
abuses of excessive passions.

Every imperative in the Law has its justification in terms of the purpose (good) it serves to foster or achieve. But this does not mean that
the justification is the authority of the law. We are commanded to help
one another because the Law recognizes that that (in part) is what the
good for man consists of. But the good of helping is not reducible to
the benefit conferred. The end does not justify the means. Maimoni-

21. The results of this mode of classification include (*a*) man's having obligations to
himself which he may fail to live up to (as need not be the case if one's obligations to
himself are conceived solely in terms of the individual's subjective perceptions of them),
and (*b*) the fact that the individual is not isolated, alienated, or cut adrift, morally speaking, in the Rambam's ethics, as so often happens in an ethic based on the concept of
personal self-perfection. Self-perfection is an obligation to the Giver of our being, with
ramifications not only in our own lives but in the lives of all we touch. Yet the significance of the obligation of self-perfection transcends both its personal and social dimensions.

des' position is a subtle one, as subtle as the difficulty it resolves: if the Law is simply an imperative expressing no wisdom but only the sheer positivity of the divine will, what relevance has it for man? But if the Law exists simply to confer benefits, does not the Law become (as in some versions of utilitarianism) the mere creature of the benefits it imparts, possessing no higher authority, no absolute standing? Maimonides' keen philosophical perception penetrates the falsity of this dilemma completely: there is no dichotomy between utility and divine authority, for what is God's absolute Goodness as applied to man if not the sum and integration of human goods? Thus, no attempt is made to divorce the Law from the benefits it confers; every law will have its justifying ground in the particular good it serves. But that particular good is not the ultimate source of the Law as law, for that particular good, as philosophers have demonstrated repeatedly, cannot define the law. It cannot, for example, judge between itself and some other, competing good. The only standard of such judgment is the Absolute Good, the Good Itself, which, in the view of Maimonides and all philosophers of the great tradition of monotheist philosophy, is the source of all relative or particular goods, and which is to be identified as God.

The Law, then, serves human goods, but it does not derive from humanity the conception of the benefits it affords. Rather, it is the declension into human terms of the divine Goodness/Intelligence. Any limitations in the rationality of the Law, therefore, must be understood as expressions of this divine condescension. The Rambam gives two examples of this. First, the law must be concrete and specific. To this end, it must contain particularities which are arbitrary (expressions of "will") with respect to the ends ("wisdom") of the Law. Secondly, the Law, in part, is tailored to the specific limitations of the culture of the recipients at a particular epoch. The sacrificial cult, paradigmatically, is a divine concession to a particular, limited conception of devotion, aimed to achieve a particular effect regarding the transference of that devotion from the local and particular to the absolute and universal Divinity. It is clear that refinement in man's form of devotion was of secondary importance until that transference was achieved. But once it was achieved, the old form of worship might well be transcended. This, however, is not the case with the mainsprings of the law. One must beware of the temptation to confuse what is addressed to the limitations of a particular level of cultural development with what is predicated upon the universal limitations of human nature. *A fortiori* one cannot play Voltaire here by applying the notion of the Torah's concession to a primitive audience to Scripture as a whole, for this would be the worst form of throwing out the baby with the bath water—ignoring the eternal themes of the Torah as well as the inner dynamic of their development, for example, in the writings of the later prophets cited by the Rambam.[1] It is crucial to the understanding of the Maimonidean method to recognize that the Rambam rejects out of hand the notion that there might be any conflict between the underlying burdens of the later and earlier revelations. The Torah, as a whole, is a dynamic unity which serves to inculcate human virtue, civil, personal, intellectual. And it does so by means which are immutable so long as human nature does not change.

The Law, then, is the divine will/wisdom adapted to the needs of human beings. It does not seek to set before mankind the inconceivable and alien goal of achieving the absolute good but, rather, it delineates the do-able good for man in natural, human terms. This means provision for man's bodily and spiritual welfare—for these are the two areas in which man's nature allows him the possibility of fulfillment. Bodily welfare begins with the matter of diet, hygiene, and personal physical regimen, but it extends to the cultivation of the virtues of character, for even bare subsistence cannot be maintained long without self-discipline, and still less can self-perfection. But the virtues are not merely personal, for man is a social animal. He cannot survive, let alone progress, without the cooperation of his fellow men. Recognizing this, the Law provides for civil as well as personal virtues. It institutes modes of behavior conducive to the cultivation of civility, thoughtfulness, consideration—the ways of living that give concrete content to the injunction of Leviticus (19:18, *cf.* Exodus 23:4), that each of us love his fellow human being as he loves himself. And

---

1. The later prophets do not, as is often claimed, add a new level of spirituality to the Torah but rather they develop the inner logic of its central themes. The same can be said, from the Maimonidean perspective, of the work of the faithful judges, kings, and sages of Israel. (*Cf. Moreh* III:32 and the treatment there of 1 Samuel 15:22, Isaiah 1:11, Jeremiah 5:12, Psalm 50:7–9.)

recognizing that virtue alone is not sufficient guarantee of the survival of society, upon which depends human survival as a whole, the Law lays down the framework of civil and penal imperatives which express the overall requirements for the preservation of human cooperation.

By laying down its moral and civil requirements, the Law has made possible not only human survival but also the gradual development of the arts or industries by which social cooperation produces progress. Thus, health and material welfare, charity and penal law, economy and security are all provided by this level of the Law. To us, I suppose, that would seem sufficient; to some, perhaps, even more than sufficient as the sphere of action of the Law. But we must bear in mind that it is not the function of the Torah to create a nation of healthy and contented, well-adjusted philistines whose morality is subservient entirely to their technology. Rather, the ethical imperatives of the Torah—above all, the commandment to love one another—are given in the context of the higher imperative: "You shall be holy, for I the Lord your God am holy" (Leviticus 19:2). If law is seen, as Plato saw it in the *Republic,* as a means of building national character, then the function of the Torah, as a system of law, is to create a holy people (*am kadosh*)—that is, a people whose every individual has fulfilled not only his material but also his intellectual/spiritual potential.[2]

Of course this is a lofty goal, and everyone would agree that this cannot be legislated. Thought cannot be legislated. But what the Torah does do is provide the framework for the thought by which man's intellectual/spiritual nature may develop and grow. It does this with a view to the limitations of the masses (for it is not the purpose of the Torah that only a few should reach fulfillment) by embodying its eternal insights in poetic form, as myths and allegories, through which the truth about God's relation to the world is symbolically set forth. To those who live intellectually on the mythic level, this poetry is sufficient. To those capable of going further, toward the concepts that lie behind the myths, the poetry of the Torah is a key to the door to true intellectual understanding, apodictic, as the Rambam says, regarding the Highest Truth.

2. *Cf.* especially *Moreh* III:31, 33, the Rambam's discussion of Exodus 19:6, and *Shemonah Perakim* 5.

BIBLIOGRAPHY
INDEX

A BIBLIOGRAPHY OF MAIMONIDES' WRITINGS

GUIDE TO THE PERPLEXED (*DALALAT AL-HAIRIN*)

Le Guide des Égarés traité de Théologie et de Philosophie par Moïse ben Maimoun dit Maimonide. Critical ed. of the Arabic text with French tr. and extensive notes by Rabbi Salomon Munk, 3 vols. Paris, 1856–1866 (repr. Osnabruck: Zeller, 1964; Paris: Maisonneuve, 1970).—Arabic text alone, ed. I. Joel, based on Munk. Jerusalem: Junovitch, 1929.

Moreh Nevukhim. Hebrew tr. of Judah al-Harizi, ed. with notes, Salamon Munk. London: Samuel Bagster, 1879.—New ed., based on Munk, by S. Scheyer. Tel Aviv, 1964.

Moreh Nevukhim. Hebrew tr. of Samuel ibn Tibbon with commentaries of Moses Duran "Ephodi," Shemtov, ibn Falaquera, Asher ibn Abraham Crescas, and Don Isaac Abarbanel. Vilna: Funk, 1914.

The Guide of the Perplexed. Tr. with intro. and notes by Shlomo Pines and introductory essay by Leo Strauss. Chicago: University of Chicago Press, 1963, 1969. "Every Arabic technical term has been rendered by one and the same English term. Wherever the original is ambiguous or obscure the translation has preserved or attempted to preserve that ambiguity or obscurity," quoted from the Preface, p. vii. Translator's introduction summarizes Maimonides' direct obligations to his predecessors. Strauss's intro. offers an approach to the exegesis of the *Guide* as a quasi-hermetic document; *cf.* his *Persecution and the Art of Writing*. Glencoe: Free Press, 1952.

The Guide for the Perplexed. Tr. Michael Friedländer *et al.*, 3 vols. London,

1881–1885; 2nd ed. rev., 1904, without the notes. A fluent translation in the nineteenth-century idiom, but containing some inaccuracies and glosses. This was the first complete English translation of the *Guide*. It includes a life of Maimonides, an analysis of the *Guide*, and a valuable listing of commentaries and discussions on the work (repr. of 2nd ed., New York: Dover, 1956).

BOOK OF THE COMMANDMENTS (*KITAB AL-FARAID*)

Le Livre des Préceptes par Moïse ben Maimoun dit Maimonide. Arabic text ed. with intro. and notes by M. Bloch. Paris, 1888.

Sefer ha-Mitzvot. Hebrew translation of Moses ibn Tibbon, ed. with notes by Hayyim Heller. Jerusalem: Mosad ha-Rav Kook, 1946.

The Commandments (Sefer ha-Mitzvot). Tr. with notes by Rabbi Charles B. Chavel, 2 vols. London and New York: Soncino, 1967. Maimonides' Arabic original of this text was translated into Hebrew three times during the author's lifetime, by Abraham b. Has-dai, Moses ibn Tibbon, and Solomon b. Ayyub. The present version, however, is based upon a modern Hebrew translation by J. Kapach, M. Y. Sachs, and M. Goshen, ed. M. D. Rabinowitz. Jerusalem: Mosad ha-Rav Kook, 1958.

COMMENTARY ON THE MISHNAH (*KITAB AL-SIRAJ*)

Sefer ha-Maor, hu Perush ha-Mishnah. Ed. M. D. Rabinowitz. Tel Aviv: Rishonim, 1948. (The Hebrew version of Maimonides' Mishnah Commentary is also found in standard editions of the Talmud.)

Hakdamot le Ferush ha-Mishnah (introductions from the Commentary on the Mishnah). Hebrew ed. with notes by M. D. Rabinowitz. Jerusalem: Mosad ha-Rav Kook, 1968. Includes the introduction to the Mishnah, the introduction to *Perek Helek* (see below), and the ethical introduction to tractate *Avot* known as the *Shemonah Perakim (Eight Chapters;* see Part Three of this book).

Perush le-Massekhet Avot (Commentary on the Sayings of the Fathers). Hebrew ed. with notes by M. D. Rabinowitz. Jerusalem: Mosad ha-Rav Kook, 1961.

Musa Maimuni's Acht Kapitel. Ed. M. Wolff. 2nd ed., Leyden, 1903.

The Eight Chapters of Maimonides on Ethics. Critical ed. of the Hebrew text of Samuel ibn Tibbon (collated with the Arabic), with English tr. and notes by J. I. Gorfinkle. New York, 1912 (repr., New York: AMS Press, 1966).

The Commentary to Mishnah Aboth. Tr. with intro. and notes by Arthur David. New York: Bloch, 1968.

"Maimonides on the Jewish Creed" (introduction to *Perek Helek,* commentary on Mishnah Sanhedrin X). Tr. J. Abelson, *Jewish Quarterly Review,* o.s. XIX, pp. 28ff.

"Maimonides on Immortality and the Principles of Judaism" (*Perek Helek*). Tr. Arnold J. Wolf. *Judaism* XV (1966), pp. 95–101, 211–16, 337–42.

MISHNEH TORAH (CALLED THE *YAD HAZAKAH*)

Mishneh Torah, hu ha-Yad ha-Hazakah ("The Law in Review" or "Strong Hand"). Hebrew text, ed. S. T. Rubinstein, M. D. Rabinowitz, *et al.* Jerusalem: Mosad ha-Rav Kook, 1967–1973.

The Code of Maimonides, Mishneh Torah. Text with standard commentaries. New York: Goldman, 1956.

The Book of Knowledge and the Book of Adoration (books I and II of the *Mishneh Torah*). Tr. Moses Hyamson. 1937 (repr., Jerusalem: Boys Town Publisher, 1962).

The Code of Maimonides. Yale Judaica Series, Leon Nemoy, General Editor. New Haven: Yale University Press, in progress. Translations of books III, V, VI, VIII, IX, X, XI, XII, XIII, XIV by various hands have appeared since 1949. This will be the authoritative translation.

Maimonides' Mishneh Torah (selections). Ed. Philip Birnbaum. New York: Hebrew Publishing Co., 1967.

ON LOGIC (*MILLOT HA-HIGGAYON*)

Treatise on Logic. Original Arabic and three Hebrew translations, ed. and tr. Israel Efros. New York: American Academy for Jewish Research, 1938.

Introduction to Logic. The Hebrew tr. of Moses ibn Tibbon. ed. with notes by Leon Roth, collated with the Arabic original by D. H. Baneth. Jerusalem: Hebrew University, Magnes Press, 1935 (2nd ed. 1965).

ON THE CALENDAR (*MAAMAR HA-IBBUR*)

Die Aelteste astronomische Schrift des Maimonides. Ed. L. Dünner. Wurzberg, 1902.

LETTERS, ETC.

Kobetz Teschuvot ha-Rambam ve-Iggerotav (Maimonides' collected epistles and responsa). Ed. A. L. Lichtenberg. Leipzig: L. Schnauss, 1859.

Responsa quae exstant. Hebrew and Arabic texts, ed. J. Blau, 3 vols. Jerusalem: Mezike Nirdamim, 1957–1961.

Iggerot ha-Rambam (Maimonides' epistles). Ed. D. Baneth. Jerusalem: Mezike Nirdamim, 1946.

Iggerot ha-Rambam (epistles of Maimonides). Contains *The Epistle on Apostasy,* also called the *Treatise on Martyrdom; The Epistle to Yemen* called *Petah Tikvah* or the "Gate of Hope"; and the *Epistle* or *Treatise on Resurrection.* Hebrew texts ed. M. D. Rabinowitz. Jerusalem: Mosad ha-Rav Kook, 1968.

"Maimonides' Treatise on Resurrection" (*Maamar Tehiyyat ha-Metim*). Ed. with notes by Joshua Finkel. *Proceedings of the American Academy for Jewish Research* IX (1939), pp. 61–105, 1–42 of the Hebrew section. English tr. by S. Morais from the Hebrew, in the *Jewish Messenger* 1859, pp. 81–82, 90–91, 98, 106, 114.

"Letter on Astrology." Tr. R. Lerner. In Lerner and Mahdi, *Medieval Political Philosophy*. Glencoe: Free Press, 1963. Pp. 227–237; ed. A. Marx, *Hebrew Union College Annual* III (1926), pp. 311–58, IV, pp. 493–94.

Epistle to Yemen. Arabic text with three Hebrew versions, ed. with intro. (in Hebrew) by A. S. Halkin; English tr. Boaz Cohen. New York: American Academy for Jewish Research, 1952.

Selected letters in *A Treasury of Jewish Letters*. Ed. Franz Kobler. Philadelphia: Jewish Publication Society, 1954. Vol. I, pp. 178–222.

"Translation of an Epistle Addressed by R. Moses Maimonides to R. Samuel ibn Tibbon." Ed. H. Adler. In *Miscellany of Hebrew Literature*. London: Trubner, 1872. Vol. I, pp. 219–27. See also ed. of A. Marx in *Jewish Quarterly Review* N.S. XXV, pp. 374 ff.

Maimonides on Listening to Music (from the Responsa). Texts and translations with commentary by H. G. Farmer. Bearsden, Scotland: pub. by the author, 1941.

"A New Responsum of Maimonides Concerning the Repetition of the *Shemonah Esreh.*" Ed. Israel Friedlander. *Jewish Quarterly Review*, n.s. V, pp. 1–15.

"An Autograph Responsum of Maimonides." Ed. P. Halper. *Jewish Quarterly Review* n.s. VI, pp. 225–29.

Uber die Lebensdauer (*Responsum on the Duration of Life*). Tr. J. Weil. Basel, 1953.

"Arabic Responses of Maimonides." Ed. D. Simonsen. *Jewish Quarterly Review,* o.s. XII, pp. 134–38.

"Responses of Maimonides in the Original Arabic" (autograph facsimile). Ed. George Margoliouth. *Jewish Quarterly Review,* o.s. II (1899), pp. 533–50.

MEDICAL WORKS

Ketavim Refuyim (Medical Works). Hebrew texts ed. with English prefaces by S. Muntner. Jerusalem: Mosad ha-Rav Kook, 1959—, in progress.

The Medical Aphorisms of Moses Maimonides. Ed. and tr. Fred Rosner and S. Muntner, 2 vols. New York: Yeshiva University Press, 1970–1971.

Treatise on Hemorrhoids (*medical answers responsa*). Ed. and tr. F. Rosner and S. Muntner. Philadelphia: Lippincott, 1969.

Treatise on Asthma. Ed. S. Muntner. Philadelphia: Lippincott, 1963.

Regimen Sanitatis; oder Diatetik fur die Seele und der Korper, mit Anhang der Medizinischen Responsen und Ethik des Maimonides. (Fi tadbir as-Siha, "On Hygiene: Physical and Psychological,'' and *Maqala fi bayan al-arad,* on fits.) German tr. and commentary by S. Muntner. Basel, New York: Karger, 1966.

The Preservation of Youth, Essays on Health (Fi tadbir al-siha), tr. H. L. Gordon, New York: Philosophical Library, 1958.

Two Treatises on the Regimen of Health: *Fi tadbir al-sihah* and *Maqalah fi bayan bad al-arad wa 'l-jawab anha.* ed. and tr. A. Bar-Sela, H. E. Hoff, and E. Faris. *Transactions of the American Philosophical Society* N.S. LIV 4, 1964, pp. 50ff.

"Un Glossaire de matière medicale" (Glossary of Pharmaceutical Terms). Ed. Max Meyerhof. *Mémoires Presentés à l'Institute d'Egypte* XLI.

Sex Ethics in the Writings of Moses Maimonides (Treatise on Cohabitation and selections from other works). Tr. F. Rosner. New York: Bloch, 1974.

Traité des poisons (Treatise on poisons). French tr. by I. M. Rabinowitz. Paris: Lipschutz, 1935.

''Maimonides' Treatise on Poisons.'' Tr. Louis T. Bragman. *The Medical Journal,* 1926.

COMMENTARY

Perush Megillat Esther' (Commentary on the Book of Esther). Hebrew tr. J. J. Rivlin. Jerusalem: Krynfiss, 1952.

INDEX

441